★ "With its focus on books and book lovers, eccentric villagers and frauds, this first mystery from the author of *The Readers of Broken Wheel Recommend* is a delightful traditional, filled with fascinating characters. Those who escape to Louise Penny's Three Pines might want to check out Great Diddling."

—*Library Journal*, Starred Review

"This quirky, twisty, quintessentially British cozy is frothy and funny with a hint of dark and menacing."

—*Booklist*

"On the charming side of humorous and self-consciously charming."

—*Kirkus Reviews*

THE READERS OF BROKEN WHEEL RECOMMEND

"A manifesto for booksellers, booklovers, and friendship. We should all celebrate these little bookstores where our souls find home… One of these books you want to live in for a while."

—Kristin Harmel, *New York Times* bestselling author of *The Book of Lost Names*

"One of the more surprisingly improbable and delightful books I've read in years. What begins as an unlikely international friendship based on a mutual love of books becomes a sweet and soulful discovery of America. Quirky, unpredictable, funny, and fresh—a wonderful book."

—Nickolas Butler, international bestselling author of *Shotgun Lovesongs* and *Beneath the Bonfire*

book references, chief among them Austen and Bridget Jones, but it is her characters that will win readers over… As in Austen, love conquers, but just who and how will come as a pleasant surprise."

—*Publishers Weekly*

WELCOME TO THE PINE AWAY MOTEL AND CABINS

"Katarina Bivald talks about her characters like you talk about your best friends. She gives her story absolutely everything she has. You'll care when you read because she really, really cared when she wrote."

—Fredrik Backman, #1 *New York Times* bestselling author of *A Man Called Ove*

"Hopeful, heartening, and humane, this is the novel I needed to read right now."

—J. Ryan Stradal, author of *The Lager Queen of Minnesota* and *Kitchens of the Great Midwest*

"A novel of irresistible characters who make you believe in the power of hard-won wisdom and second chances, *Welcome to the Pine Away Motel and Cabins* is a delight!"

—Linda Francis Lee, author of *The Glass Kitchen*

"Bivald's charming, heartwarming, and thought-provoking novel will linger long after the last page is turned."

—*Booklist*

"In a story about the lives a single person can touch, the highlight is fittingly Bivald's memorable characterizations, as she makes each person and their needs distinct and complex. This is a winning novel about the lasting impact of love."

—*Publishers Weekly*

"A celebration of life in which friendship, community, and a room for the night are gentle antidotes to prejudice."

—*Kirkus Reviews*

"The novel perfectly captures the joys and trials of small-town living... A story full of both hope and heart."

—*Shelf Awareness*

ALSO BY KATARINA BIVALD

Just Another Dead Author

Just Another Dead Author

Katarina Bivald

Poisoned Pen
PRESS

Copyright © 2025 by Katarina Bivald
Cover and internal design © 2025 by Sourcebooks
Cover illustration and design by Sandra Chiu

Sourcebooks, Poisoned Pen Press, and the colophon are registered trademarks of Sourcebooks.

Published by Poisoned Pen Press, an imprint of Sourcebooks
1935 Brookdale RD, Naperville, IL 60563-2273
(630) 961-3900
sourcebooks.com

Cataloging-in-Publication Data is on file with the Library of Congress.

Printed and bound in the United States of America.
KP 10 9 8 7 6 5 4 3 2 1

MOMENT OF DEATH

AS SOON AS I SAW *him, I thought: He must die.*

No, I didn't. I thought: *I still want him to like me.*

But no one expects literal truth in a book, do they? You're looking for a higher truth. A poetic truth. And his destiny was sealed that same moment I laid my eyes on him on the opening night of "the writing retreat that will change your life."

He was bigger than I remembered him, as if even his body had reached mythical proportions in my head. Or as if he'd eaten too much and moved his arse too little.

There you go. You preferred the first version, didn't you? The poetic truth.

The truth—an unnecessary repetition, but it's a difficult word to avoid during a confession; I'll have to edit it later—is that I've thought about that evening a hundred times and I've still not been able to determine the exact moment when I decided to kill him. I have examined every second. Every word he uttered. Every word I uttered.

I've asked myself: *Did I already know this? Was the decision already made there and then? Could he have saved himself?*

And, yes, he could have. At least I think so. But he didn't want to save himself. He wanted to barge in as usual, stamp on people's feelings, their dreams, their fragile egos (yes, he hurt mine, and, yes, it made the murder more pleasurable, but that wasn't why he died, not by a long shot). The truth—my truth, you can read into whatever you want—is that I don't even know whether I hated or admired him. Maybe both. Real feelings are complicated in that way. It's almost only in books that hate can be pure and free and untarnished by irritating positive feelings. Perhaps I even loved him? Maybe. Once upon a time.

If I had to choose a moment that decided everything, it was when I saw his smiling face. He looked so happy and unburdened. That was enough. I knew then that I had to do something.

That night I walked aimlessly across the dark fields. I followed my dreams until the end. My hands swept through the tall grass, the meadow flowers that almost looked like cow parsley, so banal, so exciting, so terrifying. I was high on inspiration. I smoked a sneaky cigarette and got high on nicotine as well.

It felt like when I was writing. The moment that you suddenly have the best idea. The world changed in less than a second. Something that didn't exist before, existed now.

An idea. A thought. A decision that was suddenly cemented in my head. *He must die.*

1

"*C'EST BERIT GARDNER, UN TRÈS...CÉLÈBRE?...AUTEUR Suédois?*
Et she wants *un café, s'il vous plaît.*"

"Of course, mademoiselle," the waiter at the Hôtel d'Aubusson replied. His English was perfect. His face expressionless. It was the beginning of a scorching day in July, the kind that drove Parisians away, leaving the city for the tourists. The man was dressed in black chinos, black shirt, black socks, black shoes, and yet he looked completely unbothered.

Like a vampire, Berit thought. *Or a true Parisian. Maybe they were one and the same.*

"Et un croissant," Sally continued laboriously.

"Naturally, mademoiselle." Again, the impeccable English. The expressionless face.

"Merciiii boocoooo."

The waiter struggled to suppress a small twitch in his right eye.

"You're welcome, mademoiselle."

Sally looked disappointedly at Berit, as if another illusion of life had just been crushed. "I didn't think French waiters spoke English," she said.

"At expensive hotels in Paris, they probably do," Berit said dryly.

The coffee arrived, refreshingly strong in a small cup, together with a plate of croissants that shattered into small buttery flakes as soon as you touched them. The waiter fled the scene before Sally had the chance to thank him again in French.

Berit lifted the coffee cup, closed her eyes, and breathed in the lovely aroma. Everything was still and quiet around them. The courtyard of the Hôtel d'Aubusson was like a secret, silent oasis in the middle of Saint-Germain. Green plants and white umbrellas offered welcome shade. A German couple was reading *Der Spiegel* at the neighboring table, but apart from them, they were alone.

Loud swear words and angry voices suddenly disturbed the calm.

Berit stretched her neck to be able to look out into the somber and dimly lit lobby, where the receptionist, the concierge, the waiter, and the doorman all tried talking to a man who was gesticulating and swearing loudly.

"Monsieur! *Monsieur!*" the concierge said. "You can't park your *vehicle*… there! Can't you see you're blocking off half of the street?" He pointed angrily with both hands and added, even more upset: "And our entire doorway!"

Drivers were honking their horns furiously. The man offered numerous creative locations where he could park his car if they didn't let him in immediately, all in explosive, smattering French. He then broke through the defense barrier, walked over to Berit and Sally's table and said, "Ah, Berit Gardner! Such a pleasure."

"What's going on?" Sally whispered and desperately tried to google the words she'd just heard: *putain, crétin, couillon, raclure de bidet, nique ta mère*…

Berit quickly put her hand over the phone. "I imagine our ride has just turned up," she said. At least she hoped so. She stretched her head up to see if anyone else was standing behind this man, but apart from the upset hotel staff, the lobby was completely empty.

The man bowed carelessly. "Antoine," he said. "Antoine Tessier, at your service."

While he was talking, he casually picked up Berit and Sally's suitcases and headed toward the entrance. "Our bags!" Sally exclaimed and ran after him, as if she thought he was trying to steal them.

Berit stood up, finished the last of her coffee, left a fifty-euro note on the table with an apologetic nod to the waiter, and followed them out.

An old, run-down, and filthy white bus took up most of the narrow street. Most of the windows were down; the sweaty faces poking out suggested there was no air-conditioning.

Standing in front of it was Emma Scott.

Berit smiled when she saw her old friend, but there was something about her appearance that bothered her. A new tiredness in her face, or some kind of helplessness in her shrunken shoulders that hadn't been there the last time she saw her.

Emma came toward Berit with her arms stretched out.

"I don't know what I would have done if you hadn't saved me," she said.

Her body felt fragile when Berit hugged her. She remembered the sinewy strength that had always been there and the thousands of boxes of books this woman had carried during her life, and she got worried. They hadn't seen each other in over five years, and those years did not seem to have been kind to Emma Scott.

"It's John Wright who is the savior," Berit said.

Emma pulled away.

"Yes," she said guardedly. "We are very grateful. Obviously. He's already at the château. He arrived yesterday."

We, Berit thought and looked at Antoine. He was loading their suitcases into the hold of the bus, taking his time. A line of cars had formed behind them on the narrow rue Dauphine.

"And you must be Sally," Emma said. "Your mum has told me so much about you. An impressive woman, Olivia. Really very…impressive," she finished lamely when she couldn't seem to think of another adjective describing the formidable literary agent that was Sally's mum, and now also her boss.

Emma looked at Berit again. "I am so grateful that you're here. I didn't know what to do."

"I would have come to the bookshop too if only you'd asked me," Berit said. "I had no idea how bad things were. If there was anything I could have done…"

Emma lowered her gaze. "Yes," she said. "In fact I tried… Olivia said you were very busy." She smiled uncomfortably. "And I'm sure she was right. But you're here now."

Antoine grabbed Berit's elbow gently but firmly, helped her up onto the bus, bowed toward Sally, and said: "Mademoiselle" with a strict kind of politeness that made her hurry up on to the bus.

He helped Emma with considerably more patience and jumped in behind the wheel. After making sure Emma, who was standing in the aisle, was holding on to the handle firmly, he skidded away, accompanied by the horns and cursing that's such a typical part of Parisian traffic.

Berit looked around in the bus. They were an odd little group, spread out across the seats. Everyone stared at Berit and Sally when they unsteadily made their way toward two empty seats in the back.

"More people will join us at the retreat," Emma assured them. She was still standing in the aisle despite Antoine's erratic driving. "A lot of them are flying straight to Lyon."

"I bet you would have done the same if you had known there was no air-conditioning on the bus," a guy in his midtwenties said from the seat directly behind Berit and Sally. He stretched out his hand between the back of their seats. "Alexander Spencer," he said. "But call me Alex."

Alex radiated a youthful optimism and seemed almost manically social.

"I'm not a writer," he said chirpily, which explained a lot of the optimism. "Jules here is, though. My boyfriend."

The boyfriend next to him was slim and svelte, dressed in black jeans and a black polo shirt. He looked as if he tried to mimic the French waiter from the hotel but had regretfully already started sweating in the stifling heat on the bus. His long, thin, black hair was stuck to his forehead. The hand that was extended to Berit was clammy, his handshake weak and lifeless.

"Julian Aubrey," he said without making eye contact. He leaned back as if he wanted to distance himself from any small talk.

"I hope you'll all get to know each other a little during the ride," Emma said. "If not, there'll be plenty of opportunity during the retreat. Cyclist!" she suddenly yelled over her shoulder.

The bus swerved. Berit offered her a hand to steady her and received a feeble smile as a thank you.

Berit looked over at Antoine behind the wheel. Romantic partner or colleague? Regardless, she was pleased he was here. She had noticed the fleeting but protective glance he'd directed at Emma when they left the hotel. It felt reassuring that his explosive rowdiness was on Emma's side.

She had a feeling Emma needed it.

In the seat across the aisle sat a woman around the same age as Alex and Julian. She had hair the color of honey, perfectly blow-dried with shimmering long blond waves falling over her shoulders. Her clothes—gray trousers, white short-sleeved shirt, stilettos—revealed a slim and fit body. On her lap was the welcome pack Emma had given them, a notebook, several pencils, and her mobile. A manicured hand held everything in place.

She looked like a mix between a journalist and an influencer, and she was staring straight at Berit.

"You're Berit Gardner, aren't you?" she said.

Berit admitted as much.

"I'm Nicole. Nicole Archer. I've read your earlier work. But not your latest ones."

"They're even better!" Sally said.

"Sally Marsch," Berit said. "My agent."

Nicole studied Sally carefully, as if weighing her status and importance. Then she looked down at her welcome pack, ticked her off the participant list, and turned toward Berit. "But I thought it was brave of you to try out a new genre at your age," she said. "Older people seldom dare to try new things. Most stagnate in their thirties, and you've got to be a lot older than that."

Berit admitted this as well.

In front of Berit was a woman in her seventies. She turned around and said quietly: "She told *me* she was pleased I was here, as it's important for older people to have a hobby. Like knitting." She smiled. "I'm Mildred Wilkinson. I *have* read your latest books."

Mildred's hair was thin and gray, and she exuded an air of patient suffering. On the hot, stuffy bus, after what must already have been a long journey, she looked the most tired but also the most stoically accepting. Berit got the feeling that she didn't expect life to be very comfortable.

"I'm a journalist," Nicole said. "And one day I will write a book that will change the world. The only thing it takes is being in the right place at the right time."

"You write nonfiction?" Sally asked with interest.

"Let's just say…based on a true story." Nicole smiled radiantly. "One mustn't let the truth get in the way of a good story. And believe me, I will succeed. I'm willing to walk over dead bodies to achieve it." Her words jarred scarily with her perfectly made-up, smiling face. "That's why I'm here," she continued.

"To walk over dead bodies?" Alex asked, but he didn't sound very shocked.

Nicole glared impatiently at him. "To become successful, obviously. By extending my network. That's how you succeed in this world. You have to know the right people." She looked greedily at Berit.

Berit instinctively leaned back farther into her seat.

"I'm in IT," Alex said over Berit's backrest. "Customer support. I always tell Jules that if he ever wanted to write a comedy, I've got plenty of material for him."

Julian didn't seem to want to write comedies.

"Why are you here then, if you're not a writer?" Nicole challenged.

"Moral support." Alex winked at Berit. "I'm here to defend him from all the other scary writers."

At the front of their little group was a woman in her fifties who looked as cool as Julian Aubrey was trying to be. She was wearing a black leather skirt, a black-and-white shirt with a graphic pattern, and bright red lipstick. Her dark hair was long and artistically ruffled, but in a way that must have cost hundreds of pounds to achieve in an exclusive salon. Her face was stiff, but whether it was from Botox or sadness, Berit couldn't tell.

Nicole's gaze constantly wandered across to her. It appeared she hadn't yet dared asking her name, but it was obvious she wanted to.

"Rebecka Linscott," the woman finally said. She turned around in her seat so she could look at Berit. The presentation was aimed at her and not the rest of the participants. She completely ignored Mildred, who was sitting between them.

Nicole looked through the paper in her lap.

"You're not on the list," she said disapprovingly.

"I joined late on in the process. Another publisher had to cancel."

"So you're a substitute?" Alex said.

She looked annoyed. "I run Linscott Publishing. I'm sure you've heard of it."

"No," Alex said cheerfully.

She looked even more annoyed. "I published John Wright's first books. I discovered him."

"I *have* heard of him," Alex said.

"Everyone's heard of him," Nicole said impatiently.

"John asked me to come here as a personal favor."

"I heard he moved to Penguin Random House," Nicole said.

"*I* heard he got millions," Alex said.

"It's true," Sally whispered to Berit. "Mum represents him."

Julian forgot to play cool and said in an excited voice: "I can't believe we're going to stay in a French château together with *John Wright*." He said it as if the name was a concept, not a person, and in his childish admiration he finally seemed slightly interesting.

Nicole leafed through the welcome packet to find the list of lecturers on the writing retreat and found John Wright immediately. Berit glanced over. His blurb started with saying that he "was a writer that needed no introduction," and proceeded with an introduction that was twice as long as everybody else's. He was a global phenomenon, had been nominated for the Man Booker prize five times, and topped the *New York Times* bestseller list multiple times. His photo filled a whole page. He stared angrily at all of them as if the photograph was a personal insult. His mouth had a condescending smirk that made Berit want to wipe it off his face.

Emma looked down at the brochure in Nicole's lap. Despite it being just a photograph, it provoked a worried frown on Emma's forehead.

Berit examined her carefully. Her blond, fluffy hair was unkempt. Her clothes were already creased after a long and exhausting day. Her lipstick had come off, apart from the bits stuck to her teeth. But there was something else as well. Something subtle yet elusive was different about Emma. Not a weakness—Berit didn't want to say that about one of the strongest women she'd ever known—but perhaps a new sense of danger. As if life had dealt Emma a few blows since they'd last seen each other, and she was now prepared for new ones.

When Berit's debut came out, Emma Scott had been a name to reckon with in the literary world. She had owned an iconic bookshop in London and had helped establish more than one famous writer. If Emma really loved a book, there was nothing she wouldn't do for it. She'd talk about it everywhere, recommend it to all her customers, review it wherever she could, and personally be the difference between success and anonymity.

And Emma loved Berit's first book. *No writer*, Berit thought, *forgets the first person who loved their book or showed it kindness.*

But as Berit's star had risen, Emma's had fallen. Berit couldn't shake the uncomfortable and completely illogical feeling that the two were connected, like a seesaw: one rose, one sank. The bookshop was forced to close last year. Berit hadn't found out until it was too late.

Emma had done more for literature and reading than anyone else Berit knew, and she hoped that the writing retreat was a sign that Emma hadn't given up. Berit would do everything she could to make sure it was a success.

She opened up her own welcome packet and got out the thick, gleaming brochure. Large golden letters on the front said:

Welcome to Château des Livres
And to the writing retreat
that will change your life!

2

THE BUS HURTLED ALONG THE road. Sally was soon uncomfortably warm. Even with the windows open, it was stuffy and sweaty on the bus. It smelled of exhaust fumes and warm tarmac.

Her mobile phone pinged. She opened the text message.

Do you have eyes on the object?

It wasn't hard to work out who the "object" her mum referred to was. The only person her mum thought of these days was John Wright.

Sally started replying: **No mu...**

Deleted. **No boss**, she wrote instead. Then she deleted that as well.

Negative, boss.

The reply came after only a few seconds, in a series of demanding texts, one after the other until everyone on the bus was staring at her.

Keep your eyes and ears open, the first one said.

Don't lose sight of him for even a second, the next one said.

Whatever you do: don't talk to him, said the last.

Sally replied that she was still on the bus, turned her phone to silent, and put it in her handbag. She glanced at Berit. For the umpteenth time she asked herself why they were there.

Not here on the warm, stifling bus, even though Sally did wonder about that too. They could easily have gotten a first-class ticket to Lyon instead of getting the train to Paris and having to travel by bus the rest of the way. But the big question was why Berit had accepted an invitation to present a series of lectures at a writing retreat in France in the first place. She had never expressed any interest in teaching before. She had been determined not to leave her cottage in Cornwall, until one day she'd called Sally and said they were going to France.

Her mum hadn't objected as strongly as Sally thought she would, but that was readily explained when it turned out that Olivia's newest acquisition, the pride of her stables (her word for the writers at her agency), John Wright, would also be there. He was the keynote speaker and would give the opening lecture on the first day, and then leave. Even though he would only be there for twenty-four hours, it was enough to make Olivia nervous.

Sally's phone vibrated in her bag.

And make sure Berit doesn't argue with him!

They stopped for lunch at a service station outside Dijon, where everybody was given a bottle of water and a dry baguette, which they ate at a couple of rickety picnic tables next to the car park.

In the afternoon they were finally driving through the ramshackle suburbs of Lyon. For a while they followed the signs toward Vienne, until they turned off again and were surrounded by vineyards.

Berit looked around.

Julian had fallen asleep with his head on Alex's shoulder. In his sleep he looked innocent and serious, and so very young. His face was pale against the dark clothes.

Nicole was writing in a beautiful notebook with a dark leather cover. When she looked up, she hungrily observed everyone and everything around her. So eager for new experiences to document, Berit wondered if Nicole had any time for living.

Finally, they turned off. They followed a long, narrow dirt track, shaded by enormous cypresses, leading to a dark and depressing building.

Berit saw the look of disappointment on Sally's face when they got off the bus. She must have imagined a beautiful renaissance castle with cupolas, pilasters, bows, and recesses.

This place was just a large, square building with a battered facade and closed window shutters. A narrow, split staircase led up to a substantial door. It was closed. The stairs were covered in leaves and debris, as if no one had walked up them in years, and on the gravel drive, weeds were growing freely.

The château was completely in the shade. The whole building had an air of lost possibilities and abandoned dreams.

Antoine herded them around to the other side of the building. When they turned the corner, the sun, literally and figuratively speaking, caught up with them.

Large vineyards stretched out in front of them, a broad and uninterrupted horizon that made Berit want to run along one of the rows of vines and continue forever. The afternoon sun wrapped the world in a soft, orange-colored light that made the château shimmer magically.

Berit's heart beat faster. She could feel the energy flowing from this place. She wondered if Emma had intentionally chosen it because of the creative energy here, or if it was just a happy coincidence that had led her to this place. Regardless, Berit felt optimistic about the retreat for the first time since she had accepted the invitation.

From this angle, the building wasn't austere and impersonal, but chaotic and surprising. Instead of being uninhabited and deserted, the château seemed to have lived a long and interesting life. It must have been extended over generations, until nothing really made sense, but everything was charmingly informal.

Two wings on each side of the building created a large courtyard, and between them were the picturesque ruins of an old barn, a wild kitchen garden, and a pool shaded by tall poplars and watched over by several statues.

Wisteria in full bloom framed a paved patio, and on the second floor right in front of them was a large terrace with sofas and umbrellas.

John Wright was standing on the terrace. Berit recognized him immediately. She looked up at the same time everyone else did. He was in the middle of a heated conversation with another man. Their voices were angry and upset.

The other man was dressed in a creased light-blue linen shirt and he talked with a worrying intensity with John Wright, who was older, heavier, and angrier. John's face was frozen in irritation. He looked as if the other man was an annoying fly that he wanted to swat away.

"It's John Wright!" Sally said excitedly.

There was something old-fashioned and literary about his corpulence and formal dark suit. He looked down at the group, and suddenly his frozen face changed to bright red in angry surprise.

"What the hell is *she* doing here?" he said.

3

"*CHARLES TATE IS AN IDIOT,*" Emma said as soon as she was alone with Berit.

Berit looked around the gorgeous, airy room that was going to be hers for almost two weeks. High ceilings. Beautiful windows facing the vineyard and the hills beyond, and open French balcony doors letting all the intoxicating scents in from outside.

John Wright and his wife were staying in the room next door. When Berit stuck her head out the window she could see their open balcony doors and flowing white curtains.

Emma added angrily: "Charles should know better than to fight with him."

Charles was John Wright's previous agent, and Berit was wondering why both he and Rebecka Linscott had agreed to attend the retreat. Very few agents and publishers had enough spare time to hole themselves up in a château in France for twelve days with a bunch of hopeful, future debut authors, and if they did, it was to look after their own bestselling writers, not to chase one that had recently left you.

Berit carefully studied her friend.

They hadn't seen each other in years, but it didn't matter. Emma had helped her when she was young and insecure, and that was enough. Maybe it was because she'd never married or had children, or because her mother had died when Berit was in her twenties, but she had decided early on that you needed more people around you than just your biological family. She'd determined that the only way to make this world a little bit better was to help others, and be helped by considerably more people than the few who were the very closest to you. Berit might pick her friends carefully, but once she counted someone as a friend, there was very little she wouldn't do for them.

Berit had received Emma's email on a lovely spring day in Cornwall. She had been at home by her Edwardian desk and was looking at the stunning rhododendrons in full bloom, feeling happy with life, and content.

The email sounded desperate, despite its formal tone. She had reached for her phone and called immediately. A few questions had confirmed what she had already suspected. Emma was in trouble. The château was rented, the deposit paid, and orders made, but two months before the retreat was due to start, she had hardly received a single booking.

Berit didn't hesitate for a second to offer her attendance, her name, her contacts, whatever she could provide. But in the end, it wasn't her who had saved the retreat. It was John Wright.

When *he* agreed to give the opening lecture, the spaces filled up quickly, despite the hefty ticket price. He was the undisputable star of the retreat, Berit thought without any hint of jealousy, and now he was here, arguing with people.

"Forget about Charles," Emma said with a credible attempt at breeziness. "I hope you will enjoy it here. If you need anything, just let me know. Welcome drinks on the terrace at six. Dinner at seven thirty. I imagine you might want a bit of rest before that."

Berit had no plans to rest. She needed to stretch her legs after the long bus trip and clear her head. When Emma left her, she walked down the steep staircase and out into the garden. It was wild and neglected, but the evening sun made it look naturally charming.

Rusty old cast-iron furniture was placed here and there on the paved patio alongside stacked, dirty white plastic chairs that Berit presumed would be used for the "literary discussions" that the program promised would take place in "the lush verdant garden" and which would "stimulate both your senses and imagination." The stacks of chairs looked precarious on the uneven slabs of stone.

Berit went through an open glass door and found the kitchen. A worn old table in the middle of the room looked inviting. *Perfect for writing*, she noted approvingly, *and if I play my cards right, I might even be able to bag some coffee and biscuits from the cook.*

Along the wall were spacious work surfaces and a wonderful old cooking stove, already fully fired up for dinner.

The cook was an admirable matron around the same age as Berit, but her body and demeanor made her seem older. She had muscular arms and strong hands that could surely butcher a rabbit with calm, confident cuts.

Antoine was by one of the work surfaces, with rolled-up shirt sleeves, slicing bacon, mushrooms, shallots, and potatoes. He was surprisingly competent with the sharp knife.

Neither of them looked up when Berit poked her head in; they were completely focused on dinner preparations.

Outside on the lawn, Rebecka Linscott was doing yoga, her thin, sinewy body enhanced by black tights. She had placed herself in the perfect spot for the rays of sunshine to fall on her long, dark hair.

Berit noticed several members of the retreat walking around with an astonished expression on their faces. Some took selfies in front of the wisteria, while others had put their phones away and gotten their notebooks out, as if they couldn't wait for the retreat to begin.

Berit understood them. There was magic in the air, a creative energy that seemed to come from the earth itself.

So why couldn't she rid herself of that restless, anxious feeling? Despite the idyllic setting and the sunshine, she sensed a darkness edging in.

The argument between Charles and John had affected her more than she cared to admit. There had been poison in John's voice when he realized Rebecka Linscott, his previous publisher who still bragged about discovering him, was there. It was the first time she'd seen the old cliché *if looks could kill* in real life.

Berit shook her head to rid herself of her melodramatic thoughts. She was just tired. Everything would feel better as soon as she'd got herself a large, cold beer.

Sally looked out the window. On the lawn Rebecka Linscott was doing the downward dog, but Sally had been in London too long to react. In the parks of London, yoga and tai chi were as common as ducks and untrained dogs.

She turned to the mirror.

I'm Sally Marsch, junior agent, she said to herself.

She had been a literary agent for nearly a year, ever since the dramatic events in Cornwall and the resulting book, and it had been a transformative time for her.

As a junior agent, Sally was naturally given all the boring tasks. Besides Berit, she was also responsible for the published authors who no longer sold well and for the pile of manuscripts that were about to be rejected.

Dealing with the published authors was the most difficult task. Most of them refused to accept their books no longer sold. They needed more time to improve the quality of their manuscripts, but financial pressure and tight contracts meant they continued to publish one or two books a year. When each book sold less than the previous one, even more books were needed to make ends meet. The advances got smaller, the time between books got shorter, and quality suffered. Many of them were stuck in a vicious circle, until the publisher or the agent had to put an end to it. No matter how hard Sally tried, it was doubtful she could do much for them, but she couldn't stop feeling bad about them either.

The writing retreat had come as a welcome escape from it all.

Her mum was more than happy that someone would keep an eye on her new favorite author. "But don't talk to him," she had instructed Sally. "He doesn't like inexperienced people. Or young women. We don't want him to think that you have anything to do with him at the agency."

Sally didn't mind. Her interest wasn't in John Wright, but in the other people at the retreat. Olivia couldn't understand what Sally wanted with a bunch of unpublished writers.

"Sooner or later, they will have finished their dreadful manuscripts," she had said with a shiver. "And they'll send them in to our slush pile. Have you *seen* our slush pile? We could spend the rest of our lives reading and still not get through all the tedious and unprintable manuscripts we've already been sent. Why on earth would you want to *encourage* them?"

But it was precisely that pile of rejections that kept Sally's dream as an agent alive: to find, develop, and nurse a new author so that one day, Sally could stand in front of stacks of shiny new books and say: *These exist because of me.*

Every night after work she spent hours plowing through the slush pile in search of that golden nugget. They still called it "slush pile," even though it had been years since the manuscripts they were sent were actually printed on paper. These days everything was digital.

So far she hadn't found anything interesting at all. It was slightly discouraging, really, how many people seemed to send in their manuscripts without even doing a spell-check and how many of them completely lacked self-awareness. *You will love my unique idea and be grateful that you took me on. The book will sell at least twenty million copies. It's about a boy that discovers he's a wizard and gets sent to a wizard school—where seagulls deliver letters.*

But at the moment, she was here. Among people who loved literature and would be given the tools needed to take their writing to the next level.

She carefully wrapped a cornflower blue scarf around her neck. It was almost the same color as the French sky.

She nodded. She was as ready as she'd ever be.

I'm Sally Marsch, she thought. *Junior agent.*

4

WELCOME DRINKS WERE SCHEDULED FOR six, but half an hour before then, most people had gathered out on the terrace. They stood in small groups with glasses of bubbly in their hands, looking nervous and insecure in the soft evening sun.

All of them, except Berit, Sally thought. Berit stood by herself with a beer in her hand.

Sally walked up to her. "What an amazing place," she said.

Berit mumbled something in agreement and had a swig of beer. She never stopped observing the people around them.

"And the writing retreat is going to be amazing too, isn't it?" Sally continued.

"Yes," Berit said. This time her voice was resolute.

Sally smiled as she imagined the days ahead. For nearly two weeks she'd be surrounded by intelligent, ambitious people who loved literature as much as she did. They would attend lectures, visit Vienne and Lyon, stay in an actual French castle…

And I'll discover a new writer, she promised herself.

She moved closer to Berit. "You're not going to get up to something while you're here, are you?" she whispered.

Berit looked at her amusedly but replied in a normal conversational tone. "What do you mean get up to something?"

"You know. *Something.* Like what happened in Cornwall."

"Are you asking me if I'm going to get involved in a murder investigation?" Berit sounded incredulous, and when she put it like that, it did sound rather stupid. No one had even died. Sally added an ominous *yet* in her mind and felt a bit silly. But you couldn't deny that things happened around Berit. The last time she had mingled with her, it had not gone great. She looked around nervously.

Nicole was staring intently at them. She must have heard the words *murder investigation.*

"I just want to know why we're here," Sally said quietly.

"I'm here because Emma asked me," Berit said. "That's why."

"Mum asked me to tell you to not get into an argument with John Wright."

Berit let out a short laugh. Her face softened when she looked at Sally.

"I'll try," she said. "But I can't promise anything. He seems to be a total bastard."

Sally looked over to where he was holding court, surrounded by participants. *Exactly* the type that Berit loved quarreling with.

John Wright was here.

Julian would have come to a halt just outside the entrance to the dining room and stared like a fool had Alex not put his warm, firm hand against his lower back. It pushed him resolutely through the dim room, toward the terrace.

John Wright's back got closer and closer. Circled around him was a group of smiling sycophants, nodding in agreement to everything he said. Julian heard their false, shrill laughter before he could even hear John Wright's voice.

He was dressed in a traditional dark suit jacket. His thin hair was combed back, and his neck was drenched in sweat. If you didn't know who he was, you'd think he was a completely normal, slightly boring, uncomfortably warm man. But not to Julian. He ignored the somewhat ordinary and sweaty shell and focused only on Wright's genius and the sharpness of mind underneath it.

Julian could hear his voice now. That last comment was perhaps slightly banal, but only because all the ingratiating and fawning people around him made him less interesting than he really was. *Mr. Wright had to lower himself to their level, Julian told himself.* It would have been different if he were talking to Julian... Yes, it would have been different altogether.

The pressure from the hand on his lower back got firmer. Julian stiffened. Would Alex, driven by misjudged compassion, force him to be a part of the sycophantic group around Mr. Wright? As if Julian was interested in standing there, stuttering some platitudes about the weather together with them! Or even worse: What if Alex went up and introduced himself to Mr. Wright? *I work in customer service. Let me know if you need any material for a comedy book. I've got tons of it.*

Julian shuddered. Alex meant well, but he didn't get it.

"Remember what you promised," Alex whispered in his ear.

He remembered. In the shoulder bag he was squeezing tightly were two hundred forty-seven printed pages. His whole future. Years of work. Everything he had to give in terms of talent, discipline, and inspiration.

He was torn between his yearning to show it to the world and finally get the recognition his words deserved, and an equally strong urge not to show it to anyone, protect it, perfect it even more.

The familiar panic was resurfacing.

What if I don't have what it takes to be a writer?

But he felt Alex's hand against his back, calming now, and his manic grip of the bag loosened.

"I remember," Julian said.

It's impossible to avoid John's magisterial voice, Berit thought. She could hear him the whole time as she moved through the crowd, carrying a silver tray of canapés. She had relieved Emma of it so that Emma could focus on being the hostess, and now she pushed the tray demandingly in front of people's faces saying "Canapés!" with a brusqueness that made most people take one. While she was circling the terrace, she was observing John Wright.

At the moment he was talking to Nicole Archer. She smiled admiringly at everything he said but raised her chin subconsciously, as if to remind herself she was as good as him.

"I'm also a writer," she said. "Journalist."

He skeptically checked out her perfect hair, the swanky dress she had changed into, and the perfect makeup. "What paper do you write for?" he asked.

"I'm freelance," she said, looking away.

He smiled condescendingly. "And which was the last paper that paid you?"

"The media landscape has changed," she said. "It's not only traditional journalism that counts anymore. People receive their news from a multitude of different sources…"

"In your bank account. The last publication that put money into your account. What was the name of it?"

"Bored Panda."

John Wright raised his eyebrow. "The latest publication that paid you was a bored teddy bear?" he said.

"It's just temporary. You have to start somewhere and work your way up in this business…"

"If an endless line of monkeys with a typewriter would sooner or later produce the collected works of Shakespeare, it would only take one monkey and one week to produce your kind of journalism." John laughed at his own joke.

Nicole's shoulders tensed, and she lifted her chin involuntarily again, but that was the only sign of her irritation. She still smiled. Her face had that polite, interested expression that many women were so good at. Berit was sure that John didn't even notice her anger; it was so fiercely under control.

The smiling mask only came off when Nicole turned away from John Wright.

Berit went up to her and offered the tray. "Canapé?" she said.

Nicole ate several with jerky, angry movements.

"I wouldn't mind walking over *his* dead body to succeed," she said quietly. "If I ever got the chance, I would *dance* across it."

"I don't trust thin people," John Wright said to a woman who looked like she'd never eaten a single french fry in her life.

"Small vessels make for narrow-minded souls," he continued.

The woman smiled stiffly. She hid her feelings behind a perfect set of teeth. "This is my first writing retreat," she said. "But I have been to several workshops about unleashing my inner creativity. I think there's a writer inside all of us. You just have to set it free."

"Jesus, no," a cynical voice said quietly in Berit's ear. "There's a bad writer in most people. Do the literary world a favor and keep it locked up." He extended his hand. "Charles Tate. No relation to the gallery. Or the boxer."

"Berit Gardner."

She eyed him openly. *Upper class, but sloppy*, she thought. Still dressed in the same creased shirt as before. Bags under his eyes. Wild, dark blond hair that should have been cut and brushed. Love handles. He looked like years of unhealthy living had finally caught up with him, but without him realizing it. He was closer to fifty than forty but still relied on his boyish charm. The dinner hadn't even started yet and he already seemed half-drunk.

The publisher Rebecka Linscott came out onto the terrace wearing a pair of enormous shades that covered half her face. All you could see was her bright red lips. She smiled stiffly using only the facial muscles that could still move and raised her hand in a theatrical wave toward John Wright.

He turned his back to her.

Her hand dropped. Rebecka brushed passed him, trying to pretend he wasn't the one she'd waved at. For a second Berit almost felt sorry for her.

"Fucking idiot," Charles mumbled. "Anyone would have realized that her turning up here was only ever going to provoke him."

He raised his wineglass to his mouth and realized it was empty. He gave it a disappointed shake, but there wasn't even a drop left.

"Mixed crowd, both the students and the lecturers," he said while he looked around for more wine. He nodded toward Claudia. "One of mine. Claudia Ramirez. She's not selling anymore. If she doesn't come up with something exceptional, I won't be able to place her next book." He grimaced. "Knowing my luck, she'll probably write an international bestseller and give it to Olivia's fucking daughter. She probably thinks some little whippersnapper can do a better job than I can."

"Perhaps she can," Berit said calmly. Charles shot her a glance to see if she was serious. When he couldn't work out her expression, he let out a laugh as if to convince them both that she was joking.

"And of course, our golden calf, John Wright himself."

"I wonder what he's really doing here," Berit pondered.

"Knowing him, probably stirring shit up. That man is so convinced of his own excellence that he can't help but judge everyone else. He probably does it in his sleep. If you woke him up in the middle of the night, he'd start listing everything that's wrong with you."

"What would he have to say about you?" she asked, but Charles just laughed unconvincingly and went to refill his empty glass of wine.

Claudia Ramirez gazed across the terrace and thought, not for the first time, that the publishing world was very anxious, and very white.

That dizzying feeling of not existing came over her like it always did when she was with a group of people and couldn't see anyone else who looked like her.

Everyone mingled nervously in the French afternoon sun, wineglasses full, smiles empty. They were all white. All middle class. And with the interesting exception of two, they all seemed heterosexual. She nodded at the two young men when they passed her. One of them raised his glass toward her.

It's going to be a long twelve days, she thought, and had a large sip.

Then she forced herself to focus on the positive, like she always did. She wrote romance novels, after all. If she had wanted to dwell upon things that couldn't be changed and moan about the injustices in life, she would have written depressing high-brow literature instead.

She needed a fresh start, and this writing retreat was her best chance. She would lead workshops in the afternoons, and apart from that she was free to work on her own projects. The fee was symbolic, but at least she was here. At a château. In France. For twelve child-free days. She would have time to write and think about her career. What was left of it.

Claudia looked around but couldn't see Charles anywhere. It wouldn't surprise her if he was avoiding her.

She had tried to get hold of him for weeks. Ever since that humiliating meeting with her publisher. *We're sorry, but we won't be able to publish your next book.*

She still felt nauseated when she thought of that meeting. Her publisher had seemed to feel as bad as she did about it, but that had only made it worse. She shivered now when she remembered the pity on their faces.

Limited market. Declining sales. Nothing personal. We wish you the best of luck with future projects.

Nothing personal! Writing was her life. What was she supposed to do now? Go back to her old job? Whoever heard of following your dreams only to turn back?

She spotted Berit Gardner, who was talking to that young agent of hers. Did Berit know her last book had been a flop? For a short, dreadful second she even wondered if Berit knew that her publisher had rejected her next book. Nothing spread as fast as bad news.

She reminded herself that a lot could happen in two weeks. All that was needed was one brilliant idea. A book could change everything. Everybody knew that.

Unfortunately, success rarely came to those who deserved it. She looked angrily at John Wright. It took all her self-control not to go up to him and throw the wine in his face.

She knew she shouldn't give him the satisfaction, but she couldn't help staring at him. His permanently raised eyebrows displayed the same condescension as the last time she had seen him. The same sardonic smirk as if the world constantly surprised him with its stupidity. She wondered if he had practiced the look in the mirror.

He must have felt her staring at him, because he turned suddenly and looked at her.

Claudia tensed. There was something almost pleasurable in standing there and openly meeting his gaze.

And then…nothing.

She tightened the grip of her glass.

He didn't even recognize her.

Claudia walked over to the bar table in the dining room, where several bottles of red wine stood. There was white wine and beer in a small fridge. A sign informed them that the bar was open twenty-four hours and that it was self-serve. You were asked to pay at your own discretion and put the money in a small tin next to the bottles.

Claudia had just dropped two twenty-euro notes in the tin when Emma hurried up to her.

"Oh no, you don't have to pay now, of course," Emma said nervously. "The welcome drinks and the wine with dinner are included."

"I know," Claudia said through clenched teeth. "This is for later."

She got out another twenty-euro note and put it in the tin. She would need it.

The last rays of sun hit the terrace just as Emma started moving everyone into the dining room. Berit knew she should go inside with the others, but it was impossible to tear herself away from the stunning scenery in front of her eyes.

John Wright had no such problems. He gave the sunset over the vineyard one glance and then, as if he found the beauty in nature too pastoral, moved toward the set table indoors.

Berit watched Julian Aubrey nervously intercept him on the way. Julian was carrying a bunch of sheets pressed against his chest, and Berit hoped that John Wright wouldn't be too savage about Julian's youthful ambition.

John Wright stared coldly at him. "And who the hell are you then?" Berit heard him ask.

Julian lost his confidence. "Nobody," he replied quickly and tried to back away. "Nobody at all."

"You don't look like a nobody," John said. He pointed to the printed sheets in Julian's hand. "A manuscript?"

Julian nodded.

"Yours?"

Julian nodded again. He seemed to have lost his ability to speak.

"You want me to read it and decide whether it's any good?"

"Y…yes," Julian said and handed over the stack of papers. Berit thought it looked like he'd handed over an offering.

John Wright grabbed a few sheets from the top.

"Five pages," he said. "It's enough to see if you have any talent. Give me twenty-four hours and I'll tell you whether you're somebody or not."

Julian looked euphoric. Or nauseated. Sometimes it was hard to tell the difference.

Nonsense! Berit thought. She turned toward the fields again. The sun had disappeared while they were talking. There was nothing left to do but to follow them into the dining room.

5

EMMA HAD ARRANGED THE SEATING plan to keep a clear line between teachers and participants. Berit looked longingly over to the other end of the table. Young people were almost always more interesting than middle-aged ones, and beginners more fun than experts. But Emma's hand on her arm was firm and unrelenting as she led Berit to her seat next to John Wright.

"John Wright, Berit Gardner," she said too cheerfully. "You might have met before?"

"No," John Wright said at exactly the same time as Berit said: "Yes, several times."

On the tables were rustic lanterns that cast a warm, cozy light over the tension at the table. The lanterns were reflected in Rebecka's shades, lit up John's dissatisfied face, and illuminated Claudia's tense neck and clenched teeth.

Emma introduced Berit to Mrs. Wright. She was clearly the devoted kind. You would have thought that a long marriage would have removed some of the romance, but she still looked at her husband adoringly and listened carefully to every word he spoke.

How damning that sort of worship must be for an already narcissistic man. A stronger person would have chosen a partner with a little more bite, Berit thought.

At least he hadn't chosen her for her looks. The woman was almost comically plain, with mouse-colored hair, slightly protruding eyes, and dull, baggy clothes. In fact, the starry-eyed admiration was the most interesting thing about her: such an open, unbridled adulation that set her apart from the slight cynicism that surrounded everyone else at their end of the table.

Rebecka Linscott's expression looked even more impassive now. Her dark hair hung loose over her shoulders. There was something ethereal in the way she just sat there, back straight, long narrow neck and a graciously lifted face, her dark shades reflecting everyone's feelings but her own. Berit saw John's face in them, red, angry, and distorted like in a fun-house mirror.

Charles smiled too much. He constantly sought John's eyes, but John made a point of not looking in his direction. Claudia, in turn, tried to catch Charles's attention, and he just as elaborately refused to look at her.

The dining room acoustics amplified all sounds. Cutlery grated against the plates, there were loud thuds when the pots and plates were put down on the tables, and the laughter from the other end of the table echoed between the walls.

The dining room opened on to the terrace through beautiful arches and stone pillars. Someone, Berit guessed it was Emma, had woven fairy lights around the railings. They glimmered invitingly at the edge of Berit's vision and made her want to get up and escape into the warm, lonely darkness.

John ate.

Berit followed with fascination every loaded forkful on its way to his mouth. Sometimes he closed his eyes and looked almost content, but then the mouthful finished, he opened his eyes, saw the group of people around him, and frowned disapprovingly.

When he wasn't eating, he talked. His jaws were constantly active.

"I can't stand functions like this," he said loudly to Berit. "Everyone's just smiling and groveling and expects you to remember their names."

He reached over to his wife's plate and finished her pâté as well. "And everyone's so young these days," he said. "Everyone's supposed to be some young literary genius without having to put any of the work in. No one has time to wait for insight or wisdom. Or work for it. And if you happen to review them negatively, they just give up and pack it all in. No stamina. No tenacity."

Alex must have said something funny at the other end of the table because everybody around him was laughing. He was surrounded by two middle-aged women and their husbands. None of them had been on the bus, but they seemed to have already made friends with Alex.

"They're not that young, are they?" Berit said.

"No, the very young ones probably can't afford to pay two thousand five hundred pounds to be here. Two thousand five hundred! Insanity. In my days, one *read* if one wanted to learn how to write books. But no one does anymore, do they? Everyone wants to write books, no one wants to read them."

Charles reached for the bottle again. John finally looked at him and sarcastically raised his eyebrow. Charles blushed and froze in a comically pitiful way with the wine bottle heading toward his glass. Then he defiantly filled it.

Claudia's glass was also empty, but since Charles purposefully refused to look her way, he didn't notice. She had to reach across his plate to grab the bottle.

Charles's movements became more and more jerky until he nearly knocked over Rebecka's glass. She looked disdainfully at him and moved it to the other side of her plate. When he spoke, he was well articulated, but his voice was much too loud. Pearls of sweat had formed on his forehead. Neither John nor Rebecka listened to what he had to say.

The main course was served: Rabbit à la Lyonnaise that smelled deliciously of bacon, rosemary, thyme, and garlic and was served on a bed of creamy mash.

John continued to talk in his magisterial tone. "There are two things an author must be extremely careful with," he said. "The first is one's literary reputation. The other is one's money. Don't let anyone waste away either of them."

While he was talking, he stared straight at his old publisher. Rebecka Linscott's jaws were so tightly clenched that Berit's own teeth hurt.

She had had enough. Berit got up and went down the staircase, out into the warm summer's eve. Through the open arches facing the terrace above she could hear clinking glasses and cutlery and the odd laughter. She was congratulating herself on having escaped when she suddenly heard footsteps behind her.

She turned around and expected to see Emma, but it was John Wright who had followed her.

"I also needed to get away from them," he said and lit a cigar.

Berit breathed in the smell of it. For a moment they stood there in silence.

"I apologize for not recognizing you up there," John said gruffly. "I didn't mean to offend. It's just I'm bloody lousy at remembering faces. I wouldn't even recognize myself if I met me at one of these parties!"

Berit waved it off. "No offense taken," she said.

"I know who you are, of course," John said. "I've read several of your books. With some pleasure, I should add."

She had read his work too. In essays and reviews he had a knife-sharp ability to reveal pretensions, but he lacked empathy. His novels were hard and brilliant like diamonds but lacked compassion.

"It's this bloody industry," he said. "The longer I'm involved in it, the more cynical I become. And now a new generation is apparently making its way in, but without creating something at all innovative or original. We've seen it all before, haven't we? Nothing surprises us."

"On the contrary," Berit said. "People surprise me all the time."

"I used to believe in this industry. God, listen to me: industry! Everything has to be about business these days, hasn't it? We might as well be selling vacuums." He shook his head. "One day my memoir will be published, and then everyone will find out exactly what I think about the people who make a good living off other people's talents and hard work. Jokers and charlatans, the lot of them. One day, I'll reveal all their dirty secrets."

"Not here at Emma's retreat, I hope," Berit said. "I suspect it might dampen the mood."

He made a dismissive gesture with his hand. "What do I care about that? Actions must have consequences. That's the problem with today. You're not allowed to write about anything, but you can do whatever you want unpunished."

"What actions?" Berit asked. "And what consequences?"

For a while it looked like John was about to answer her question, but Mrs. Wright came running out with a scarf in her hand. She tried to wrap it around her husband's shoulders, even though the dark evening was still warm.

"Stop coddling me, woman," John hissed, and sent both the scarf and her away. "Wait for me in our room. I'm going to have a walk before I go to bed, and I don't want you following me around all the time like a sad puppy."

When she'd left, he looked sheepishly at Berit.

"I know what you're thinking," he said.

"I doubt it," Berit said.

He smiled briefly, a surprisingly disarming smile. "You're thinking that a person of my physique shouldn't balance on a pedestal."

"I don't think anyone benefits from being placed on a pedestal," Berit said cautiously.

"I know I'm not treating her right. But once you're up on the pedestal it's damn hard to get down."

"She's not the only one placing you on a pedestal," Berit said. "The students here, they do it too."

John dismissed it with a wave. "I don't care about their admiration," he said.

Perhaps he should, Berit thought. In its own way, admiration could be a feeling just as lethal as hatred.

She frowned. Something had popped up at the back of her head and was troubling her, but she couldn't quite reach it. Not a real memory, more of a fragment, something her subconscious had observed without even informing her about it.

Years of experience with half-forgotten ideas had taught her that the only thing to do was to wait. Either the insight returned, or it didn't.

She looked at John Wright. "Sooner or later all pedestals are knocked down," she warned.

"I'll keep that in mind," he said.

Berit had just managed to go to sleep when she was woken by angry voices outside her door. She lay disoriented in the darkness trying to distinguish them, but after the first loud outbursts, the people outside had been careful to keep their voices down.

Then they went completely silent. The sound of footsteps trailed off, heading toward the staircase and down the stairs.

Berit wrapped her duvet around her, opened the door, and poked her head out. The hallway was deserted.

She knew who one of the voices belonged to at least. The door to John Wright's room had closed just before the footsteps had faded.

And she had heard what someone had said to him.

I will destroy you.

6

THE WATER WAS FREEZING WHEN Berit dived in.

The shock made her eyes open wide. Above her head the world was a distorted and shimmering green. She stretched her body. She was free and weightless, and nothing existed apart from the pressure in her ears when she held her breath and the bubbles in the water around her when she let it out.

I will destroy you.

Her hands touched the slippery tiles on the opposite side of the pool, and she turned around. When she finally reached the surface, she gasped for air. She shivered. The sun's rays had not yet reached the pool. When she started swimming a long, strong crawl, her body and brain came to life from the cold and the motion. While she swam, she listed everything she didn't know about the conversation from last night.

One: Who'd uttered the threat. All she knew was that it was a man. She had been woken up in the middle of the night with the words already planted as a memory in her head. The tone had been cold and controlled, which made the threat even more unsettling.

Two: Who had received it. When she played it over in her head, she had automatically seen John Wright's face, but now she reminded herself of the importance of not assuming anything. The voices had come from the hallway outside the bedrooms, and she had heard John Wright's bedroom door slam shut. That was all she could be sure of.

Three: If she had dreamt the whole thing.

Four: What she would do with this information.

She parked the last question for the moment and focused on the third. She didn't *think* she had dreamt it, but she had to admit to herself it was a possibility.

When her muscles and lungs started aching, she left the pool, dried herself and quickly changed, so that she could have breakfast before everyone else turned up. She brought her lecture notes and found the cook, coffee, and freshly baked bread in the kitchen.

It was a large and bright room, made for work. The large wooden table had marks from generations of cooking. The wooden floor was scuffed but recently oiled. The work tops were large and sturdy. There were brown and white eggs in a big bowl next to jugs of milk and orange juice, waiting to be served.

Berit took a coffee and a piece of baguette, sat down on the patio, and pondered the last question. What to do with this information?

She had a sip of hot, strong coffee and let her subconscious go to work. Wonderful scents of lavender, rosemary, and thyme wafted over from the kitchen garden next door. Old fruit trees cast a shadow over the paved patio. The wet prints from her feet were still visible on some of the stone slabs. Should she warn Emma? She disregarded the idea almost immediately. No need to worry her before Berit knew more. She had enough to think about as it was.

She finished the baguette and the coffee and decided the question would have to wait until after her lecture.

Emma came into the kitchen just as Berit was leaving. She'd made an effort and put on some lipstick, but it was her energy that suddenly made her beautiful. It was as if she had a newfound vitality. For the first time since they had arrived, Berit recognized her old friend.

"Today we start in earnest!" Emma said enthusiastically. "Isn't it going to be exciting? Who knows what insights John Wright will share with us during his lecture! I'm actually looking forward to it."

It was obvious she was thinking about the author John Wright rather than the man.

"And your lecture, too, of course," she added quickly.

She grabbed a tray to carry a plate filled with two boiled eggs, one croissant, half a baguette, butter, cheese, smoked ham, and a large cup of brewing tea leaves in steaming water. "We're not supposed to do room service," Emma said. "But it's hard to deny John anything. You will be there at his lecture, won't you?"

Berit nodded.

They were both supposed to be speaking on the same topic: The writing life. The idea, she presumed, was that they would introduce two different aspects of the experience of living and working as a writer. He in the morning, she in the afternoon.

"Emma…" she said hesitantly.

Emma stopped in the doorway with the tray in her hands. Berit had no idea what to say, but she had a foreboding feeling after hearing John's words yesterday and the threat against him. She desperately hoped nothing would happen that would crush Emma's newfound hope.

"Just be careful, okay?" she ended weakly.

Emma smiled, perplexed. "I'll see you at John's lecture, then. Ten o'clock in the movie theatre."

"Ten o'clock in the movie theatre" might have confused Berit if she hadn't read up on the history of the building in the welcome packet.

A writing retreat was only one of the château's many uses in the recent decades. It had, in turns, been a hotel, a conference center, a boarding school, and the regional headquarters of a production company that apparently couldn't afford Cannes and the Riviera.

The hotel had installed the swimming pool and bought the old, slightly sinister, stone statues surrounding it. The conference center had built the two wings in a somewhat incongruous style. The boarding school had provided the wings with vinyl flooring and the smell of depression, teenage sweat, and institution that still lingered. And the production company had made a lasting impression by adding a movie theatre.

It was located at the far end of the eastern wing, and Berit made her way there now, in plenty of time before John's lecture was due to start.

She wasn't the only one who was early. The room vibrated with expectation. Berit took a seat in the front row and turned around so she could study the rest of the audience.

Most of them were sitting bolt upright in eager anticipation, some with laptops on their knees, others with old-fashioned notebooks and pens. The room was filled with an intense murmur, but everyone fell silent when John Wright entered the room.

He walked down the aisle along one of the walls, up the low steps, and out onto the small stage in front of the screen. He was formally dressed in a dark suit, white shirt, and a bow tie.

The audience leaned forward, as if they couldn't wait for his words to reach them.

John Wright lifted one hand and pressed a button on a small remote control. His PowerPoint presentation lit up on the screen behind him.

In large black letters it said:

"If you have any young friends who aspire to become writers, the first greatest favor you can do them is to shoot them now, while they're happy."

—Dorothy Parker

Nervous laughter spread among the audience, but it subsided when they realized John Wright wasn't smiling. Berit wondered if he had misquoted Dorothy Parker on purpose. Killing them was actually only the second greatest favor you could do an aspiring writer. The first was to give them a copy of *The Elements of Style*. But it was just like John Wright to ignore the positive part and focus solely on the negative.

"When I received the request to take part in this writing retreat, my first impulse was to decline," he continued. "Writing is an art form. It can't be taught like painting a wall or replacing a roof. If someone suggests it can be, they're only after your money.

"But then I thought maybe it was my duty to attend. Maybe it is every thinking human being's duty to do what they can to stop this insanity. So here's my piece of advice: Stop. Give up before you've wasted any more time. Find yourselves another hobby. *Read* a book instead, if you still remember how to."

The spotlights fell on his chronically disappointed face.

"You won't succeed!" he said. "Not any one of you. There's no point trying. You will lose out to a celebrity's shitty ghostwritten book; I can guarantee you. Publishers don't care about quality anymore, and agents only care about money."

As he sauntered slowly back and forth across the stage high above the audience, he perfectly embodied the lone prophet he saw himself as. But his voice, when he spoke again, just sounded quarrelsome. Berit thought that what he was saying would have more impact if his voice had been deeper and more serious, but he seemed to be too stuck in his grievances with the state of the world to care about what effect he had on the audience.

"And the booksellers? They're more interested in selling cappuccino than quality literature! They're probably more interested in the interior design than books. Pastel-colored walls with insipid quotes in cursive fonts is so important to them that they don't have room for actual bookshelves. And they won't be around much longer anyway. Not when Amazon sells off books for next to nothing and would just as happily sell toilet paper. And the readers? They haven't got a clue what good literature is. They would probably be just as happy *reading* the toilet paper."

He pointed at the audience and moved his finger in a sweeping motion as if he wanted to address each and every one of them. "None of you will make any money. You can forget about having a pension. If you think you can live off admiration alone, you're wrong. And you won't have much of that either. Newspapers don't review books anymore. The judges of the literary prizes wouldn't know quality if it hit them in the face with a hardcover. Regardless of what you write, someone will take offense. Especially if you're a white, middle-aged man. No group are under more attack than us."

He looked out across the audience. "And yet here you are. Victims of the oldest fraud in the world: the business of peddling false dreams. The people trying to teach you how to become a writer are the charlatans of our time! A hundred and fifty years ago, they would have sold miracle cures for hair loss or impotence. Now they're selling dreams to anyone who can cough up the money."

He raised his voice. "Listen to my advice! Give up! Quit now! Believe me, you will do yourself and the world a favor."

And with those words of wisdom, John ended his lecture and went down the steps without giving so much as a glance at Emma, his wife, or the audience.

No one said a word.

7

THE WRITING LIFE, RIGHT, BERIT thought as she gazed across the auditorium. It was five to two, and everyone was still finding their way back to their seats. She had a few moments to collect her thoughts before she got started, and she needed every minute she could get.

Her heart was pounding as she stood on the stage. It wasn't out of nervousness or stage fright. No, it was John Wright's words that had shaken her, and the audience's reaction to them. When they went to have lunch, they had been quiet and withdrawn. Several of them looked almost scared. Others seemed resolved but distant.

Berit involuntarily looked over at Emma, who had just entered the cinema and taken her seat. Her face and neck were still red and flushed and her hands manically squeezed the armrests of the red velvet chair.

Berit forced herself to think about the lecture again. She reminded herself that she could have talked about the writing life in her sleep. She was used to living and analyzing life at the same time, experiencing things and noting them somewhere inside her, ready to be used in a book one day, and she had no problems turning it into a lecture.

If she were to describe her life chronologically, she would say it consisted of three phases. The first had been her childhood years in Sweden, distinctly defined by age and geography. She had never felt like she belonged there, and it hadn't exactly been a happy upbringing, not with her parents' unhappy marriage and her mother's low moods, but when she looked back on those years, they were still filled with joy. What she hadn't got from home, she'd found in books.

She remembered autumnal days at the city library, where the old books seemed to create a space and time just for her. She used to walk along the shelves and look at the different sections of books in Finnish, German, French, Russian, Polish and think about how many stories there were, in so many languages, that she would never have time to read. *Not even if I was locked up in the city library*, she used to think, and then lose herself in a fantasy about being able to stay there with the books.

The second phase in her life had started when she moved to London, the city of her dreams. A time of dreaming and seeking. For the first time in her life, reality began to compete with the books in terms of absurd adventures and intricacies. She had been happy, broke, and often hungover, and if she closed her eyes, she could still see herself as she was then: jeans, leather jacket, the long curly blond hair. So full of life and confidence and curious about everything. And so very young.

The third phase was the writing. It stretched from the thrilling moment she first held her own book in her hand, until now, standing in a cinema in a castle in France looking out across a sea of slightly nervous faces. She desperately hoped she could give them an alternative to John Wright's jaded cynicism.

She wanted to convey to them how every new book was a miracle that still filled her with amazement. How the smell of a freshly published book was more sublime than the smell of a brisk autumn day, a flowering meadow, your lover's perfume, hot coffee on a cold morning…

At one minute to two, John entered the room. He looked cross and irritated before Berit had even begun to speak.

Emma turned around, and her face distorted in a hateful snarl. Her fingers twisted as if she imagined strangling him.

After John, Nicole came in, with a look of interest on her face, followed by Claudia, who looked like she had done something outrageous that she would certainly come to regret. No Mrs. Wright in sight.

John Wright looked over at Berit's PowerPoint presentation, and his face scrunched up even more, as if he had swallowed something revolting. The picture showed a black hat seen from the side, with a rounded crown and long, thin brim.

Berit sat down on the edge of the stage and dangled her legs. "Does this picture scare you?" she asked.

She looked out over the audience to see how many of them understood the reference. Mildred was the only one who smiled. John Wright definitely understood but rolled his eyes.

In the end Nicole was the one who impatiently answered her: "Why would we be scared by a picture of a hat?"

Berit reached for the slim, unassuming edition she had found in the castle's library, and she told them that the hat was really a boa constrictor who had swallowed an elephant.

She read from Antoine de Saint-Exupéry's classic, *The Little Prince*:

> "Grown-ups never understand anything by themselves, and it is tiresome for children to be always and forever explaining things to them."

She clicked on the small remote and a quote from Astrid Lindgren came up on the screen.

> "Everything great that ever happened in this world happened first in someone's imagination."

The next picture was of Astrid Lindgren herself, with the quote:

> "Where in Moses's law does it say that old ladies can't climb a tree?"

She clicked again. New quote. This time it was a reader's question to an author:

> "I want to become a writer when I grow up. Am I mad?"

This time, several people laughed.

The next picture had the author's answer:

"Yes. Being an adult is extremely overrated. Become a writer instead."

John Wright had sat down in the front row, right in front of Berit. She wondered if he'd done so just to make her nervous. At his feet sat a large cup of tea, untouched.

"When writing is at its best, it lets us imagine things and play like a child," Berit said. "It lets us see the world with the wide-eyed fascination of a child, talk to imaginary friends inside our head, travel all over the world without leaving our chair, befriend dragons, find love, save the world."

She stood up and walked slowly across the stage.

She still remembered the days when she struggled with her writing on the evenings and weekends. When the publishers returned everything she sent them, and she thought no one would ever read anything she wrote.

"Is it going to be difficult?" she asked and answered her own question: "Yes, almost all the time. Will you be rejected? Yes, probably by all the publishers you know of, and quite a few that you haven't even heard of yet."

She shook her head and continued: "Will you be broke? Good god, yes. Will you live your whole lives in a frustrating mix of hubris and self-doubt? Definitely."

Most people in the audience smiled at her questions and answers. They were young enough not to be put off by hardship, probably because they still thought it would be temporary and fleeting, rather than a constant part of life.

"Is it worth it? I've never doubted it for a second. If people stopped reading my books and the publishers stopped publishing them, I would still write. Fredrik Backman once said that he wrote like middle-aged men played guitar, alone, late at night, just for themselves. And I do too. I write because I have to. To me stories are as necessary as air, and the imagination is a muscle that needs constant exercising in order not to wither away. Socrates said the unexamined life is not worth living, and I feel the same thing about the unwritten life."

John Wright made no effort to try to hide his disinterest. His eyes were apathetic. His body slouched. He let his chin drop to his chest, as if her lecture wasn't even worth staying awake for.

"The writing life is a way to relate to the world, not a finished result," Berit said. "It's not financial security or validation or status. It's always looking for stories and being aware of the unfolding tales around us. About asking questions, being curious, observing people and places with inquisitiveness and interest."

Opposite her, John's arms dropped down the sides of his chair.

If he starts snoring, I'll throw the remote at him, Berit thought.

"You can invent whatever you want," she continued. "That's the great thing about the writing life. Sure, sure, there are drawbacks as well. You're constantly going to doubt your own ability to put your visions down on paper, and you're right in doubting, because you're never fully going to reach the goal. It's a disastrous, boring, panic-filled, passive life that will most likely never make you rich."

And on top of that, Berit thought, *it might take them to the darkest corners of the human psyche.*

That was flipside of creative curiosity: how affected you became by feeling empathy with your characters. She was often overwhelmed by a sort of existential dread when she identified with the lives of her lonely and damaged characters, until she agreed with Strindberg that human beings are indeed to be pitied.

"It's only worth it if the stories are worth it," she continued. "If we can find happiness in imagination, if somewhere inside us we still daydream like a child and climb trees and draw boa constrictors that swallow elephants. John Wright was right in trying to put you off writing. If you can think of something you'd rather do with your time, your imagination, your insanity, please, go on, do that. All I can say is that it's a privilege and a blessing to get to make things up for a living. And one day you'll meet people who will have heard the voices you planted in their head. What you saw, they see. What you felt, they feel. They will laugh and cry with you, and that, my friends, is a gift and a miracle, something of the most wondrous things people can achieve: to imagine the world as it could be and see it through somebody else's eyes. That's all."

She'd come to the end she'd prepared, but Berit didn't finish her lecture. Instead, she slowly looked at her audience, from left to right, as if she was trying to observe each and every one of them individually. Most of them met her gaze, interested in listening to what she had to say.

"There is one thing that writing does," she said, "that's not altogether positive. It can blur the perception of what feels real and expand the limits of what is possible. This can be positive, if it makes you see the world through new eyes, but it can also be harmful, if it makes you no longer able to tell right from wrong. Behavior that should be unthinkable no longer is. There are boundaries that should exist in real life, albeit never in writing, and we abandon them at our own peril."

She looked at them again, soberly and sternly. "If anyone here is planning something…something desperate, think again. It's never too late to change your mind. Don't do something that cannot be undone. Don't cross any lines that once crossed, you can never go back on."

Berit looked for signs of someone understanding what she was talking about, but all she got was surprise and puzzled faces. From all of them except John Wright. He was asleep.

No one seemed to understand what she meant by her warning. She wasn't sure she knew herself, but she had to do something to prevent a catastrophe she felt more and more certain was hurtling toward them.

When they realized she wasn't going to say anything else, they clapped slowly, confusedly.

She frowned. People started collecting their things and getting up, and John Wright just sat there, not moving. The color of his skin was an unnatural, doughy white.

Berit jumped down from the stage without using the steps and carefully touched his shoulder. Then she felt for his pulse.

Damn it, Berit thought. She was too late. She looked instinctively for Emma.

"Call the police," she said. "John Wright is dead."

8

COMMISSAIRE BÉATRICE ROCHE OF THE Police Nationale in Lyon opened the fridge door and stared miserably inside. On one shelf were individual portions of onion soup ready to be gratinated. On another were bowls filled to the brim with fresh pasta. There were steaks, fresh fish, oysters, charcuteries, a whole chicken, a game pie, a bowl of berry mousse, and a small plate of bomboloni coated with sugar and finely chopped hazelnuts, decadently inviting.

She stared at the excess downheartedly and then back at the small kitchen table by the window, perfect for two people.

It was set for one.

Her daughter wasn't at home. Obviously. It was Saturday. And she wouldn't be back until much later, probably not until after two in the morning.

When the phone rang, she picked up immediately. "Yes, boss?" she said way too eagerly.

There were a few seconds of silence before her boss said: "You're home alone, aren't you?"

Roche confessed.

"It's Saturday, your day off. Why aren't you out enjoying yourself?"

"Do you have a job for me or not?"

In the background she could hear laughter and commotion and cheerful chatter. Roche imagined luxurious elegance, dressed-up women and handsome men drinking champagne or cocktails, smoking e-cigarettes. She heard the clicking sound of stilettos on a stone floor, then the background noise faded out.

"Meet me at the office in half an hour," her boss said. "I've got to be back in time for the starter."

Roche put on a blazer, combed her hair, and went back into the kitchen. She reached for a Post-it note, which seemed to be their only form of communication these days, and wrote: *at work*, in the unlikely event that her daughter would get home before her.

She drove the few blocks to work, turned into the fenced-off area around the police station, and parked. She felt her energy return as soon as she saw the modern gray building. *Police Nationale* was written on one of the walls. She automatically straightened her back for the French flags, fluttering in the air high above.

This was her life. She had spent more time with her colleagues here than at home with her daughter. She refused to admit that perhaps that was part of the problem.

She ran up the stairs two steps at a time. The office where her team worked felt alive and chaotic, even on a Saturday afternoon. Seven desks were crammed into the room, with printed sheets of paper, notes and connections jotted down, case files and old coffee cups spread out everywhere. The cycling shirt hung over a file cabinet told her Janvier was there.

She went straight into her boss's office. The desk was completely empty and manically tidy, almost as perfect as the boss herself. Chief Superintendent Sylvie Pelissier was nearly the same age as Béatrice Roche, but that's where their similarities ended. Pelissier had studied at an expensive private school, was married to the head of a hospital, and had two perfect children who looked incredibly neat and polite in the framed photos on her desk.

Roche was a single mum to a twenty-one-year-old. On her desk was, if you could find it in the mess, a photo of her daughter when she was twelve and going through her punk phase. She looked like a young Gene Simmons.

"We've got a dead Englishman out at Allard's old place," Pelissier said.

"The production company?" Roche asked.

"It's been sold. Apparently, it's full of writers now."

"And was the cause of death suspicious?"

Not that it mattered. She would check it out, even if the dead person was a hundred and ten years old with a history of heart problems. Suddenly, her Saturday was rescued. And if the cause of death was not suspicious, she could spend tomorrow morning making her daughter a breakfast she would refuse to eat anyway.

"Suspicious enough," her boss said. "The victim's name is John Wright. That much we know. We've informed the consulate. They'll want to know when we can release the body. The coroner is already on his way. I've told him to hurry up. The gendarmes were first on the scene, but they have already handed the case over to us. Lack of resources."

So, at least they had felt something was wrong, Roche thought. The local police station wouldn't have handed the case over if the man had died of natural causes.

"Next of kin?" she asked.

"His wife. On site. That might speed things up a bit."

It would help with the bureaucracy if nothing else, Roche thought. And, if it turned out to be murder, the wife was always the prime suspect.

"Any signs of violence?"

"No. As I understand it, he died during a lecture. But the woman who reported the death clearly thought something was wrong. One Berit Gardner. *I want to report a murder.* That's what she said."

"Maybe she killed him herself?" Roche suggested. It wasn't that unusual that the perpetrator called it in.

"It's possible. Regardless, we have a building full of tourists. Apparently they were in the middle of a writing retreat when their star writers dies. If there's anything suspicious about the cause of death, I want us to have a clear picture of the sequence of events before all of them return home."

Roche nodded. Tourists were a nightmare to investigate. "Drugs?" she said.

"We don't know anything yet. Writers didn't used to be that wild in my day. And he died sometime between two and three this afternoon, during a lecture. Hardly the standard time to have a line."

"Money?"

Pelissier shrugged. "Who knows?"

Roche waited. She knew her boss well enough to know there was more coming.

"When the case was called in, I was with Monsieur le Maire," Pelissier began. "He felt, and I agreed, that this was an excellent opportunity for Philippe to find his feet. He's eager to prove himself. I don't need to mention that we all predict a brilliant career for him."

"Of course," Roche said, trying to maintain a neutral face.

Philippe Delavigne was the mayor's son. He had started working for them fresh out of the police academy a matter of weeks ago.

"And it won't hurt you either to be able to do Monsieur le Maire a favor. It won't hurt any of us, I might add. I specifically mentioned that he would be working with one of my best investigators."

"Yes, Madame." Her boss seemed to expect something else, so she added: "Thank you, Madame."

"He might not be that bad. Off you go."

Constable Janvier stopped Roche in the corridor and jogged slowly next to her down the stairs. "I heard The Mayor's coming out with you," he said.

"Are you still trying to win the Tour de France?"

"You have to keep in shape." Janvier had passed thirty a few years ago. He had recently started losing his hair and developing a beer belly, and it had encouraged him to take up exercising and dress much too youthfully.

"What are you doing here on a Saturday?" Roche asked. "Shouldn't you be at home with your family?"

"My mother-in-law is visiting."

"Ah." Roche used to say that their team of seven was like a family, and Janvier used to object and say they were much better than that. Because, unlike with family, there was no mother-in-law.

"So, what do you think?" he asked.

"About the case?"

"About The Mayor."

She shrugged. "He's probably fine."

Janvier followed her all the way to her car. "Shall I start the background check?" he said with hope in his voice. "The victim's economy, his closest friends, that sort of thing?"

"Do you speak English?" she asked.

He hesitated, like he considered lying. "No," he admitted.

"Go home," Roche said and got in her car.

He rested his hand on the roof of her car and leaned down. "You better behave yourself," he said. "Otherwise, The Mayor will tell on you."

"*You* better behave," Roche said just before she slammed the car door shut. "Otherwise, I'll tell your mother-in-law."

Commissaire Roche drove up a dark and depressing tree-lined avenue leading to the dilapidated château. She noted the tracks in the gravel that the gendarmes had left behind and drove slowly around the corner. She parked halfway up the lawn next to the coroner's battered old Citroën and got out.

Around thirty people were spread out on the paved patio between the two wings. They looked like a group that had just been evacuated because of a fire alarm. But with one difference: instead of shock on their faces, there was some sort of eager curiosity.

"Who's responsible here?" Roche asked loudly.

She spotted a stern looking woman her own age, with steely gray hair and a confident posture. She was dressed in a dark green linen suit with a beautiful red silk scarf around her neck and both hands in her jacket pockets.

Her cold, clear blue eyes met Roche's gaze and held it, as if she was trying to see straight into her soul in order to decide what kind of a person she was. Finally, the woman nodded toward an ordinary looking, insecure woman who broke away from the group.

"Emma Scott," said the woman in the green suit, as if the woman couldn't speak for herself.

Roche turned to face her. "Madame Scott," she said. "We'll need to speak to you later, if you could make yourself available."

"Of course. Naturally. Whatever you need."

"I understand the…" She searched her memory for the English word for coroner but gave up. "That Dr. Laurent has already arrived? Can you take me to him and…the body?"

"This way," Madame Scott said, and hurriedly led her to the entrance of one of the wings.

Inside, she opened the doors to a movie theatre. They entered at the top, so in order to get to the stage they had to walk past rows of real cinema chairs in red velvet.

It should smell of old popcorn in here, Roche thought when she walked down the aisle. But it didn't.

The coroner was at the bottom by the front row, hunched over the body. His face was only millimeters away from the dead man.

"Aren't you getting a little too friendly with him?" she said. "You've only just met."

Laurent straightened up. "Roche," he said. "How decent of you to finally turn up."

There was something sickly about the color of Laurent's face, very similar to the victim's. Roche always thought of the autopsy room when she saw him. As if the harsh light, the stainless steel, and the smell of corpses had somehow rubbed off on him. She wondered what his private life was like. If he even had one.

But who was she to say anything? She was grateful to be spending her Saturday night in a movie theatre with a corpse.

The victim was a burly man in his sixties. He was dressed in a tailored suit jacket, dark trousers, white shirt, bow tie, silk scarf in his jacket pocket, polished black shoes, black socks. But none of those things could save him from the undignified moment of death.

The man was slumped in the chair, chin resting on his white shirt, his mouth wide open, and his eyes like glass. It was impossible to get an idea of what he'd been like as a person. Death hadn't only deprived him of dignity, but also of all his personality.

Roche focused on seeing him as a human being. Later on, she'd be as ruthless as necessary, but during this brief moment she allowed herself to feel empathy for the unknown Englishman who had died so far away from home.

It was true that you couldn't be soft or sentimental to cope with a job in law enforcement, but she knew that you couldn't be too tough either. She had seen many colleagues hide behind a ruthless, insensitive protective shell for so long that in the end, there was nothing left behind it. No wonder so many police officers ended up divorced.

Justice, in itself so harsh and impersonal, needs compassion, she thought.

Roche lightly touched the dead man's hand, ignoring the coroner's disapproving look.

"Any theory about what killed him?" she asked.

"Yes," Laurent said.

"Any chance he died of a natural cause?"

"I'm pretty sure nature was helped along this time." He looked around and picked up a paper cup from near the victim's feet. He smelt it.

"Interesting," he said.

"What is it?"

"Cold tea," he said and put it down. "Run tests on everything he ate and drank."

Her phone rang. The new guy had arrived. He was on the other side of the house and had knocked on the door several times. Nobody was answering, he complained. Roche wondered if it was the first time he'd come across a door that wasn't immediately opened for him.

"Come around the back," she instructed and hung up.

Idiot, she thought.

"I have to go and rescue the new guy," she said.

"I hear they're already calling him The Mayor?" Laurent said.

"Of course."

"In my profession you learn not to judge people until you've seen what's inside them."

Roche shuddered. He meant it literally.

"I'll remember that," she said. She looked around the movie theatre. "To think that he died here, surrounded by people, and not one of them noticed."

"One person must have seen something," Laurent said.

Roche raised an eyebrow.

He nodded toward the stage. "The person who gave the lecture. He or she must have stared straight at him as he was dying."

9

ROCHE'S NEW INSPECTOR WAS DRESSED in a dark suit that had probably cost as much as her monthly wage. The shoes were Italian and doubtlessly impossible to run in. His hair was combed back.

He looks more like a yuppie than a police officer, she thought.

He also looked incredibly stiff. His face was completely expressionless and his back so straight it seemed as if he thought he was in the military rather than the police.

"I heard they call me The Mayor down at the station," he said, raising his chin when he spoke, as if he was on the warpath to defend his dignity.

"I'm sure they wanted you to hear it," Roche said drily. "But in my experience, it's better to find out what they call you behind your back straight away."

His jaw dropped a little when he thought about what she had said.

She sighed. "Are you expecting me to do something about it?" she said. "Because the best you can do is just to ignore it. You won't make many friends if you run to the boss every time someone makes a joke about you."

"No, no." He looked appalled. "I'm not *telling*. I just wanted you to know that I'm not expecting any favors because of my family connections. I have always been very clear that I—"

"Well, you'll get them," said Roche, shrugging. The way the world worked wasn't his fault. "Relax," she added. "They'll accept you when you've shown them what you're made of. You don't have any siblings?"

He looked at her with a combination of respect and unease. "How... how did you know?"

"Get used to being teased," she said. "That's my advice. Do you speak English?"

"Of course. And Mandarin. My father insisted I learned several languages. Tourism will always be part of the future of Lyon, and regardless of what career path I chose, he said, there would always be international connections."

She patted him on the shoulder and said: "Another piece of advice, Mayor." *If that's what they called him behind his back, he'd better get used to it,* she thought. "Try not to mention your old man in every sentence."

The cook was a sturdy woman of indeterminable age. Roche suspected that she was one of those women who had been a matriarch all her life. She had that warm, soft type of body you could easily imagine spoiling children and grandchildren with homemade food and freshly made biscuits.

But right now, she was deeply enraged. It was a frightening sight. Roche understood why The Mayor took two steps back until he was protected from her behind Roche's back.

"Take samples, of my food?" the cook said, her face alarmingly red. "Are you suggesting something I served, something I *cooked*, killed Monsieur Wright? I have never heard anything so upsetting. And slanderous!"

Roche held her hands up. "Do you have a manager here, Madame?" she asked calmly.

The woman stopped abruptly. "A manager?"

"Yes. Someone who bosses you around and tells you how to do your job even though they wouldn't be able to cook a *poulet au vinaigre*, even if their life depended on it?"

"I've had bosses like that," the cook admitted. "When I was younger. But I've learned that you have to teach them straight away, so they don't get ideas. No one tells me what to do anymore. And it's not needed, I assure you. Nothing *I* cook—"

"I salute you, Madame. But you're way ahead of me. I still have a boss, and she will tell me it doesn't matter how brilliant a cook you are; we'll still need samples of the food. Strictly protocol. You know what it's like. Everything needs documenting these days."

"Oh, I see. Well, I guess that's different."

"What did Mr. Wright have for lunch?" Roche asked again.

This time the cook answered. "Same thing as everybody else. Sole *meunière* with parsley, lemon, and lots of melted butter. With that, boiled potatoes and a freshly made summer salad."

Roche glanced over her shoulder to make sure The Mayor was writing it all down. He wasn't. She frowned at him and nodded toward his pocket until he eventually understood what she meant and pulled out his notebook.

"Did anyone complain about anything?" Roche asked in a neutral voice. "Something that tasted strange? Someone feeling sick afterward?"

The cook tried to make herself as tall as possible; she hardly measured five feet three. Her face turned red again.

"For the protocol," Roche reminded her. "Purely routine."

The cook answered through gritted teeth. "No," she said. "No, no one complained."

"Were there any leftovers?"

"I told you there was nothing wrong with the food I cooked! There's not going to be any leftovers when you cook sole." She looked triumphant. "But even so, it *couldn't* have been the food, because I always taste what I cook, and I feel just fine."

"Someone could have put something in it afterward," The Mayor said.

The woman seemed insulted by the mere thought that someone would tamper with her food, because she glared angrily at The Mayor, who took a further step back behind Roche.

"What my young colleague is trying to say is that you can't possibly be held responsible for what people do to your food after you've cooked it," Roche said. "In case it turns out there is something in it. You hear about people doing all sorts of things."

"That's true," the cook said. "One wonders where the world is heading. People show no respect these days."

"What about the plates? The pots and pans that were used?"

"Do you think I leave unwashed plates sitting around for hours while I relax? Sunbathe? Have a foot massage, perhaps? This is an efficient, well-organized, and *clean* kitchen, I'll have you know."

She showed them the spotless cast-iron pots, pans, and stacks of clean, dried plates and bowls.

"Where did they have lunch?"

"We set up a buffet in the dining room upstairs. Most of them ate out on the terrace."

"So everything came from the same serving plates? They helped themselves to what they wanted?"

"Yes, but Monsieur Wright didn't eat with the rest. No, no, not him. He insisted on being served in his room."

"You went up there with a tray?" Roche asked.

"Me?! I don't have time to run around with trays for people who think they are above eating with everyone else."

"But you prepared the tray?"

"Madame Scott did. Here in the kitchen. I'll give her this much; she prepared a lovely looking tray. A small vase with flowers and everything. Neatly folded napkin." The cook nodded approvingly. "She's very meticulous, is Madame Scott."

"Did she take the tray up herself as well?"

"Of course. Madame Scott always took his food up. She does everything herself here on the writing retreat: washing, cleaning, serving. You'd think she'd have her hands full without having to wait on that Monsieur Wright. But that's just the way it is. Some people can't say no. They have no sense of dignity." She hesitated. "But she must have been fed up with waiting on him in the end. When she was preparing the lunch tray, she was muttering to herself like a lunatic." The cook shrugged her shoulders, as if nothing English people did really surprised her.

They found Madame Scott in the garden. Spread around her on the lawn were young people with notebooks and computers. Seated at a few tables were the people who were too old to work sitting down on the ground.

Commissaire Roche took a seat at the rickety table where Madame Scott was sitting. The Mayor sat down beside her.

"They're writing," Madame Scott said in a quiet voice. "They've had a terrible shock, of course, but, well, life must go on."

She looked naive and innocent from across the table. She leant forward as if eager to do whatever she could to help them.

"Such an *awful* tragedy," she said breathlessly.

Roche offered a vague murmur in agreement. "Madame Scott," she continued, "tell me exactly what happened. Include as many details as you can think of, please."

"Please call me Emma," she said eagerly. Then she was quiet for a while. Roche wondered if she was nervous, but when she started talking, Roche realized she had just been gathering her thoughts.

"It was Berit who first realized he was dead," she began.

"Berit?"

"Berit Gardner. One of the teachers at the retreat. She gave the lecture, so she was staring straight at him."

"Madame Gardner gave the lecture?" Roche asked. She suddenly had a vision of clear blue eyes looking down on the Englishman while he was dying.

Emma nodded. "When the lecture had ended, she suddenly jumped down off the stage and said: 'John Wright is dead. We have to call the police.' Or something along those lines."

"And you did?"

"She did. I was in a state of shock."

Roche made an encouraging movement with her hand. "And then what happened?"

"Berit made sure everybody left the theatre and that nobody touched the body. I felt we shouldn't leave him all alone in there. It seemed so cold. I suggested maybe we should move him to his bedroom instead."

"But you didn't?"

"Berit said it was best not to touch anything until the police turned up."

"How very kind of her."

"And then…I realized we'd have to tell Mrs. Wright that her husband had died. She wasn't at the lecture, you see, so she wasn't aware of it. She had no idea."

"Were you the one who told her?" Roche said in earnest sympathy. It was the worst part of her job. She was grateful that she wouldn't have to do it this time.

"Berit did. I…I just couldn't."

Roche nodded. "We'll need to speak to Madame Wright," she said.

"No, you can't!" Emma burst out. "Not right now, I mean. Berit gave her a sleeping pill. She thought it was best. When she left Mrs. Wright's new bedroom she said: 'I hope she gets to sleep for a while. There's no reason for her to be in a rush to wake up to her new reality.'"

"Mrs. Wright's new bedroom?"

"Berit thought you'd want to look at Mr. Wright's room, so she was moved to a different one."

The Mayor raised his eyebrows.

"Madame Gardner seems to have been very helpful," Roche said in a neutral voice.

"Yes," Emma simply said. "I couldn't have done it without her. We accompanied Mrs. Wright so she could collect a few things from their room. She picked up her toilet bag and all the black clothes she'd brought with her. When she got the clothes out of the wardrobe, she buried her face in her husband's clothes. Berit whispered to me to allow her. It could be the last time she ever smelled him, and I had to leave the room in order not to cry. She took his pajamas as well."

"Did you bring John Wright his lunch earlier?" Roche asked.

"Of course. We weren't supposed to have room service. We're short-staffed. But it was hard to deny John anything. And it was only for a couple of days. He was due to fly back later this evening."

The Mayor and Roche glanced at each other.

"Did he finish his lunch?" Roche asked.

"Of course. The tray was empty when I picked it up an hour later."

"Did he have any complaints about the food?"

Emma smiled feebly. "John Wright might have complained about most things, but he devoured the food. And the wine."

Roche hesitated. "And were you… Were you upset about something when you prepared the tray?"

Emma opened her eyes wide and said in a high-pitched voice: "Upset? Why would I be upset about anything?"

Madame Gardner was Emma Scott's opposite, Commissaire Roche thought. Emma had come across as restless and slightly detached from the world, whereas Madame Gardner was calm, focused, and constantly observing everything.

She sat down where Emma had been, crossed her legs, and regarded both Roche and The Mayor with alert attention. Roche had a strong feeling that not much got by Madame Gardner unnoticed. For a moment she felt uneasy when she thought about what Madame Gardner might see in her.

"Madame Gardner, tell me about John Wright," Roche said.

"Call me Berit," she said, before carefully considering Roche's question. "John Wright was…the powder keg, I suppose you could say."

"And we're looking for the match?"

Berit nodded. "As a writer I've learned to become sensitive to different atmospheres. So, I know that several people…felt things about him." She seemed disappointed in her inability to find the right words but continued: "Intense feelings. And several people needed him. Strong desperate needs. It was a very…volatile mix. I felt it on the first night and became even more convinced when I heard someone threaten him."

The Mayor twitched. "Threaten?" he said.

Berit nodded. She told them about what she'd heard when she'd woken up in the middle of the night. The Mayor seemed disappointed that she couldn't be more specific. "So it could have been anyone?"

"It was a male voice. I know that."

"If you even heard it," The Mayor said skeptically. "You might have dreamt it."

"It's possible," Berit said calmly.

"Tell us everything you did, from the time the lecture started," Roche asked.

Berit did, clearly and carefully, but even though she had been standing right in front of Wright, she didn't seem to have noticed anything.

"You saw nothing?" Roche could hear the disappointment in her voice. She could have sworn Berit Gardner was someone who saw everything. If she had to describe her favorite type of witness, they would have been very similar to the woman sitting calmly opposite them. And yet—nothing. Nothing at all.

"I must have been blind. Like a kitten." Berit's voice sounded irritated. "I believed he was asleep, you see. He looked peaceful."

"But then you thought it was murder?"

"Yes, like I said, he provoked extremely strong reactions in people. He liked to stir things up. It seemed completely unfathomable that a person like him would die from natural causes in a context like this."

"What did you do before the lecture?"

"All day?"

"Start from lunch."

"I had lunch in the kitchen. I always try to be on my own before a lecture. To focus."

"So you must have seen Madame Scott preparing John Wright's lunch tray?"

"Yes," Berit said expressionlessly.

"Did she seem agitated in any way?"

Berit hesitated. "I was focused on my lecture," she said. "But I believe John Wright's lecture stirred up a lot of emotions in many people. Like I said. The man was a powder keg. All set to explode."

Roche noticed she hadn't answered her question, but she didn't press her. "And afterward?"

"After lunch I went to the cinema where the lecture would take place. I needed to connect my PowerPoint presentation and prepare a little. The lecture started at two. By three, John Wright was dead."

Roche drummed her fingers on the table. "And you didn't notice anything strange or out of place?"

"Not then. Not during the lecture. But later I discovered somebody had stolen his briefcase. It felt like too much of a coincidence to not be related to his death."

Roche leaned forward.

"His bag was missing?" she asked sharply.

"I found out when Mrs. Wright collected her things from her and John's room. I asked her if anything was different than when she'd last been there."

"Apart from her husband being dead?" The Mayor said.

Berit pulled a face. "Apart from that," she agreed. "Mrs. Wright remembered his briefcase had been below the table before the lecture started. Now it was gone. It contained his computer, all his notes, everything. And it had never been by his feet in the cinema during the lecture. I remembered that."

"Did Madame Wright know when she'd last seen the briefcase?" Roche asked.

"At lunch, she remembered it clearly. He was working at the desk when the lunch tray arrived. Computer, sheets of paper, and a notebook on the desk. Before he ate, he packed everything up and put his briefcase under the desk. And after his death, it was gone."

10

JOHN WRIGHT'S ROOM WAS MORE of a suite, consisting of one big bedroom with open wardrobes, an unmade bed, and a living room, with French balcony doors overlooking the vineyard and the rolling hills beyond. The suite was bright and airy with white wood wall paneling and a dark oak floor. Delicate curtains fluttered softly in the wind from the open balcony doors.

"Berit Gardner is hiding something," The Mayor said and walked up to the large wardrobe.

"Do you think she lied to us?" Roche said. Her own impression was that Berit had been honest and helpful. A bit too helpful, granted. Roche had met more than one perpetrator who had gone out of their way to help the police.

The Mayor frowned. "Perhaps she didn't lie. But she didn't tell the whole truth. I'm sure of it."

"They rarely do," Commissaire Roche said. She thought of Berit's completely expressionless face when she had asked her about the lunch tray and the way she'd studiously avoided answering her question.

The Mayor carefully put on disposable gloves and pulled out a clothes hanger with a black blazer on it.

"Good quality," he said. He sounded grudgingly approving, which made Roche think it was probably of extremely good quality.

Women's clothes were strewn on the chaise longue. The Mayor picked up a salmon-pink dress with his thumb and index finger and looked at it in abject disgust. "*This*, on the other hand, is not. Cheap polyester."

Roche went to the desk. There were piles of books. All the titles were by John Wright himself. She opened one from the top of the pile. It was signed.

"What's your impression of Emma Scott?" she asked.

He waved dismissively. "She seems to be pretty organized," he said. "But not particularly full of initiative, don't you think?"

Roche wondered how many competent women looked after and kept his family in check. "She prepared the lunch tray," she said. "And delivered it. It would be the simplest thing to add something to his food on the way from the kitchen to his room."

"What would her motive be?" The Mayor asked.

Roche shrugged. "We haven't even scratched the surface yet." She smiled. "And you heard the cook. Perhaps she hated waiting on him. I bet more than one housewife has dropped something in her husband's food. Or at least fantasized about doing it."

The Mayor did not smile. "That's hardly the case here," he said. "Emma Scott and John Wright weren't married. It was only for a couple of days. And he was an important author. She was lucky he attended her little retreat."

"Either way, she was the one who prepared the tray," Roche said. "And there's something about her that bothers me. All that innocence, that naivety. It feels…perhaps not feigned but forced. I bet she's shrewder than she wants us to believe."

The Mayor didn't reply. There was an irritated frown on his forehead and an absent look on his face, as if half his brain was thinking about something else.

"Trace the thought back," Roche said.

He seemed surprised. "Boss?" he said.

"You're trying to remember something. Trace the thought back and see if you can catch it."

He looked embarrassed. "It's just stupid. Something feels slightly off, that's all, but I can't put my finger on what it is."

"When you go through a victim's room you have to use all your instincts.

Don't trust them blindly, you still need to evaluate them, but use them. That's the best way of forming a picture of the person who's died."

"Yes, boss," he said hesitantly.

"You commented on his suits. Expensive, good quality. And her cheap polyester dresses."

"That's it! The wives' outfits are usually more expensive. Or at least as expensive. Who's ever heard of a man who buys expensive clothes for himself and then ruins the impression by dressing his wife in cheap rubbish?"

Roche shrugged her shoulders. "Maybe he was a cheapskate."

"Then he would have bought cheap clothes for himself as well. And believe me, those suits are not cheap. Several of them are from Saville Row. That's as good as it gets in England."

"I believe you," Roche said dryly.

The door to the room opened, and The Mayor hurried to stop the person coming in. "You can't come in here," he said. "A police investigation is underway."

He sounded extremely pompous for his age and was just about to close the door again when Emma calmly said: "I understand, but Mrs. Wright has woken up, and I thought Commissaire Roche might want to speak with her."

Roche nodded to him to let them in, and he grudgingly opened the door. He seemed upset that his only attempt at exerting authority had failed. Roche wondered how he would be when he had his own team—which he most certainly would one day.

After Emma, Madame Wright stepped in through the door. Even though Roche had never seen her before, she easily recognized her. Her face, totally devoid of expression, spoke of a new sadness, so unbearably fresh that both her body and soul were still fighting reality.

"Madame Wright," Roche said. "I'm so terribly sorry."

Madame Wright stared blankly at her, as if words no longer had any meaning.

"Would you be okay answering a few short questions? I'm afraid we'll have to ask them at some point, but I could come back tomorrow if you'd prefer."

Madame Wright moved her hand apathetically, as if answering some questions was the least of her problems.

Roche looked around. "But not here," she said. She placed a careful but firm hand on Madame Wright's elbow and guided her slowly to the library at the end of the hallway.

"I understand how difficult everything must be right now," Roche said when they had sat down. "And if you feel you can't go on with the interview, we can end it at any point."

Madame Wright nodded.

"Has your husband been worried about things lately?" she asked.

"Everyone was after him! Everyone! No one knew what he had to put up with. No one cared about him but me."

Roche seemed surprised. "What did he have to put up with?" she asked.

"Oh…lots of things."

Roche nodded encouragingly, but the short outburst seemed to have drained Madame Wright of her last bit of strength. She sat slumped and quiet in front of them.

"You had lunch in the room?" Roche said.

Madame Wright didn't seem to notice the sudden change in subject. She answered mechanically: "Yes. John was tired of people." When she mentioned his name, her face temporarily came alive. The memory of him softened her eyes and brought on a smile, despite the grief.

"What did you have for lunch?" Roche asked.

"Fish. Lemon sole. A fresh salad. It was delicious. He gave me some to taste."

"Taste? Sorry, but you didn't get your own lunch?"

Madame Wright answered as if it was completely normal: "John insisted on eating in the room, so they sent him up a tray. But I didn't want to bother anyone, so naturally, they only sent up one portion. But I just ate his salad. He didn't want it anyway. I could have gone outside to eat with the others, of course, but I didn't feel like seeing other people either. We had some white wine with it. I picked up a bottle from the bar."

"But you didn't try the fish? Or the potatoes?"

"I wasn't particularly hungry," she said. "Sorry, but what is this about? Are you saying it was something he ate? I thought… Emma said…something to do with his heart, maybe?"

"There are some…questions. Which means, unfortunately, there will have to be an autopsy." Roche studied Madame Wright closely to see how she would react. Some people had religious objections to autopsies. Others felt the thought of it was distressing for personal reasons. You could never predict how a person in shock would react.

And some didn't want the police to find out how they had killed their beloved husband.

Madame Wright just looked confused. "An autopsy?" she said.

"It's routine in cases like this," Roche said. She pushed away all thoughts of how the partner was always the first suspect, and kept her voice slow and calm. She didn't want any form of mistrust or questioning to reflect in her body language or tone of voice. You always found out the most if they weren't on the defensive.

"Who receives your husband's inheritance, Madame Wright?"

Madame Wright paled. Her hands trembled. She had to lay them on her lap in order to control them. Her whole being slumped. She looked defeated, in a way that the grief hadn't been able to achieve.

"I…I don't know," she said. She kept tugging at the sleeve of her jumper. "I would imagine there's a will. His lawyer would probably know."

"You would be the natural heir, wouldn't you?"

"Yes. No. Maybe. I told you I don't know!"

"Do you have the contact details for his lawyer?"

Her voice was almost inaudible by now. "No."

"If you can arrange it, I really need a copy of his will," Roche said.

"I…I can try."

"Just a formality, of course," Roche reassured her. There wasn't really a way of asking for the will without causing distress. Even completely innocent people would get upset. Perhaps especially them.

But Madame Wright didn't seem to get upset in the normal way. Something was off. Roche glanced at The Mayor to see what he was thinking. He met her glance and raised an eyebrow.

"Olivia probably knows who his lawyer is," Madame Wright said eventually in a flat voice. Her pale face looked lonely and sad, as if she'd only just now realized she was alone in the world. "I think…I think I would like to go home now."

"Olivia?"

"Olivia Marsch. His agent. John used to say that she always knew exactly how much money he had. Down to the last penny."

"And how can we reach this Olivia?"

Madame Wright shrugged her shoulders apathetically. "Berit probably knows," she said.

Roche gave Madame Wright her card. "If there's anything else I can do… or if you have any questions. Anything at all. Just call. I'll make sure you'll get your husband home soon."

Madame Wright stared blankly at her. The dignified grief had been replaced by helpless confusion. "I was the only one who really understood him," she said.

After a few seconds, she continued: "He was going to write such fantastic books."

"Can I ask you something?" The Mayor said when they were heading back to their cars. The sun was going down over the vineyard. The evening was almost painfully beautiful.

"Please, who am I to stop you?" Roche said. She paused to admire the view one more time. It was probably her last chance for quite some time. Once they'd confirmed it was murder, she wouldn't have time to stop and admire any sunsets.

"Haven't we spent quite a bit of time on something that could be a completely natural death? The coroner hasn't even performed the autopsy yet."

"It wasn't a natural death. Believe me. Dr. Laurent was much too intrigued."

"The autopsy might just prove that he was an overweight man with a heart problem."

"Those men can be murdered, too."

Roche's eyes were drawn to the people who had gathered on the lawn, where the evening shadow had just reached them. The colorful lanterns and fairy lights created an illusion of security. They all seemed drawn to them like moths to a flame.

Slightly apart from the rest, Berit Gardner and Emma Scott stood staring at Roche and The Mayor. The intensity of their attention sent shivers up Roche's spine.

"Something is really wrong here," she said. "I can feel it."

Emma followed the police cars with her eyes when they left. "Do you think they'll return?" she asked.

"Without a doubt," Berit said.

Emma swallowed nervously. "They asked so many questions," she said, as if to herself.

Berit looked sharply at her. "They'll ask more," she said. "Someone murdered John Wright. I'm sure of it."

Emma let out a groan. Then she met Berit's eyes and hesitated. "Berit, what shall I do?" she asked helplessly.

"I don't know," Berit said.

In the light of the colorful lanterns she studied Emma and tried to force herself to see things differently. The only thing she saw was a tender trust, an extremely misplaced trust, in Berit's ability to somehow sort everything out. But there were things not even Berit could make go away, despite how much she wanted to.

I could kill him.

Berit quickly looked around. There was no one nearby. "Emma," she said quietly. "I *heard* you."

"Oh?" Emma's voice was light and composed.

"After John's lecture. When you prepared his lunch. You said: *I could kill him.*"

"Oh, that. But that's just things you say, isn't it? Obviously, it didn't mean anything."

Emma had been standing at the work surface in the kitchen preparing the tray. Her neck and face had been red with anger. When she thought no one was in earshot, she had hissed those words to herself. Once again, Berit cursed John Wright and his bloody lecture.

"Emma," she said. "It's me you're talking to. I know you. I know you don't say things like that, not about another human being. I don't even know if I've ever seen you angry before."

Emma let out a short, harsh laugh that made Berit feel almost as uneasy as the words she had heard her say in the kitchen.

"No, of course not," Emma said cynically. "The nice, helpful Emma Scott who never gets angry. She does everything she's asked and never complains. Just tell her what you want, and she'll run and get it immediately."

"That's not how I meant…" Berit tried to object, but then she realized Emma might have been closer to the truth than she would want to admit.

Emma's face suddenly distorted with…grief? Anger? Berit didn't know, but the raw emotion she expressed made her back off.

"How dare he?" Emma said. "How *dare* he?"

She seemed to force herself to lower her voice, because when she continued talking, she hissed: "What did he know about running a bookshop? I worked so hard! I loved the pastel-colored walls. It wasn't my fault that nobody wanted to buy books. People loved to *talk* about books. Tell others about everything they'd read, and they were always keen to hear my recommendations. Then they just went straight home and ordered them online. But that's life. Nobody cares."

"You always used to tell me that you had to have a burning love for books. That it was the only way to survive. That's what you said. *Let them be their own reward,*" Berit said.

"Well, that's the only reward you'll ever get," Emma said, her face twisted in a bitter grimace, making her almost unrecognizable.

"You're wrong when you say no one cares," Berit said quietly.

"Am I?"

Berit nodded. "*I* care."

11

THE WRITERS HAD GATHERED ON the patio. Perhaps they had been driven by some urge to stay together. Berit went into the kitchen and asked the cook for a cup of coffee, then she sat down at the well-lit kitchen table. Her eyes were drawn toward the people outside.

She was thinking about what the French police would make of their strange group of wannabe writers. It was no easy thing to investigate people who were basically in training to become liars. Their whole career, perhaps it was even a vocation, was about making things up. It's what they did.

Could she help Commissaire Roche? She wasn't sure.

The only reason she had been able to help the police with the murder in Great Diddling was that she had moved to the village before it happened and had been able to observe those involved in their natural habitat. Here, she was clutching at straws. She didn't know anyone at Château des Livres. Everyone was disconnected from their everyday life and the things that would normally give them structure and routine. Here, during two beautiful summer weeks, they could be whoever they wanted.

Berit had felt it herself, the intoxicating existential freedom a new and beautiful setting could offer. A creative energy, not only for writing, but for reinventing oneself.

She briefly thought of her cottage in Great Diddling and her safe, familiar life there.

Since Sally had moved back to London and started her new life as a junior agent at her mum's agency, her own life had plodded along in a satisfyingly slow fashion. She had watched the shifting colors of autumn from her desk, spent Christmas in her comfortable long-serving armchair, and seen spring bring new life outside her window.

She felt herself acutely longing for the safety in knowing that each day is going be the same as the previous one and that every morning you will drink your coffee out of your favorite coffee cup.

Berit shook her head at herself. The opposite of freedom isn't obligations, she thought. *It's comfort.*

She got the list of attendees out of the welcome pack and put it on the kitchen table in front of her. It was divided between faculty and participants.

The list of teachers started with Claudia Ramirez, romance and crime writer. She had written seventeen books, but the conference material only mentioned a few of the later titles—a detective series Berit had read and thoroughly enjoyed. In the photo, Claudia was staring straight into the camera with an open, almost defiant, look that challenged the viewer to criticize her or her books. She had big dark eyes, broad cheekbones, and thick, lustrous hair that she had combed away from her face.

The next person was Sally Marsch, junior literary agent. She would hold a workshop with Emma, but also read texts and listen to the students' sales pitches at the end of the retreat. Berit skipped the introduction but lingered on her photo. Sally had a trustworthy, honest, and open face that even the forced situation of being photographed couldn't take away from her.

Then there was Charles Tate, literary agent. In the photo he looked carefree. Boyish fop, expensive clothes, jaunty smile.

Berit looked up from her papers. No wonder he'd lost clients. If she had been writing her debut novel, she doubtlessly would have chosen Sally over Charles. It made no difference how much he bragged about having represented John Wright "and several other bestselling authors" that weren't even mentioned by name.

Charles had argued with John on the terrace last night, Berit remembered.

But as she thought about it, she wondered if it had actually been an argument at all—at least not from Charles's point of view. Berit had heard his tone of voice and watched his body language, and he'd come across as pleading. Perhaps John had refused to give him what he wanted, and Charles had killed him for…what? Revenge? Berit shook her head. What would killing John solve for Charles?

She couldn't be bothered reading John Wright's bio again.

Instead, she got out her pen and neatly added Rebecka Linscott, publisher, to the list of faculty members. Once upon a time she was known for discovering John Wright—now for losing him. No one knew why he had left her, and without the facts, all that was left was gossip.

Now that Berit had met Rebecka, she understood why people talked about her so much. Rebecka's pale, marble-like face seemed to invite gossip and speculation. Something beneath that cold surface felt chilling, although Berit couldn't put her finger on what it was.

Emma Scott's introduction was very short and only described her as a former bookseller who had turned retreat promoter.

Berit composed her own version in her head: A stalwart in the world of literature. One of those people who had always been there and fought for books and literature. Emma had run a much-loved bookshop, but that was only part of it. She had also organized literary festivals, published a magazine about books (that, admittedly, only survived a few issues), run several book clubs, and had started her own publishing house that specialized in translating French novels. She had even written a book many years ago, a slim, moving tale that had been well received but quickly forgotten.

But it was the bookshop that occupied Berit's thoughts. It had resembled precisely the kind of bookshop John Wright had ridiculed in his lecture. And Berit had seen how upset she was when she prepared the lunch tray. *I could kill him.* Her neck and face had been red with anger. When she thought no one was in earshot, she had hissed those words to herself. Once again, Berit cursed John Wright and his bloody lecture.

But would Emma really jeopardize the whole writing retreat by committing murder? No one could foresee how the students would react when they found out that John Wright had been killed. And for what? Her wounded feelings?

Berit moved on with the list. Instinctively, she was more inclined to suspect the faculty rather than the students, as it took time to work up enough murderous feelings to kill someone. She was pretty certain John Wright had known his killer before he'd arrived in France, and that made it more likely that the murderer would be one of the teachers.

But she didn't want to cross anyone off the list yet, so she went through the list of participants as well. Not that it enlightened her much. The only people she knew anything about were Nicole, Julian, and Mildred.

She wrote down what she knew:

Nicole, young, extremely ambitious. Hungry to succeed and become famous. John Wright had insulted her, and even though she had made sure not to show him how she felt, Berit was sure it must have stung. She had heard Nicole say that she'd gladly dance across his dead body, but surely, it must have been metaphorically speaking. She hoped.

Julian, the complete opposite of Nicole, his ambition detached from the world. Berit had seen the adoring looks he had given John Wright. No one benefited from being put on a pedestal, but there were certain people one should definitely think twice before placing there, and John Wright was one of them.

She shook her head. None of this was reason enough to kill him, not all of a sudden after being acquainted with him for just one day.

Mildred. She had nothing to say about Mildred. As far as she was concerned, Mildred had nothing to do with John.

The pop of a champagne cork cut through the quiet evening like a gunshot.

She looked over at the people who had gathered outside the kitchen garden. The colored lights made it look inappropriately festive.

"We're not just grieving John's death," she heard Emma say defensively while Antoine poured the champagne. "We're also celebrating his life's work."

In the program, this evening's event was called *A get-together for perspective*. As a way of getting to know the others at the retreat and get ideas, the aim of the event was to look at the evening from different people's perspective. But Emma had been wise enough to realize that the only thing people would talk about was the death, so she had changed it into an improvised memorial ceremony for John Wright.

"The retreat will continue as planned," Emma said firmly. "I hope we won't let this tragic matter overshadow the joy of writing. We're all here because we love to create. We have some amazing, action-packed days ahead of us."

With an admirable poker face, she added: "That's what John would have wanted."

Champagne glass in hand, Berit observed the participants. They were all wide-eyed and consumed by that general *isn't-it-awful* feeling that resulted in gossip, loud voices, and laughter. But they were all dressed in black.

Only among writers, she thought, *could you improvise a memorial on a summer's trip to France and still be sure that everyone would have something black to wear.*

The setting was so idyllic, Berit had to remind herself that one of them was a murderer. Evening sun, vineyard, *murderer*. Clinking wineglasses, an old transistor radio playing Edith Piaf, *murderer*. Laughing people, smiling people, *murderer*.

Mrs. Wright, in a pair of dark blue trousers and a black blazer, was standing on her own slightly away from the others, looking lonely and lost. So often when people were unsure of what to say, they did the worst thing they could possibly do and said nothing.

Apart from Mildred, Berit noticed, pleased. Mildred took Mrs. Wright over to a table and sat down next to her. After a while she stood up to fetch something to drink. On her way she passed Berit.

"At my age, you're much too familiar with widows," Mildred said wearily. "So many of my friends have lost their husbands. And it's always too soon."

"You as well?" Berit asked.

"Yes, but that was different."

"How come?"

"My husband wasn't much of a loss."

Then she guiltily put her hand over her mouth and looked horrified.

Rebecka Linscott outdid Mrs. Wright where clothes and styling were concerned. She was wearing a black suit, black blouse, and a white silk scarf wrapped around her neck. Her face was yet again hidden behind her dark sunglasses—this this time, undoubtedly, to feign grief—but her lips were still carefully painted a bright red.

Grief suits her, Berit thought.

"I discovered him," Rebecka said to Berit, loud enough for everyone to hear her. "As soon as I read the first pages of his first manuscript, I knew I'd come across an exceptional talent. I can tell immediately, you know. Five first pages. That's all it takes."

The words reminded Berit of what John had said. "John Wright insisted he could do the same," she said.

Rebecka looked annoyed that she wasn't unique. "I don't doubt for a second that he thought he could," she said. "John was an amazing writer, but it's a completely different thing establishing whether someone has what it takes or not. Especially from an unedited manuscript."

"Yes, I don't think anyone could do that in five pages. Not with confidence."

"Well, I can. I did. The text was unpolished, naturally, but the voice was there. Inimitable. I guided him through the whole process. He sharpened his claws on me."

What a strange way of putting it, Berit thought.

"Do you know what it's like, after years of hard work in this industry, to finally get the recognition you deserve?" Rebecka wasn't expecting an answer. "It wasn't the money, it never meant anything to me, apart from being able to publish more books and market and package them in the way they deserved. No, the important thing was that I was suddenly treated with *respect*. I was someone to reckon with. Even the editors at the major publishers asked how I knew John would become a huge name. As if I ever thought about that! I just knew he was brilliant. They would have known too, if they had cared more about quality and less about their sales trajectory and their quarterly reports."

And then the respect and the success had been snatched from under her feet. Berit wondered, *Was it a possible motive?*

"I can't believe he's dead," Rebecka said suddenly, and for the first time during the retreat it felt like she was actually telling the truth, even to herself.

Her voice was thin and whiny, as if it was an annoying inconvenience for her that John had decided to die. She said it in a way as if someone had destroyed a piece of artwork. But John Wright was a human being with all the inherent capacity to irritate, annoy, provoke, and threaten.

And Rebecka Linscott knew that. Berit was sure of it.

12

CHARLES RAISED HIS GLASS IRONICALLY to Berit. "If the *Titanic* had been full of writers, everyone would have been standing there with a glass of champagne in their hand as the ship went down," he said.

"Is that what you would have done on the *Titanic*?" Berit asked.

"Of course. Champagne is the only right way to face disaster." He looked disdainfully around at the people mingling. "I wonder why I even do this anymore," he said.

"It's a memorial. You couldn't really have avoided it."

"No, I mean all of it. The job. The publishing world. One awful writer after another. And it's gotten a hell of a lot worse during my time."

"Sure," Berit said dryly. "Most things get worse when you get old."

"I'm not old," Charles snapped. It was possibly the first real emotion he had exhibited. She wondered what else he hid underneath that cynical, sozzled surface.

He strained a smile. "I guess that's what all middle-aged men say just before they buy a sports car. But I don't think it's that. I just don't see the point anymore. Why are we doing this? Maybe Olivia Marsch was right. Maybe I *have* lost the spark."

"Olivia?"

"Apparently that's what she said about me to John. I wasn't 'hungry' enough. Because of my upbringing. Born with a silver spoon in my mouth, been handed everything for free, used to relying on the boys from my private school days, so I can't navigate the modern world."

"Did it work?" Berit wondered.

"Evidently so. Olivia is fucking clever. She used all the things John once chose me for and turned them into a disadvantage. John was a snob. He liked my private school upbringing, that I knew which fucking fork should be used for which dish. Shooting weekends at some posh old schoolmate's estate. Oh, he loved it, don't think for a moment he didn't."

Berit noted how easily the past tense came to him. He didn't have to try to remember that his old writer was dead.

"Olivia could never have given him that, so she used it against me and turned it into a weakness. As I said: clever. A bit too clever for her own good. Do you want to know something?" He waved his glass in Berit's direction and didn't even notice that he spilled some wine on her hand.

Berit quickly pulled away. "Sure," she said.

"He would never have stayed with her. He might have admired her cold-heartedness and her pushiness for now, but he preferred men. He would never admit it to himself, of course, but he was never comfortable with women."

"But his publisher was a woman."

"Only because she got her claws in there early on. And that relationship chafed; it was like an unhappy codependent marriage. He believed her when she said she was the one who made him into the writer he was. And he couldn't stand her, precisely because of it. I always had to mediate between them. And then she dragged me down with her."

"What really happened between you, Rebecka, and John?"

For a moment it looked like Charles was about to answer, but he wasn't drunk enough to be completely honest with her. "Ask Olivia, if you want to know it so much," he muttered and downed his wine.

Emma and Antoine put two large plates of sandwiches on the table, and all of a sudden everyone seemed to realize how hungry they were.

Everyone except Julian Aubrey, who stayed behind next to Berit beneath the colored lights. Alex returned with a glass of bubbly in one hand and a plate of sandwiches in the other, but Julian just shook his head and dismissed the offer of both food and wine.

Berit had one of the sandwiches instead.

"Look at them!" Julian said. His cheeks were covered in angry red blotches, and he spoke with a strange and slightly worrying intensity. "How can they stuff their faces at a time like this? None of them care. They never appreciated him in the way he deserved."

"He probably wasn't the easiest man to like," Berit said. She took a bite of her sandwich. Ham, cheese, and an amazing mustard.

"Why should he have cared about being liked? He despised the middle classes and their anxious facades."

Julian gripped Berit's arm hard. "You talked to the police earlier on. Have they found his notes?"

"No," she said.

So, everyone already knew that John's notes were missing. It was impossible to keep a secret among a group of writers.

"Well, have they looked? They must be somewhere."

"I'm sure they're doing their best."

His gaze fell on Mrs. Wright. Mildred had managed to persuade her to have a sandwich, and she was now eating heartily.

Too heartily, Julian seemed to think.

"And *she* will have control over his literary estate," he said. "Why should she be the right person just because they've slept together for a few decades?"

"I believe a marriage is a bit more than that," Berit said.

"Sure. Washing up, cooking, fighting about whose parents you'll spend Christmas with, awkward silences at breakfast. It doesn't exactly bring some deeper understanding of his literary qualities. Heterosexual relationships are weird. They barely seem to understand each other. How can you be together that long without sharing everything?"

"Is that what you do?" Berit asked.

"Everything that's important," Julian said, at which Alex instinctively grabbed his hand.

"She doesn't even care about his books," Julian continued. "The only thing she cares about is her own feelings and her selfish grief."

Berit thought of Mrs. Wright's raw and passionate loss. *Was it a sign of innocence? Not necessarily.*

She remembered how DCI Ahmed had once explained how it was possible to kill someone and hardly be aware of what you'd done. Many perpetrators were shocked when they found out what they had done. And more than one man who had killed his wife had seemed genuine in their grief afterward.

"Detective stories are false, you see," Julian suddenly said. "The murder is always the starting point, and the solving of the case the most important. The detective is the main character. But that's not what it's like in reality. In reality, the death is the only thing that matters. Not the victim, but the *death*. And death is the *end*. The motive, the killer, all that is pointless."

"Not entirely pointless to the family, I suspect," Berit said.

Julian dismissed Berit's pragmatic view. "We cling to the illusion that a life is worth something, that it matters what happens to individual specimens of the human race, but the reality is that we're all disposable. The only thing that matters is what we leave behind. What we have *written*."

Berit wandered among the participants and tried to form a picture of them. But it was difficult. There were too many of them, and they were too unfamiliar to her. Smiling faces merged into an anonymous mass.

In Great Diddling, Berit had thought that writers were unusually adept at solving murders. They had an interest in observing their fellow human beings and eavesdropping on everything they said, an instinct for secrets and conflicts, and perhaps also some sort of insight into humanity after thinking so much about the tragedies and joys of the individual.

For the first time she asked herself if writers were also particularly suited to *commit* murder. She thought about all the writers she knew who, on paper, had killed enemies, for example, past teachers, parents, and anyone who had made the mistake of doing them wrong. Would any of them actually cross that line and do it in real life?

She knew of at least once when it had happened. A writer had published a book, *How to Murder Your Husband and Get Away With It* and had consequently been arrested for the murder of her husband. *Which just went to show the importance of research for a writer,* Berit thought.

Footsteps in the gravel from the other side of the lawn made her tear herself away from the rest of the group. She quickly walked through the shadows, past the dark pool with the stone statues, and reached Nicole Archer just in time to stop her from sneaking under the police tape outside the theatre.

Berit blocked the door, crossed her arms, and said, "They've already moved the body."

"I know. But I want to see the room. Take in the atmosphere. I need it, you see, for my book."

Nicole was dressed in a fitted black suit and a pair of thick dark-framed glasses. There was something exaggerated about her professional look, as if Nicole had dressed like she thought a writer or a journalist should look. Berit wondered if there was really anything wrong with her eyes or if the glasses were just part of the outfit.

She stared intently at Berit. "John Wright was murdered, wasn't he?"

"I know as much about that as you do."

"He must have been. Infuriating old men don't suddenly die in a château from natural causes." Nicole did a little twirl as if she was consumed by inspiration. "A real live murder!" she said. Her voice was full of conflicting feelings: joy, eagerness, determination, a hint of anxiousness which contrasted with her confident exterior.

"For the first time I'm finally in the right place when something's happening," she said. "I'll be able to follow the entire police investigation close up. The death of John Wright will be a perfect book."

Berit raised her eyebrows. "Don't you care that a person has died?"

"There wouldn't be much of a book if he had survived," Nicole said. There was a glimmer in her eye. "Do you know who the first person I would suspect if I was the investigator?" she asked.

Berit shook her head.

"You," Nicole said. "Think about it. You're the last person anyone would suspect. You were on stage the whole time as he was dying. You're practically the only person who *couldn't* have committed the murder, and we all know how suspect that is. And you have already started helping Commissaire Roche. It's always the helpful, sympathetic bystander who's guilty, isn't it?"

"I've only answered some of the commissaire's questions," Berit said.

"You're going to help her more," Nicole said. "Just wait and see. People will tell you things they would never tell the police."

13

DR. LAURENT WAS WAITING FOR Roche outside the forensic institute at 12 avenue Rockefeller in the Eighth District when she arrived at just after nine the following morning. He had an espresso in one hand and a cigarette in the other.

Roche looked longingly at the coffee. She'd been working since six o'clock.

Laurent stubbed his cigarette out on the ground when he saw her. He led the way into the building and down dark and quiet corridors. Energy-efficient lights went on one after the other as they traveled down the corridors. Everything was still and deserted on a Sunday morning.

Laurent's office looked like an ordinary GP's; a desk, an exam table, medical posters, and the faint smell of disinfectant. Roche shivered. She didn't like hospitals.

On the wall was a portrait of Alexandre Lacassagne and Professor Louis Roche, no relation. Laurent gestured toward the portrait and said: "Very apt, come to think of it. Professor Roche specialized in toxicology. He made huge advances in how we relate to poisons in forensic investigations. And here I am about to go through a toxicology report with another Roche."

"Get to the point, Laurent," Commissaire Roche said, without expecting too much.

The coroner saw himself as a combination of Sherlock Holmes and Dr. House. He was nearly as irritating as both of them put together, but because he was also as brilliant, it almost always paid off to listen to what he had to say. He made himself comfortable before delivering what would undoubtedly be a long lecture.

"Hemlock," he began, "or *Conium maculatum*. It's a biennial belonging to the Apiaceae family. It grows to two meters in height and flowers from June to August, with beautiful white flowers, and looks similar to cow parsley."

"Impressive. Lovely. Beautiful. If I need a flower arrangement, I'll come to you."

"I wouldn't recommend it. All parts of the plant, including the flowers, are very poisonous. The plant contains several poisonous alkaloids, coniine among others. Six to eight leaves from hemlock contains enough coniine to kill a person. The seeds and the roots are even more poisonous. Around one hundred and fifty to three hundred milligrams of coniine is enough."

"So it was hemlock that killed him?"

Laurent nodded. "The toxicology report showed deadly levels of coniine. The poison attacks the central nervous system. High doses lead to respiratory arrest and muscle paralysis."

The restless and constantly active Roche stilled.

Murder.

The beginning of a murder investigation was the only time she felt completely calm. She was consumed by an intense feeling of peace, which she thought was related to being exactly where she should be, at the beginning of something big and important. At this stage everything was still simple and uncomplicated. She had one task to perform. The strangely vulnerable, well-dressed man in the red velvet seat was her responsibility.

"What are the symptoms?" she asked.

Laurent ticked them off one by one with his fingers. "Symptoms include excess salivation, vomiting, thirst, difficulties speaking and swallowing, muscle weakness, tremors. Hemlock attacks the central nervous system, first stimulatory, then later depression. A progressive paralysis starts in the legs and spreads through the body. Eventually you die from respiratory or cardiac arrest. And you remain conscious throughout. It's a pretty gruesome death."

Roche remembered the victim's smooth and peaceful face and told Laurent it didn't seem to fit John Wright's death.

He nodded eagerly. "I was fascinated by that, too," he said.

"Hemlock." Roche suddenly remembered. "Wasn't that…?"

He looked at her approvingly, as if she were one of his students who had suddenly said something intelligent. "The poison that killed Socrates," he said. "It is relevant to the seemingly peaceful death of our victim, and why I am pretty certain it wasn't an accident. When people were executed in ancient Greece, the common, simple criminals were given wolfsbane, aconite, which resulted in a more excruciating death. The powerful and mighty, on the other hand, were given a poison chalice, called a *kôneion* in Greek, after…"

Roche put her hands up. "No," she said. "No way. I'm just about willing to accept a historical lesson about ancient Greece, but I draw the line at linguistics."

"As you wish. In any case, the chalice contained a combination of hemlock and poppy."

"You're telling me that someone has found both hemlock and morphine at that château?"

"I think they've compromised and used something slightly more modern. The blood samples showed high levels of diazepam, meaning…"

"Valium," Roche said.

"Exactly."

Roche remembered Emma Scott and the meticulously prepared lunch tray. "Do you think it was served at lunch?"

"Normally, that would have been my best bet. The plant looks similar to parsley, and there are several cases where people have died simply because they've made a mistake. Did he complain about the taste?"

"No."

"He would have done, believe me. In the cases where it has been mistaken for parsley, the victim immediately realizes he or she has made an error. It tastes like shit. Unfortunately, often there's not much you can do. There is no antidote. All you can do is put the patient on a ventilator and hope they survive until the poison has left the body. But the timing is off. Digestion had already begun when he died. He ate at least an hour before, maybe two."

"Hmm," Roche said. "So somebody drugged him with Valium and poisoned him with hemlock, after lunch?"

"It seems that way."

"In his tea?"

Laurent shook his head. "Coniine doesn't dissolve well in water. Especially not hot water. It does, however, mix well with alcohol. And I found about two hundred milliliters of a reddish-brown fluid in his stomach."

"Red wine?"

"Exactly. It's an extremely interesting method of murder." He seemed pleased.

"How fast does hemlock act?"

"It depends. It's a notoriously unreliable poison. But in these quantities…he would probably have been dead within an hour. Let's say two, max. But it's irrelevant. He had such high doses of diazepam in him that he would have become unconscious long before then."

Roche became aware that Laurent was observing her while he was talking, so she leaned back in her chair and waited. If you were patient enough, it wasn't unusual for Laurent to share his thoughts on the case, and those thoughts were almost always rewarding.

"Are you sure it *was* murder?" he asked finally. "He didn't commit suicide?"

"It's possible, I guess," Roche said. But she thought something felt off. It wasn't just the absence of a suicide note or apparent problems in his life, but something about the scene, how he'd been sitting there in the front row…

"The reason I'm asking is that there's something almost compassionate about the method," Laurent continued.

"*Compassionate?*" Roche said. She thought of the list of symptoms he had listed.

"The Valium suggests a strong wish to alleviate the suffering at the moment of death. If indeed it was murder, the killer wanted to give him a peaceful death. A dignified death."

"Like Socrates?" Roche said slowly.

"Interesting, isn't it?" Laurent said.

Roche remembered Berit's words. *I thought he was asleep.* "So I'm looking for a merciful killer?" she asked.

"With knowledge of ancient Greece or botanicals. And, yes, with an aversion to causing another human being suffering."

"Or at least *this human being*," Roche said. "But not merciful enough not to kill him." In order to not draw any conclusions too early on, she added: "Unless he did it himself," and Laurent nodded approvingly.

She shook her head. "There's something about this case that worries me," she admitted. "Hemlock. You only kill someone like that in a book."

Laurent smiled sympathetically at her. "And you have a whole château full of writers."

The Mayor met Roche outside the depressing facade of the Château des Livres. As they walked around the building, Roche recounted what Laurent had said.

"If he wasn't poisoned at lunch, maybe Emma Scott isn't the perpetrator after all," she concluded.

"She could have given it to him in something else," The Mayor said.

"It's possible. But if I'd been her, I would have sprinkled it over the salad and pretended I thought it was parsley."

"Then Madame Wright would have died instead," The Mayor pointed out.

Roche froze. "Do you think the killer knew he never ate his salad? No, it's a bit too far-fetched."

"Either way, we have to find out what everyone was doing the last half hour of the lunch break yesterday," The Mayor said. "It shouldn't be too hard for people to remember."

Roche didn't share his optimism. Fifteen years in the force had taught her that people could forget pretty much anything.

She waved at Emma.

"Are you going to question her again?" The Mayor asked.

"You heard the cook. If John Wright wanted something, he asked Emma. Who knows, maybe he felt like a glass of red wine after lunch and called his private room service?"

"Murder!" Emma said.

They were in the same room where Commissaire Roche and The Mayor had conducted the interview with Mrs. Wright yesterday, the one Emma called the library.

It was an almost perfectly cubical room, whose impressive proportions had been ruined by a new dividing wall for the dining room. But the ceiling height was still striking, with beautiful coving along the top, which added further elegance. A large, mullion window made the room feel bright and airy despite the cheap, ugly bookshelves lining the walls. They were made for a more modern ceiling height and were easily two meters too low.

"We're going to need a list of all the participants at the retreat," Roche said.

"Of course. Anything... I just can't take it in... Who would want to murder John? And *why?*"

"You can't think of a reason?"

Emma glanced nervously around. "No," she said too quickly and added, more calmly: "No, not at all. He was a brilliant writer. Everyone admired him enormously."

She's lying, Roche thought, *and not particularly well either.*

"We'll need all the information you have. The program, a list of the attendees..."

Emma rummaged around in her bag, found a thick, shiny brochure, and gave it to Roche. She flipped through it, found the list of the participants, and pushed it back across the table.

"Could you please mark everyone who had met him before?"

Emma got out a pen, examined the list with a frown, and finally drew an asterisk next to one of the names on the list.

"Charles Tate is John's previous agent," she said.

At the top of the list, she added a new name and drew an asterisk next to that as well.

"Rebecka Linscott was his first publisher. She joined late, so she's not on the official list," she added.

"So, she knew John Wright would be here when she agreed to join?"

"Of course. But everyone did. He was our main attraction."

"Did you contact her, or did she invite herself?"

"Now that you mention it, she got in touch with me. She'd heard from Charles Tate that I was looking for people in the industry who would guide the talents of the next generation."

"*Was*," The Mayor said suddenly.

Both Emma and Roche stared at him: Emma confused; Roche interested.

"Madame Linscott *was* his publisher? Charle Tate is his *previous agent?* Did this change recently?" he asked.

"A few months ago," Emma said.

"I imagine they weren't particularly pleased about losing him?"

Emma smiled feebly. There was a flash of something cynical in her eyes, but so brief that later Roche wasn't even sure she had seen it. "I wouldn't have thought so," she said, amused. "Shortly after, he signed a seven-figure book deal with a different publisher. And a different agent."

Without having to look at The Mayor, she knew they were both thinking the same thing. Money was one of the most common motives for killing someone.

"Any others who had met him before?" Roche asked.

Emma looked down at her list again and added question marks next to the ones she thought might have, or could have. That list was longer and included Berit Gardner, among others.

"She said they'd met," Emma said. "But Mr. Wright said they hadn't."

Roche reached for the list and studied it closely. "You haven't marked your own name," she said. "Had you not met him before the retreat?"

"Oh. Yes. Of course. I just didn't think about myself."

Roche borrowed Emma's pen and drew a neat asterisk next to her name.

"Madame Wright isn't on the list either," Roche pointed out.

Emma looked confused. "No, but obviously she had met him before... they were married."

"What I meant was: She's not on the list at all."

"Oh, I see what you mean. No, but she wasn't a participant."

She smiled kindly at Roche, as if she was pleased that everything had been explained.

"At the retreat, I mean," Emma expanded. "She just came along. For a small fee you could upgrade to a double room and bring your partner. Well, not that Mr. Wright was paying. But you know what I mean. Generally, that's how it was."

"And are there other people here that 'obviously' aren't on the list?"

"Sure. Three of the participants brought their husbands."

Roche pushed the list toward her again. "Could you please add their names?"

Emma did.

"Had any of them met John Wright before?"

"I wouldn't think so. One of them works in customer service. The other two are just here for visiting vineyards. I don't think they were even here when John Wright died."

"Any others missing?"

Emma skimmed through the list. "Antoine, he owns the estate. Antoine Tessier. There is a cook as well. Does she count?"

Roche nodded. Cooks counted. "We've met her," Roche said dryly. "Tell us about this...retreat."

Emma cleared her throat. "Over the course of almost two weeks the participants have a unique opportunity to develop their own writing and their network in the industry. Each day during the first week, they'll go to lectures and have workshops with famous writers. On Tuesday we go on an inspiring trip to Vienne and a nearby vineyard to practice using setting in writing, and on Friday we visit Lyon. The idea is that they'll have more time toward the end of the retreat to work on their own projects, but naturally with faculty at hand, in case they have questions. Next Wednesday, they'll get the chance to pitch their novels in real meetings with agents and publishers, followed by a big party to celebrate everyone's hard work."

Emma gasped for breath. She hadn't paused to breathe during the whole presentation. *She sounded like a walking commercial*, Roche thought.

"So…a combination of writing retreat and luxury holiday?" The Mayor asked.

"Not a holiday," Emma objected. *"Research."* She leaned forward eagerly. "There's never been a writing retreat like this! It will change their lives."

"Not for John Wright," The Mayor said wryly. "It ended it. Although, I suppose death is also a kind of change. The biggest of them all, one might say."

Roche tried to stifle a smile. "Was John Wright your biggest name?" she asked.

Emma looked back and forth between them as if she didn't know who to answer. Roche nodded encouragingly at her.

"Yes," Emma said. "Without comparison. He was the star of the retreat. Everyone was here to listen to him. That's why this is all so strange."

Not everyone, Roche thought. *One person was here to kill him.*

"Did you serve John Wright red wine yesterday, at lunch for example?"

Emma looked confused. "Red wine? No, of course not. We had fish. And I know John Wright drank white; the bottle and the glass were on the tray when I collected it after lunch."

"I meant after lunch. Maybe he felt like a glass and asked you to go and get one for him?"

Emma looked annoyed. "No," she said through gritted teeth. "He did not."

"What were you doing in the thirty minutes leading up to when Berit Gardner's lecture began? From one thirty to two o'clock?"

"I was serving coffee, all right? Someone actually has to do that. The lunch was a buffet, so everyone helped themselves, apart from John Wright, of course, who was above everyone else. But we served coffee in the garden. With a madeleine. The cook thought it was suitable. For the literary connection, you know."

"We? You served coffee with someone else?"

"Yes, Antoine helped me with the coffee. We were together all the time. Everyone can corroborate that."

"Right, well, there goes our suspect," Roche said. "She has an alibi."

"But you were right about her being a bitter hostess. She really didn't like that comment about John Wright asking her to get him a glass of wine," The Mayor said.

Roche nodded. She had intentionally provoked a reaction.

"She couldn't stand him, that's for sure," she said. She looked at The Mayor. "Forensics are arriving soon. We can't be sure where he ingested the poison, but most likely it would have been in his room. We know he had his lunch there. We'll have to find out what he did between then and the lecture. Who knows, perhaps he went downstairs and got a coffee himself."

"Unlikely," The Mayor said.

"Yes, he doesn't seem to be the type to get his own coffee."

"No, I mean he brought a cup of tea to the lecture."

"True. Either way, it was from his room where the computer, the notebook, and his notes were stolen. So let's start there. I want you to make sure forensics go over the room with a fine-tooth comb. Prints, whatever they can find, anything that suggests someone, apart from his wife, has been in there. Send all the glasses off to the lab. I saw two in the bathroom yesterday. Even if someone has tried to clean them, there might be traces."

"Will do, boss."

"We have to talk to everyone," Roche said and got up. "Find out where they were, if anyone had access to diazepam, and find the person who wanted to kill him and was crazy enough to use hemlock to do it."

The Mayor nodded. "Motive, means, opportunity," he said as if quoting a textbook.

"Exactly." She looked around. It felt like the calm before the storm. "Let's go."

14

"LOOK AT THEM!" EMMA SOUNDED upset, but it was unclear if she meant the forensic vans or the idle retreat participants who followed every step of the police investigation with a dedicated interest.

She and Berit were standing by themselves beneath a fig tree. Emma was holding the program, constantly looking down at it as if to remind herself what they were supposed to be doing. A lecture in the cinema on *How to Create Memorable Characters*.

"If the police continue like this, we're going to fall hopelessly behind schedule." She looked at her wristwatch. "It's gone eleven, the lecture should have started ages ago."

"No point in having it now," Berit said. "John Wright was murdered. We have to accept it's going to disrupt the schedule."

"John Wright is still causing me problems, even from beyond the grave," Emma said.

Berit looked at her. "What did the police ask you?"

"They wanted to know if I had served him red wine! As if I did nothing all day but run around waiting on him. Though, honestly, it's not far from the truth," she added gloomily.

"Red wine?" Berit asked sharply. "Didn't they ask you what he had for lunch?"

She thought about the carefully arranged tray, Emma's murderous face, and how her knuckles had gone white when she'd grabbed the handles to bring him his lunch. And what she had said to herself, when she thought no one was listening.

"They asked about that yesterday. Today it was all about the red wine."

"Did they know what time he might have ingested it?"

"They asked me what I did during the last half hour of the lunch break."

"And…" Berit hesitated. "What were you doing?"

"I was serving coffee, obviously. With Antoine."

Mrs. Wright's new room was in the wing that used to house the students in the days of the boarding school. *It was small and sparsely furnished, but at least it wasn't filled with memories of her dead husband,* Berit thought. The door was open when she arrived, clothes were strewn everywhere. Mrs. Wright was packing.

"I refuse to stay in this awful place," she said and pulled a thin blouse from the hanger and threw it in the suitcase. She didn't look at Berit but kept on talking. "I'm going home. What are they going to do? Arrest me?"

Berit bent down, picked up the blouse, folded it neatly, and put it back in the suitcase. "Won't it be easier to arrange everything if you are here, on site?" she asked.

Mrs. Wright sank down on the bed. She sat right on top of a pile of clothes but didn't even seem to notice. "I should never have come. I knew it was a mistake, but I couldn't resist. I wanted…to be out in the light just once in my life."

Berit wasn't sure if she meant metaphorically or the actual French light that shone through the windows, making even this old student room seem magical and shimmering.

"What did John do during the last half hour of the lunch break yesterday?" Berit asked. "Were you together?"

"No, we weren't. Perhaps I should have stayed with him, but I wanted a coffee. Emma had told me there would be madeleines. John never liked cakes, but I was still hungry, so I left him."

Berit hunched down in front of her and took both her hands. "It's not your fault," she said.

Mrs. Wright pulled her hands away. "I know," she said. "But I still wish I had stayed with him."

Berit stood up with some effort. "Did you see anyone when you went to get coffee? Were people still eating in the dining room?"

Mrs. Wright thought for a moment. "No," she said eventually. "Most people had already finished. When I walked past the dining room it was practically empty. There were two middle-aged men by the wine. And that young guy whose partner is on the retreat."

"Alex," Berit said.

Mrs. Wright looked out through the window. "Do you know what the last words John spoke to me were?"

Berit shook her head.

"He said: *Go away and stop bothering me, woman.* And now he will never say anything again."

The two middle-aged men who had been in the dining room were called Harry and George. They were there with their wives Helen and Susan, who were on the retreat. Berit had got their names mixed up as soon as she was introduced to them at the drinks reception. But she liked them; they were nice, good-natured people, the type who'd created a comfortable life for themselves and were now enjoying it wholeheartedly.

She found the men at a table outside the kitchen. They had persuaded the cook to give them a silver coffee jug and some leftover croissants from breakfast and generously offered to share it with Berit.

"Nicole calls us the plus-ones," Harry or George said cheerfully. "Where our wives go, we follow."

"The government decides," the other one said. "We obey."

"You were in the dining room at the end of lunch, weren't you?" Berit asked. "Standing by the wine?"

"Yes. We were discussing what we'd been drinking the night before. At the reception."

"Local. No label on the bottle. A young wine, but with a long life ahead of it."

"Was Alex there with you?"

"Yes. Nice chap," Harry or George said cheerfully in a voice that suggested they didn't understand him at all, but it didn't bother them. "We started talking about wines during dinner and one thing led to another. He didn't have anything to do during the lectures either, so we asked him if he wanted to come with us."

"When did you leave?"

"It must have been around the same time as your lecture started. Around two? I remember standing here discussing the wine, then we went downstairs, got our things together, and left."

"And when we got back there was a hell of a scene," George or Harry said. "Police everywhere."

"Are you visiting more vineyards?"

"That's the plan."

"Is Alex coming?"

"Alex is *not* coming." Alex himself answered. He came over to join them. "I'll never forget the shock on Julian's face when he came toward me. I was terrified something had happened to him. In the future I will stay right here."

"Well, Susan and Helen don't get in a tizz so easily. They won't thank us for hanging around them all the time either."

"But you're staying until the end? You're not going home?"

"Susan and Helen have been looking forward to this all spring. A little murder isn't going to drive them away."

Harry or George nodded. "Susan and Helen love detective stories. Wouldn't surprise me if they decide to write one after this."

"Jules and I have dreamt about this for years," Alex said. "Not this particular retreat, but something similar. Going away together. Being surrounded by writers. Making contacts. We won't leave early, not for anything."

"Did you see anyone else in the dining room?" Berit asked.

"No, everyone had gone downstairs for coffee and cake by that time," Harry or George said.

"Apart from that ambitious young girl... What's her name?"

"Nicole," Alex said.

"Exactly." Harry or George nodded vigorously. "She was in the library with her notebook. I remember thinking: at it again, as always."

Nicole intercepted Berit before she'd even had a chance to look for her.

"So, we were right!" she said enthusiastically. "It *is* murder. What are the police saying?"

"I haven't spoken to them."

"But they spoke to Emma, and I saw the two of you together afterward. But I couldn't hear what you were saying," she added in a tone that suggested she'd tried.

At least that's something to be grateful for, Berit thought. "Nicole, were you in the library toward the end of the lunch break, before my lecture?"

Nicole nodded eagerly. "Yes. I wanted to write down some notes from John Wright's lecture while they were still fresh in my mind."

"And did you see anything? Anybody? John Wright, perhaps, or someone going over to his room...?"

Nicole's face became calculated. "What did the police ask Emma? Is she one of the suspects?"

"No, of course she isn't." Berit sounded irritated. She added more calmly, "Obviously I don't know what the police are thinking."

Nicole smiled gleefully. "Very well. Then I won't tell you who went into John Wright's room, after his wife had left..."

"Nicole!"

"But let me just say: One of the faculty at the retreat clearly had a much more...*intimate* relationship with him than she led us to believe."

15

REBECKA LINSCOTT CONCEALED HER INSECURITY behind a mask of lighthearted superiority. *Probably conceals it to herself as well,* Roche thought. *Nothing is as powerful as the lies we tell ourselves.*

Rebecka had all the features required to be a conventional, timeless beauty: high cheekbones, big eyes, clear skin, but somehow, she didn't quite achieve it. Her nose was too big and hawklike, her forehead too wide, her mouth too small. In her youth, her type of beauty would have been called "interesting," now she had "character." She accentuated it with thick black hair, bushy eyebrows, and bright red lipstick. *And so much Botox that even blatant lies wouldn't move her face,* Roche thought cynically. A small involuntary twitch by her right eye was the only feature that revealed any feelings. She seemed aware of it herself; she constantly moved her fingertips to the disobedient eye as if to calm it down.

"John and I were always friends. No, more than that, we were literary soul mates," Rebecka Linscott said. "No one understood him like I did."

She was dressed head to toe in black, as if she believed herself to be the grieving widow.

"I discovered him," the woman continued. "None of the majors wanted to publish him. I was the first one to believe in him. I *created* him. Without my guidance he would never have achieved what he did."

"But in the end, he left you," Roche said.

Rebecka Linscott's right eye started twitching again. She nervously touched her eyelid with her fingertips. "I assure you it was a perfectly amicable split. We both agreed that a change of…of direction was good for John at this point in his career. And we still had a very special relationship. We always had it."

"Did you know each other privately?"

"More…on an elevated level. Two consciousnesses in constant contact with one another."

"Perhaps you visited each other's homes? Invited each other for dinners?"

"Not…exactly. You have to understand, John Wright was a very self-sufficient man. He thought he didn't need anybody else. And he was very strict about separating work from his private life. We communicated on a higher, literary level. Far, far beyond things like dinners in stately homes and having to make small talk with each other's partners."

"Naturally," Roche said wryly. "How did Mr. Wright react when you showed up here?"

"I…I don't understand?"

"It's a pretty straightforward question? Was he happy?"

"He… I guess he didn't react at all."

"I thought you said you were…how did you put it…literary soulmates?" The Mayor imitated her pretentious voice with devastating likeness.

"It was only a misunderstanding." She sounded distressed. "Everything would have been fine if only we could have had more time together. If we could have sat down and *talked* to each other."

"What was a misunderstanding?" Roche said softly.

But it was like hitting a brick wall.

"Nothing," Rebecka Linscott said. She said it in that self-assured, categorical way people use when they're lying to themselves. Her face was completely blank. Like granite. She was so preoccupied with lying to herself, she didn't have to make much of an effort to lie to them.

"What did you do at the end of the lunch break?" Roche asked.

"Lunch break?"

"Just before Berit Gardner's lecture. Say, half an hour before it started."

"Oh, I…I can't remember. I guess I was getting coffee? And I smoked a cigarette. I needed to calm my nerves."

"What was wrong with your nerves?" The Mayor asked.

"Nothing! It's just an expression. I don't remember."

Charles Tate had an unusually wide and animated mouth. All his feelings were expressed through the involuntary movements of his lips. His clear blue eyes looked small, set in such a tanned, puffy face. The pink linen shirt was at least one size too small for him, and his white belly peeked through the gap of buttons. Despite his hair thinning, it was too long. He would have looked disheveled if it wasn't for his confidence making up for the rest.

The Mayor seemed to take offense to him immediately. Roche wondered it if was because they were both born into privilege, but only one of them had worked hard to do something with it.

"You were John Wright's agent, weren't you?" Roche asked.

"Yes," Charles Tate said pleasantly. "We parted ways a few months ago."

"Amicably?"

"Very. He was coming up to a new phase of his writing. Sometimes a writer needs a fresh start. Completely normal. Happens all the time. I wished him well for the future."

They had *not* parted ways amicably. And Charles had *not* wished him well. But she didn't know enough about the industry to ask the right questions to get behind the facade.

"He was very successful, wasn't he?" she said.

"Very. He was also incredibly talented."

"Did he have a lot of money?"

The agent smiled cynically. "Well, that's not always the same thing. But in his case, it was. He was a fantastic writer, and the readers rewarded him by buying his books. It's always encouraging when that happens."

"Did you get along on a personal level?"

"Of course. We'd known each other for years."

"Did you see each other socially?"

"I wouldn't say so. John was an extremely private person. But we had a professional friendship. We respected each other's work. I wished him all the success he could get."

He's repeating himself. It sounded like the kind of sentence you taught yourself in order to keep up appearances and had been repeated so many times it came automatically. But that didn't make it true.

"Sounds to me like he was your most important client," The Mayor said. "Losing him must have been devastating for your agency."

"If you knew anything about the industry, you'd know that there's nothing unusual about a writer who wants a change in direction and moves to a new publisher, and even agent. It was *I* who suggested he would be happier at a new agency when I realized which direction he was going."

"You suggested it?" The Mayor sounded skeptical.

"Yes. I wasn't convinced it was the right way for him to go, this new style he wanted to try, but I respected his choice. I'm still not convinced he made the right decision."

"And then he made loads of money?" The Mayor said. "Was that because of his new agent?"

"I could have negotiated just as big a deal if I knew all he was interested in was money!" Charles sounded upset. "Jesus, Henry the fucking VIII. There are thirteen writers to the dozen who write about the Tudors, and everyone imagines they're the new Hilary Mantel."

"Did any other writers leave you after John Wright did?" The Mayor suddenly asked.

It wasn't a question Roche would have thought to ask herself, but it provoked an immediate reaction. Charles glanced nervously around, and his confident smile suddenly became anxious.

"A couple," he admitted. "Writers are like lemmings. They follow quickly where the leader takes them. And they have no sense of loyalty, however hard you've been working for them."

"Enough to cause financial problems for your agency? Problems with the cash flow, perhaps?"

"An agency isn't like a…car dealership. Our product is our knowledge, our vision, ideas, and contacts. And it's all volatile. One book can change everything. The only thing you need is a story people suddenly realize they've been hungering for."

"Will you benefit from his death in any way?" Roche asked.

"Benefit! His death couldn't have come at a worse time!"

"For you or for him?" The Mayor asked drily.

Charles blushed. "It's obviously a complete tragedy for everyone. I meant that for personal reasons, I would much rather see him alive. There was a slight possibility that John would want to…collaborate again. We had made plans to arrange a spontaneous workshop, here during the retreat. A writer and his agent, the relationship that's the key to success, and so on."

"Shouldn't he have held that with his current agent instead?" The Mayor asked.

"Well, she's not here, is she? Besides…well, a lot of things can happen in ten days."

"Come on now," The Mayor said. "He left you, and you hated him for it. And then you killed him."

"Killed him?! I'm telling you I needed him alive!"

"How come?"

Charles wiped his forehead with his hand. He glanced over at a side table, got up, and poured himself a large glass of lemonade. The hand holding the carafe was trembling. He downed the lemonade in a few gulps and stared out the window.

"Writers aren't just herd animals, they're an extremely frightened herd. Insecure and neurotic. I never objected when John left, but I needed his help restore their confidence. Show a united front. Show them we were still friends. That sort of thing."

"Restore their confidence," The Mayor said. "That's an interesting choice of words."

Charles made a disgusted face, like he was trying to swallow something repulsive. "Certain…rumors had started circulating. Nothing substantial. Definitely nothing that was true. But, well, you know what it's like. People talk."

"And what were these rumors?" Roche asked in a neutral voice.

But Charles was not prepared to speak any more on the matter.

"I needed John Wright alive," he insisted. "That's all."

"She's lying," Roche said at exactly the same time as The Mayor said "He's lying."

"I'm already getting the feeling that *everybody's* lying to us," Roche said.

The door opened, and a forensic technician poked his head in.

"The only glasses I found were the two in the bathroom," he reported. "I've sent them away for analysis. But I've already found something interesting."

"Yes?"

"There are no fingerprints on the door handle."

The Mayor looked surprised. Roche let out a whistle. "None at all?" she clarified. "That means someone has cleaned the door handle on the way out. On both sides, I presume?"

The technician nodded.

"But you think you can find something?"

They almost always did. The days when you could get away with just wiping a surface were long gone.

"Wouldn't be surprised," said the technician.

Roche nodded smugly to herself. "Every contact leaves a trace," she quoted.

"Edmond Locard." The technician sounded unimpressed. "We will need everyone's fingerprints in order to eliminate them from the investigation. How do you want to do it? Do you want them to come down to the station or shall we do it here?"

Roche stood up resolutely. "Might as well get it over and done with," she said. "Unlike the people here, fingerprints don't lie," she said.

16

THE QUEUE TO HAVE THEIR fingerprints taken was long and snaked at a slow pace around one of the wings. Even with the little shade the orchard offered, it was warm, stuffy, and humid.

Claudia Ramirez involuntarily touched her fingertips against each other, as if she could still feel the scanner on them.

This time, Claudia, she thought, *you've really fucked up.*

"How long do we have to stay here?" Charles asked.

The teachers had their prints taken first, and they were now waiting for the participants a short distance away.

When Claudia believed no one could see her, she allowed herself to close her eyes for a short moment. She thought about her wife back home in Bristol. What was she up to right now? Working, she imagined. The boys were probably at their grandparents', who lived only a few blocks away.

"That fucking cop is pretty rude," Charles continued.

"Did they put pressure on you then?" Claudia said spitefully. It was a small comfort that Charles also seemed to be in the shit. "I'm sure they can't stop you if you want to go home," she added. "But they would probably wonder why you were in such a hurry… They'd think you were hiding something."

"No one's going home!" Emma said in an upset voice. "You agreed to your assignment. You can't just leave."

"No one said anything about a murder when we accepted." Charles was sulking.

"The retreat will continue as normal," Emma insisted. "With certain… practical adjustments, of course. The theatre won't be available for a while. Berit will give her lectures here in the garden instead. And in the afternoons, Claudia will hold her workshops according to plan. We've lost half a day, but we'll make up for it later."

"Instead of one lecture and one workshop, Claudia and I could just hold a shared workshop on how to create memorable characters," Berit said.

For a brief moment, Claudia relaxed in the collegial friendship. *This* was what she liked about being a writer. Female colleagues supporting each other.

She longed for the safety of her family, but she had no choice. She had to come up with an idea for a new book series that could restart her career. And personal catastrophe or not, this was the perfect place to do it.

"We'll just have to see it as a possibility to do some research," Claudia said in such a chirpy voice, she annoyed herself.

Charles glared at her. "Let's see how much you'll enjoy it when you're in the front seat of a police investigation."

Claudia looked away. Sooner or later, they would come after her, and when they did… She forced herself to think about something else.

"Commissaire Roche would never be believable in a book," she said instead.

"Why not?" Berit was interested.

"Too normal. No inner demons, no trauma. Not even a hint of alcohol problems. I bet she had a perfectly fine childhood. Readers expect a certain darkness in their detectives."

Charles shot her a scornful glance, as if he was dying to remind her that she was hardly the right person to determine what readers wanted. She grimaced.

"So, are we agreed?" Emma said firmly. "Everything continues as normal, and with a bit of luck, the students will realize what a fantastic opportunity this investigation is. I mean, what writer wouldn't want some insight into modern police work?"

Claudia would have given almost anything to avoid it.

It was her bloody temper. She had always known it would land her in the shit. And that's where she was now. So deep in the shit she could swim in it.

"Do they know having their fingerprints taken is voluntary?" The Mayor asked as he observed the queue eagerly waiting in front of the forensic technician's table. "And that we store their prints for as long as the investigation is ongoing?"

"Yes. That was the prosecutor's requirement for him to agree, and I have repeated it to them several times. Their only concern has been not having to pay extra for the experience. Apparently, Emma Scott had emphasized what an exclusive insight into modern policing they would get."

The Mayor looked at his phone again. He had hardly taken his eyes off it since they started fingerprinting.

"Finding anything interesting on there?" Roche asked sarcastically.

"You tell me," he said and showed her the phone. He was on Amazon and had found one of Claudia Ramirez's titles: *Death Comes to Tea.*

"You figured I needed some reading recommendations?"

"The hemlock made me think of it. I remembered Agatha Christie used it in one of her books, so I wanted to find out about the writers here. Read this."

He clicked his way to the blurb:

During the Christmas holidays, ten people are gathered at a stately home. One by one they are murdered, poisoned by hemlock. Death has come to tea.

Roche whistled. "That would mean…"

"That she knows a thing or two about hemlock," The Mayor said. "Writers do a lot of research for their books, don't they?"

17

CLAUDIA RAMIREZ WAS IN FULL control of her facial muscles, but she kept crossing and uncrossing her legs. It was the only thing that revealed she was nervous.

"What I thought about John Wright?" She stared straight at Roche. "I hated him. And I wasn't the only one."

Yet another strategy. The exaggerated frankness. It could conceal as much as refusing to say a word did.

"John Wright was a bastard," Claudia continued. "And I can't stand people who idolize bastards. Not even after their death. Why should we tiptoe around it just because he's dead? I can guarantee he wouldn't have shown the same respect had one of us died."

She looked back and forth between Roche and The Mayor. "Did you know that the advance he got for his latest book is more than I received for my last ten books put together? And it wasn't even written yet. I've written historical fiction for years, and people were behaving as if he'd invented the whole genre."

"I thought you wrote detective stories," Roche said.

"I do. But before that, I wrote historical fiction. And before that, romance."

"Productive," Roche said. She wondered to herself who had the time to read all those books.

"Do you know why it's so much harder for women writers to write a bestseller?" Claudia asked.

"The patriarchy?" The Mayor said sarcastically.

Claudia ignored him. "Because women read both male and female authors. Men only read books by other men." She leaned forward toward Roche.

"What's it like in your line of work?" she asked. "It's got to be rife with sexism too. I bet you can think of a dozen incompetent men who were promoted ahead of you. How does that make you feel? Are you angry? Upset?"

I don't exactly lose sleep over it, Roche thought.

"That's the way the world works," she said. "No point getting hung up on things you can't change."

"Why did you become a police officer?" Claudia asked.

"Camaraderie." Roche surprised herself by telling the truth.

"Did you want to be part of something bigger? A higher purpose? Serve justice, that kind of thing?"

"I liked the jargon and the banter, that's all," Roche said, which was true, but it wasn't the whole truth. Being in law enforcement was the first time in her life that she felt like she fit in.

There was something calculating about the way Claudia Ramirez listened to everything Roche said. As if it was analyzed, written down, and recorded for future purposes. As if sooner or later, everything she happened to divulge would end up in a book.

"Tell us about your book *Death Comes to Tea*," she said instead.

Claudia looked surprised. "It's a standalone novel set during Christmas. I had great hopes for it. People like a murder mystery. They love cozy crime. But it didn't sell as much as I hoped it would."

"The killer in the book uses hemlock?" Roche said.

"Yes, a decoction from the leaves. Hence, the deathly tea in the title."

"Did you know that hemlock is not water-soluble?" The Mayor asked. "*Especially* not in hot water."

Claudia made a face. "Well, I know that now," she said. "More than one male reader got in contact to let me know. Apparently, I should have diluted it in alcohol. But I sell entertainment, not chemistry."

"In wine, perhaps," Roche suggested, just to study her reaction.

"The title wouldn't have worked," Claudia said dismissively.

"Cozy murders," Roche said when Claudia had left. She shook her head.

"Someone should show them a junkie being punched to death by their dealer in a parking lot, then let's see how good they feel about it," The Mayor agreed.

"But she didn't react when I mentioned the wine," Roche said.

"What do we do now?"

Roche looked at her watch. Coming up to one. "We're about to meet a botanist from the University of Lyon and talk about the local flora."

The botanist had parked up at the end of the tree-lined avenue outside the château and was inspecting the bark of one of the trees.

"Fine specimen," she said and tapped it carefully. "Will stand for a hundred years, unless something happens."

Laurent, the coroner, had put Roche in contact with her and given her the number of the university where she worked. When Roche called her to book a meeting, the botanist had offered to cancel her midmorning lecture and come out straightaway "if it was urgent." She sounded excited, as if she wanted to live in a world where botanists were called out just like the fire brigade or the paramedics. Roche had disappointed her and said it was no problem if she turned up after the lecture.

The botanist was wearing corduroys and a T-shirt. She was carrying a tattered rucksack with a water bottle swinging from it. Her walking boots were sturdy. A baseball cap protected her face from the sun. She smelled of sunscreen and mosquito spray.

Roche thought of a soldier, not because of her military posture or discipline, but because of the meticulous preparation. The botanist's rucksack was probably always in her office, ready to go, in case there was an urgent field trip. Roche asked her about this.

"Yes, I have a rucksack ready in the office," the botanist said impatiently. "For my *excursions*. And if I understood you correctly, you need my help in finding hemlock?"

Roche nodded and started walking over to the other side of the building. "I need to know if it grows on the grounds here," she said.

When they reached the glade, the participants all turned in unison toward them. The botanist came to a halt, while Roche and The Mayor continued forward. Several of the students stared at them, then frenetically typed on their laptops, as if they were taking notes on everything they saw. One girl appeared to be taking photos, but Roche glared at her until she put her phone away.

Roche took the botanist's arm and led her away from the future writers. "How do you know Dr. Laurent?" she asked to distract her from the staring eyes.

The botanist glanced over her shoulder. "We're in the same book club," she said.

Roche stopped involuntarily. She tried to imagine Laurent in book club, but failed.

"Right now we're reading a book about the plague," the botanist continued. "*The Great Mortality*. Absolutely fascinating. Before that it was about murders by poison throughout the ages."

That explains it.

"Fascinating," she said lamely.

When they were out of sight behind a small grove, the botanist seemed to relax. She looked eagerly around. "*Conium maculatum*, which is the Latin name for hemlock," she said, "is often found where drainage is poor, next to streams, ditches, or roadsides." She looked around, toward the fields in the distance and the wilder meadow nearby. "Or at the edge of farmland, like here."

"Will you be able to find it? We have to prove that hemlock grows here."

"If it's here, I'll find it. It's not particularly difficult to identify. The stalk is completely smooth and…" the botanist started.

Roche had never met an academic who couldn't resist an unnecessary presentation.

"Smooth and with reddish purple spots," the botanist continued. "The lower leaves look similar to cow parsley, but they are bigger, dark green, and completely smooth. They can grow to one and a half to two meters and flower from June to August. A very beautiful plant, really."

"But deadly," The Mayor said flatly.

The botanist seemed to think it wasn't the plant's fault if people were stupid enough to eat it.

"We'll leave you to entertain yourself for a while," Roche said.

The botanist looked excited about being out in the field. Roche imagined she was grateful to escape her office and that she would recount the story of how she had helped the police in an investigation for many years to come.

"Let me know if there's anything you need," Roche said.

The botanist tapped on her rucksack. "I've got everything I need in here."

Of course she did.

"Look at them," The Mayor said. He and Roche were leaning against the wall eating sandwiches they'd snagged from the kitchen. Their eyes were drawn to the group of people over in the glade who were all staring at them.

"It's not that I can't handle people staring," he continued. "Any cop is used to it. But this is different."

"Clinical," Roche said. "It's like we're being scrutinized. Analyzed. Weighed up."

The botanist waved at them from the little grove. Roche and The Mayor finished off their sandwiches and hurried over to her.

"I've found the hemlock plant your killer picked their poison from," the botanist said with due pride in her voice.

"Are you sure?" Roche asked. The botanist looked at her with disdain.

She crouched down and gestured at Roche to do the same. Then, with a glove on her hand, she carefully touched a plant.

"Look at this," she said. "The stalk is broken, and several branches have been removed. Leaves have been removed. The killer has even dug up the ground looking for the roots. Look. Here's the hole. And tried to rip them out, so whoever did this didn't have the right tools. Suggests the decision to use hemlock was spontaneous, wouldn't you say?"

Fantastic. An amateur sleuth. Just what we needed.

18

BERIT AND CLAUDIA WERE SITTING on the patio outside the kitchen, planning their joint workshop on memorable characters they were about to give soon. But Claudia was distracted.

"That bloody young cop needs to learn a thing or two about manners," she complained.

"I guess you can't be concerned about stepping on people's toes if you're a police officer."

"Yes, yes, I know. I have written the scene many times myself. Good cop, good cop doesn't really work, does it? But it's definitely different being on the receiving end. They behaved as if I was a common suspect!"

"Aren't we all?" Berit said.

"Do you know what the problem is?" Claudia asked.

"No."

"John Wright. He's the problem. Insufferable in life, insufferable in death."

"I wonder what they've found behind those trees," Berit said pensively.

"Hemlock."

The answer came quickly and confidently. Berit looked at Claudia with interest.

"They asked me about a book I wrote," Claudia continued. "*Death Comes to Tea.*"

"I've read it," Berit said.

Claudia was surprised. She seemed to hesitate, then she asked: "What did you think?"

"I liked it. A lot."

Claudia looked grateful, and relieved.

"So, John Wright was murdered with hemlock," Berit mused. "Dissolved in a glass of red wine, I wonder?"

"Well, it wasn't tea, that's for damn sure," Claudia said darkly.

Berit quickly stood up. "Can you do the workshop on your own?" she asked. "There's something I've got to check."

Claudia looked up at her. "Sure," she said surprised. "What are you up to?"

"I'm going to try to track down a bottle of wine."

"Save me a glass," Claudia said. "I'll need it after today."

Berit found Antoine in the restroom on the student corridor, on his knees in front of a toilet seat in one of the cubicles.

"Three times I've warned them," he muttered. "Three! But do they listen? No. English people! They have no respect for French plumbing. The pipes are delicate. They need to be treated with respect. You can't just flush down everything like they do in England. It will cause a blockage."

Berit leaned against the tiled wall by the sinks. "Could you tell me where the wine is kept?" she asked. "Is there a wine cellar?"

"There is a cellar," Antoine replied. "No wine. At least none worthy of mentioning. The previous owners were a production company. Do you think they left a full wine cellar? But I'm slowly restocking it. Nothing especially exclusive, but quality through and through. Young, lively wines with potential."

"But the wine served here is kept in the wine cellar? Who has access to it?"

"Me, Emma, and the cook. And anyone who knows where it is. It's not locked. Like I said, there are no valuable bottles there."

"But others would have to know where it is," Berit said. "I doubt the students at the retreat know."

"No, if they want a glass of wine or a bottle, they'll just help themselves from the free bar in the dining room."

"Can you show it to me?"

Antoine looked down into the toilet basin, shrugged his shoulders, and got to his feet with difficulty. He was wearing shiny polished shoes, gray suit trousers, and yellow rubber gloves.

"What did you do before you bought this place?"

"I sold my soul," he said and added: "Real estate agent."

He took his gloves off, left the bucket of cleaning products, and led Berit to the main house, up the stairs, past the room where the police had locked themselves in earlier, and out into the dining room and the improvised bar.

"Open twenty-four hours a day," Antoine said. "You can't expect people to be able to write without access to alcohol."

Berit leaned down to inspect the wine bottles. "Can you see if any are missing? What happens to the empty bottles?"

"They get thrown away. No one's keeping count. I restock it if we're running low."

"Have you restocked it already?"

"Of course. You're a thirsty lot, you writers. But honest." He explained the system with the honesty box. "I empty it at the same time. So far there's been more than enough to cover what's been drunk."

"So anyone could grab a bottle from here and just throw it away anywhere when they're done?"

"Yes. That's the idea."

"What happens with the empty bottles after that?" she asked.

He shrugged his shoulders. "We take them to the kitchen and rinse them out. They're probably still down there somewhere."

Berit made a mental note to let Roche know. That's where she would have hidden the bottle if she was the one getting rid of the murder weapon: in plain sight among all the other bottles.

"The bar is only a few meters away from John Wright's room," Berit said to herself. "But it's not on the way to the lecture theatre. You'd have to call out for him to come over here."

By the bar was where the plus-ones had been standing. Two were friends from before, one was a stranger. An unlikely constellation for committing murder, unless you were Agatha Christie and could get away with it.

"What are you thinking?" Antoine asked. "That someone called him over? Gave him a glass of wine?"

Berit looked sharply at him. She wondered how much Emma shared with him. Everything, perhaps? She studied the hallway. Anyone coming up the stairs would have been able to see them. "It would have taken nerves of steel," she said. "Ice cold."

"Yes," Antoine agreed. "Or just plain stupidity. But if you'll excuse me, I have a toilet to fix."

He left to go back to his cleaning bucket and toilet, and after a second's hesitation, Berit followed.

Antoine seemed surprised to find her following behind. "What do you want now?" he asked, not impolitely but not in a helpful way either.

"Emma says you served coffee together at the end of the lunch break yesterday?"

"And? Someone's got to do it. And we're not exactly overstaffed here." He shrugged. "Emma and I do most things ourselves. *Merde*," he said when he'd reached the toilets and was looking down the seat.

"And neither of you left at any point?"

"How could we? Everyone wanted coffee."

"Did Emma ever talk to you about John Wright? About what she thought of him?"

"Are you asking me whether she could have killed him? The answer is no. Never. He was a bastard, and he deserved it, but she could never have done it."

"But she thought he was a bastard too?"

Antoine laughed, the sound coming out of him was raw and contemptuous, emphasized by the setting they were in. "Everybody thought so. The man was an idiot. And not just an idiot, but the worst kind of idiot."

"Which one is that?"

"A condescending idiot who thinks he's above everybody else. I heard him going on about all sorts of things. He was an expert in every subject. He alone was the savior of the literary and cultural world. Ha! The man didn't even speak a word of French."

"I guess you could say the same about the French," Berit pointed out. "Surely there's many in France that don't speak English?"

"That's not the point. The point is he didn't speak any other languages either. How can you think you know everything about literature if you only have your own country, your own limited experiences to refer to? But John Wright wasn't a man aware of his own limitations, which is a sign of a very limited intellect. The man was completely lacking any kind of refinement." Antoine scoffed. "Cultural! He didn't appreciate music, the beauty of nature, food, drink…"

"He seemed to appreciate food and drink reasonably well," Berit said sarcastically.

"Oh, he ate the food, but he didn't appreciate it. Not genuinely. And he quaffed the wine. He probably ordered expensive wines in a restaurant and drank them as if they were water. It should be illegal to sell certain wines to tourists."

"How did you and Emma meet?"

Antoine sighed theatrically, to let her know how annoying her question was, but he answered, nonetheless.

"When I was working as a real estate agent," he said, "I specialized in international companies looking for offices or accommodation for their employees. The business lunches were a hopeless darkness of uninspiring conversation. The only conversations international businessmen conduct concern money and golf. They want to go the most expensive restaurants, but only because they're trendy, then they drink so much alcohol they can't even taste anything. Just like your John Wright."

"He wasn't *my* John Wright," Berit said. "Is that how you met Emma?"

"I found the premises for her French publishing house. It was a…what is it the Americans say? Pro bono project. She was here to launch her book. We were at the same party. The following day I saw her rummaging through the book stalls along the Seine."

Unintentionally, Antoine had straightened his back and put down the plunger. The cynical lines in his face disappeared when he talked about Emma. "I have never seen anyone look as happy as Emma, that day in Paris, surrounded by books. We had an espresso, we talked about life, she reminded me that there are values more important than money. Much more important."

He must have thought he'd revealed too much about himself because his face seized up again, and he went back to trying to clear the toilet blockage.

"And let me tell you one more thing," he said hunched over the toilet seat. "Many people at the retreat didn't like John Wright. They smiled and laughed at his jokes, but when they thought no one was watching, they glared at him as if…"

"As if they wanted to kill him."

He nodded. Then the toilet made a gurgling sound, and he swore.

"*Regardez!*" he said. He was so upset he automatically switched to French. He pointed with both arms outstretched at the toilet basin. "*Une forêt!* Someone has flushed down a whole bloody forest!"

Berit looked down on a mess of chopped up grass, twigs, and roots. And leaves. Everything was an unpleasant reddish-brown. Apart from the general smell from the sewage, another, sharp, foul, acrid smell seemed to come from the weeds in the toilet.

Like cat piss.

"Get Commissaire Roche," Berit said.

19

"SHE'S CRAZY," THE MAYOR SAID. It was the third time he'd repeated the same words. "Why on earth would we want to inspect a blocked sewer?" He looked disgusted.

"It wasn't my idea," Antoine said as he led them to a part of the building that looked like an old students' hall. It smelled of vinyl floor covering, teenage angst, and oppression.

Roche said nothing. In her experience, toilets were a part of the job. A surprising number of crimes was committed near them. It's just the way it was.

She entered the cubicle ahead of The Mayor and looked down the toilet basin.

She didn't wince at the stench, but she thought that if the taste was anything like the smell, Laurent's comment made sense. You would very quickly discover your mistake if you ate it by accident.

For a moment she even doubted it was murder. How did you get anyone to drink this? But she had found no evidence that John Wright was a man in crisis. Quite the opposite, in fact. He'd just signed a contract for a new series of books, worth millions. He had left his old agent and publisher, which suggested initiative and optimism about the future. And there was a certain joie de vivre in wanting to cause so much dispute.

One thing, however, did perhaps point to suicide. John Wright seemed to have been a man who, if driven to suicide, would have liked to see himself as a modern Socrates. A prophet who provoked people with logic and wisdom and was killed by a narrow-minded contemporary world.

"We'll need samples of that," Roche said and nodded toward The Mayor. "Get your gloves out."

His face was a sight to behold.

Commissaire Roche found Berit on her knees behind the staircase in the main building, examining first the checkerboard floor, then the whitewashed walls.

They had sent the samples from the sewer off for tests, but Roche already knew what they would find. This was the hemlock someone had put in the red wine to create the poison that would kill Monsieur Wright. The red wine had been poured back into a bottle or a glass, and the killer had flushed the rest down the loo to get rid of the evidence. Or tried to flush them down. She thanked French plumbing for this new piece of evidence.

The plumbing, and Berit Gardner.

Roche leaned against the banister and said: "*I want to report a murder. That's what you said when you called in the death.*"

Berit nodded distractedly without taking her eyes off the wall.

"Because John Wright provoked too many strong emotions to die from natural causes?"

Berit nodded again.

"You never considered a third alternative?"

"Which one?"

"Suicide."

Berit's answer was immediate: "No."

"Would you say Monsieur Wright was a man who would never attempt suicide?"

"I don't think there's anyone who couldn't be driven to suicide. But why flush the remnants down the toilet all the way over there? Why not use your own, or just leave the bottle?"

"Maybe someone else tidied up after him. Someone who wanted to protect his reputation?"

Berit looked up. She seemed to consider this. "No," she said eventually. "I'm not saying he would never have taken his own life. You can't say that for sure about anyone. But John Wright would never have committed suicide *in this way*. Anonymously in the dark, but at the same time unnoticed as part of an audience and disgracefully on display for everyone to see? I didn't know him well, but I knew this much about him: John Wright wanted to be either on his own, or the center of attention."

That's what had felt wrong about where he was sitting. Who chose to commit suicide as part of the audience? It was too public and too private at the same time.

"It was just a thought," she said. "It would have explained why he finished the whole glass of wine. You smelled that stuff? It must have tasted bloody horrible."

"I did think about that," Berit said. "And I wonder if I might have an explanation."

She told her about Antoine Tessier's description of John Wright as a man who gulped down his food and his wine. She had seen it herself during the dinner and reception.

"I actually do think it must have tasted bloody horrible, but that he'd have had several big sips before he could stop himself. And I think he was murdered right here. Look. Red wine stains. I think he drank it, then spat it out, but by then it was too late. He'd already ingested a large enough quantity of the poison."

She pointed at the wall, and when Commissaire Roche leaned closer she saw it. Dark red stains on the rough wall.

It looked like blood.

20

"SO WHAT HAVE WE GOT?" Roche asked. She was pacing up and down in the library. She liked that way of working, summing up together what they had found out so far and going through the plan of action. It was too easy to lock into one lead too early on and not realize you were going in the wrong direction until you were helplessly lost.

"We know the scene of murder," The Mayor said. And added grudgingly: "Pretty good work by that Madame Gardner."

"And most likely the spot where the killer found the wine bottles." Berit had informed them of the free bar in the dining room. It would have been easy to pick up a bottle the night before or in the morning, prepare the brew, and intercept John Wright on his way to the lecture.

"A hell of a gamble, though," The Mayor said. "How did the killer know he would be on his own? The wife could have been with him. Or someone else from the retreat?"

Roche nodded. "Yes. It all feels a bit too impulsive. Don't forget the killer had to run up to John's room and steal his briefcase as well. If it wasn't done afterward, that is. There would have been plenty of time in the ensuing chaos when people discovered he was dead. Easier to sneak up then, perhaps."

"We haven't found the diazepam either," The Mayor said.

"No, that will be our next task. Interview all the participants, list all the ones who were using any kind of prescription drug containing diazepam, and find out where they were at the end of the lunch break. We need a clearer picture of how people moved around. Was the killer likely to be uninterrupted under the staircase?"

"Yes, but—" The Mayor began but didn't get any farther as the door to the room suddenly opened.

A scrawny young man with black hair stood before them. He was dressed in tight black jeans and a black T-shirt and looked lost and out of place in the summer heat. His body was tense, and his hands fidgeted constantly.

But his gaze was frank and focused, consumed by some inner purpose.

"Have you found them?" he asked.

"Pardon?" Roche asked.

The Mayor got up to show the lad out, but Roche gestured to hold back. "His briefcase. The notes."

"What's that got to do with you?" The Mayor asked.

"Five of those pages are mine." When he realized they didn't understand what he meant, he said, "He had the first five pages of my manuscript."

"Let me guess," Roche sighed. "It was the only copy? No back up?"

"What? No, of course I've backed it up. I've got it saved on the computer, on an external hard drive and in the cloud. But he said he would comment on them. He might have done that before he died. It's my only chance to find out whether I've got what it takes to be a writer. I have to *know*."

Roche pointed to a chair for him to sit down. "What's your name?" she asked in a friendlier tone, hoping it would calm him down.

It just made him more annoyed. "What does it matter? *Have you found them?*" When they didn't answer, he said impatiently: "Julian Aubrey. My name is Julian Aubrey."

The door opened again.

"It's like rush hour around here," The Mayor commented dryly. "We'll have to set up a queuing system outside."

"What are you questioning him about?" the new arrival asked. He was the same age as Julian, but the similarities stopped there. He had a carefree, boyish appearance and ruffled blond hair.

"It's mainly him questioning us," The Mayor muttered.

"And you are?" Roche asked, amused.

"Alex. Alex Spencer. His boyfriend."

"Very well, why don't you take a seat?" Roche shrugged her shoulders. They would need to talk to everyone, and they might as well start with these two.

She turned toward Julian. "No," she said. "We haven't found any notes, yours nor anyone else's. But we haven't given up looking. It would help us if you could tell us where you were during the last half hour of the lunch break."

"I was on my way to a vineyard," Alex Spencer said. "And Julian was downstairs drinking coffee with the others. Weren't you, Jules? I saw him there on my way out. He was there the whole time."

Julian shrugged. "Sure," he said.

"Did you talk to anyone?" Roche asked. "Or remember anyone standing close to you?"

"I try to avoid talking to people if I can help it. And there were people all around me. I wasn't really paying attention. I was thinking about if John Wright had read the first pages of my book yet."

"What are you writing?" The Mayor asked.

"A novel," Alex answered for him. "He's exploring loneliness and anonymity in the contemporary urban environment. An honest and crushing account of the existential emptiness and—"

"Do either of you take some form of psychotropic medication?" Roche interrupted. "Benzos? Antidepressants? Sleeping pills?"

"Yes," Julian said and glanced around nervously. "Diazepam."

"He won't be the only one," Alex said. "All writers are neurotic. I reckon every poor sod here is on something."

It turned out to be depressingly true. Of the eighteen participants, twelve were on some form of sleeping pills or antidepressants. Seven took diazepam, Julian Aubrey being one of them. And, as The Mayor pointed out, anyone could have gone into a room and stolen a few pills. No one seemed to have any idea of how many pills they had, and the doors were such a hassle to lock, most people just left them unlocked.

No one could recall seeing John Wright in the half hour leading up to the lecture, and they were all convinced they would have remembered.

Most people had left the dining room as soon as they'd finished lunch and gone straight to the garden where the coffee and cakes were served. A few of them had commented on the madeleines. They seemed to be even more lyrical about the way they melted in your mouth than any literary associations.

"Somebody must have seen him," The Mayor said, annoyed.

Roche got up and walked around the chair to stretch her legs. The sharp sunshine ruthlessly revealed how dirty and run-down everything was. Dust was dancing across the worn floor in the afternoon sun. She assumed it was the production company that had been so reckless: There were drill holes, scratch marks, and discoloration everywhere. The window was open, but all it did was let warm air in.

"Who's next on our list?" she asked.

Mildred Wilkinson was different from the rest of the participants in many ways. She was forty years older than most of them, but that was only part of the difference. She waited respectfully for Roche and The Mayor to ask their questions, listened politely, and most importantly, she made no attempt to get her notebook out during the whole examination. Roche found her refreshing.

"What did I do during the lunch break?" Mildred repeated Roche's question to herself. Not, Roche believed, to gain time or to prepare a lie, just to be sure she answered correctly. She reminded Roche about one of those dutiful girls at school who were still expecting life to hand out gold stars if they behaved well and never used swear words.

Roche had never been given any gold stars, but then real life hadn't come as a shock to her either.

Mildred Wilkinson swallowed. "I had lunch with everybody else," she said. "It lasted for an hour or so. Then I went to the toilet. That must have taken about five minutes, no more. Then I went to get coffee. Emma and Antoine had already started serving, and most people were taking it outdoors." She looked like she was trying hard to remember everything correctly.

"Sally sat next to me, I'm sure of that. Such a sweet girl. I had a madeleine." She added guiltily, "Two, actually. I didn't think anyone would mind."

"I'm sure that's fine, Madame Wilkinson," Roche said. The woman still looked guilty. She was fidgeting with her blouse.

"Did you know Monsieur Wright before you arrived?"

"Mr. Wright? No. No, of course not. I'm just a housewife. Widowed, now."

Roche hadn't expected her to have known him. "Thank you, Madame Wilkinson." She dismissed her.

The woman looked relieved. "That's all? I can go now?"

Roche gestured at the door in a sweeping motion as if to say "please."

Mildred got up so hurriedly she knocked her bag over. The contents fell out on the floor. Her knitting, several balls of wool, Cavendish & Harvey fruit pastilles, and a notebook. Roche bent down to pick up her notebook.

"May I have a look?" she asked and Mildred looked helplessly at her.

On the first page was written what appeared to be a shopping list:

Toothbrush

Toothpaste

Those little shampoo and conditioner bottles you're allowed in the hand luggage

Reading glasses unless I find the other pair

Sunscreen

On the next page were rows after rows of: *tea, toast, baked beans, tea, toast, baked beans, tea, toast, baked beans.*

Roche looked confused.

Mildred Wilkinson looked mortified, completely mortified. "It was just a writing exercise," she said desperately. "I couldn't think of anything to write, so Emma told me to choose a sentence at random and write it over and over again until I thought of something. It was supposed to get my subconscious going, she said. So I just wrote down things I missed from home."

Roche turned the page. Mildred must have changed the sentence, because it read: *I should never have come here I should never have come here I should never have...*

And on the following page:

People I should have killed:
My husband
My brother
My sister-in-law
John Wright
That annoying little brat in Spar
My manager at the bank (if only I could remember his name! Is it James?)
Maureen Swainsbury

"My husband" and "John Wright" were neatly crossed out.

21

COMMISSAIRE ROCHE AND THE MAYOR both stared at Mildred.

"Who's Maureen Swainsbury?" Roche asked eventually.

"My neighbor."

"And if I may ask…why?"

Mildred's voice was so weak it was barely audible. "She's always giving me unsolicited advice on my begonias," she whispered.

Roche couldn't imagine how that would be a valid reason, in anyone's world, to kill someone. She glanced at The Mayor, who looked just as baffled. "Why is John Wright's name crossed out?" she asked.

Mildred looked surprised. "Because someone actually did it," she said. "He had to come off my list."

Roche wasn't sure if she felt he had to come off for moral or pragmatic reasons. She shook her head and looked at the notebook again. "And your husband?"

"Well, he's also already dead."

Like a ticked-off item on a to-do list, she thought.

"I'm going to have to keep this," she said.

Mildred looked nervously at them. "C…can I go now?" she asked.

"Don't leave the country," Roche said.

Mildred collected her things with trembling hands and fled the room.

The Mayor stared at her. "It's like what that Alex Spencer said. They're all crackers, the whole bunch."

From Roche's experience, everyone reacted differently to being questioned by the police. Some became defiant or got overly cocky. Others clammed up. Others looked so guilty you could have sworn they had done it, even when you knew they couldn't have committed the crime. But she'd never met anyone who reacted like Nicole Archer.

Nicole sat down opposite them, got her notebook out, and stared at Roche eagerly.

"Do you have a business card?" she asked.

Roche and The Mayor glanced at each other. *It couldn't hurt*, Roche thought and gave her one.

Nicole carefully wrote down Roche's name and rank on a new page in her book. Then she put the business card in her mobile phone case.

"Did you know John Wright?" Roche asked.

Nicole nodded as if to say she'd understood the question and then answered carefully. "Not personally. I knew of him, of course. Everyone did. He's probably the reason ninety percent of us signed up."

"Would you say he was liked by the other students?"

"He was enormously respected as a writer."

So not very well liked. "Can you tell us what you did during your lunch break?"

She noticed from Nicole's face that she stored this new information in her memory: The lunch break was important. Something had happened then. Her hand instinctively reached for her notebook. She wrote in it without looking while answering the question.

"There was a buffet in the dining room. Most people had their lunch out on the terrace. After lunch they served tea, coffee, and cake in the garden. Practically everyone left the terrace and headed down there."

"Including you?"

"No, I happened to stay up here."

"Where, out on the terrace?"

"No. Precisely here. In the library. In the exact chair that you're sitting in right now."

Roche got up, walked over to the door, and opened it. Then she sat down again.

From here there was a clear view of John Wright's door.

"Did John Wright stay in his room?"

"Yes, the whole time. He didn't go downstairs for coffee."

"His wife?"

"She did. About half an hour before Berit's lecture was due to begin." There was a sparkle in her eye. "So no, his wife *definitely* wasn't there at the end of the lunch break."

"Did you see anyone else going into John Wright's room?"

"No."

Nicole Archer answered quickly. Too quickly. She was lying.

And she wasn't as good at it as she imagined, Roche thought. Nicole looked her straight in the eye when she replied, probably because she thought it would make her seem more reliable. Beginner's mistake. Only professional criminals and crooks looked you straight in the eye.

And only when they lied.

The Mayor glanced at Roche again, as if to let her know Nicole hadn't told them everything she knew. Roche agreed. She knew something, and for some reason she was keeping it to herself.

She reached for Nicole's notebook. "May I?" she said, and before Nicole had a chance to answer, she started flipping through it. From her expression it was as if Roche had asked to read her diary, but perhaps she thought the police had the right to, because she didn't object.

The notebook was bound in fake leather, and the pages were plain and cream-colored. Roche flicked through a few. Nicole had filled several pages with unintelligible notes from Berit's lecture. The headline: *Lecture with Berit Gardner at Château des Livres* were the only neatly written words, presumably written down before Berit started her lecture.

On another page it said: *Why do women have affairs with men they can't stand?*

Roche sent the book over to The Mayor. He read the note and raised his eyebrows. They both had a fairly good idea who the man in question was.

"Who was the woman John Wright was having an affair with?" Roche asked.

Nicole opened her eyes wide in feigned surprise. "Was John Wright having an affair? But his wife is here!"

The Mayor leaned across the table. He was about to say something when Roche intervened.

"Mademoiselle Archer," she said sternly, "this is an official police investigation. Lying to us is very serious..." She held her hands up to quell any potential objections. "Or withholding vital information. I'll ask you again. Who was John Wright having an affair with, despite not being able to stand him?"

Nicole suddenly looked much younger than her twenty-five years. Maybe she remembered the young girl she once was that used to admire the police and respect authorities. Roche thought that a part of her longed to relinquish the responsibility...

And just like that, the moment was gone. Nicole opened her eyes wide and said unconvincingly, "What woman? It was just a general reflection. Could I have my notebook back, please? I don't think you have the right to keep it. I'm a journalist and—"

Roche pushed the book back.

Madame Wright still looked unremarkable, and her clothes were still cheap and badly fitted, but her demeanor had changed; she carried herself with a newfound dignity. It was as if grief had granted her a grace that didn't call for expensive suits or ironed shirts.

The dignified impression lasted until Roche asked her first question.

"Tell me about your marriage," she said. "Was it a happy one?"

Madame Wright froze. She looked back and forth between Roche and The Mayor as if she was trapped. "Yes!" she said finally, too emphatically. She lowered her voice. "Yes," she repeated. "It was. Very."

"You don't think… You had no reasons to believe your husband was having an affair?"

"An affair! My John? He loved me! He…"

Roche put her hand on Madame Wright's. "I have to ask these questions," she said. "I know how upsetting they must be."

Madame Wright pulled her hand back. "Well, you're wrong. John would never do that to me."

"Where did you go after you had your coffee?"

Again, that trapped, nervous look. "What do you mean?"

"It's a simple question. Toward the end of the lunch break, you went downstairs to get a coffee. What did you do after that?"

"Well, I drank it, I guess."

"You went back up to yours and John's room?"

"No. I drank the coffee outside. It was such a lovely day; I wanted some fresh air."

"Were you at the lecture?"

"No. I attended John's, obviously."

"Did you talk to your husband again, well, before he died?"

"No." Her voice was almost inaudible.

"You never saw him again?"

"No."

"Thank you, Madame Wright, that was all."

But the woman remained seated for a while, staring unseeing straight ahead. The Mayor had to put his hand on her elbow and help her up.

"John loved me," she said, without looking at either of them. "I know it. *I know.*"

"Do you think she knew about his infidelity and lied to us?" The Mayor asked when they were alone in the room.

"She could have been lying to herself as well," Roche said. She went over to the big mullion window. The only thing she could see outside was a large horse chestnut tree. It made the whole room feel like a tree house.

"We don't know for sure that John Wright *was* unfaithful," she said. "That note could have been about anyone."

"It was about him." The Mayor was convinced. "Who else?"

"If he was unfaithful, the mistress is as much of a suspect as the wife," Roche said. "Perhaps he refused to leave his wife?"

The Mayor shook his head. "What I don't understand is why he brought both his mistress and his wife to the same conference? Everyone knows you only bring one or the other."

Roche looked amused. "Oh, yeah, everyone knows? But maybe he didn't know the mistress was coming? She could have turned up here without his knowledge or approval."

"Maybe he dumped her before the retreat," The Mayor suggested. "You know what they say about hell and a scorned woman."

"No, pray tell," Roche said sarcastically. "What do you say about them?"

"'Heaven has no rage like love to hatred turned,'" The Mayor recited. "'Nor hell a fury like a woman scorned.' William Congreve."

Roche massaged her forehead.

"It's a possible motive," she admitted. She looked at her watch. It was almost six o'clock. She had one last debrief with the boss at seven, then she'd call it a day.

She patted The Mayor's shoulder. "Good work today," she said.

MAGNUM OPUS

THERE THEY ARE, WORKING ON their little narratives. I could tell them what's really creative.

Murder.

Writing is power, that's true, but it's nothing compared to knowing you've taken another person's life. Apart from being a parent and having created someone, I can't imagine a greater power.

And I haven't just changed John Wright's life. I've changed the lives of everyone around him. I've taken a star off their night sky, and they are freer now that they are no longer in his orbit.

But they don't realize it yet. Not fully. They're still unsure of their new freedom. Still in shock. But they will soon blossom. That's my gift to them.

Part of me wants to tell them about it. Sometimes I think they would understand. We could treat John Wright's death as the literary project it is. They'd give me feedback, and I'd listen politely. Not that any of them could have done it better, of course.

Then I think of Berit Gardner's gaze, so cold and penetrating, as if she already knows what I'm thinking, and the illusion dissolves. *She* wouldn't understand. She suffers from a terribly old-fashioned morality, despite her being a writer herself. She should know that the petty rules of ordinary people don't apply to us.

So I'm writing this instead. My magnum opus. The book that will never be published. The masterpiece that no one will ever read.

22

BERIT WAS LYING ON THE bed, her head at the foot and her feet on the pillow, when Sally found her. The French balcony doors were open to the delightful evening breeze.

"Now that we know the murder method, we can start work in earnest," she said when she saw Sally's silhouette upside down.

Sally went over to the window doors. Below, Emma had gathered the students to summarize the day. She longed to be down there with them, hearing their thoughts about Claudia's workshop. She guessed it was loyalty that made her stay up here instead, thinking about murder.

It was the first time Sally realized how much she'd been affected by the experiences from the summer in Great Diddling. She had appreciated the work with Berit and the chance it had given her to invest in her future as a literary agent, but she had hoped she would never again be involved in a murder.

She loved books, the safety and comfort they gave her, and she knew she wanted to secure the future of great stories. But preferably without having to witness another dead body.

She shivered. She had left the auditorium as soon as she'd realized what had happened, without the slightest smidgen of curiosity or interest in seeing more than she already had.

Berit Gardner had stayed in there, of course.

"What I could really do with," Berit continued, "is a whiteboard." She got up and walked over to Sally. Then she put her hands on her shoulders and led her back to the chair in front of the desk.

"Sit here," she said. "I need to think out loud. I'm going to throw stuff at you and see what comes back."

Sally didn't reply.

"First of all: It was not out of mercy that the killer mixed diazepam with hemlock. If the killer had cared about minimizing John Wright's suffering, they wouldn't have made his death so humiliating and public."

"Do we have to talk about this?" Sally said. "Can't we, I don't know, just let the police deal with it?"

Berit looked at her.

Sally averted her eyes to avoid seeing Berit's thoughts in her expression. But you could tell from her voice when she started talking anyway. Pity, sympathy, and impatience: a combination exclusive to Berit.

"An awful thing doesn't get less awful just because you try not to think about it. Quite the opposite, in fact. When we attempt to continue as normal and pretend nothing's happened, we only grant the tragedy more power over ourselves. The only thing that really works is looking reality straight in the eye and doing what we can about it."

Sally nodded. It was probably true. But sometimes you just didn't want to. "How did the killer know hemlock grew here?" she asked.

"They didn't. It seems to me the murder was impulsive and unplanned. If you traveled here specifically to kill someone, surely you would have come up with a better method than to rely on the local flora? No, let's write 'impulsive' on our mental whiteboard."

"Everyone knew John would be here," Sally said.

"Yes. I think we can cross out revenge as a motive. If you wanted to avenge a previous wrongdoing, you would have planned ahead."

"So, either John Wright did something on the only day he was here," Sally began.

"Or he was murdered to prevent him from doing something in the future," Berit concluded. "There's one thing we do know, however: The murderer had enough knowledge about ancient Greece to know that Socrates was killed by a combination of hemlock and poppy, but they created their own concoction with a modern twist. I say they must be boastful with niche knowledge. Awkward. Overly complicated. What does that make you think of?"

"A writer."

"Or someone who has worked with writers long enough to start thinking like us. Because, equally, it's *not* normal for writers to suddenly start killing people spontaneously. We're inherently passive. Our nature is sedentary. We mull over things rather than act out our aggressions. We go crazy or we start drinking." Berit considered this and corrected herself: "Or both."

There were a few examples of writers who had been driven to violence, Sally thought. Norman Mailer had got so upset by a review of his book by Gore Vidal he'd punched him at a party. Vidal had got up with a bleeding nose and said, "Norman, once again words have failed you." Perhaps the best comeback in the history of literary arguments.

"Why would anyone want to kill John Wright?" she asked. "That's what I don't understand. I've not been in this industry very long, but I've already learned that there are many unpleasant middle-aged men. And women, for that matter. But that's no reason to *kill* them."

"No," Berit agreed. "Fortunately not." She shook her head.

Sally got up and leaned against the railing of the French balcony. She took a deep breath. *If a Monet had a scent, this would be it*, she thought: flowering meadows, lavender and sunflower all mixed together to make the afternoon air intoxicating. Below, the participants were leaving to change for dinner.

Sally couldn't explain her sudden feeling of sadness, even to herself. Missing out on a work trip was in itself a kind of grief, she realized. The writing retreat was still taking place, but it wasn't the same anymore. Something dark and disturbing had crept in among them.

"Sally," Berit said behind her.

"Yes?"

"I understand. I really do. That's why I have to solve this. Whatever it is that's hiding here in the shadows needs to come out into the light. That's the only way we'll be able to move forward."

The dinner was quiet and subdued. Everybody seemed exhausted after having been seated all day, making things up, and the excitement about the investigation had deprived them of all their social reserves. *Probably more than one of them*, Berit thought, *was longing for home, even if a good night's sleep would likely make them forget the feeling.*

The police had left over an hour ago, but they had left behind a sense of suspicion. Mildred twitched at every sound.

Emma struggled to keep the conversation going, but from most people all you got was the clinking sound of the cutlery and porcelain while they mechanically shoved the delicious food into their mouths. The cook had exceeded herself with pig's cheek cooked in red wine gravy accompanied by exquisite small potatoes and parsnip crisps, but Berit felt she was the only one who appreciated the effort that had gone into the meal.

"The police think Mr. Wright was poisoned," Nicole suddenly said, loud enough for the whole table to hear.

Mildred dropped her fork on the floor.

"Nicole, please," Emma said.

Everyone stopped eating except Berit, who took another bite of the tender meat. "Whoever the killer is, he or she is unlikely to want to kill us all," she said.

"Exactly," Emma said, relieved.

"Besides, there's nothing to suggest that he or she would use the same method as last time," she continued.

"Right," Claudia said feebly. She pushed her plate away. She didn't seem to be the only one who had lost what little appetite they had.

"Of course the killer won't strike again," Emma said unconvincingly, as much to herself as to the participants. She was about to say something else when the doors to the dining room swung open.

In came a woman in her fifties who carried her years with confidence. She radiated the allure of someone who had long stopped caring about what other people thought of her. Her hair was neatly arranged, her suit jacket expensive, tailored, and bright red. Big gold buttons matched gigantic bracelets and a similarly oversized necklace. In her hand she was holding a large, wide-brimmed sun hat. An expensive handbag hung over her shoulder.

The woman seemed completely unfazed by everyone staring at her. She just raised an eyebrow and swept the room with her eyes.

"Okay," she said. "Which one of you slept with my husband? And which one of you killed him?"

23

THE REAL MRS. WRIGHT SAT on a Louis XIV-style sofa in pale blue fabric and swirling golden woodwork. On the beautiful table in front of her was a silver jug of coffee, an ivory white china cup with a golden rim, a silver bowl of sugar, and a smaller silver jug of warm milk.

Squeezed together on the opposite sofa were Emma, Berit, and Sally.

Mrs. Wright raised an eyebrow and drank some coffee.

"Quite the delegation," she said sarcastically. She made no effort to order them coffee.

They were in the luxurious lobby of one of Lyon's best hotels. It was nearly two o'clock.

Berit had delivered her lecture on *Dramatic Plot Twists*, almost mechanically, before lunch, handed over the baton to Claudia, and persuaded Emma and Sally to accompany her to the hotel.

The arrival of the real Mrs. Wright on the scene had changed everything. Berit knew it must have reinforced the police's original suspicion about the woman everyone had thought was John Wright's wife, but the woman seated in front of her also had a pretty good reason to kill her unfaithful husband.

Berit had tried talking to the fake Mrs. Wright the night before, but she had locked herself in the room and refused to see anyone. Berit assumed she would have to come out soon to talk to the police.

Up until now, they seemed to have prioritized talking to the real Mrs. Wright. Berit, Sally, and Emma had been told to wait in the lobby until the police were finished with her.

She still looked angry and impatient, and in a way, Berit could understand her. *It couldn't have been easy finding out that your husband had been unfaithful, then lose him before you even had a chance to have a go at him.*

"We just wanted to make sure you have everything you need," Emma said and awkwardly reached out for her hand. "If there's anything we can do, on a practical level perhaps, in the contact with the police or other authorities… So awful…"

Her voice faded. *Perhaps she'd realized it wasn't fully clear if she had referred to the mistress or the dead husband.*

Mrs. Wright removed her hand and waved it dismissively. "The consulate will give me all the help I need. One of my cousins is stationed here. So you, I take it, are Miss Scott?"

Emma nodded.

"My husband talked about you." She didn't elaborate. Her gaze moved across to Berit. "And you? Who are you?"

"Berit Gardner," Berit said calmly. "Writer. I'm sure your husband never mentioned me. He didn't remember me at all when we met."

Mrs. Wright laughed. The sound seemed to surprise even her. "No, I bet he didn't. John was completely useless at both names and faces. I used to say to him: 'John, old boy, it's bloody lucky you didn't pursue a career in diplomacy.'"

She turned to Sally. "And you?"

"Sally Marsch. I work for Marsch Agency, we represent…"

"Marsch! You must be related to Olivia Marsch?"

"My mum."

"That woman knows no shame," Mrs. Wright said angrily.

"No," Sally agreed. "What's she done this time?"

"She called me the day after my husband died, to make sure she would continue making money off him now that he was dead!"

"I'm sure—" Emma tried nervously to smooth it over, but it was doomed.

Mrs. Wright interrupted her. "She thought I was that, that *woman*! That's how I found out that there's apparently a little slut here passing herself off as Mrs. Wright. And now Olivia's sent you, I understand, to persuade me? I'm going to tell you what I told your mother: I have never been interested in discussing my husband's financial dealings, and I'm definitely not interested in doing it *now*. For God's sake, woman, my husband is not yet cold in the grave."

She turned toward Berit and Emma. "We can continue this conversation if she leaves, but if she stays, I'll leave. I'm not spending another minute in her company."

Then she pointed furiously toward the hotel doors as if she personally could decide who was allowed in there.

Sally slowly stood up. "I wouldn't dream of staying if you don't want me here, Mrs. Wright," she said, and left with considerably more dignity than Mrs. Wright had managed to muster.

Emma seemed to teeter between the urge to follow Sally and comfort her and to stay with Mrs. Wright. Berit nodded toward Sally, so Emma got up, excused herself, and left hurriedly.

Berit called a waiter over. "I don't know about you," she said to Mrs. Wright. "But I could use a drink."

Mrs. Wright relaxed. "God, yes," she said.

"Gin and tonic?"

Mrs. Wright nodded.

After only a few minutes, the waiter came back with their drinks.

Mrs. Wright took a deep sip and closed her eyes. "I needed that," she said. "Did you know the police think I killed my husband out of jealousy? Jealousy!"

She shook her head as if it were a personal insult that she should have had any strong feelings for her husband.

Berit said in a normal conversational tone, "Did you know your husband was having an affair?"

Mrs. Wright smiled wearily. "I did not kill him out of jealousy, if that's what you're asking. As I've already explained to the police, I was at a wedding when my husband died. Four hundred guests can corroborate that."

Berit noted that she hadn't answered the question. She waited.

"No, I didn't," Mrs. Wright said irritably after a while. "If you must know, it came as a pretty big surprise. I could have sworn John wasn't that interested in sex."

She had another sip of her drink. "The police should talk to that woman instead of bothering me. *She* most likely killed him. If anyone had a reason to kill my husband, it would be her. He never cared about her; I promise you that. If they were having an affair, it was all her initiative. And he never would have left me."

"Because he loved you?" Berit asked.

Mrs. Wright raised her eyebrows condescendingly, as if her kind of people didn't concern themselves with such feelings, let alone talk about them with strangers.

"Because I left him alone," she eventually said. "I had my horses and my dogs, and he had his literary life in London. Just like we both wanted it. He would never have risked his comfortable existence for another woman."

"Did your husband say anything about the writing retreat?" Berit asked. "Did he mention any of the teachers or students?"

"I'll tell you exactly what I told that French policewoman: I knew nothing, and cared less than that, about my husband's work. I don't have time to read books. He took care of all those things in London, then he came home to me to get away from it. He always said he needed to escape all the failed writers who contacted him and wanted him to read what they'd written, and all the substandard manuscripts, as he called them, that they'd sent to his office, even though he never asked for them."

What a lovely way to think of your writer colleagues. Berit had always been met with kindness and support from colleagues, and she felt a strong need to extend that help to others.

She thought about Julian Aubrey, who had handed over his manuscript with so much respect to his idol. *Carried it over to him as a gift, or an offering.* What would a man like John Wright have done with it?

"And he didn't say anything before he left? Nothing about the participants or the retreat itself?" she asked.

"Only that it was a waste of time. His and theirs. 'There are already too many bad books out there. Why encourage people to write more? We should discourage them instead!' Something like that."

It really was an excellent imitation of John Wright, Berit thought. She wondered what it was like to be married to someone you saw with such merciless clarity. Was it a sign of strong, or tepid, feelings, that she could know him so completely and still stay?

"And you never met Charles Tate or Rebecka Linscott?" Berit asked. "His previous agent and publisher?"

"No, why would I want to do that? When John spoke of them, they sounded really boring. You have to understand, John despised the publishing world. Perhaps not from the start, but definitely toward the end."

"Did he keep a diary?"

"He wrote everything down. He was annoyed when Knausgård had so much publicity. 'When my diaries are published, no one will give a toss about him,' he said."

"So he was planning on publishing them?"

"Of course. He talked about it every time Knausgård released a new volume, but like I said, I wasn't interested in John's writing. I never really listened when he started going on about it."

"And did he do that a lot? Go on about it?"

Mrs. Wright considered this for a moment. "More and more, actually, now that you mention it. He got worse and worse. I think something happened that made him even more cynical."

"But you don't know what?"

"No, but I do know things seemed to be going well for him. That new agent he found—awful woman—appeared to have negotiated a good deal for him. Not even John could find anything to complain about."

Berit stood up. "Regardless of what Olivia Marsch lacks, you're wrong about her daughter," she said. "Sally has never tried to make a penny out of a writer her whole life. Dead or alive."

"She can't be much of an agent in that case," Mrs. Wright said.

"On the contrary," Berit said. "She's brilliant."

24

THE FAKE MRS. WRIGHT SAT across the table from Roche and The Mayor in one of the interrogation rooms in the police building. She looked gray and blurred in the ruthless strip lights. As if her identity and her contours were dissolving in front of their eyes.

Her passport was laid open on the table in front of them.

"Sarah Briggs," Roche said.

She studied the passport photo closely. If you'd only seen that photo of the ordinary and serious-looking woman in the picture, she would have been the last person you'd suspect turning up at a French château as the mistress of a famous man. Roche wondered how she'd ever caught Monsieur Wright's attention.

"Miss Briggs. It is Miss, isn't it?" Roche asked.

"Yes."

"And you were John Wright's mistress?"

"Yes."

"How long had you been in a relationship with him?"

"Seven months."

"Let me guess. He promised he would leave his wife for you?"

Sarah Briggs's mouth formed a weary, ironic smile. "I'm not as stupid as you think, and John was never that banal."

"Why don't you tell me how things really were, then?" Roche said.

"What does it matter? You wouldn't understand."

"So you're telling me you knew he would never leave his wife?"

"Of course I knew."

"And it didn't upset you? Didn't make you angry, or frustrated…?"

"No."

"You killed him." It was The Mayor. He sounded harsh and judgmental. Roche wondered if Sarah Briggs's ordinary appearance offended him. In France, mistresses were usually more beautiful.

Sarah Briggs met his stare calmly. It was as if she found an inner strength from his overt antipathy.

"No," she said.

"Believe me, I understand," The Mayor said. He didn't sound like he did. His tone of voice was an insult even if the words were not. "You got jealous. A moment of insanity. It happens. If you cooperate with us, the prosecutor may agree to a more lenient sentence."

"No."

"Otherwise, you'll get life in prison. Trust me when I say you're not tough enough for a French prison. You wouldn't stand a chance with the women in there. They've also killed people, but not out of some romantic idea of true love. They kill for drugs. For pocket change. Because they feel like it."

Sarah smiled softly, as if his anger amused her.

"What's so funny?" he asked irritably.

"Trust *me* when I say that if you're going to threaten someone, you shouldn't do so when the absolute worst thing that could possibly happen to her, already has. Prison! John is dead, and you're wasting your time. You already knew what I did in the time leading up to his death. I was having coffee. At the same time someone was killing my hus…my John, I was having coffee. I was in the kitchen garden. I'm sure someone can confirm it."

She turned to Roche. "What did I have to gain from his death? I loved him. And now his wife will get everything. You should talk to *her* instead."

Chief Superintendent Pelissier's voice had an unfortunate tendency to go into falsetto when she got angry. This, in turn, made her mood even worse. It became a vicious circle that would have been comical if it wasn't aimed at Commissaire Roche. She had already spent half an hour being shouted at in her boss's office, and Pelissier showed no signs of slowing down.

"I've had it up to here with the different Madame Wrights!" Pelissier said. "The whole investigation is a joke. The consulate has already had a go at me. Apparently, they are deeply concerned on behalf of Madame Wright. She found out about her husband's death from his agent. 'Is this how the French police normally handle these things?' he had the nerve to ask me."

Roche made a face. Maybe she should have been more sympathetic to Madame Wright. But the woman's personality made it difficult. She was steeped in the English style and smiled when she insulted you.

Roche had never understood the expression *stiff upper lip*. It seemed to her that English people handled everything with ironically curled lips.

She felt her boss glaring at her and quickly uttered: "Yes, Madame," as a test. When the glaring didn't stop, she corrected herself with: "No, Madame. Of course not."

"When the press finds out about this, they're going to have a field day. We've been fawning over a common mistress!"

"Not fawning," Roche objected. The wives were always the prime suspects when rich men died. She imagined the mistresses came in a good second. "So far no one's spoken to the media. I don't think they are very keen to go public with the affair. It doesn't exactly make them look particularly good either."

"Small mercies!" The chief superintendent's voice was so loud and high-pitched, Roche had to lean farther back in her chair. With great effort, Pelissier tried to calm herself down.

"So, who killed him?" she asked. "The wife or the mistress?"

"Neither, it seems. The wife didn't come as a surprise to the mistress, who swears she was aware he would never leave the missus. She loved him unconditionally and wouldn't have touched a hair on his balding head." Her boss actually smiled at this. "If the wife had been killed, the mistress would have been the first to be locked up, but as it is, I can't find a motive. What would the mistress gain from killing him? She won't inherit anything, I've checked. She lives in a small flat in a small town. No particular income and no fortune to speak of. She would have gained more from keeping him alive."

"And the wife?"

"The wife's alibi is watertight—387 guests at a wedding. The May… Philippe, has spoken to seven of them who all confirm that Madame Wright was there all weekend. The airline has confirmed that she arrived late yesterday afternoon. The ticket was booked the same day."

"She could have hired someone."

Roche smiled feebly. "No one at the retreat comes across as a pro exactly. But we're double-checking everyone."

"Triple-check them."

"Will do, boss."

Berit knocked on Sarah Briggs's door. Emma had told her that was her real name.

"Miss Briggs?" she said.

No answer.

Berit moved her ear closer to the door and could hear the frenzied breathing of someone who was fighting a panic attack.

She leaned against the wall and said in a quiet voice: "Mrs. Wright?"

From the other side of the door came a faint reply: "Do you know what it's like to stand beside life? To always be the one who's looking on?"

"Yes," Berit said simply.

"All the others seemed to have it so easy. They hang out, laugh together in the pub, go on dates, get married, have kids, move into terraced houses… And all the time I was outside, in the cold, looking in. That's what it felt like."

"And then you met John Wright?"

"Yes. Yes, then I met John."

The door opened. Berit went inside and sat down on the only available chair. Sarah was sitting on the foot of the bed.

"When did you meet?" Berit asked.

"Seven months, two weeks, and three days ago." She smiled wearily. "I've been keeping count. You tend to do that when something changes your life."

"How did you meet?"

"At a literary event in Southampton. He gave a speech in the theatre there. I'd booked a ticket and traveled there. I like doing things where I'm surrounded by other people. It makes me feel less alone. It turned out we were staying in the same hotel. He had just been made aware of a betrayal on an enormous scale. His whole world had been shaken to its very foundation. And when I saw him sitting there, alone and bitter in the hotel bar, my world shook as well."

She turned to face the window, but Berit knew she didn't see a beautiful French summer's evening, but a dark hotel bar, where a lonely man was drowning his sorrows…

"How was I brave enough to go up to him? I still don't know. I just knew I wanted to look after him, listen to all his problems, comfort him. There was something lost and abandoned about him that spoke directly to me. I said: *'You look like you could use another drink.'* Can you imagine? Just like in a film!"

Berit smiled. She could see the whole scene in her mind.

"'*God, yes, you could say that again,*' he said. So I called the bartender over, like this." She lifted one arm up as if she were an actress in an old black-and-white Hollywood film, waving down a taxi. "And then I said: *'Another one of those.'* Because, clearly, I had no idea what he was drinking. It turned out to be whiskey. I ordered the same for myself; I didn't know what else to have. And then he said: *'A woman who appreciates a good whiskey. That's my kind of woman!'*"

Sarah put her hand on Berit's knee and whispered: "But I didn't! I had to pour it into the flower pot when he went to the loo. Poor flower."

Berit smiled. "It's probably been through worse."

"We talked all night." A romantic shimmer came over her. She already knew the next line, it was clear. She was telling Berit her favorite story, her very own fairy tale that she had probably recounted over and over again in her head. "And then he said: *'I don't suppose you fancy coming up to my room?'*"

A small wrinkle appeared on her forehead at the unromantic choice of words, but it disappeared as quickly as it had formed. "But I did! We went upstairs together; no one else saw us, only the bartender, and he didn't care. Sometimes I almost wish that someone had witnessed it. I wanted someone to see plain old Sarah Briggs walk straight up to a man in a bar and then leave together with him."

"I can see it clearly," Berit said, and she did, even the details that Sarah had left out and perhaps had never existed: the worn bar top wood, the bored bartender who couldn't care less which lonely travelers left together, the carpet in the corridor.

"After that, we saw each other every time he was in London," she said. "I went up just to see him. Took time off work. It was worth it. I said my mum was ill. No one cared." She smiled bitterly. "Perhaps I'll say she's died now, when I go back."

Berit frowned. "What was the betrayal he talked about? Did he ever tell you?"

"Of course. Rebecka Linscott, his publisher, had betrayed his confidence. Abused his trust completely. He was in a state of shock. It's beyond me how she had the nerve to turn up here. John was terribly upset about it too."

"In what way had she betrayed his confidence?"

"He…never said. But I know it was bad. That's why our relationship was so important to him. It was never about sex for either of us. He needed someone to talk to, someone who listened and was on his side. He was faced with one of the biggest decisions in his literary career. Should he leave Linscott Publishing and replace Charles with a new agent? And I was there, and I listened to him."

"What happened then?"

"He obviously got really busy when he'd finally made all his decisions. And later in the summer he would be in the countryside with his wife. I got it. I really did."

She got a faraway look in her eyes and said, almost breathlessly, "A love story like ours…it couldn't last! All major love stories end in tragedy. I knew he would never leave his wife. He needed her in order to be able to write. But when it was all over, I would have my memories. I would have *lived*. And he would continue to write his amazing books, and I would always know that I had contributed. And perhaps we'd bump into each other in the future, and our eyes would meet in the queue to get my book signed…"

Berit thought wearily that this vision of future meetings probably wouldn't have been as appealing to John Wright as it was to Sarah. Few people liked to be reminded of their earlier mistakes.

"Whose idea was it that you should come here?" she asked.

"It was his, of course. It was meant to be the end. I know that. A sort of farewell gift. One last magical experience." *She looked eagerly at Berit.* "So you realize, I could never have killed him. Never! He was the love of my life. No, more than that. My raison d'être. With him I had a purpose. My life meant something. And now it's over."

How precarious it was to live for just one person. Berit recalled her last conversation with John Wright. *Sooner or later all pedestals will be knocked over.* But who had torn down his?

Sarah's shoulders sagged. Her eyes filled up with tears again. "I want to go home," she said and sounded very much like a homesick child.

Perhaps her old life, where nothing ever happened, suddenly seemed more appealing. Berit leaned forward and touched her hand.

"I'll see what I can do," she promised.

The Mayor was at his desk with a stack of English passports and a copy of the list of participants. Every passport had to be checked against Interpol and directly with the British police, and then with airlines, hotels, anything they could think of.

"It was hardly our fault that John Wright lied about who he was married to," he said and glared at Pelissier's closed door.

"Shit happens," Roche said in English. Every time she spoke another language for a length of time, she began mixing up expressions. In a few weeks she would start dreaming in English.

"What do we know?" she asked.

"I was just talking with Mrs. Wright's lawyer. He confirmed that she inherits everything. Money, his literary estate. The lot."

"She seemed to have a decent amount of money even before."

The Mayor nodded. "The lawyer confirmed this as well. He's her old family lawyer, so he knew her background well. He helped write the prenup when they got married, and it was more to protect her than him."

Roche slumped into the chair behind her cluttered desk. Then she pushed it out and swung around so she could stare emptily in front of her.

"Why this whole charade of pretending to be his wife?" The Mayor seemed irritated. "English people are so prudish. Why not just be open about it and tell everyone he's brought his mistress? Nobody expects you to bring your wife to a place like this."

Roche had no idea who you were expected to bring to one of these conferences, but she trusted his expertise.

"It's not just her," she said. "All these writing people. No one is who they seem. And the fact that they're so far away from their natural environment makes it worse. It's as if the people at Château des Livres are only visitors in reality! What I need," she pondered, "is a guide. Someone on the inside who could explain how these people work…"

The Mayor had been staring at his computer screen when she spoke. But at this he suddenly looked up and said: "If you're thinking of Berit Gardner, I wouldn't if I were you."

"Why?"

"Look at this."

He turned his screen around. On it was the headline from an old newspaper article.

Swedish writer named person of interest in the Cornwall bomb murders!

25

"SHE'S MENTIONED SEVERAL TIMES IN the article," The Mayor said. "Apparently it was a double murder in Great Diddling, her home village. Someone else went down for it in the end, but can we be completely certain she wasn't involved in some way? And if she was involved and got away with it, what would stop her from trying again?"

Roche thought about everything Berit Gardner had helped her with. The wineglass. The hemlock flushed down the toilet. The psychological insights into the victim. Had she found the murder site so easily because she had been the one waiting there, offering him the red wine on the way to her lecture?

"The theatre," she said. "She was there preparing for her lecture when he must have been given the wine. Several people confirmed it. She couldn't have done it."

"She could have arranged it some other way," The Mayor said, but neither of them had any idea how. "Another thing. In both cases she was the one calling in the murders."

I'm Berit Gardner, and I want to report a murder. Roche spun around on her chair, logged on her own computer and googled *The Murders in Great Diddling*. There were several results straightaway.

Roche clicked through the search results. She found several postings about the case, made by bloggers, news reporters, and true crime podcasters.

She skimmed through some of them until she had a pretty good idea of the case.

The Devon and Cornwall police had been in charge. DCI Ian Ahmed had led the investigation. He'd had very little to say to the press. She smiled. She rarely did either.

The only thing she couldn't understand after reading the reports was what role Berit Gardner had played. Several journalists had tried but failed to interview her. Whatever she might be accused of, she hadn't used it for publicity. She seemed to have been a reliable and factual witness. That was it.

A photographer had captured her leaving the courthouse after the sentencing. The tanned face that Roche knew so well looked serious and drained.

She looked over to The Mayor, who was hunched over his computer screen, and wondered what his smooth, shimmering skin would look like when they were finished with this case. She felt an illogical urge to protect him from it all.

She looked at the photo of Berit again. She didn't see a hint of triumph or satisfaction that someone else had gone down for a crime she'd committed. But that didn't necessarily mean anything.

Roche clicked her way through to the Devon and Cornwall police's website and looked at her watch. Five thirty. With a bit of luck DCI Ahmed would still be in his office.

She dialed the non-urgent number, and a very talkative person in reception explained that DCI Ahmed was on holiday ("he's probably roaming the back of beyond as usual"), but that DI Rogers was there. Did she want her to connect her? Roche did and thanked her for her help.

"Detective Inspector Linda Rogers."

The voice was sharp and impatient, as if it wanted to warn whoever was calling not to waste their time.

"My name is Béatrice Roche, Commissaire with the Lyon police. I'm calling about a double murder investigation I believe you were involved in."

Two seconds of silence. "You're talking about the murders in Great Diddling, aren't you?"

"Yes. I'm right in the middle of my own murder investigation, and I have reasons to believe you also investigated someone who's…" She tried to remember how that papers had put it and continued: "Who is a person of interest in my own investigation."

"Okay?" Again, the short tone of voice.

"A writer by the name of Berit Gardner?"

The silence told Roche that DI Rogers had one or two things to say about Berit Gardner, but also that she hadn't yet decided whether or not to share it.

"Was she ever a suspect?" Roche finally asked.

"A suspect?" Strangely enough, DI Rogers sounded amused. "No, the boss never suspected her."

"DCI Ian Ahmed?"

"Yes."

Her voice was reserved.

A loyal colleague, Roche thought. "It sounds like he did a brilliant job," she said. "And led a very complicated investigation."

Silence again.

Roche realized she hadn't actually asked a question. "What was your opinion about Berit Gardner?"

"I didn't have one."

"And what did your boss think?"

"He told me once that he couldn't have solved the case without her."

"I doubt that," Roche said. It wasn't individuals, no matter how brilliant they were, that solved cases. It was grueling police work, persistence, and often very tedious bureaucracy.

DI Rogers seemed to share Roche's opinion. "Well, that's what he said anyway. I never understood it during the investigation, and afterward I asked him just what that help was. He said she helped him to think more freely. That Berit Gardner had an unusual ability to envisage several possibilities. She saw different realities all the time. That's what he said." Rogers sounded as if she had no time for things she didn't understand.

"I see," said Roche, who didn't understand it either.

"He said something else as well. He said he enjoyed going over the cast of characters with her."

"Cast of characters?"

"That's what he said."

Just as Roche was about to hang up, Rogers surprised her by saying: "Do you want his mobile number?"

"I thought he was on holiday?"

"I'm sure he wouldn't mind a call from you. Especially if it's about Berit Gardner. Besides, he's not that far away from you."

"No? I thought he was hiking?"

"Yes. And at the moment he's hiking Mont Blanc."

Roche called Chief Inspector Ahmed three times while driving to Château des Livres. No answer. She left a message and asked him to call her when he had a moment.

She found Berit on the terrace with a cold beer in her hand. She looked serious and so tired that Roche was put off her stride for a second.

"I spoke to Mrs. Wright," Berit said. "The old Mrs. Wright, that is. The first one. The one we thought was Mrs. Wright." She grimaced and took a large gulp of her beer as if to gather strength before she continued. "She wants to go home, and I promised I'd ask you if she could. She can leave her contact details. You've got a copy of her passport. Do you have any reasons for keeping her here?"

Just the mention of Sarah Briggs seemed to drain her, as if the tragedy sucked the energy out of her. She hardly knew the woman, but still made an effort to help her. *An extreme form of empathy.* Roche suddenly felt for Berit. Maybe that thin-skinned compassion for other people came from the writing. You couldn't go around thinking about all the tragedies you were faced with as a cop, that was for damn certain. If you did, you'd never make it. It was as simple as that.

She sat down next to Berit and said in a kinder tone of voice than she had intended: "Why didn't you tell me about Great Diddling?"

For the first time since Roche met Berit, she looked embarrassed. It made her seem very human, underneath all that quiet confidence.

"I couldn't just declare that I was involved in a double murder in Cornwall," she muttered.

"Why not? Didn't it feel pretty relevant to mention when people began to die here as well?"

"Because…it… For God's sake, you can't go around bragging when it concerns someone's death!"

"Brag? So you're saying you actually had something to do with solving the case?"

"A little bit."

"Are you being modest?"

Berit made a face. "A little bit."

Bloody hell, it was like pulling teeth.

"Let's just say I helped DCI Ahmed reach certain conclusions," Berit said.

Then she seemed to become aware that there were people on the terrace, pre-dinner, enthusiastically listening in on their conversation.

"We can't talk here," Roche agreed.

"A drink in town?" Berit suggested. She looked wearily at Roche and sighed. "Or do you prefer to talk at the station?"

"I can do better than that," Roche said.

26

AFTER THE CALM AND TRANQUIL countryside, the lights and sounds of Lyon came as a shock.

Roche's idea was to take Berit to a *bouchon*, one of those small hole-in-the wall restaurants in Lyon, which Berit remembered served very good traditional food.

Roche parked her car in rue de la Charité and led the way to one of the unremarkable-looking restaurants in a back street near Place Bellecour.

Despite it being a Monday night, the place was almost full. At eight o'clock they were in the middle of the first sitting. Families, groups of friends, and couples of all ages were crowded around the small tables.

The maître d' hurried toward them. "I didn't know that you were coming today… That is…she never mentioned it…"

"Relax, Mathieu. She doesn't know either. Do you have a table for us?"

"A table? A table! Yes, of course. This way, Madame le Commissaire."

Even though the restaurant was full, he managed to magically produce a table out of thin air, moved a few things around, made his apologies to the young couple next to them, and seated Roche and Berit. *"Et voilà!"* he said, pleased with himself.

A minute later a waiter came rushing out with a bread basket, a plate of thin slices of salami, and a carafe of the house red.

"Gabrielle will be out any minute, Madame," he promised. "I'm sure she'd love to see you."

"No rush," Roche said magnanimously.

"Who's Gabrielle?"

Roche smiled. "The chef," she said.

"Do you come here often then?"

Again, that fleeting smile. "It happens," Roche said.

Berit hadn't had Roche down as a regular anywhere. She could have sworn Roche was the kind of cop who lived off sandwiches and junk food, when she didn't forget to eat altogether. But Roche had relaxed as soon as they stepped in through the doors of the restaurant. She looked so comfortable that Berit had to reappraise her perception of her. Roche had her own anchor outside of her job, something that made sure she didn't end up off course.

The waiter brought their starters without them having ordered anything. He must have brought the whole menu: pâté, cheese, poached egg in a red wine sauce, mushroom ravioli, snails, and a *salade lyonnaise*. "Adam insists it's on the house," he said.

It all looked delicious. Berit tried a snail swimming in garlic sauce.

Roche stuck her fork in the ravioli and said: "I want you to know I don't believe in psychology."

Berit raised an eyebrow as she helped herself to more food. "Categorically? As in not the science, the profession, the human psyche?"

"In policing," Roche said. "Most murders are two things: excessively violent and glaringly obvious. A drug dealer gets shot with seventeen bullets. An alcoholic husband beats his alcoholic wife to death. Neither the perpetrator nor the victim is particularly loved. But we keep on going. We do what is needed of us."

Berit nodded. The young couple at the next table had just gotten their entrées. The very beautiful woman had ordered *andouillette*, Berit noted with admiration. The man had chosen a much more pedestrian skirt steak with new potatoes and red wine sauce.

"I had…" Berit noticed how Roche went through the options in her head before she settled for a slightly ironic "…the privilege to observe an FBI profiler at work once. I sat in on a debriefing in Chicago. The knot on the FBI guy's tie was as big as my wrist."

She held her arm up in demonstration. Her fist was clenched.

"He studied the killer's method, then he brainstormed the hell out of it. The killer is not married. Or maybe divorced. Or perhaps married to a woman who wears the trousers. He's scared of women. Probably unemployed. Or, if not, in menial work. Low status. Bitter about his lot in life. Problematic relationship with his mother."

Roche made a face. "I've heard better profiling from a second-rate fortune teller. Nothing could be disproven, and nothing was specific enough to actually help finding the killer. You can't look for an unmarried, divorced, or possibly unhappily married working-class man. Well, you can look. Just as you can look for a needle in a haystack."

"Did they ever find the killer?"

Roche smiled. "*Mais oui*. She was a thirty-four-year-old woman. A teacher. Well educated. The motive was purely economical. The victim, an older woman, kept her savings in an old coffee tin in the kitchen. She was killed over one hundred and sixty dollars."

"And what did the profiler have to say?"

"That he was right, of course. She was unmarried. And she never could stand her mother."

Berit shook her head and had another sip of wine. "So no psychology," she said. She tried the pâté. It tasted delicious.

Roche nodded. "But I do need help. I'll willingly admit it." She seemed to hesitate. Then she said, "I spoke to the Devon and Cornwall police."

Berit looked at her with interest. "With Chief Inspector Ahmed?"

Roche shook her head. "He's on a hike. I spoke to a Detective Inspector Rogers. She said you'd helped her boss...how did she put it?...*go through the cast of characters?*"

"Is that what you want to do?"

"I need background information. I need to understand these people."

Berit nodded slowly. "Okay," she said.

" So anything you can tell me about them. Anything at all."

"Well, I spoke to Sarah Briggs. And she said that John Wright had been upset that Rebecka Linscott had 'betrayed' him. Very upset. The betrayal happened months ago, but apparently he had been furious when she appeared here, without warning."

Roche whistled. "So, he didn't know she was going to be here?"

"No, seems that way." Berit told her about his initial reaction when he had spotted her.

"Sounds like he was angry with Charles Tate as well," Roche commented.

"Yes. And I think those two things are related. When his publisher let him down, maybe he took it out on his agent too."

Roche ate her poached egg in silence. It was clear she was going over something in her head. When her plate was clean, she said, "Could John Wright have had another mistress? Apart from Sarah Briggs?"

"Surely not?"

But she couldn't be completely sure. The discovery of the new Mrs. Wright had shaken her. There were other things she could have missed.

"I don't even think he *liked* women all that much," she continued. "To be honest, I'm surprised he even had one mistress."

Roche seemed to hesitate again, but in the end told Berit about Nicole Archer's notebook. "Could Nicole have realized Sarah Briggs wasn't his wife?"

"*I* didn't realize," Berit said. "So, no, I don't think Nicole knew. What exactly had she written?"

"'*Why do women have affairs with men they can't stand?*'"

"Good question," Berit said.

Roche raised her wineglass in agreement. "The man…" she said.

"Must have been John Wright. I agree. But the woman was definitely not Sarah Briggs. She worshipped him. So I'm pretty sure Nicole must have missed something. I can't believe he had *two* mistresses here. Although I wouldn't eat poison to prove it. So to speak."

"Be careful what you eat and drink," Roche said.

"In the company of crime writers, I always wait for someone else to eat or drink first. You never know what research they're doing at the moment."

"You don't think that someone killed him just to see what happened? As *research*?"

Berit considered the question seriously.

"No," she said eventually. "He wouldn't have died so discreetly, then. The writer would have wanted to see the effect of the poison. What's the point of doing research if you can't witness the result?"

Roche regarded her in a strange way.

"What?" Berit said. "Of course I wouldn't murder someone for research. Obviously not. But *if* you did it…"

"You'd want to witness it completely. Yes, I see what you mean."

At the next table, the young woman had left half of her offal sausage uneaten. The man generously shared his more palatable plate of meat and potatoes.

Berit smiled. That was true love.

As they finished off their starters, Berit observed Roche. She wondered if they were about to cross the line between a professional relationship and friendship. She had respected the Commissaire; now she was beginning to like her.

Suddenly Roche's face changed. It became warmer, softer. A smile started somewhere in her eyes and ended in a very slight movement of her mouth. Berit got the feeling she was witnessing something very private.

She followed Roche's gaze.

A young woman in chef's whites was bringing out their main courses. Her gait was confident and purposeful, her face open, strong, and intelligent. And right then, annoyed.

"My daughter, Gabrielle," Roche introduced her. "Gabi, this is Madame Gardner, a famous Swedish writer."

"Not that famous," Berit said uncomfortably.

Gabrielle nodded politely and put their plates on the table in front of them.

"Gabrielle is the youngest sous-chef in the restaurant's history," Roche said.

"Mum, you can't keep coming here all the time," Gabrielle said. "We talked about this. Once a week, okay? No more. I need to be able to work in peace."

Roche made a vague gesture with her hands. "What's stopping you?"

"She works too much," she said when Gabrielle had gone back into the kitchen and they had started eating. "She says she has to put up with the long hours now while she's still making a name for herself. But, when I ask her if there are any famous and well-established chefs with reasonable work hours, she just tells me I don't understand."

"I imagine you know quite a bit yourself about putting in long hours?"

"That's different." Roche grimaced. "Or at least, it doesn't mean I want the same life for her."

"There's nothing wrong with enjoying what you do. Or finding meaning in it."

"It's an obsession."

"A vocation, perhaps? Not unlike being a detective…?"

"Believe me, it's worse. Being a detective is nothing compared to being a chef." She shook her head. "It's my own fault, I guess. I worked all hours when she was growing up. Weekends, holidays… I was always busy. It's the only life she knows."

"Not necessarily a bad life."

"But lonely. And she's young. Shouldn't she, I don't know, travel? Party? Fall in love with someone completely inappropriate? All she ever thinks about is work. It's not natural."

"She'll find her own way in life," Berit said. "They always do."

Roche still didn't look convinced, so Berit changed the subject.

"Who's Adam?" she asked and topped up their glasses.

Roche looked at her, surprised.

"One of the chefs here," she said.

"A good friend of Gabrielle's, it seems," Berit said and looked at their plates.

Roche shrugged her shoulders. "Oh, that. I did him a favor once."

Berit waited.

"I cleared up a minor misunderstanding, that's all. His son had got dragged into something really stupid. Teenage stuff. Nothing I couldn't sort out."

Berit had another sip of wine and said nothing, but Roche seemed to take her silence as a question.

"What, you think the rich French kids don't get help all the time, from their parents, their network, their own personal lawyers? That's how the world works. But hard-working youths like Adam's son get done for the slightest mistake. So I offered him some help. A friend of my daughter's, why not?"

They finished their dinner, and Berit studied Roche carefully.

"If you're after gossip, I just realized who you should talk to," she said. "But not here. Let's go somewhere a bit quieter."

Roche got up. "Thanks for tonight, Mathieu," she said when the maître d' came over. They were given coffee in two takeaway mugs and left without even seeing anything resembling a bill.

Roche suggested they walk down to the Rhône. She moved with a natural confidence, secure in herself, by being in just this spot.

Berit followed. For some time, they walked in the dark next to each other in comfortable silence. "Are you from here?" she asked after a while.

"Lived here all my life."

And would most likely continue to do so. Some people had no need for movement.

The Rhône was dark and still. On the opposite side of the river, the grand houses were reflected in the water. Lyon had always been defined by its rivers, and to Berit the whole city reminded her of adventure and freedom.

"I lived here for six months once," she said.

It was between her third and fourth book, so she must have been coming up to forty. Her writing had neither led to the failure she had feared nor the success she'd dreamt of. She was a grown-up, living on her own, working in a profession she'd chosen herself, perhaps not rich, yet far from poor.

Her friends had grown up as well. Children and careers had shrunk their lives until there seemed to be no room for adventure and surprises. A new kind of fear had crept into their lives: suddenly they were scared of losing things, rather than never getting them.

In hindsight it was easy for Berit to see how bored she had been.

And as always when she had become stuck, she had picked up her things and left. Escaping was her go-to method of dealing with life.

"Did you like it here?" Roche asked. "Was it a good time in your life?"

Berit smiled. "*Like*" was definitely the wrong word. She had lived here, fully, and she'd been in love.

"Places where you've been in love are always interesting," she said. "You always carry them with you somehow."

"Do you?" Roche said slightly amused. "I try and forget mine as soon as possible."

The difference between a cop and a writer, Berit thought. Roche neither had the time nor the energy it took to mull over everything that happened to her. She had a job to do. To Berit, mulling over things was her work.

At the same time, she could tell that Roche was a person who shared her basic values in life. Things were what they were. No point regretting them.

Roche and Berit sat down on a bench next to the dark river. Berit got her phone out, opened her contacts, and found the name *Don't answer!!!*

"Olivia Marsch, Marsch Agency," a professionally impatient voice answered.

Berit switched to video call and waited for a moment until Olivia had done the same. Then she introduced the two women to each other. "Olivia Marsch, agent. Béatrice Roche, commissaire. Olivia, we need some information."

"Nice to meet you," Commissaire Roche said in her almost perfect English. The faint French accent only made her seem more sophisticated. Berit caught the scent of her leather jacket and the elegant French perfume she was wearing. And something else that Berit realized must be a hint of nicotine, lingering on her jacket. They had the phone between them and a notebook each resting on their legs.

"Tell us what happened between John Wright, Charles Tate, and Rebecka Linscott," Berit said.

"Regardless of what Charles might have said, I did not steal John Wright from him," Olivia said. "That's not how it works. Writers can come to me, but I don't chase them or lure them away from their previous representation. John Wright was furious when he came to see me. If it had been up to him, he would have pressed charges against Charles, Rebecka, and everyone who worked for them, down to the secretaries and the trainees."

Roche and Berit quickly looked at each other. "Pressed charges?" Berit said.

"Rebecka used his royalties to finance her misguided literary ventures. When John came to me, he wanted to report her for embezzlement."

Embezzlement. That would ruin any publishing career.

"When was the last time you spoke to John Wright?" Roche asked.

"On Saturday. The day before he died. He called me, upset about Rebecka Linscott turning up. I had managed to persuade him to sign an agreement with a repayment plan. No scandal, no police, everything terribly civilized. And what does that stupid woman go and do? Turns up and provokes him with her presence!"

Berit leaned down toward the phone. "Did he mention the police when you talked to him? Did he want to report her now, too?"

"That ship had sailed," Olivia said. "But he was consumed by some crazy idea of writing a revealing exposé of the publishing world."

"Jokers and charlatans," Berit recalled.

"Something along those lines. But it reeked of bitterness. Impossible to sell. I told him to focus on his novel, that success was the best revenge."

"Did he listen?" Berit asked.

"No, but he would have done so, eventually. I can be pretty persuasive."

"This exposé of his," Roche said. "Would it include Rebecka Linscott?"

"Rebecka Linscott *in particular.* If he had persisted in writing that book, it would have been devastating for her. And she would have dragged Charles Tate down with her. Charles should have realized what she was doing long before John did. The royalty reports were a mess. The rest of the accounting too. I should know. We've had auditors go over everything, as part of the agreement."

Berit thanked Olivia and ended the call.

"Finally," Roche said. "A real motive. If it had come out that Rebecka Linscott had embezzled his money…"

"Even without a lawsuit it would have ruined her career," Berit agreed. "The accusation would have been enough."

"John Wright threatens to reveal everything. Career ruined. Possible prosecution. She kills him. We've got enough for a warrant."

"Don't forget about Charles," Berit said. "In a way his motive is just as strong. He would have exposed his incompetence as well."

"Rebecka stole the notes and the computer because John had written down what she'd done. It has to be. It fits. Is it tomorrow you're going to Vienne?"

Berit felt her jacket pockets and found her crumpled up copy of the program. Tuesday promised "a fantastic opportunity to develop the way you used settings in your novels," by a visit to the "nearby, incredibly beautiful" town of Vienne.

Berit nodded.

"Excellent. We'll search her room while you're away. I'm sure the prosecutor will agree with me."

"Don't just search Rebecka's room," Berit said. "Search everyone's."

"Yours too, I take it?" Roche said skeptically.

"Of course, mine too."

Roche thought about it. "The prosecutor would never agree," she said. "We have enough grounds for a warrant to search Rebecka Linscott's and Charles Tate's rooms, but we can't start searching everybody's room. Not without cause."

"You could if they gave their permission," Berit said.

"And why would they do that?"

"Group pressure. Try it. What have you got to lose? If nothing else, you get a chance to study the expression on their faces when you ask them."

"Facial expressions can't be used as evidence," Roche said, but at least she didn't say no.

It was eight thirty in the evening, and the only thing Philippe Delavigne saw in the office window was the reflection of himself, hunched over his desk. He had John Wright's phone records in front of him, a totally pointless task since the killer hardly would have called him. Why would he? They were in the same place.

He flinched when someone punched him in the shoulder. *Ah, Janvier, the office idiot.*

"So the boss has deserted you?" Janvier said.

"Sure, sure." Philippe massaged his shoulder where Janvier had hit him.

"Do you know what she's up to while you're here, slaving away?"

"She's the boss. She can do whatever she likes."

"She's having dinner with that writer, Berit Gardner. Has taken her out to a restaurant and all." Janvier waived his phone around as if to suggest he and the boss were in constant contact with each other. "Apparently, she's been given some very valuable information too."

"And?" Philippe said.

"How do you feel about her preferring Berit to you?"

"I'm sure she's got her reasons."

"If you say so," Janvier said and seemed bored of teasing him. "See you, Mayor," he said with one final perfunctory wave over his shoulder.

Philippe comforted himself by noticing how ridiculous Janvier looked in his Lycra shorts. "See you, idiot," he muttered.

Then he put away the stack of phone records. If his boss was out having fun with potential suspects, he wasn't going to stay in the office.

A MURDERER'S MEMOIRS

DO YOU RADICALLY CHANGE WHEN you take someone else's life?

I suspect most people believe so. They want to think something happens to their soul. As if you can't kill another human being without killing something inside yourself.

It's such a banal train of thought. An intellectual comfort blanket. An old wives' tale for children.

John Wright would be the first to point out that people kill each other all the time. We always have done, and we always will.

If you found out that you could save another person's life, ninety-nine times out of a hundred, you just ignore it and continue on as if nothing had happened. What's the difference when it comes to me? You're passively killing loads of people. I killed one man in a slightly more active manner.

Don't believe me? How about every war and famine you ignore? The refugees drowning in the Mediterranean, climate change that will drown whole islands, every nameless beggar outside Marks & Spencer who will freeze to death this winter while you buy yourself yet another winter coat. *Help us, we're dying! I can't, I need a soy latte.* So get off your high horses, that's all I'm saying.

And do you feel different afterward? More pleased, probably, with your gorgeous winter coat and your lactose-free latte.

The same say that every life counts. In reality, hardly any do. I could probably have killed roughly 80 percent of the world's population without consequences. I'm guesstimating here, so don't bother coming to me with some paltry arguments about percentages.

Historically, people's lives have never been worth very much. We've kicked the bucket—as some would put it—for thousands of years without anybody giving a toss. That's why people had so many children in the old days. For spares.

And nobody cares. No more than God does when the proverbial sparrows fall.

Where was I? I need to edit this page later, for the pacing. More excitement. You readers never have any patience. No unnecessary refinement, thank you very much. Literary ambition unwanted. You only have time to listen to the audiobooks for as long as it takes to fold the washing.

Where was I? People's lives. Do you want to know what my crime is, my real crime, the one I will be punished for if I ever get caught? I killed a rich white man. Perhaps the only life that has consistently mattered. Even historically.

And did I feel different afterward? I hesitate here. Perhaps I did. I didn't regret it. Not then, not now. If I feel anything, it's pride. I look around and realize that everything that happens from then on, happens because of me.

Thanks to me, I should say.

If I'm different in any way, I am freer. I have shed yet another of the world's expectations. I have fulfilled a dream. I have achieved something.

And it's not just my own destiny I've changed. Everyone at the retreat is freer now. It's going to be a success, thanks to me. The participants have experienced a real-life murder investigation close up. Who would have wanted to miss out on an experience like that?

I can see it in their faces, how they suck up the information. The clever ones pick up on the details. The less clever pick up on their own feelings. Less interesting in the long run, but something might come of it too. But to communicate those feelings, they'll still need all the details. Light, color, taste, smell. Show, don't tell, as we say in this industry.

One day I might even tell the story of what happened, how it felt, and, yes, how it affected me.

A psychological portrait of a killer, if you want. An account of a soul in transit. A murderer's memoirs.

27

COMMISSAIRE ROCHE INTERRUPTED EVERYONE IN the middle of breakfast.

"Good morning," she said. She sounded alert, rested, and efficient. Her working day had probably begun hours ago. "I hope you've all slept well," she added politely.

No one answered. Sally slowly put down her baguette with apricot jam. Charles and Rebecka glanced furtively at each other over their cups of tea.

"Madame Scott has informed me that you're going on a trip to Vienne."

"What if we are?" Charles said aggressively. "What's that got to do with the police? Or are we under house arrest, perhaps?"

"Not at all. I'm sure you have an interesting day ahead of you. Vienne is a fantastic town, with a rich and fascinating history."

"For God's sake, you're hardly here to talk about our travel plans," Charles said.

"Very well. I'm here to ask your permission to search your rooms."

Berit quickly looked around. The expressions varied between upset (Rebecka), nervous (Emma), and confused (most of the rest). Only Charles looked angry.

"It's just a formality," Roche assured them. "We're just want to make sure that Monsieur Wright's briefcase isn't in anyone's rooms."

Charles seemed to have made himself the spokesperson for the group. "And if we refuse?" he said. His fingers gripped the teaspoon so hard, his knuckles whitened.

"That's fully within your rights, Monsieur. However, we won't be able to eliminate you from the investigation in that case. Should we need to, we'll return later on with a search warrant."

"Of course we don't mind," Emma said. "We've got nothing to hide." She looked around the group. "Do we?"

Charles made an irritated gesture with the teaspoon. "Yes, yes," he said. "Search my room, if it amuses you."

In the end no one refused.

As if they had an unspoken agreement, they all met by the bus as soon as they had finished breakfast. They had been allowed to collect what they needed for the day from their rooms and had been offered to stay behind to attend when their rooms were being searched. No one had taken the police up on the offer.

The group waited around nervously, staring at the police officers who had gathered around Roche for the briefing.

Charles was on his own, away from the others, smoking a cigarette. When he was done, he put it out on the ground, picked up his briefcase, and walked over to the bus.

"I'm tired of standing around waiting," he said loudly. "We might as well wait on the bus until we're ready to leave." He nodded toward Antoine. "Open up, will you?"

Antoine shrugged his shoulders. "It's not locked," he said. He hadn't finished his cigarette.

"Excuse me, sir," Roche said, who had hurried over when she saw Charles heading toward the bus. "Before you board, we need to search your bags. With your permission, of course." She smiled disarmingly at everyone. "Purely a formality, but there would be little point in searching your rooms if you could take away whatever you wanted on the bus. You have the right to refuse, of course."

Charles handed over his bag. "You never give up, do you?"

Roche quickly and systematically went through the bag. "Thank you very much, Monsieur."

"Perhaps you want to do a full body search as well?"

"That won't be necessary, Monsieur. We're looking for a briefcase and a computer. There's hardly room enough underneath your shirt."

"You'll want to look through mine as well," Claudia said and handed over a large handbag.

Roche lifted up a bright pink laptop case. She opened the case, pulled out the laptop with an enormous rainbow flag sticker stretching across the whole cover, and then put it back down again.

"Not exactly John's style, I think," Claudia said dryly.

They all queued up to have their bags searched before they boarded the bus. Roche carefully went through them, one after the other. Notebooks, computers, water bottles, sunscreen, phone chargers.

None of the notebooks looked like the one Mrs. Wright had described: leather bound, with a golden inscription and his initials on the spine.

Mildred was the last in line. Her bag contained neither computer nor notebook, so it didn't take long to search. Commissaire Roche lifted out the knitting and the wool, dutifully looked inside the bag, and handed it back.

She poked her head inside the bus and said politely: "I hope you all have a nice day."

No one answered.

The doors closed.

Berit looked around. There they were. All their suspects, gathered in one hot, rattling bus.

Antoine was driving. Emma stood next to him at the front of the bus and was being thrown from one side to the other as the bus swayed. She held a crackling microphone in her hand and tried to drown out the sound of the engine.

"Vienne is one of the richest towns in France for Roman and medieval history," she said. "There's an old Roman amphitheater and several mosaics, as well as several medieval buildings…"

"I can hardly wait," Charles muttered. "Christ, are we being taken on a sightseeing trip?"

He and Rebecka sat at the front of the bus, expressing an almost hostile disinterest. Charles glared at Emma; Rebecka ignored her.

"No one is forcing you to be here," Antoine said angrily from the driver's seat. "I can stop the bus and let you get off right here."

They were driving on a deserted country road, surrounded by fields.

"This excursion is completely optional," Emma assured them quickly. Even though it was only day three of the retreat, her face already looked haggard. Her voice was tense. "At any time, you can return to the château…"

"And watch the police search our underwear drawers?" Charles said. "No thanks."

"So shut up and enjoy the trip," Antoine suggested.

Rebecka suddenly spoke. "I don't believe in being a tourist when I travel," she said. "It feels so false and commercial. I prefer seeking out more authentic places."

"*C'est des conneries!*" Antoine said to himself. "*Tojours les mêmes conneries.*"

Emma drew her breath and said with forced enthusiasm: "And afterward we'll have lunch at an amazing vineyard."

"You should at least appreciate that," Nicole said to Charles, loud enough for everyone to hear.

The rest of the participants were spread out on the bus. The only ones who had seemed to form some kind of a group were Nicole, Julian, and Alex. They were in the back, reminiscent of the cool gang in school.

Nicole looked greedily around as if she'd had the same thought as Berit: The killer must be on the bus at this very moment. It was almost as she expected them to stand up any second and blurt out: "It was me! I did it!" When nothing happened, she looked disappointed.

Julian seemed to vacillate between hoping that the police would find the first five pages of his manuscript and despairing that they might be lost forever. Only Alex seemed to look forward to today's trip with uncomplicated joy.

Berit reminded herself how little she really knew about the people on the bus. Their personalities, backgrounds, histories—all of that could be tweaked or concealed in an environment where nobody knew you.

Berit had previously thought that the teachers were more suspect than the participants, since they were more likely to have met John Wright prior to the retreat, but Sarah Briggs had challenged that theory too. Any one of them could have met John Wright at one of the countless literary festivals and events he'd attended during his career.

She looked around. She planned on using this day trip to observe all the people on the bus. Faculty member or participant, it didn't matter—while they were examining Roman ruins, Berit would examine *them*.

Two questions occupied Berit. Who had met John Wright prior to coming here? And who was capable of murder?

28

THE BUS PARKED NEAR THE train station, and they walked toward the amphitheater on rue Victor Hugo. Emma had paid their entry fees in advance, so everyone just walked straight in. She'd also bought the program and led them up onto the stage at the bottom of the amphitheater and read about its function and history. They all stood facing the steep rows of stone benches as if they were actors in a timeless play.

Rebecka went all the way to the edge of the stage, pulled by an invisible audience only she could see. She laughed. "I did a bit of acting in my day," she said. "And to stand on a stage in France…"

"It affects you, doesn't it?" Emma said understandingly.

Her kindness only seemed to provoke Rebecka.

"You're wasting your time here anyway," she said. "You can't teach people how to write. They either have what it takes, or they don't. It's an art, not a craft."

She said it loudly in front of everyone, indifferent to who could hear her.

Emma smiled stiffly and put her hands together. When she started talking, she sounded like sounded like a stressed preschool teacher. "And it is this beautiful and fascinating setting that we are going to use today. Our first writing exercise will be to write a scene that takes place in this Roman theatre. Contemporary, historical, during a Roman play or the archaeological excavations or a tourist expedition—it's up to you. You don't have to write the whole scene if you don't want to, but take note of which details you would use. What are the emotions you want to evoke in your scene? What details are you using to help convey those emotions? What can you do to transport the reader to the time and place you've chosen? Spread out, sit wherever you want, and we will reconvene in about forty-five minutes. And remember: specific details!"

"They're just going to place dead bodies everywhere," Rebecka said dismissively.

With difficulty, Berit climbed up all the stairs until she stood at the top of the amphitheater.

The rows of seats led down to the stage in a steep incline. Birds circled below her, and beyond the amphitheater, the town of Vienne was crouching in. The attractive sand-colored cathedral tower stood out among the red roofs, and between them glittered the turquoise water of the Rhône. In every direction Berit turned, hills spread out in the distance, clouded in mist.

Emma was busy checking in on everybody. The wind made her hair move in every direction, and she was sweating under the hot sun as she walked up and down the steps, but it didn't stop her from giving each person her full attention. She had a nice word to say to everyone, or an encouraging pat to offer, and if any of the students got stuck, she sat down next to them and guided them through it.

Berit helped her. She asked the ones sitting on the highest rows how they were doing and if they needed help, and it turned out Rebecka had been right about the dead bodies. It was slightly disturbing seeing the attentive, focused faces and realizing they were all struggling with describing how blood splattered all over the stage, or the exact moment when the retractable theatre knife-that-proved-to-be-real sank into soft human flesh, or the poison chalice that was raised…

Only one of them wasn't writing. Nicole Archer was standing at the top of the amphitheater, but Berit wondered if she was even appreciating the breathtaking view. Her face was turned toward the sun, and she seemed caught up in her own thoughts.

She must have felt Berit's gaze because she turned around and stared straight into her eyes.

She could do it, Berit realized with sudden conviction. *She really would walk over dead bodies if that's what it took.*

There were very few people about whom Berit could say with certainty that he or she could kill someone. It wasn't a moral assessment, but a practical one. Was the person strong enough, mentally, and in themselves, or determined or crazy enough to take another human being's life?

Nicole was definitely strong enough.

"What are you thinking about?" Nicole asked.

"Whether you could kill someone."

Nicole smiled but didn't answer the unspoken question.

"Had you met John Wright before coming to the retreat?" Berit asked.

Nicole's smile widened. "If I was the killer, I would hardly divulge such an important detail, would I?"

Charles was running up the rows of seats. He attacked them in a stride that became slower and more labored the higher he got.

As he passed Berit, he stopped and clutched his side.

"I have to start going to the gym again," he gasped. "I could have run up and down these rows when I was at Oxford."

Berit looked disapprovingly at him. "Why aren't you helping out?" she said. "You could do your job. Once upon a time you were good at it."

He looked offended. "*Good?* I was brilliant."

Down below, on the stage, Rebecka was lifting her arms up in the air letting the theatrical side of her free. Berit could easily imagine how a young John Wright had been dazzled by her cultural luminosity. Dressed in a long, billowing dress, with those bright red lips and the long, wild hair, she looked like a modern-day Boudicca.

And like a killer, Berit thought, and added Rebecka Linscott's name to her list.

Next stop on the agenda was the cathedral in Vienne.

Emma had prepared excerpts from *The Hunchback of Notre Dame* and *Madame Bovary* and asked them to analyze the descriptions of Victor Hugo's and Gustave Flaubert's cathedrals, followed by a writing exercise to describe the cathedral in front of them in their own words.

"We're unlikely to find the next Hugo or Flaubert in this group," Rebecka said sarcastically from behind her dark sunglasses.

Berit wondered if she was actually unaware of what an unpleasant impression she was making or if she really just didn't care.

Berit withdrew to the side entrance and lit a candle for John Wright's soul, or perhaps for her own.

"I didn't think you had any patience for religion," Sally said.

"I'm not conceited enough to imagine myself knowing everything about the universe, or humanity's place in it," Berit said. Even their whispers seemed to echo in the vast room. She shook her head. "But I've never understood the meaning of praising God with this much stone. It feels more like human vanity, trying to outdo him."

Sally looked at her doubtfully, and Berit was reminded that young people were often more categorical when it came to faith.

Whether they believed or not, they did it wholeheartedly. In Berit's experience, you became less sure of things as you got older. Life had the ability to take your stubbornness and transform it into a joke at your own expense. That was the strongest proof Berit had found that God, if they existed, at least had a sense of humor.

"Either way, anyone who's ever struggled with a deadline should respect the story of creation," Berit said. "I couldn't even write a novella in six days."

"You had something to do with the police letting Sarah leave, didn't you?" Sally said.

Berit shrugged. "Roche had all the information she needed."

"But you persuaded her."

"I talked to her about it," Berit said. "That's all."

"I didn't think you cared about what happened to her."

Berit looked at Sally in surprise. "I care what happens to all of them," she said.

"And what happens to the retreat," Sally guessed. "For Emma's sake."

"For everybody's sake. There are plenty here who need it, both among the teachers and the students."

Sally nodded. "Me, too," she said. "I feel free here, in a way. *Felt* free. Before all of this happened."

Freedom could be extremely revealing. When you were unable to hide behind your everyday life and your set identity, you might accidentally reveal the murkier parts of your personality that were normally kept strictly under control.

She had thought that the unfamiliar setting would make it harder to get to know the people here, but travel could also be a crash course in discovering people's personalities. Exhaustion, strange food, the lack of routines. All of these things could bring out sides you normally managed to hide. But how could one use it…?

The first hint of an idea started forming in Berit's head when they suddenly heard upset voices from the chapel next door.

"I was an idiot to let you join the writing retreat." Emma's voice was quiet, but she was clearly distressed. Berit placed a finger over her lips to hush Sally up and crept behind a pillar in order to see and hear better.

"You were happy enough to accept my help," Rebecka said dismissively. "Grateful, and desperate."

"Help?! You haven't helped a single person here. You don't read any of the texts, you give no feedback, hold no workshops! I thought you would engage as a publisher."

"With *this* group? You're not exactly giving me much to work with."

Emma put her chin out. She had to stand on her toes to reach Rebecka's height. Her bright red face was reflected in Rebecka's sunglasses. "I took a risk when I let you come here, and it almost cost me the whole retreat! If you don't get a grip of yourself and start pulling your weight, I'll…"

"You'll what?" Rebecka sounded worried.

"Let's just say I know one or two things about you that I think the police would be very interested in finding out!" Emma said.

29

MILDRED'S FEET WERE SORE. THE vibrations from the bus made her want to close her eyes and take a little nap. But everyone else seemed sprightly. Where did they get all their energy from?

After the amphitheater and the cathedral they had been dragged around on a sightseeing tour. Every mosaic and stone relic from ancient Rome and beyond had been pointed out to them. It was interesting, of course, and the sweet Emma had been so thoughtful and looked after her when she'd gotten tired, but still. The only thing Mildred wanted now was to take her shoes off and massage her feet. And a cup of tea. God, she could kill for one. She thought of her own kitchen, the flowery curtains, the begonias on the window sill, her own teapot.

Her eyes welled up. She had to blink quickly to stop the tears from falling.

The bus drove into a vineyard, and Mildred hobbled down the steps along with everyone else.

She blinked in the bright light. Even the sun was different here. The English one was mild and lovely and, she had to admit, very reluctant to show itself. The French sun was hot and burning with no sense of modesty.

A wine tasting was followed by a lavish lunch with more wine. Afterward, some people wandered around, while others stayed in the cool restored barn where they had been eating. As always in similar situations, Mildred didn't know what to do, so she stayed seated, even though everyone else around her had escaped.

Everyone seemed to have forgotten that the police might be searching their rooms right this minute. Mildred knew they wouldn't find anything in her room. But it didn't stop her from constantly thinking about it. The same had happened in the airport on the way here. As soon as she got near security, she became convinced she had accidentally hidden drugs, weapons, and a couple of bombs in her handbag.

Berit waved from the other end of the table to come over and join them, and Mildred scooted over.

Alex, Julian, and Nicole ordered another bottle and poured Mildred a glass as well. She accepted, even though the wine she'd had with lunch was already giving her a headache.

Alex looked around admiringly. What in Mildred's eyes was an old barn was apparently the height of style in his, right down to the bare concrete floor under their feet. The refectory table was made from thick wooden beams, held together with heavy-duty iron nails that would ruin any tablecloth that was spread on top of it.

The bench they sat on had no backrest. She was the only one who seemed to be annoyed by it. Her kitchen chairs back home had backrests. Her living room sofa did as well. And the armchair, she thought longingly.

"Isn't it amazing?" Alex said. His smile included Mildred, in a warming way that eased her tiredness a little bit.

"Good wines, France, a summer's day," he continued as if had just counted his blessings. "And to experience it with like-minded, passionate, creative people."

"All writing about the same subject," Nicole said darkly. "Every person here seems to want to write about the murder."

"Writing is such a lonely profession you need other people who have experienced the same thing," Alex said. "That's what we've been missing. Isn't it, Jules? This is how we'll spend our time in the future. Perhaps I could be both muse and sponsor, but you need context. No truly amazing artist operates in a vacuum."

"I just wish everyone hadn't experienced my murder," Nicole said. Mildred shuddered. "The race is definitely on. I have to be the one who finishes first."

"Do you think the police will find John's briefcase with his notes?" Julian said.

Alex looked impatient. The expression only lasted a split second before he regained control over his emotions and patted his partner's hand.

"Fuck John Wright," he said. Despite the swear word, he sounded happy and enthusiastic. "We've got wine, bread, and butter, what more could you want in life?"

"He was going to read my manuscript. I would finally have found out if I'm a writer."

Claudia sat apart from the others and wasn't drinking wine. She looked slightly disoriented and had been quiet throughout the whole conversation. *She looks how I feel*, Mildred thought.

But now Claudia turned to Julian. "You write, don't you?" she asked, a slightly belligerent tone in her voice.

"Yes."

"And you've written a full draft? From the very first chapter, to the end?"

"Yes."

"Well, then. You're a writer. You don't need an idiot like John Wright to tell you. If you want my advice, it's this: Find a sensible person to read what you've written. But don't put your trust blindly in someone else's opinion. Believe in yourself. This industry is full of idiots."

"There's one less in it now," Alex said. "What?" he added when he saw their expressions. "We all know it's true."

"I don't care what you say," Julian said. "I admired him. He was an amazing writer."

"Shame he was such a horrible human being," Claudia said.

Mildred giggled. Alex topped up her glass.

"I admire you young people," she said suddenly. Her voice was slurred, but she didn't care. "In my day, we were taught to be nice and quiet and not take up any room. Or believe we were something special. Us girls, that is."

"Wait until you find out what they taught gay men," Alex said.

"Oh, there weren't any. I mean, I didn't know of any."

Alex winked at her. "We were an exclusive and secret society in those days."

Mildred nodded eagerly. "I wouldn't have known how to join," she said seriously. "I knew nothing about life. I still don't. Not like you do. You write about your lives, and you're not afraid to be seen, and if you think of something you post it immediately on Facebook."

"Not anymore," Alex said. "They say it on TikTok now."

"But you stand up for yourselves." Mildred had picked up steam. "You stand up for each other! You're outspoken. You're not afraid to say what you think."

"You could, too," Claudia said. "You just have to stop caring about the consequences."

"Me? Good god, no. It's too late. I wouldn't even know where to begin." She leaned closer and said: "Sometimes I get so *angry*. I've wasted so many years of my life being nice."

"So stop, then," Alex said. He downed his wine. "Write about how you really feel instead. You're in the right place to learn."

"No one would want to read about my feelings."

"Just channel your inner diva," Nicole said.

Mildred was fairly certain she didn't possess one of those. "Sometimes I *swear*," she confessed. "But only in my head, of course."

"Well, at least no one knows what's going on inside your head. They can't read your mind," Claudia said.

"My mother can," Mildred said. "She's been dead fifteen years, but I'm still convinced she hears everything I think and knows immediately if I'm about to do something I shouldn't. God might too, but I'm less sure about him."

"I don't believe in God," Nicole said dismissively.

"I don't think I do either!" Mildred objected. "I just believe in an invisible power that watches over me."

Nicole suddenly smiled at her. "Of course, you're under constant surveillance here," she said and nodded toward Berit. "Berit listens to every word you say and is probably asking herself right now: *Is Mildred the killer?* What do you say, Berit? Is she?"

Mildred flinched guiltily. *She can't know that I lied,* she told herself, but she couldn't be sure. There was something in Berit's gaze that seemed to be omniscient, just like her mother's. But much less judgmental.

"I'm only here as a teacher," Berit said.

Mildred nodded nervously. She squeezed the handbag on her lap even harder. She wasn't going to let her guard down again.

"I don't know if I'll ever let anyone read what I've written," Julian said. "I've been working on this book for five years, and no one has read it. Not even Alex. Only John Wright, and he—"

Nicole interrupted him impatiently. "Fuck John Wright's comments," she said. "What we should be discussing is his death."

"What do you mean?" Alex asked.

Nicole looked around the table. She looked each person in the eye, as if she wanted to make sure she had their full attention.

"I'm going to do it, you understand," she said.

"Do what?" Alex asked.

"Find out who killed him, of course! Solve the murder. Find the killer."

Alex scoffed. "You're hardly going to solve it before Berit," he said. "She's solved murders before. That double murder in Great Diddling? I followed the whole trial."

"Everyone did," Nicole said dismissively.

"Then you should both know that it was the police who solved it," Berit said sternly. "It's by no means a task for amateurs." She seemed to realize she sounded a bit hypocritical, because there was a sparkle in her eye when she added: "Apart from in books, of course. A Poirot or Miss Marple is always needed in them."

"I know Berit's solved murder before, but she's not getting any younger." She smiled cheerfully at Berit. "No harm meant," she said, as if it was a miracle phrase that wiped away every insult.

"Berit can't be much more than fifty," Mildred protested.

"Exactly," Nicole said in agreement. "And she has lost the spark. The hunger."

Berit smiled. "I don't think I've ever had much spark," she said. "And even less hunger."

"Besides, I happen to have something she doesn't," Nicole said triumphantly.

"What?" Claudia asked, apparently drawn in to the conversation again against her will.

Nicole met her gaze and smiled smugly. "Information the police don't even know about!"

On the bus heading back, Emma asked if anybody would volunteer to read to the others what they had written. They had to shout to make their voices heard over the rattling noise, so while the bus bumped its way through the French countryside in the glorious afternoon sun, they were inundated with dead bodies. Bloodied corpses were discovered in ancient Roman amphitheaters, in cathedrals, in back streets, and on vineyards. They'd been stabbed, shot, poisoned, and disturbingly often naked. Sometimes they were lying in the blazing sun, sometimes they were discovered in the eerie moonlight illuminating pale naked bodies. One was crucified in the middle of the cathedral.

Berit noted that almost all of the dead bodies were female, as if none of the writers could imagine male bodies naked and mutilated. She wondered what it said about our society that we could so easily kill off women for our entertainment.

When they arrived at Château des Livres, the afternoon sun hit the roof and the tops of the trees lining the avenue, making even the front of the house seem warm and inviting.

Commissaire Roche came toward them with brisk, determined steps. The usually pleasant sound of footsteps on gravel sounded suddenly ominous. She was carrying a clear evidence bag containing an expensive dark leather briefcase.

"Madame Linscott," she said and held the bag up. "Could you be so kind as to explain what Monsieur Wright's briefcase was doing in your room?"

30

THE INTERROGATION ROOM WAS WARM and stuffy. The air-conditioning only ever worked during winter. This was a space that had seen more social realism than Honoré de Balzac. Thousands of banal, tragic crimes had been dealt with in here, and the criminals usually looked as gray and shabby as the surroundings.

Rebecka Linscott, in her designer sunglasses, expensive sun hat, and maxi dress with a graphic pattern, was an anomaly. It was almost like she changed the whole feeling of the place with her bright red lipstick alone.

But in the end, institutions always won, Roche thought. Individuals didn't stand a chance. The fluorescent lights on the ceiling made her face look pasty, and the dirty gray walls slowly sucked any remaining color from her.

"Would you like some tea?" Roche asked. "Coffee? No? No, I wouldn't drink the cat piss we serve here either."

A vague reaction from Rebecka Linscott: disapproval of the vulgar language.

Roche made a mental note of it. She wanted to provoke a reaction, and she had succeeded.

She put a large plastic bag on the table. In it was John Wright's briefcase, a handsome thing made of expensive leather, with the initials *J. W.* in gold in one corner.

"Do you recognize this?" she asked.

"Of course I do," Rebecka said in a matter-of-factly way. "It's John's bag. I gave it to him to celebrate the success of his first novel."

Her gaze caressed the briefcase in the plastic bag. She stretched her hand out as if to touch it. The Mayor instinctively leaned forward to prevent it, but Roche put a protective hand on the plastic bag.

"What I don't understand, Madame, is how Monsieur Wright's bag ended up in your room."

A friendly question. No accusation in her voice.

"It's a misunderstanding, that's all," Rebecka said.

"A misunderstanding," Roche repeated. "And it's not the only one, is it?"

Rebecka looked at Roche in a polite but quizzical way. Her body language was relaxed. *She wasn't worried in the slightest.*

It annoyed Roche, but she continued. "I've spoken to Olivia Marsch."

That worked. Rebecka tensed up. "She stole John from me!" she shrieked.

"She said that she did you a favor. That it was only because of her that John didn't press charges against you."

Rebecka's face became expressionless and closed. "Lies," she said unconvincingly. "All lies."

"Why did you decide to come here if you knew how much John Wright disliked you?"

"He didn't! It was all her fault. She turned him against me. If it wasn't for her, he never would have written as he did."

"Written what?"

"A letter. An awful letter. She was behind it all, I know she was."

"What did the letter say?"

"N…nothing. It was just a misunderstanding."

"More lies?" Roche's voice was deceptively appreciative.

"Yes!"

"Was it the letter that made you come here?"

"We could have sorted it all out. We just needed to talk."

"And did you? Talk?"

"No. He…didn't react in the way I had thought he would. But it was just a matter of time until I found a way to reach out to him."

"You threatened him?"

"What? No! I would never hurt him. Who told you that? It's a lie!"

"You were going to destroy him?"

She looked at them in confusion. Roche could have sworn it was genuine. "Destroy him? How? I had no means to do that."

I can't get to her. Not really. She was hiding behind that facade of hers, and Roche couldn't find a way through it. Perhaps it was because Rebecka lied to herself as much as to the police.

The Mayor shifted impatiently in the chair next to her. "What did you do with the computer?" he suddenly asked.

"His computer?" Rebecka looked surprised. Surprised and insulted. "Do you think *I stole* John's stuff?"

"You had an affair, didn't you?" The Mayor said. *He thinks we're doing the good cop, bad cop scenario.* Or in this case, more like smart cop, stupid cop. She stamped on his foot, hard, but he continued anyway: "And when he dumped you and left your publishing house, you killed him."

"Sex?" Rebecka said. "Is that what you think John and I had? You... you...*filisté!*" She straightened herself. "I discovered him. I was the first one to realize his greatness. I—"

The Mayor slammed his fist on the table. "You embezzled his money! And then you killed him when he threatened to go to the police."

"You have no idea what John and I shared. You would never understand. It's pointless trying to explain it to you. The only thing you think about is money and sex. I would never have killed John. The mere thought of it is absurd. Absurd! Should I have denied the world all his future works? I gave him to the world! All this talent. Wasted!"

Roche stamped on The Mayor's foot again, even harder. He twisted his legs so that his feet were farther away from her, but at least he kept quiet.

"Why don't you tell me what actually happened?" Roche asked. Her voice was soft, friendly, inviting even.

"He...we..." For a brief moment it seemed as if Rebecka was balancing on the brink of being honest with herself. But self-deception won. The curtains fell behind her eyes. "It was just a misunderstanding," she said.

Chief Superintendent Pelissier was observing Rebecka Linscott from behind the mirrored glass. "Has she said anything else?" she asked.

"No," Roche said.

"I think we should put some pressure on her," The Mayor said for the third time.

Roche shook her head. "That will only result in her sticking to her version of reality even firmer."

"What proof do we have?" Pelissier asked.

"Not much," Roche said at the same time as The Mayor said, "The bag was found in her room!"

"In the room that anyone at Château de Livres has access to," Roche said impatiently. "A five-year-old girl could have picked that lock. And what has she done with the computer and notebook?"

"Destroyed them. Buried them."

"But kept the bag?"

"Maybe she didn't have time to destroy it. Or it has sentimental value. You heard her. She gave it to him. That woman is crazy enough to do anything."

"It's possible, I guess," Roche said, doubtfully.

"What was she doing at the time of John's poisoning?" Pelissier asked.

Roche double-checked her notes. "Drank coffee, smoked a cigarette. Thought there were people around her, can't remember who. One of the participants remembers her asking for a lighter but couldn't remember what time it was."

"The consulate has been in touch," Pelissier said. "They want to set up a meeting."

"Later," Roche said dismissively.

"Keep me posted. You've got the rest of the evening. We can't keep her overnight unless you have more evidence than this."

Pelissier left with a final nod toward the interrogation room.

The Mayor's phone rang. "It's reception," he said. "He's saying Berit

Gardner is down there asking after you. Apparently, she has some insights into the cast of characters she thinks you might be interested in."

"Excellent. Send her up. I'll meet her at the lift."

"Are you sure that's a good idea?" The Mayor asked. "I thought we were interviewing Rebecka Linscott. You heard the boss. We've only got until tonight."

"If we're ever going to get anywhere with her, we'll need all the help we can get."

"From *Berit Gardner*? From a writer who knows nothing about police work and will possibly use whatever she sees and hears in a book?"

"By anyone who knows something about these people. She's spent three days with Rebecka. It won't hurt to listen to what she has to say," Roche said.

He was about to raise further objections, but his phone rang again. "There's another English woman downstairs," he told Roche. "Says her name's Nicole Archer. She wants to know what Berit Gardner is doing here. Shall I tell them to send her up as well?"

The last question was clearly sarcastic, but Roche ignored it. "Tell them to send her home," she said.

31

ROCHE OPENED THE LIFT DOOR and led Berit to one of the department meeting rooms.

"Do you have something for me?" she asked. "We found the bag in Rebecka Linscott's room, but we're getting nowhere."

Roche's face looked tired. Berit wished there was more she could do to help.

"Only psychology, I'm afraid," she said.

Roche smiled. "Right now I'm so desperate, I'll take anything."

"I was thinking about what Olivia Marsch said on the phone. She had persuaded John *not* to report Rebecka to the police. So she was safe. She narrowly avoided being charged with embezzlement. Then she turns up here only a couple of weeks later, to see the man who still hates her. What kind of person does that?"

Roche massaged her temples. "A person who lives completely in her own reality," she muttered.

"Exactly! She's probably been living in denial at least since John Wright left her. And I think she started lying to herself long before that. Perhaps since the first time she needed money and helped herself to a small amount of his royalties to keep the publishing house afloat. Telling herself something would turn up, it's only for a short time, just a loan, I'll pay him back soon, and either way, it's only because of me he's made all this money. Dug herself deeper and deeper. If you push her too hard…"

"She'll just cling to her story even more. That's the feeling I've got, too," Roche said.

Berit nodded. "Insistence creates resistance."

"Do you think she killed him?"

"I don't know. She's educated in the classics. She adored John Wright, in her own way. She could have thought of and appreciated the Socrates angle. And she would have wanted to give him a merciful death. But still…there's so much that doesn't add up. Why come all this way just to kill him here? And why take his briefcase afterward?"

Roche looked even more tired. She'd probably already asked herself the same questions. "So how do I reach her? That's the big question."

Berit drummed on the table with her fingers. She went through everything she knew about Rebecka in her head. "'*I discovered him*,'" she said. "Rebecka Linscott says it all the time. Start there, with her own truth. When we write we put ourselves in our characters' world. It doesn't matter whether it's true or not, as long as it's logical in its own way. As long as it follows its own specific laws. I think it's the same with her world. You have to put yourself in it. Learn how it works. Find out what's true for her."

Roche got up. She was leaving the meeting room when Berit said: "Could you tell me what you found in Mildred Wilkinson's room?"

"No. Absolutely not. Out of the question. It's a breach of privacy just searching it. I can't reveal what we found in anyone's room."

"Could you confirm what you didn't find?"

"What?" Roche asked curiously.

"A notebook. Or pens."

"You mean John Wright's? No, we still haven't found the computer, the notebook, or the rest of his documents. Right now I wonder if we ever will. The killer probably destroyed them immediately. What's that look? You disagree? You think the killer kept them and ran the risk of them being discovered?"

"Someone kept the briefcase."

"Yes, but…" Roche didn't say what went through her mind, but it was clear she too wondered if Rebecka really was stupid enough to keep it in her room, if she was the killer. But someone could have planted it there.

"Did you find any other notebooks in Mildred's room?" Berit suddenly asked. "Or pens?"

"That's none of your business," Roche said and left. She returned after only a few seconds. "No, to both," she said. "But you didn't hear that from me."

Berit stepped outside into the modern, gray courtyard surrounding the police station and closed her eyes wearily.

It had been a long day. Somehow it had taken her to a Roman amphitheater, a cathedral, a vineyard, and a police interrogation room. Even though it was quarter past seven in the evening, the air was still stuffy and humid. It smelled of tarmac and dust, and in the distance, you could hear the sounds of rush hour traffic.

Berit's feet ached. Her skin was warm and sticky. All she wanted was to be alone with her thoughts, but a nagging feeling at the back of her head told her it would be a while before she'd get that.

Someone was watching her.

She got out her phone and called a taxi. Then she calmly looked around, phone still in hand. Very few people moved through this area at night. She stayed put, only a few meters from the main entrance of the police station.

When the taxi stopped in front of her, she quickly walked up to it. When she was in the back seat, she finally relaxed.

The car door swung open before she had a chance to slam it shut.

"Hi, Berit," Nicole said. Her voice was overly cheerful, her smile a dazzling white.

The taxi driver looked at them angrily in his rear mirror. "Are we leaving or are you talking?" he asked.

"Leaving," Berit said and moved over to the other side of the car. Nicole jumped in after her. She put her seat belt on and turned toward Berit.

"Do the police think Rebecka killed John Wright and stole his briefcase?"

Nicole failed to hide the smugness of her tone. It was obvious she thought the police were wrong.

"I don't think they think anything at this stage." Berit sounded reserved.

Nicole shot her an impatient, superior look, as if Berit was wasting her time with her careful platitudes.

Nicole's personality was even more overwhelming in such a confined space. She was young, beautiful, and confident. Even after a long and intense day, there wasn't a hint of her perfect veneer cracking.

Berit was acutely aware of how tired, uncomfortable, and sweaty she was. Her shirt was creased. She needed to be on her own and think. She wrinkled her nose. And shower.

"Why did John leave Rebecka's publishing house?" Nicole asked suddenly.

"I don't know," Berit lied.

Nicole stared sharply at her. "I bet you do know," she said. "You're just not going to tell me."

Berit leaned her head against the window. It was refreshingly cool against her cheek.

The vineyards outside the car closed in on them like a dark sea. Only the immediate surroundings were lit up by the car's headlights. If she closed her eyes, she could imagine they were on the road to anywhere.

"And she managed to get herself to this writing retreat, even though I don't think John would have wanted her here…" Nicole was thinking out loud. "You have to question why Emma allowed her to come. Do you think Rebecka has something on her? Or was she just desperate?"

Berit didn't answer.

"If Rebecka did kill John and stole the briefcase, it wasn't very clever of her to leave it in her room."

Nicole's voice sounded deliberately innocent. When Berit said nothing, she looked away, disappointed.

The taxi stopped outside Château des Livres, and as Berit was paying, Nicole stepped outside. But she leaned over Berit's car door and said:

"The most interesting question is: *Why Rebecka Linscott?*"

"What do you mean?" Berit asked pretending to sound distracted.

"If the killer planted the bag there to frame her, why her? Someone clearly dislikes her. Maybe it was someone she had a fight with recently?"

She studied Berit carefully to see if she could read something into her reaction. Berit hoped her face didn't show anything.

"I meant what I said in Vienne," Nicole said. "I'm going to solve this murder, and I'm going to do it before you."

32

IT HAD JUST GONE EIGHT in the evening. Rebecka Linscott had been in the interrogation room for three hours. Half an hour ago she'd been given a dry ham and cheese baguette in plastic wrap and a cup of tea in a plastic cup from the vending machine in the corridor.

Commissaire Roche was sitting opposite her, alone. On the table between them she spread out sheets of paper, blank side up.

From the corner of her eye, she could see how Rebecka followed all her movements. She slowly turned over the papers to face up, one at a time. Rebecka's eyes were drawn to the pictures. In one, she was at a drinks party, smiling next to a much younger John Wright. He looked shaken, with a stupid smile on his face. The next photo showed them at a book fair. John was signing books. The queue in front of him was long. Rebecka stood next to him, with her arm protectively placed on his shoulders.

From the observation room, Chief Superintendent Pelissier and The Mayor looked at each other. "The boss made me print them out from her Instagram account," he said. "But she didn't tell me what she needed them for."

In the interrogation room, Roche said, "You discovered him."

Rebecka stretched her hand out and touched one of the photos. A smile spread across her face. "As soon as I'd read his manuscript I knew. It had that unique something you're always looking for. The voice. The perspective. And something else, something magical you can't really explain, not even to yourself. You just know."

"How many books of his did you publish?"

"Ten. Each one better than the last."

"Did you love him?"

"Love. It's all today's society can think of. And when they say love, they mean sex. So unoriginal. So incredibly unoriginal."

"But you shared something."

"We created together."

"What did you create?"

"Oh, masterpieces. Masterpieces! For too short a time, we were the final defense against a dark and heathen world. We were like…monks during the Dark Ages, who still maintained some form of education and culture. Did you know Linscott Publishing is the only independent publisher that still publishes poetry? Not only poetry, of course, natural science, fiction, and philosophy as well. But never crime."

Roche remembered that John had signed a deal for a series of historical crime novels before he died.

"He had such high ideals in the beginning. He used to say he'd rather be with a small, *exclusive* publisher than with one of the major houses where anyone could be published as long as they'd written a crime novel. And then he left for Penguin Random House the minute he got the chance…"

It's easy to want to be small and exclusive when it's your only option, Roche thought cynically.

"John shared my views of the publishing industry. We could have revolutionized it if only we'd had more time together!"

"But instead, he left you," Roche said.

"I had invested some money in a couple of books that…that didn't quite work out as well as I thought they would. People have no taste, you see. No one cares about quality anymore."

You embezzled his money. You let his royalties finance your failed ventures. Roche didn't need to vocalize it. The accusation hung in the air between them. She thought of Berit's words. One lie after another, from that first questionable transaction.

"Tell me about the misunderstanding," she said.

Rebecka glanced around nervously. Her voice was low when she answered, as if she was talking to herself. "I just did what all publishers do. The income from the commercial titles finance the unlucrative ones." She leaned across the prints on the table. "There were… mistakes in accounting. But I didn't kill him. I could never hurt him. In my eyes he'll always be that lost, insecure debut writer I looked after. I tried to protect him! But I failed, didn't I?"

She blinked back some tears which seemed to embarrass her more than the confession about the embezzlement. "I couldn't protect him," she repeated.

"Did Charles Tate know about your…investment in other books?"

"Know about them? They were all his writers, every single one of them!"

The Mayor left the observation room as soon as Roche came out of the interrogation room.

"Charles Tate is here. He wants to talk to you," he said.

"How convenient," Roche commented. "I want to talk to him too."

"Before you do, you should see this. I found it when I was going through Linscott Publishing Instagram account." He showed her his phone.

She whistled. "Interesting?"

"What do you want me to do with Madame Linscott?"

"Give her a ride home. You heard the boss. We have no choice," she added when she saw the skeptical look on his face.

"But you nearly broke her! You should put some more pressure on her."

"Mayor, could you for once stop arguing with me and just do what I say?" Roche said tiredly. "Or is that too much to ask for?"

For a split second she thought there was a look of hurt on his face, but she ignored it. He was a grown man. He'd get over it. Besides, she had a headache, and she wanted to get home at some point this evening.

Charles Tate had flung himself down in the cheap office chair, looking confident. When Roche entered, he slammed his hand on the table and said: "You're all a bunch of idiots if you think Rebecka killed John. Of course she didn't. Why would she be so stupid and leave the briefcase in her room, if that were true?"

"Yes, why, Monsieur?" Roche said and sat down opposite him.

"Someone's trying to frame her, that's why."

Roche raised her eyebrow questioningly. "Of course, that's a possibility," she admitted.

"So you do have some sense, after all?"

"One tries," Roche said modestly. "It must be someone who knew she had a motive."

"Excuse me?"

"The person who hid John Wright's briefcase in Rebecka's room. The killer. They must have known there was a reason to suspect Rebecka. Why choose her room otherwise?"

"Well, yes, clearly, but—"

"You knew, of course, that John had accused her of embezzling his money?"

"Yes, but—"

"In reality, it was your writers who got the money, wasn't it?"

"What? Is that what she's saying? Listen, she wanted to publish literary writers who were impossible to sell. I represented them as a favor to her. I knew she wouldn't make any money from them. And neither did I, damn it. I had nothing to do with all that!"

"But John Wright thought so? Wasn't it actually Rebecka's fault that he left you?"

"In a way, but—"

"Did it make you angry?"

"No, I—"

Roche nodded. "You forgave her," she said. "And John Wright too?"

"Of course I forgave him. And remember, I needed him alive."

"Why? He'd left your agency. He was never coming back. And he made all your other clients leave as well."

"Not all of them!"

"Do you know what hemlock looks like?"

"Why would I know anything about plants?"

She leant back in her chair. "*Poison in Nature and Literature*," she said. "Does that mean anything to you?"

Charles Tate swallowed. His voice was almost inaudible now. "It's a book."

"You represented the writer?"

"Yes."

"It specifically mentions hemlock?"

"I guess. It might. I don't know."

"With pictures?"

Nervous glance. "I can't remember. But I don't read all the books I represent!"

"Who published it?"

"Linscott Publishing, I think, but—"

"John Wright held you responsible for the embezzlement, didn't he?"

"I guess he thought I should have discovered what was going on."

"You threatened him."

"No!"

"You said you'd destroy him."

"What? What's this? Who said that? That's a goddam lie. If I had wanted to kill him, I would have come right out and said it." He saw Roche's raised eyebrows and added quickly: "No, no, I didn't, to make it clear. I never said such a thing!"

Charles looked anxiously at Roche.

"I begged him, okay? I needed his help, if you really have to know, and I wasn't too proud to grovel at his feet. That's the only thing I ever did, I swear. Not that it made any difference. I should have remembered; sympathy never was John's strong point."

33

DINNER WAS ALREADY IN FULL swing when Berit and Nicole entered Château des Livres. Nicole went straight into the noisy dining room, but Berit was not in the mood for a big, heavy dinner surrounded by everyone, so she sought out the relative calmness of the kitchen.

The warm darkness from the kitchen garden seemed to enter the kitchen with Berit. Only the stove and the work top at the back of the room were properly lit. The washed-up pots and frying pans from today's dinner preparations and individual portions of crème brûlée that only needed torching were stacked up on it.

The cook threw a glance at her tired, flagging figure, put the blowtorch away and got out a frying pan instead.

Berit sank exhausted into a chair and enjoyed just sitting there, watching the cook at work. From a basket next to the stove, she got out two eggs that she cracked open in one hand. She added a dash of milk, salt, and pepper to the bowl, whisked it, and poured it all into the frying pan together with a big dollop of butter.

Through the open kitchen doors, the wind brought with it the aromas from the kitchen garden, a magical combination of dry soil, thyme, rosemary, and lavender. Sometimes it carried loud voices down from the dining room upstairs and every time, Berit was grateful that she was here in the quiet and cozy kitchen instead.

The cook expertly moved the frying pan back and forth on the stove. When the omelet was starting to set, she threw in a handful of grated cheese and tilted the frying pan slightly so that somehow, the whole omelet ended up in a roll at the bottom. With a determined, competent movement, she turned it over onto the plate, then she placed the whole buttery, golden creation in front of Berit. As a last touch, she sprinkled some fresh parsley on top.

"Eat," she ordered her and nodded at the plate. She poured some red wine from a carafe by the cooker into an old, chipped glass. "Drink," she said. Then she thought better of it and poured herself one too.

As soon as Berit took the first bite, she realized she was starving. It was the most delicious omelet she'd ever tasted. When Sally entered the kitchen five minutes later, there wasn't a single morsel left.

The cook, pleased, nodded and got out her blowtorch again. Sally jumped up on the chair next to Berit. "Did Rebecka do it?" she asked. "Nicole said the police were still interrogating her when she left."

"I don't know," Berit said. She had another sip of the red wine and felt like a new human being. *Well,* she though, *as a better secondhand one, at least.*

"You don't sound convinced," Sally said.

"No. Something feels wrong." Berit shook her head in frustration. "I have to think. I've let myself be swept along by everything that's happened. First Mrs. Wright turning up out of the blue, then the police finding John Wright's briefcase in Rebecka's room, which focused everything on her. I've never gone through everything systematically."

Sally's phone started ringing. She glanced at the screen, turned the volume off, turned the phone over, and ignored it as it vibrated on the table.

"I really could do with a whiteboard," Berit said and stood up again. "Okay. Let's pretend this table is my whiteboard. In this corner"—she started at the top of it where she was standing—"is Rebecka. With an apparent motive to kill." She told Sally about the embezzlement.

"I knew there was more to John's transfer than Mum let on," Sally said. "But to steal money from a writer…! I can't believe any publisher would do that. And how could Emma let her attend the retreat if she knew?"

"Maybe she wasn't aware," Berit said, but they both remembered the conversation they'd overheard in the cathedral in Vienne. Berit focused on

Rebecka again. "I can't escape the feeling that she's too smart to let John's briefcase lie around in her room. What did she even want with his computer and notebook?"

"Maybe he'd written something about her? And she didn't want anyone to find out she'd taken his money?"

"But that's just it. We still found out. She must have known Olivia knew everything. Then there's Charles."

"Who also had a motive, if what you say is true. Rebecka took him down with her."

"Yes, and he might not have known about the deal Olivia negotiated with Rebecka. Maybe he took matters into his own hands?"

"Maybe he wanted to protect her?" Sally suggested.

Berit nodded. "I've thought about that too. But they weren't the only people who disliked John, were they?" Berit moved alongside the table and pointed to another place on it. "We've also got Claudia. She couldn't stand him."

"But did she hate him enough to kill him?" Sally asked. She stared down at the big wooden table as if she could actually see Claudia's name written there. "It seems crazy. There are so many disagreeable old men in the world of literature. And women! But they don't get killed."

"True!" Berit said with a slight note of regret in her voice.

"I know someone else who didn't like John Wright," the cook said and placed two portions of crème brûlée on the table just where Claudia's name would have been written. "Antoine Tessier. Every time he helped in the kitchen he just stood there, muttering about what an idiot that man was."

"I know," Berit said. "But he has an alibi."

"Served coffee and cake right in front of my own eyes," the cook agreed. "Together with Emma."

Berit was about to say something else when Emma stepped into the kitchen. "I was just going to fetch desert," she said and looked at Berit and Sally in surprise.

"I'm hiding," Berit said.

Emma laughed. "From what? Not me, I hope?"

"From other people."

"Clearly necessary sometimes," Emma said. She put the finished individual portions and two silver jugs of coffee on a large tray and went upstairs to the dining room.

Berit waited until she was out of earshot, then she went over to the other end of the table and said: "Over here are the participants. I realized something in Vienne that I should have thought of sooner: I don't know enough about them. I thought I could dismiss them because they didn't have a history with John Wright. But how do I know? Their paths could have crossed before."

Sally's phone vibrated. She pushed it farther away. "Which participants are you interested in?" she asked.

"All of them, at this stage. There's the mysterious Mildred, for example."

"Mildred?" Sally said skeptically.

"Who attends a writing retreat without bringing a pen or a notebook? And I've never actually seen her write anything. And then there's Nicole Archer, who does nothing but write and talks constantly about solving the murder. It's not a bad disguise, pretending to solve a murder you've committed yourself. She might have enjoyed the Socrates connection."

"She scares me a bit," Sally admitted.

She scared Berit too, but she suspected for different reasons.

"I think it's her ambition that feels so creepy," Sally continued. "She reminds me of my mum. But worse!"

"Younger and hungrier," Berit agreed. "Even more willing to do anything it takes to succeed."

"You should have heard her up there in the dining room. She made it sound like John Wright's murder was the best thing that could have happened to her," Sally said.

For a moment, Berit almost felt sorry for Nicole. It was a dangerous thing, valuing success for success's sake. You could so easily become hostage to luck and circumstances outside your control.

"I asked her if she didn't think it was awful that a person had died," Sally continued.

"She does *not*," Berit said.

"She replied, '*Do you know what's really awful? Churning out yet another*

Fifty ways to waste your time on pointless articles-*angle for the great braindead masses.*'"

"She's going to use John Wright's murder as a way to be taken seriously as a journalist," Berit said. "I wonder why she hasn't already spoken to the press about it... Why not one of them has?"

"Well, it's because she wants to write the whole book," Sally said. "She told me, just like that. And she's convinced everyone on the retreat that it's in poor taste to talk to the press. All of a sudden, we should care about his family and respect their privacy."

"And people agreed?"

In Berit's experience, most people couldn't resist the temptation to be seen in the media.

"Nicole bosses everyone about," Sally said. "She pretends to be friendly but sooner or later she gets her way with most people. The younger students think they admire her, but they're getting increasingly anxious when she's around. I think they're scared of her." She added resentfully: "She calls me *Junior.*"

"A mean joke," Berit said.

"Yes...but actually, people have called me worse things."

Sally stared down at her crème brûlée, then glanced up at Berit. "I guess what really upsets me about the nickname is that it's not true. I'm nothing like Mum. But Nicole is. Mum would love her."

Berit smiled feebly at the thought of Olivia Marsh and Nicole Archer in the same room.

"Perhaps," she said, although she rather thought they would detest each other. In her experience, people who were too similar rarely got along.

"I suppose I'm just jealous," Sally admitted.

"I doubt it," Berit said. "I don't think you really want to be either of them."

"I *couldn't* be either of them, you mean. I'm sure you were as ambitious as Nicole when you were young, weren't you?" Sally ate mechanically while she was talking and seemed to find some kind of comfort in the silky-smooth custard and the brittle caramelized sugar that cracked under her spoon.

"Hardly," Berit said. "I was much too lazy to chase success, and definitely too lazy to want to catch it. It's extremely exhausting being successful, at least if you mean in the traditional sense: acclaim, status, money. No, I've always wanted other things in life. Your mother says I'm hopeless."

"What is it that you want then?" Sally asked.

"Oh, many things. Interesting life experiences, continuing to learn new things, enough peace and quiet to hear my own thoughts, being able to read a book uninterrupted, drink coffee in bed in the mornings, and watch the seasons come and go in my own unkempt garden..."

"You want independence and freedom," Sally summarized, and Berit supposed she was right, even if "a comfortable everyday life" was just as true, and much less grandiose.

"Find in your life what's important to you," Berit advised. "And work out the best way to get it."

She looked down on the big wooden table. "Julian," she continued, pointing at the other corner. "He was obsessed with John Wright. He admired him, looked up to him as a hero. And..."

Sally's phone went off again. This time Berit managed to catch a glimpse of the screen before she put it down. *Mama-Boss* it said.

"Olivia?" Berit said sympathetically.

"Sooner or later she'll give up," Sally said.

If Berit knew Olivia it would be later rather than sooner.

"She's worried about Mrs. Wright," Sally confided. "She wants me to go to the hotel and force her to talk to us. But I refuse. I'm not going to bother her with unimportant things when her husband's just died."

Berit pushed her dessert over to Sally, who gratefully accepted it. She looked up again after a few bites and asked: "How are you going to get to know the participants if you're hiding down here in the kitchen?"

"I've got another idea," Berit said.

"Is it going to involve me?"

"Almost certainly."

LIFE AS IT WAS SUPPOSED TO HAVE BEEN

I TELL MYSELF NO ONE is ever going to read what I've written. Still, I can't stop fantasizing about the success that would follow if they did.

If the book was published, I would be terrifically successful. I know that. More successful than anyone at this retreat could even dream of. I wonder who would play me in the movie? Would it feel strange seeing myself in a beautiful and glamorous Hollywood production? No, I rather think it would feel *right*. Like coming home. Life as it was supposed to have been.

I didn't kill John Wright to write a book about it, I keep reminding myself, but now that I've started, I can't stop.

Sooner or later you write about all your experiences, Berit Gardner says. So who knows, perhaps I'll write a fictional version of it one day. Change enough details in order to get away with it.

Once again, I have to remind myself that no one can ever read what I've written. That everything I've fought so hard for would be over the second they did. But it's pointless. The dream of success has eaten its way into my consciousness.

I can almost taste it. Delicate, sweet, with a refreshingly bitter undertone. The gushing reviews. How journalists would love me! They've never experienced anything like me. They'd sit there with their bloodless lives and be drawn by all the gory details. Deep inside they'd ask themselves: *Could I do it? Could I kill someone?* And I'd answer them: I don't think you have what it takes.

Everybody would have an opinion. It fascinates me, the thought of being talked about all over social media. Everybody would know my name. They'd all have an opinion. No one would be able to remain neutral.

And the bestseller lists. Do you know what it feels like to walk into a bookshop and see giant stacks of your own books there? Your own name on the cover. A sumptuous, thick, glossy book.

I've seen it happen to so many unworthy writers. Any old rubbish sells these days.

Isn't it about time it happens to someone who deserves it?

34

THE FOLLOWING MORNING BERIT DID twenty laps in the freezing-cold pool and felt reinvigorated afterward. Over breakfast she talked to Emma and Sally about her new idea. Instead of a lecture, Berit suggested the students should work independently, and instead of working on their existing projects, they would have to work on themselves.

She called the exercise *Portrait of a Writer on Fire*, and it would involve using the techniques they'd learned earlier to create a memorable character based on themselves.

"If you think that's for the best," Emma said hesitantly.

"Our personalities and experiences provide the richest material we have to draw from," Berit said. "Regardless of whether we know it or not, we write ourselves into our books all the time. Better to do it consciously and realize what a bottomless well we have to drink from."

Berit based the exercise on the workshop she and Claudia had prepared on developing characters, so she started their day by going through all the questions they could ask in order to get to know every nook and cranny of their characters. Or themselves.

How would the students describe themselves from a physiological, sociological, and psychological perspective? What did they look like? How did they walk? What was the first thing about them that people noticed? What was their background? How was that perceived? What did they dream about? What were their innermost needs and fears?

"Artists make self-portraits all the time," Berit said. "Why shouldn't writers as well?"

Some of them looked inspired, others terrified. But all of them got to work immediately. Everyone but Nicole, who quickly got up and disappeared as soon as Berit had ended the briefing.

Sally walked over to Berit. "Do you think it will work?" she whispered.

"They're going to divulge more than they think," Berit said. "Nothing is as revealing as writing."

Nicole made sure Berit was busy with the workshop before she followed Charles and Rebecka to the ruin just beyond one of the wings. Wild fruit trees grew in abundance here, providing her with cover.

Charles stood in front of a collapsed stone wall. He had a firm grip on Rebecka's arm. "What the hell did you tell the police?" he asked. "After they'd spoken to you, they were convinced I had something to do with the embezzlement of John's mon…" Nicole crouched behind an overgrown apple tree, held her phone up, and started recording.

Rebecka broke loose from his grip and slapped him. The sound was so loud in the surrounding silence, Nicole worried the rest of the group must have heard it too. She didn't want anyone, least of all Berit, to interfere.

But no one looked their way.

Charles touched his red cheek. A smile flickered in his eyes. Nicole would have sworn he'd get angry, but he looked impressed.

"The police have nothing," he said. "They're just fishing. We'll be fine as long as we stick together."

The students worked on their self-portraits all morning, but during the lunch break, Commissaire Roche's presence was felt everywhere. She led a group of local police in a search of the surroundings.

Everybody knew the police had interrogated Rebecka and Charles all evening the night before, but no one knew any details. Not until after lunch, when suddenly everyone seemed to know that John Wright had accused Rebecka of embezzlement.

Berit didn't know who'd found out and spread the news, but she didn't like it. When they continued working after lunch, the atmosphere was somewhat altered.

They were spread out across the estate. Some on the lawn, one on a fallen tree on the outskirts of the garden, and a few had found cool shade under the umbrellas up on the terrace. They wrote on computers, in notebooks, and on their phones. Everywhere you looked there were focused faces and bent backs.

There was something inherently ruthless about how all writers were used to bending the truth to suit their needs and wishes. An intoxicating habit of playing God, of being able to control reality, change it, stretch it according to their own ideas and wishes. She couldn't help wondering if any of them had taken that omnipotence a step too far.

If that was the case, she would find signs of it in their self-portraits. People said love and a cough cannot be kept secret, but Berit thought conceit and an inflated belief in one's own capacity were even harder to hide.

They always trickled out in everything you did, she thought and looked around the glade, where the warm afternoon sun made everything seem soft and idyllic.

Alex sat leaning against a tree, chewing on a straw. Julian rested his head on his lap, chewing on a pencil. A bit farther away, Nicole was tapping furiously on her laptop.

Mildred Wilkinson sat alone at a table for four and did nothing.

None of what I write now can ever be published.

As soon as the realization hit Claudia, inspiration started flowing. Her head was drowning with ideas, sentences, scenes, whole chapters, and several plot twists.

She sat down under an umbrella in the shaded part of the kitchen garden, got out her laptop, opened the folder *Fiction*, and the subfolder *Better than Mantel*. She created a document she named *Background*, one called *Characters*, and another one for everything to do with the murders.

She felt rejuvenated, born again, as if she'd risen from the ashes of her stone-cold career like a phoenix.

Strange how a person's absence could change everything. And the place. She was at a château in France, with a vineyard right in front of her eyes and the scent of lavender and rosemary in the air. The warmth made her soul relax.

Her new idea was a combination of Emma's little speech at the amphitheater in Vienne and Berit's existential questions. As soon as she'd heard Berit tell them about the workshop, she had felt ill at ease. She didn't write to wallow in her own petty problems but to escape them.

But she had taken the exercise seriously. She was here for a reason, and she respected Berit as a colleague. And she wasn't going to behave like Rebecka, who apparently was above being a part of anything.

So she had taken herself, everything she had experienced and dreamed of, her many insecurities and her few strengths, other people's opinions about her and her own self-doubt, and placed the whole mess in the past, slightly exaggerating it along the way. She would witness Henry VIII's court and excess, the luxury and the intrigues. From the kitchen.

Henry VIII's food taster had just been appointed, and she was a Black woman. That should shake up a thing or two.

She wrote for hours until she had to get up and stretch her legs and move her shoulders. Her head felt hazy, but not in an unpleasant way, just a little stuffy because she had spent so many hours inside it.

She was on her way to the kitchen to get some coffee, just as Berit was coming out with a French press and two cups. She had even brought a small jug of hot milk.

Claudia sat down again and closed her laptop.

Berit nodded toward it. "A new project?" she asked.

Claudia smiled. She wondered what Berit would say if she knew the truth. "A new project," she repeated to herself. "Yes, you could say that. It's definitely new."

"Are you going to show this to Charles, since he's already here?"

"This project will never be published."

She'd said it before she had a chance to stop herself.

There was a glimmer of interest in Berit's eyes.

"Did Roche talk to you about Rebecka?" she asked.

"Sure. She wanted to know if I knew of the 'irregularities,' as she called it. I didn't, but I wish I had. Just imagine! Rebecka's been up there on her haughty high horse all this time, and she's just a common criminal? Did you know she rejected two of my books? Just as well, in hindsight."

Claudia had perked up at Rebecka's fall from grace, but not as much as she would have done yesterday. She was too consumed by her new project to really relish in Rebecka's misfortune.

"I guess it was inevitable that it should come out," Berit said, sounding displeased.

Claudia looked at her in surprise. "That she embezzled money? Gossip of that caliber can't be kept secret forever. Nicole told everyone about it at lunch."

"I don't like it," Berit said. "No group benefits from gossip. It hurts the ones who gossip as much as the person they gossip about."

Claudia averted her gaze. "No group benefits from secrets either," she muttered. "And there are already too many of them here."

"You might have a point," Berit said. She looked over at Mildred Wilkinson, who was sitting some distance away from everybody else, idly doing nothing.

Claudia looked at Berit incredulously. Surely, Mildred's secrets would bore anyone unlucky enough to have to listen to them? But she didn't say anything. She intensely hoped Berit's sharp eye wouldn't be directed at her.

Mildred flinched guiltily when Berit pulled up a chair and sat down next to her.

On the table in front of her was a cup of black tea, even though it was still a swelteringly hot day, and a plate with several thick slices of *gâteau marbré*. That was it. No notebook or computer.

"Mildred," Berit said, "do you have something you want to tell me?"

The woman stared at her miserably. Then she said, as if she could no longer keep it a secret: "I'm a fake!"

Berit patted her hand. "We all feel like that from time to time," she said and helped herself to a slice of cake. "Why don't you tell me everything and get it off your chest?"

Mildred looked around. Then she leaned forward and said quietly: "I'm not a writer. I can't even write!"

"You and me both," Berit said. She felt like that every time she started writing a new book. And every time she was amazed that she managed to finish it.

"You don't understand. I have no talent whatsoever!"

"You can't rely on talent anyway. What you need is stamina. And being able to sit on a chair for a prolonged amount of time."

Mildred looked around again, as if she suspected Emma or the police would turn up from nowhere and forcibly drag her away from the château. She lowered her voice and whispered with desperate intensity: "I've never written a thing in my life! I won my place on this retreat in a competition. I don't even like writing. I like reading. Laura from the bookshop told me about the competition. She had been given one place by Emma and was organizing a contest. I think the contestants were meant to write a short story or something, to win a place here. But Laura said…" Mildred lowered her voice even more and whispered painfully: "Laura said I could have it. Because I'm always in the bookshop. It's such a cozy place, you see. And it's so nice to leave the house now and then. She often gives me proofs from the publishers to read. But this! It was too much. I tried to say no, I promise. But she insisted. She didn't have time to organize a competition, she said, and she said I could use a holiday."

"Why did you agree to come, if you don't write?" Berit asked.

"I've never been abroad," Mildred said simply. "And I love French writers like Fred Vargas, Tatiana de Rosnay, Anna Gavalda…and that man, the one with the president's hat!"

Berit smiled. "Antoine Laurain."

"I wanted to experience something, anything, so badly. But as soon as I arrived, it was just awful. I've been plagued by my bad conscience. And lovely Emma is looking after me. Imagine if she knew!"

"Do you know, Mildred, I don't think she would mind, really."

Mildred shook her head again. "I'm a fake," she repeated. "I've deceived everyone."

"I'm serious," Berit said. "Being a writer is not a protected professional title, like being a doctor or a lawyer. The only thing it takes to be one is to *write*. And it's never too late to start. Why don't you give it a go and see how it goes?"

"I tried," Mildred said. She shivered. "And it was *awful*."

"We all feel that way in the beginning, but…"

Mildred leaned forward and grabbed hold of Berit's arm. "No, you don't understand. *I* was awful. I think it's all the movies I've watched. Action movies. With *swearing* in them. I hear them in my head all the time, and sometimes I can't hold them back. I've been so nice and proper all my life, always done what's expected of me, and now I feel like I'm about to implode."

"Better to explode," Berit advised. "Healthier in the long run than trying to keep everything inside. And much more fun."

"I swear in my head all the time. Saying fuck and arse and…" She put her hand over her mouth in shock. "Look! It's coming out. Do you think this is why my begonias are dying?"

She opened her eyes wide and looked at Berit helplessly.

"I wrote I wanted John Wright to die!"

35

MORALE ON ROCHE'S TEAM WAS low. Taking a suspect in for questioning had injected some new energy into the investigation, but by now both the energy and the lead had grown noticeably cold. What remained was an irritated frustration Roche knew was bad for any investigation.

She had spoken to everyone at the retreat who might have known something about Rebecka, Charles, and John Wright, without finding out anything else apart from that Emma Scott had definitely known about "the unfortunate circumstances" surrounding John Wright's move to another publisher, as she had expressed it. *It had made it sound like Rebecka was pregnant,* Roche thought. Claudia Ramirez hadn't known, but the news had definitely cheered her up.

Roche and her team had searched every square foot of the grounds to try to find John Wright's notebook and his computer or any signs of something being buried recently. She had even asked Antoine Tessier if the killer could have tried to flush the book down the loo, as they had done with the hemlock, but he'd just scoffed at her.

When her boss called her into her office, Roche frowned. She went over everything she might have done, or more likely, not done that might have upset her boss.

Found the killer, for example.

"What's this I hear about an English writer becoming involved in the investigation?" Sylvie Pelissier said in an irritated voice. "What do you think this is? An episode of *Murder, She Wrote*?"

"Swedish."

"Pardon?"

"A Swedish writer."

The chief superintendent gave her an ice-cold look. "For heaven's sake, Roche. The May… I mean, Inspector Delavigne has complained to his father, who mentioned it to his dear friend the commissioner, who called me. What do you think you're doing?"

The little shit.

"He didn't mean it, boss," Roche said through clenched teeth.

"Is that right? He didn't mean it?"

"No, boss. Trust me. He did not. I'm sure it never even entered his stupid little head to run to his dad and criticize his group leader behind the back of his whole team. If you want, we can call him in right now, so you can ask him to his face. But I warn you, if this comes out, if his colleagues hear as much as a whisper of this, it will ruin any chance he has of becoming one of the team. You know what they're like. They don't like being criticized by outsiders."

"The commissioner is hardly an outsider!"

Roche made no comment. "The chances are he'll just get even more to run home to the old man to complain about. And if the team doesn't accept him, it could affect his future advancement negatively."

"Popularity isn't needed to rise through the ranks. If it was, nobody would ever be promoted. Including myself." The chief superintendent sighed. "What do you suggest?"

"Let me handle it. Discreetly. You won't hear any more complaints from him. I guarantee it."

"There'll be some sort of punishment, I guess. It was the same in my time. Yes, well, but *solve* this, Roche. *No more complaints.*"

"Trust me, boss. You won't hear a squeak."

There was nowhere in the station for this conversation, so Roche walked past The Mayor's desk and in a terse voice told him to follow her. She walked ahead of him out of the building, across the parking lot, and out of the fenced courtyard. On the back of the fence was a long footpath. Trains passed by just beyond it and drowned out their conversation to passersby.

A dog walker went past with a yapping lapdog. Roche forced a smile and waited until the man and the dog were out of sight. Then she walked up to The Mayor, pressed her lower arm on his chest, and pushed him up against the tall wooden fence.

"You listen to me very carefully," she said, her face an inch away from his. Her voice was controlled with restrained anger. "You can think I'm an idiot. If you want, you can say it every morning, noon, and night to me or the other guys on the team. It's your prerogative. But you will bloody well keep it within the team, do you hear me? You don't go around criticizing our work to anyone on the outside, okay? If you have a problem with how I lead this investigation, you bring it up with me. You don't run to Daddy and complain like a spoiled brat, do you hear me?"

"I…" A slight flush spread across his face. "Yes, boss," he said.

She loosened her grip but kept her arm pressed against his chest. "Do you understand how your position in the team could have been affected if the others had found out? It's bad enough as it is."

"Yes, boss. It won't happen again, boss."

"Make sure it doesn't."

A guy on a bicycle surprised them both. He rode past them at a high speed and slammed on the brakes a few yards away. Roche let go of The Mayor and showed him her police badge, but that just made the guy reach for his phone and started filming.

"It's okay," Roche shouted and nodded toward The Mayor. "He's also police."

The Mayor adjusted his suit jacket and got out his own badge. "Clear off," he said.

The guy put his phone away. "Sure, sure," he said. "You just keep going. Don't let me stop you." It was obvious he didn't mind a bit of police brutality as long as it was internal.

Roche shook her head. "What a little shit," she said.

"Why have you got it in for Berit Gardner anyway?" she asked, in a considerably more friendly tone.

"She's an outsider! She's not even French. Yet you listen to her more than me, a member of your own team."

"Tell me, Philippe, how much do you know about those crazy writers who are holed up in Allard's old place?"

"Okay, perhaps not that much, but you have to admit that I've dug up a fair bit of info on them."

"What do you want, a medal? It's not a competition. I needed some background information, so I spoke to her, that's all. Next time you have a problem with something I do, you come to me. Say, boss, you're behaving like an idiot, and then we'll talk about it."

He looked at her doubtfully. It was obvious he wasn't sure if she was serious.

"No more complaints to your old man," she clarified, and started heading back to the station. "Well, then. That's that dealt with. Let's get back to work. Priority number one is to speed up the lab with the report on John Wright's bedroom. We need some real, technical evidence."

"I'll call them immediately," The Mayor said quickly.

"Tell them I don't care how much they've got on their plates. I want that report tomorrow. If they have any complaints, they can bring it up with the boss." *Might as well give Pelissier something to do as well.*

36

THROUGH THE OPEN BALCONY DOORS, fragments of today's final lecture *Literary Conversations in the Garden* could be heard. Berit was on the bed leaning against the wall, with half of today's writing exercises on her lap. Sally was at the small desk next to the open doors. In front of her were the remaining literary self-portraits.

It made for interesting reading. Berit was fascinated by both the quality of the writing and the lack of introspection of the characters. The female writers completely underrated their charisma. When they described themselves, they used words like ordinary, average height, medium blond hair, and they never even got close to capturing that inspiring mix of youth and enthusiasm, joy and engagement that she saw in many of them. The middle-aged women were even worse. They described themselves in relation to others: their husbands, their kids, their grandchildren, and their own parents and used words such as "like people in general."

Berit shook her head. Of their dreams and fears they'd written much more, and it was considerably more interesting.

She was deeply immersed in a text when Sally suddenly said: "I think I've got something here."

"Who's written it?"

"Annie."

Berit couldn't remember who Annie was.

"One of the youngest. Blond hair. Pale eyelashes. Freckles," Sally described her. "She writes about being truthful. Interesting text. Even quotes the Quakers' theories about truth and writes that silence can also be a type of lie. To be honest, the text is pretty confusing, and that in itself is pretty interesting. Sometimes it's a sign that the subject is *too* personal to the author. It makes me wonder if she's hiding something."

"You think she might know something she hasn't told the police?"

"It could be worth checking out?"

They waited until the conversation in the garden was over, then they walked over to Annie. Sally managed to separate her from the other participants without drawing attention. Sally also mentioned her writing exercise and how impressed she had been.

The girl couldn't be more than eighteen and looked even younger to Berit. There was still a slight awkward insecurity in her arms and legs, like she hadn't fully grown into her body.

Sally sat down in one of the empty chairs and patted the one next to her for Annie to sit on. Berit picked a chair farther away so the girl wouldn't feel crowded by them.

"We read your text," Sally said. "The importance of truth. And the complexity of it."

Annie nodded. She glanced nervously around her, and Berit noticed her eyes were constantly drawn toward Emma. Berit recognized the expression on her face. She had looked at Emma in the same adoring way, she knew that, when *she* was the one being seen, noticed, and softly guided toward her full potential.

"She's amazing, isn't she?" Annie said.

Berit nodded gravely. "Yes, she is."

Annie seemed to hesitate. She was much too young to be able to hide what she thought and felt. Berit saw all the emotions on her face: anxiousness, nervousness, guilt, the irresistible urge to confide in someone.

Sally didn't seem to know what to say next. She glanced at Berit.

"Start just before the beginning," Berit suggested.

"Before the beginning?" Annie repeated nervously.

"Just like in a novel. Near the inciting incident."

And all of a sudden the words poured out of the young woman, randomly, like it was a first draft. That she'd always wanted to write, how she followed several writers on TikTok and Instagram, that she'd seen an ad for the retreat and contacted Emma, how she'd never been abroad before and how everything was just *the best*, wasn't it?

"I didn't even know air could feel like this," she said. "And I've never seen light like this. And Emma says I can write about anything and travel anywhere I want."

Eventually, the stream of words dried up and she seemed to get closer to what she really wanted to talk about. "I heard something." She glanced over at Emma again. "I heard them argue."

"Who was arguing?" Berit asked calmly.

Annie swallowed nervously. "Emma and John Wright. He said he would report her to the police."

"When did this conversation take place?"

"The first morning. I was still exploring the château and wanted to take a selfie in the library before John's lecture. Emma had just delivered his breakfast tray."

"Do you remember exactly what they said?" Berit asked.

"No, I couldn't really hear everything. They were in his room. The door was ajar. But I heard John using the word *police*, I'm sure of that. It's not a word you forget. Especially after…well, you know."

Berit nodded. She knew.

"But it doesn't mean anything, does it? I mean, she can't have had anything to do with the murder. She was serving coffee. I saw her myself."

"You did the right thing telling us this," Berit said, and Annie left, her steps light and unburdened, now that the responsibility had been lifted from her delicate shoulders and placed on Berit's solid ones.

Berit followed her with her eyes and found Nicole staring at them. She was leaning against a tree just next to them, dressed in a black suit jacket and dark sunglasses, looking like a mafia boss. When she caught Berit's gaze, she waved.

"Shame," Berit said later.

All around them, people were heading up to the terrace for a drink. It had become an unspoken tradition to gather there before dinner.

But Berit stayed with her face turned toward the evening sun. This was her favorite time of the day. The French evening sun was more beautiful than anywhere else in the world.

"What?" Sally said.

"That it proved to be a dead end."

Sally looked at her in surprise. "Are you sure it's a dead end?"

"They must have been talking about Rebecka. John threatened to report her to the police. Emma probably objected. You heard what Annie said. She had overheard their conversation and came to the conclusion it was about Emma. In reality, Emma probably tried to protect Rebecka."

Sally's phone rang. She put it in her pocket without even looking to see who it was.

"You have to pick up at some point," Berit said.

"I'm not going to disturb Mrs. Wright with minor details like this. I won't become my mother."

"Sally, no one thinks you're like your mum."

Confusingly enough, Sally seemed hurt by the comment. She blinked a few times in rapid succession and turned away from Berit so that she couldn't see her face.

"You're already at least as good," Berit clarified. "With a bit more time and experience, you'll be even better. Until then you don't have to compare yourself to her, and you definitely don't have to defend yourself for something she's done. But Olivia is right about one thing."

"What?"

"She represented John Wright. Not his wife. Ask yourself if John would have thought his literary estate was 'a minor detail.'"

Berit gave Sally a friendly pat on the shoulder when she walked past her. "If I were you, I wouldn't let either Olivia or Mrs. Wright bully you. I think they both could use some pushback."

37

SALLY'S TAXI STOPPED OUTSIDE THE hotel.

She looked out the window. The hotel looked even more imposing in the evening. Floodlights lit up the beautiful white renaissance facade.

The taxi driver said something fast in French and pointed at the building. "Arrive," he added impatiently in English.

Sally paid with cash and hurried out of the car. A doorman bowed gently as she entered. The concierge explained that he believed Madame Wright was having dinner in their restaurant. If Mademoiselle would follow him...?

Sally almost wanted to make an excuse and turn around, but the concierge continued into the dining room. "Madame Wright," he said with pride after he'd taken Sally all the way up to the table. Mrs. Wright was sitting on her own at a table in the middle of the room.

Sally sat down opposite her before she could object. She presumed Mrs. Wright would rather play along than cause a scene in the middle of the restaurant, but she couldn't be completely sure.

"Mrs. Wright," she said, "I understand you're angry. I would be too. Not only at my mother, even though she really deserves it, but at the whole world that has taken your husband away from you and then continues to spin around like nothing's happened, even though your world has shattered. But I..."

"Shattered is a bit of an exaggeration," Mrs. Wright interrupted. "But it's definitely inconvenient to have lost one's husband."

"What do you live for, Mrs. Wright?"

"Live for?"

"What will you leave behind when you die?"

"Oh… Well…my dogs, I guess. Amazing gun dogs. Sought after all over the country. Their bloodline will live on long after I'm gone."

"Your husband's legacy is his books. You saw one side of him, the private side, but you must have known how much the other side, the working and writing one, meant to him."

"The only thing he did was to complain about London, publishers, the PR machine, book bloggers, all the superficial people who thought books were just another commodity. They were only interested in what was selling at the time. He despised the lot of you."

Sally nodded. "I know," she said. "Because he knew that his own contribution was *timeless*. His books belong in the history of literature. But his legacy will need curating. Someone must preserve it. It was part of him, perhaps the most important part, and it will live on forever."

"I would rather have his snoring. I can't sleep without it."

Sally didn't know how to respond to the surprisingly private information. "I understand," she said after a while and stood up.

Mrs. Wright seemed to hesitate. "Don't go," she said. "Eating alone is even more boring than sleeping alone. Sit down and tell me what's so amazing about my husband's books."

Sally sat back down. She unfolded the heavy linen napkin and opened the wine list. "I'll gladly do that," she said. She waved at the sommelier. "But in that case, we need more wine. I hear they have an excellent wine cellar."

She had picked up a thing or two from her mum, after all.

Rebecka made her entrance after the starter had been served. She was strikingly dressed all in white: wide, flowing cotton trousers, a long-sleeved shirt, and she even wore white tennis shoes instead of her usual stiletto heels.

All the conversations came to a halt when she appeared in the doorway. She stopped for dramatic effect and gazed around the room, where all of a sudden everyone appeared exceedingly interested in their appetizers and refused to look her in the eye. Everyone apart from Berit, who observed her with calm interest, and Emma, who tried to look friendly but seemed mostly anxious.

Rebecka remained in the doorway for a while, but when she couldn't handle the apparent lack of attention any longer, she slipped over to Emma's end of the table, like she was drawn toward the only friendly face.

There wasn't a seat there, but Rebecka didn't care: She grabbed a chair on the way and squeezed in between Emma and Claudia.

Claudia moved farther away.

The only sound was the cutlery scraping against the plates.

When the main course had arrived, Rebecka couldn't contain herself any longer. She gestured impatiently to the group.

"I just wanted to give this world some more incredible literature," she said. "Is that really such a crime?"

Claudia coughed. "No, but embezzlement is," she said under her breath.

"No one buys good literature anymore!" Rebecka continued. "We've become a nation of savages. Cheap savages. With the attention span of a spoiled three-year-old. Everything has to be free and instantaneous."

No one said anything.

Rebecka stood up angrily. "John Wright was a genius!" she said. "I discovered him. I *created* him. And you're sitting here thinking you can judge *me*?"

She stormed out of the dining room, the wide shirt sleeves fluttering behind her.

Gradually, the sound of people talking returned. Everyone leaned closer to each other and whispered about Rebecka's outburst.

Only Berit seemed to notice Nicole getting up and silently sneaking out. Berit, and Charles, who sat quietly, staring at the door Rebecka had disappeared through.

38

REBECKA WAS STANDING COMPLETELY STILL by the pool when Nicole found her.

The fairy lights reflected in the dark water lit her face from underneath. The long day and night seemed to have aged her. Her face was pallid, with deep, tired lines. There was a thirty-year age gap between Rebecka and Nicole, and at that moment, every one of those years was written in Rebecka's face.

The white clothes that had made her entrance so dramatic made her skin look thin and transparent now, as if at any moment she could cease to exist and dissolve into nothing.

Nicole tried to look humble and unthreatening, but her inherent confidence must have shone through because Rebecka said: "You think you know everything, don't you?"

Nicole opened her mouth to object, but Rebecka continued without waiting for an answer: "You turn up here with your cocky, youthful confidence to lecture me on what I should do. But life will break you in the end, don't you worry."

She smiled a nasty smile and seemed to take comfort in imagining Nicole's crushed dreams and lost youth. Nicole could feel how she was aging in front of Rebecka's eyes. Her hand involuntarily touched her face, as if she was worried she'd discover new wrinkles.

"You should tell your side of the story," Nicole said. She had rehearsed this bit in advance, but faced with the real Rebecka, her words suddenly sounded absurd. Her next sentence was going to be: *I can't help you unless you confess*, but she found herself unable to say it out loud.

"My side of what?"

"Of…all of this. The murder." *The murder that you committed*, she thought. "Your side of everything you've done," she said instead.

"What I have *done?*" Rebecka looked at Nicole with disdain. "I can tell you one thing and that is what happens to impertinent little girls sticking their noses in things that don't concern them. Coming here and trying to interrogate *me!* I've been in this business longer than you've been alive. I've seen young girls come and go, and I can tell you one more thing: You will *never* make it. You don't have what it takes. First sign of a setback, and you'll be running back to your temp job."

Rebecka smiled. Nicole had never seen a smile like hers before. It was grotesque.

"John didn't like the fact that you were here, right?" she said. "Was he worried you'd embezzle our money too?"

Rebecka didn't react.

Nicole faltered. Everything—the conversation, Rebecka's constant smile, the white clothes fluttering in the wind against the dark pool—made her feel ill at ease.

She took an involuntary step back, until a sudden noise made her flinch and stop.

Charles came out of the shadows behind her. She was stuck between him, the pool, and Rebecka.

"That's enough," he said. Nicole wasn't sure if he was speaking to her or to Rebecka. "You've said what you needed to say." His nodded toward the direction of the château. "Run along now."

Nicole considered standing her ground, but she'd had enough. She wanted to get back to people and real, bright light.

"If you want to tell me what happened, I'm here," she said as she backed away. "I'm not going to talk to the police until my book's finished. They can read about it in print like everybody else. But if you don't talk to me, then, well I might have to tell them everything I know…"

Then she turned around and fled in a positively undignified way. She didn't care. She would edit everything later. This wasn't how the conversation would transpire in her book.

"The bloody gall," Charles said, amused, watching her leave. He held out a bottle of champagne and two glasses. "Bubbly?"

Rebecka folded her arms around herself and nodded feebly. Her face was illuminated and white, like the moon, and her lips bright red. *Like blood*, he thought, and felt like an idiot for thinking it. What was it about this place that made everyone so ridiculously melodramatic?

"Come on," he said, as much to himself as to her. "Relax. You screwed up, but you got away with it. You were lucky."

"*Lucky?*"

"Do you know what your real mistake was?" He continued without waiting for her reply. "You expected loyalty, but writers are only loyal to themselves. He left you, and he was going to cause a hell of a scene, you know he would, and now he's dead. Like I said. You were lucky."

"Me, Charles?" It actually felt good to hear the slight superior tone in her voice. He didn't like seeing her insecure.

"Both of us then," he admitted. "We were both too careless with the goose that laid the golden eggs."

He had a sip of the champagne. It had been a long time since he was inspired by his surroundings, but when he saw the colorful light reflecting in the pool and the magnificent starry sky above, he felt something very similar to excitement.

He had thought that was a feeling that belonged to young people. Like infatuation. If he had to be honest, he wasn't sure he approved of it. Life was more comfortable when you didn't care about things. There were advantages to navigating through life somewhat numb. But he couldn't deny that he was feeling something. He had another sip to make sure it wasn't the delightful champagne that was causing it.

"I'd gotten stuck in a rut," he said and thought he was being generous by using *I* instead of *you*, but when she didn't object, he got angry and changed it to: "*We* were stuck. I thought I was dependent on John, but we created him once upon a time, didn't we? We can do it again."

"What do you mean? John is gone. There's nothing we can do."

Charles waved his hand dismissively. "I don't mean the actual John. No, like I said, we were lucky. John alive would have caused us problems. John dead can't threaten us. I mean someone new. We could discover a new star. Maybe even here, at Château des fucking Livres."

Rebecka was just about to object when he continued: "Why not? One of them should have at least some talent. Statistically speaking. And we're here to support and develop talent. I was going to try and talk John into holding a workshop with me, but why don't you and I do it? We can talk about how publishers and agents support writers together. Use John as an example. Let him turn in his grave if he wants."

"In the morgue."

"Excuse me?"

"He's not in his grave yet."

Charles glanced at her. Sometimes she was a bit too morbid for him. "Sure, sure," he said. "Let him turn in the morgue then." He chuckled. "I hope he actually does. A spinning corpse would give the police something new to focus on."

"When do you suggest we'd hold this lecture, then?"

"Why not tomorrow? Let's ask Emma now. The day after tomorrow we're going to Lyon, and on Saturday that annoying Sally is holding her workshop. I want to do it before her. I want everyone to know who the real star agent here is."

"And star publisher."

"Of course."

"And Nicole?"

"What about her?"

"What are we going to do about her? You heard how she threatened me!"

"That little whippersnapper?" Charles shrugged. "I think together we'll be able to deal with her."

Sally moved quietly through the dark château.

Everybody had gone to bed by the time she came back from dinner with Mrs. Wright, but she was too wired to be able to sleep.

When she walked past the spot where John Wright had swallowed the poison, she shivered, but carried on. She had a job to do.

Throughout her youth her mum had sent her off to various boarding schools, work experience, summer jobs, and overly long stays with school friends she hardly knew, just so that Olivia could work undisturbed during both school terms and holidays. It meant Sally had seen an infinite number of offices and old buildings.

She had learned how to quietly become one with the walls. And how to find cellars and unused rooms where you could hide, out of the way.

By now she knew how these places worked. She almost felt a kinship with the old building and its checkered past. Production company, boarding school, writing retreat. And Sally knew that neither places nor people changed form without retaining some of their old selves. There was always junk and clutter hidden away somewhere.

Odds are there's one here somewhere, she thought. The only problem was finding it.

39

WHEN ROCHE GOT TO WORK at seven thirty the next morning, the lab report was on her desk.

There was also a takeout café au lait.

The Mayor was already at his desk across from hers.

"Any surprises?" she asked and nodded toward the report.

"One," he said.

She skimmed through it. No traces of wine or hemlock in either of the glasses. The fingerprints were all from who they expected: John Wright, Sarah Briggs, mislabeled Mrs. Wright after the forensic technicians' original notes, Emma Scott, and Antoine Tessier, who had both admitted they had been cleaning the room.

The surprise came from the prints on the door handle someone had try to wipe off. Forensics had managed to lift one. It belonged to Claudia Ramirez. Roche whistled.

"I wonder what business she had in John Wright's room," The Mayor agreed.

"How about we find out?"

Commissaire Roche drove. Philippe glanced at her when he thought she wouldn't notice. As always, her expression was completely impenetrable. She had sounded pleasant enough when discussing the lab report with him. But she hadn't drunk the coffee he'd bought for her and left on her desk.

The coffee was a mistake, he thought. *Too ingratiating. Like he was groveling, which, let's face it, was exactly what he was doing.*

For the twentieth time he cursed himself for whining in front of his dad like a surly teenager. He'd had no idea his father would repeat the complaint, but he should have had. Nothing put his father in a better mood than being able to throw his weight around and force people to dance to his tune. He never stopped to consider how it affected his son.

"I ran Antoine Tessier's prints through our database as well," he said. He made an effort to sound normal, but it came out overly cheerful. He grimaced.

"Did you find anything interesting?" Roche asked.

"One assault conviction." He continued apologetically: "But I don't know if there's anything to it. I looked up the case. Just a regular brawl in a bar. No indication of who started it. But only Antoine Tessier went down for it."

"And why was that?"

Philippe was careful to control his facial muscles. "The other man was a judge."

"Ah." Roche shook her head. "Of all the idiots to punch in the face."

He glanced at her. "You can understand the impulse, though," he tried cautiously.

Nothing. No reaction whatsoever. Not a hint of a smile.

So she hasn't forgiven me yet, he thought. *Damn.*

Claudia Ramirez leaned across the little table eagerly. They were in the library, and Philippe was pleased to see that she wasn't trying to act tough this time.

"I know it looks bad that my fingerprints were found in his room, but I can explain."

Roche looked at Philippe. "Please do," she said. "We are, how do you say it, all ears?"

Philippe nodded.

"I went over there because I wanted to talk to him."

"What did you want to talk to him about?" Roche asked.

Claudia hesitated. She seemed to be debating with herself over how much to divulge. Perhaps she was wondering how much they knew.

Nothing, Philippe thought, and she seemed to arrive at the same conclusion.

"Nothing important, really," she said.

"You disliked Mr. Wright, didn't you?" Roche said.

Claudia swallowed. "I've never denied it."

"Any particular reason?"

"He was unpleasant, that's all. The kind of man—"

Roche interrupted her impatiently. "Sure, but it was hardly for feminist reasons you couldn't stand him, was it?"

"The man was a scumbag," Claudia said. "I can name a dozen people who hated him, but none who liked him."

"But those people didn't go to his room just before he was killed, now did they?" Roche said.

Claudia swallowed. "I...I wanted to ask him if he was pleased with himself," she eventually admitted. "If he liked criticizing younger female colleagues."

"And did he?" Roche asked.

"I never found out. He threw me a glance and said the bed needed making and that he wanted clean towels. Then he left. He thought I was the *cleaner*."

"That must have made you angry."

"Yes, but not angry enough to kill him. He was alive when he left. I left a couple of minutes after. Nicole saw it. She can confirm it."

"I don't understand why you're so excited about their workshop," Alex said. "One of them is a cynical, chronically sloshed agent going nowhere, the other..."

"I like her," Julian interrupted. "She has…an eye for quality. After all, she was the one who discovered John Wright."

"And then embezzled his money!"

Julian shrugged, as if money was just a worldly thing that meant nothing to him.

Charles and Rebecka had picked the terrace for their workshop, and Alex soon had to admit that they were surprisingly good together. They had worked as a team for such a long time, and they were able to offer up some fascinating insights into John Wright. Despite what everybody knew about them, Charles and Rebecka both managed to come across as professional and engaging, and it was plain to see how much they had loved working with John Wright's books.

"His books changed my life," Rebecka said, and Charles agreed, with not a hint of irony.

Alex looked around at the rapt audience. He shook his head. *They've all forgotten about the embezzlement accusations.* It would have amused him if he hadn't seen the look on Julian's face just then. Jules stared greedily at Rebecka in exactly the same way he'd been looking at John Wright.

After the workshop, Jules got out his unfinished manuscript, all crumpled up after being carried around for almost a week, and walked up to her. Alex nervously followed behind.

Julian offered the pile of sheets to Rebecka. "I want you to read it," he said.

She looked surprised, and almost human. "Why me?" she asked.

Jules's face shone with a quiet confidence that Alex hadn't seen before. "Because I want to change people's lives with my books," he said.

Just act normal, Claudia thought and sat down at her usual table in the shaded part of the kitchen garden and opened her laptop. She was pretty sure she'd gotten through the interrogation unscathed. At least she hadn't been arrested. Now she just had to pretend nothing had happened until it all blew over.

She went through her latest document, smiling to herself as she read through yesterday's notes. Then she stopped abruptly. What was she doing? Nothing was more suspicious than a writer in front of their computer, smiling!

She glared at the screen instead.

Right. That was better. Just an ordinary writing session. She opened another folder called *Historical research* and started reading.

"I know what you've done."

The sudden voice made Claudia jump. She quickly closed her laptop and leaned her elbows over it. "What have I done?" she asked.

She tried to look at herself from the outside. The vaguely interested smile. The gaze that didn't express her inner emotions. She even managed successfully to raise one of her eyebrows nonchalantly. Not even Berit would have guessed how painfully hard her heart was beating.

She nodded, pleased with herself. She hadn't thought she was that tough anymore. She thought her comfortable middle-class life had made her weak, but apparently the survival strategies from her childhood were still there.

"You had an affair with John Wright." Nicole's voice was convinced and smug. She observed Claudia intently to gauge her reaction.

She was completely baffled. She even forgot to look cold.

"I had what?" she said stupidly.

"You slept with him. Perhaps you were in love with him, perhaps it was a one-night stand, but you sure as hell didn't want anyone to find out, did you?" Nicole looked down at Claudia's hand. "You're married, aren't you? What would your husband do if he found out?"

"One wonders," Claudia said feebly.

"The one thing I don't understand," Nicole said, "is *why* you slept with him."

"Yes, that is a good question…"

Nicole shook her head in disappointment. "I don't understand women who sleep with men they can't stand. Why reward men for their bad behavior? You'll only encourage them!"

She might as well have been talking about dog training.

"And think about the next woman they meet. They're going to be even more obnoxious with them."

That was entirely true. Claudia caught herself nodding in agreement.

If more women had thought twice about the men they slept with, the world would have been a better place.

"So you had to kill him to silence him," Nicole continued. "And you had to steal his diary to prevent someone finding out. I presume you've destroyed it. I saw you," she clarified. "You were carrying a black bag when you left, but not when you arrived. I can't swear it was the same as the one that was found in Rebecka's room, but it definitely looked similar to me."

Damn, damn, damn. If Nicole had told the police… She looked at Nicole. Why hadn't she told them?

"As I see it, you only have two choices," Nicole continued. "You either confess everything to me, which means you'll have control over your side of the story. Or I'll tell the police everything. I'm sure they will be very interested. Think about it for a while." She got up and nodded toward the computer. "As a writer you should understand the importance of telling your story in your own words."

Claudia watched her leave.

It had been so close. She had seen the glimmering vision of a new series. She could have written it. And what's more, she could have *sold* it.

Her agent…no, not Charles; that would never work. She would have to change agents, but that wasn't a particularly difficult decision. In fact, it was probably best to do it soon, before he thought of dumping her. *Advance not recouped* her royalty statements had said a bit too often lately. A new agent, a titillating idea for a series, who knows, maybe a large advance…

And then it had all been snatched away from her because a cocky twenty-year-old thought she had slept with John Wright.

The irony made Claudia want to cry.

40

SALLY LED BERIT DOWN A short, narrow staircase to a dark and forgotten cellar.

It was just after lunch, but the cellar was dark and dim. The previous owners had thrown all sorts of junk down there until it was all threatening to topple over, but Sally confidently led the way past the discarded conference tables, the cheap folding chairs, and the clothes rack with several dusty eighteenth-century dresses that must have been used for extras.

"I've worked in plenty of offices," Sally said. "When I was younger, that is. Mum always forgot it was the school holidays and would place me in the postal department of some publisher or as a run-around at some accounting firm she used."

Berit's pitiful look reminded her that perhaps her upbringing hadn't been completely normal, but in hindsight, Sally thought her mum had probably done the best she could.

"I learned a lot, in my own way," she said. "And one thing I learned was that nothing ever gets thrown away in places like this. There's always a lot of old junk hidden away."

There was no electricity in the cellar, but through the small window slits some sunlight trickled in. A single lightbulb hanging from a hook in the ceiling was attached to an extension cord that seemed to make its way over to the staircase. Sally connected it, and a ghostly light spread from the lightbulb.

"So I thought there must be one somewhere," she said. "And I was right. But I'm afraid it could do with going over with a cloth." She pointed to the wall at the end.

There was a giant whiteboard hanging on it.

Berit and Sally spent the next hour moving all the junk to one side of the room and creating a large, open space in front of the whiteboard. Berit said that the imagination needed air and space to move freely.

They wiped the board with warm water and soap, until Berit declared it was good as new.

As soon as they were done, she went to get the whiteboard markers she always brought with her when she traveled (in addition to multicolored pens, pencils, and thicker marker pens—she was convinced inspiration came if you were prepared). Finally, Berit wrote in the middle of the board:

Why here?
Why now?

"That's what I would really like to know," she said. "Why go all the way to France to commit a murder when the killer must have known they would be one of the main suspects just by being here? Writers aren't rock stars; it's not particularly hard to meet us. Book-signings, events, visits to libraries, there's plenty of much easier ways than going to a writer's retreat in Lyon."

"John Wright did something here that upset someone?" Sally suggested.

"Yes. Something has been gnawing at the back of my mind," Berit said and sighed. "A detail. Something I've missed. And I think something was wrong as early as that first dinner. The threat against John Wright in the night only confirmed what my gut feeling had already tried to tell me."

"You think something happened here that led to the murder?"

"Yes, I do. So, in a sense, the answer to the first question is a given. The murder happened here because it had to happen *fast*."

They stared at the whiteboard in silence for a few moments.

"One person is missing," Sally pointed out.

"Who?"

"Emma Scott."

Berit crossed her arms over her chest, as if she physically wanted to stop Sally from grabbing the pen from her hand and adding the name to the board. "Emma's as innocent as you and me," she said. "I'm completely sure of that."

"But *how* can you be sure? How can you know?" Sally wondered.

"She just couldn't kill someone. It's as simple as that. She's not... She's not the type."

Sally said nothing. Everything she didn't say hung in the air between them.

"She had no motive to kill John Wright," Berit said. "And especially no reason to do it *now*. She couldn't know if the writing retreat could continue as normal after a murder, and she'd never do anything to jeopardize it."

"It's for her sake we're doing this, isn't it? Everything. Being here. Trying to solve the crime."

Berit didn't deny it.

"But why, Berit? Why is Emma so important to you?"

"She taught me everything I know about the publishing world and living in it."

Sally waited. Berit seemed to be lost in her memories. She said in a faraway voice, as if she was telling a story to herself: "She always used to tell me: 'Don't compare yourself with anyone else. Don't care about what other writers have. There will always be ones that have more. But everyone forgets that there are also many who have so much less. Focus on what you have. Focus on what you can control.'"

"Sound advice," Sally said, but she wasn't sure Berit even heard her.

"She also said: 'Choose your colleagues, and choose the nice ones. There are a lot of idiots in this industry, but you shouldn't have to deal with any more than is absolutely necessary.'"

"I guess they exist in all industries," Sally said.

"And then she said: 'There are no nicer people than book lovers.'"

"That's true."

"She looked after me when I was a young and insecure debut writer," Berit said finally. "I don't think I'd still be a writer today if it wasn't for her."

"She's your Berit," Sally said.

Berit shook her head. "Much more supportive. She's one of life's natural mentors. I don't think she can help but supporting people."

"Neither can you. But I guess you're more like one of life's involuntary mentors."

Berit laughed.

Sally hesitated. "Are you sure you did the right thing when you dismissed Annie's statement? That of John and Emma talking about a police report?"

"But that was about Rebecka," Berit said stubbornly. "We know that."

"Yes, but something doesn't add up. He had already signed an agreement allowing her to pay back what she owed in installments, and even if he had changed his mind, why would he tell Emma? He was hardly the person who'd politely inform her before he reported one of the teachers on her retreat. And why now? He wasn't going to report her to the French police."

Berit said nothing.

"And there's something else," Sally said. "I spoke to Mrs. Wright about it when we were having dinner, and I told her about the threat you'd heard the night before he died. *I will destroy you.*"

Berit nodded. That's what she'd heard.

"She didn't buy it."

"Pardon?"

"Mrs. Wright. She didn't believe it. She said John wasn't a man who would tolerate being threatened."

"Whether she buys it or not, that's what I heard," Berit said.

"Yes…but she said that if anyone came out with the threats, it was John. And it cleared something up I've been wondering about but not been able to put my finger on. The choice of words. *I will destroy you.* Not kill or hurt or stop. *Destroy.* I don't know. It seems like a threat John would make. Maybe what you heard was John threatening someone, and maybe that someone was Emma."

41

EMMA AND ANTOINE WERE IN the kitchen helping out with dinner preparations. There was a mountain of carrots, potatoes, parsnips, and onions in front of them. Next to them, the cook was dicing the meat and bacon for this evening's stew. A bowl of perfect little mushrooms was placed between them.

Berit looked at all the vegetables, and then at Emma, then she shrugged her shoulders, hung up her beautiful green summer scarf and got to work.

When all the vegetables were peeled and chopped, Berit asked Emma to join her on the terrace for a glass of wine before dinner. Emma hesitated as there was still a lot to do in the kitchen, but Antoine gestured encouragingly for her to leave.

"Well, perhaps a small one then," Emma said and removed her apron.

Upstairs in the dining room, several people had already sat down at the dining table, helping themselves to bread and butter and the thin slices of salami and smoked ham the cook always put out before dinner. They seemed ravenous and relaxed after a long day of writing. Everyone was looking forward to tomorrow's trip to Lyon's old town.

Alex passed the wine bottles around and told everyone about things to see there. Julian was constantly glancing over to the terrace where Rebecka was reading his manuscript. She was leaning over it with her reading glasses on and a pencil in her hand.

"Relax," Alex said and squeezed Julian's shoulder. "She'll love it."

Right at that moment, Rebecka drew a line over a whole page with her pencil. She turned the page. Drew another line all over it.

"She'll love most of it," Alex corrected himself. He quickly topped up Julian's glass.

Nicole was talking to Annie. Annie looked full of both admiration and anxiety at the same time.

"I want to know *everything* about you," Nicole said encouragingly. She gazed over at Berit almost triumphantly, but Berit was too caught up in her own thoughts to give it much notice.

She grabbed a beer and a glass while Emma poured herself a wine, then they headed out to the terrace and sat on a sofa. In the warm evening sun, Berit suddenly had a vision of what the writing retreat could have been had it not been for John Wright. She took a sip of ice-cold beer and cursed him again for dying during Emma's writing retreat.

Emma looked at the group of people inside the dining room. Every time someone laughed or leaned across the table to say something, there was a sparkle in her eye that Berit couldn't quite read. Not exactly happiness, but not exactly sorrow either.

She looked like someone in love the evening before a farewell, she realized suddenly. But what was it that was ending?

Not the retreat. Not yet. Tomorrow they would go to Lyon, and then the students would start working. Several unscheduled days of writing before Emma and Sally would hold their workshop on networking. On Wednesday was the event that everybody had been waiting for: the chance to try out their pitches on the publishers and the agents, and the grand closing party, of course. No, Emma's sorrow ran deeper than that. Perhaps she grieved the whole publishing world, or the person she'd once been?

"You and John Wright were talking about something when you delivered his breakfast on Saturday," Berit said. "The word *police* was mentioned. What was that about?"

"Rebecka, of course," Emma said lightheartedly. "What else would it have been?"

Berit shook her head. "That was my first thought as well, but it doesn't add up. John had already agreed not to report Rebecka to the police, and he definitely wouldn't have reported her to the French police, so why would he be talking to you about it?"

Next to her, Emma froze. Berit wanted to take back everything she'd said, but she had to continue. "But the conversation didn't start that morning, did it? It started late the night before."

Emma didn't reply.

"He threatened to destroy you, didn't he?"

Emma's face contorted with bitterness. "Me. The retreat. Antoine," she said. "Anyone he could think of he would destroy. I *need* this retreat, Berit. It's all I've got."

"And then you tried to reason with him when you dropped off his breakfast. But he refused to listen, didn't he?"

"Listening wasn't his strongest point, no," Emma said bitterly.

"In what way would he destroy you? What did he have against you or the retreat or Antoine…?"

Emma suddenly grabbed Berit's arm and stared at her. She didn't even seem to notice that her fingers were digging in to Berit's skin.

"Don't you ever wonder why we keep doing this?" she asked with terrifying intensity in her eyes. "Why do we keep on writing, reading, and spreading our little stories when the world is on fire?"

Berit softly placed her hand over Emma's. "Precisely because the whole world is on fire," she said. "That's why we do it." She carefully loosened Emma's grip on her arm, but she kept her friend's hand in hers.

The danger with idealistic people, Berit thought, *was that they burned so brightly and reassuringly for such a long time, it seemed they always would.* But suddenly the flame would start to flicker, and if nothing was done, it would die. All that was left was a darkness that seemed even more frightening since you'd been so used to the light.

"Do you never doubt?" Emma asked. There was a hint of restrained desperation in her voice.

"No," Berit said simply. "I doubt almost everything else, the world and its people, myself more than anything, my own ability—but never the writing itself. Sometimes I think it's the only thing I actually believe in. The way the world is going, we need books and stories more than ever. And in any case, at least we're not causing any harm. There's not a lot you can say that about these days."

"But is it enough?" Emma said quietly.

Berit stood up to join the others for dinner. She held out a hand and helped Emma stand up.

"More than enough," she said.

It was only halfway through the boeuf bourguignon she realized Emma never answered her question.

Commissaire Roche was still at the police station; Philippe had known she would be. He went up to her desk and remained standing there, awkwardly.

"What do you want, Mayor?" she asked without looking up from her screen.

He made a face. He had almost got used to his nickname, but after the incident with his dad, it felt like criticism.

"Well, I was thinking… We have to eat, right?"

"What? What are you talking about?"

"Dinner. We have to eat dinner." He hesitated. "Can I…can I buy you dinner, as an apology? For, well, you know. I know I'm not supposed to mention my father's name all the time, but there are several Michelin star restaurants where I could put it to good use. Why not reap the benefits of the old man for once? We could get a table in half an hour."

Roche didn't answer immediately, but she turned around on her office chair and looked at him. Even though he was standing up and she was sitting down, he felt like the underdog. Like he was being scrutinized and deemed inadequate.

"I've got a better suggestion," she said eventually. She reached for her phone. "Gabi, I need a table for two. Tonight. In half an hour. I know what you said, but it's an emergency. For work." She looked Philippe straight in the eye and added: "Oh, and tell Adam he'll have to let us pay tonight."

She stood up and collected her jacket and things.

"You're paying," she said to Philippe.

42

IT WAS PAST MIDNIGHT, BERIT was sure of that, even though she'd lost track of time a long time ago.

After dinner she'd gone straight to her whiteboard, and she was still there now. She was lying on the floor, staring up into the ceiling. The concrete was cool under her back, the night warm and breezy.

All the smells were more intense during the night. The wind carried with it the smell of grass, rosemary, thyme, and something mildly flowery Berit couldn't place.

And the sounds. All these sounds old houses made, but you never thought of in the daytime: rattling pipes, creaking floorboards, trees outside rustling in the wind, twigs suddenly snapping, by animals or by your own imagination.

Berit stretched her arms out. The lone lightbulb was facing the white-board which turned a dazzling white from the sharp beam. Only Berit's feet were in the light. The rest of her was in darkness, dimly lit by the moon outside.

"Hi, Nicole," she said out loud.

New sounds: feet that no longer tried not to be heard. The gentle swooshing of a summer dress. And the scent: a modern, female blend of face cream, perfume, and hair products.

"Oh, you're alive," Nicole said. Her voice sounded completely neutral when faced with this fact. "When I first saw you, I thought the killer had got to you too."

"Sorry to disappoint," Berit muttered from the floor.

"It's okay. But if he *had* killed you, it would have made a fabulous second act."

Berit raised her arms up, and Nicole helped her get on her feet.

"Since you're not murdered, you can still be the murderer," Nicole hopefully.

"If you really believed I was the killer, you wouldn't down here with me, alone in a dark cellar in the middle of the night," Berit said.

Nicole looked uncomprehending in a way that made Berit worry even more. Young people were always convinced nothing bad could ever happen to them.

"And if you *are* the killer," Nicole said coaxingly, "you could tell me your story. Give me your side of it. I would do all the work. With the writing, I mean. The only thing you'd have to do was to tell me how you went about it."

She waited, hoping she'd find out that she was alone with a murderer, then she said: "If you didn't kill him, we could solve the murder together."

"No," Berit said, but she couldn't help admiring the impertinence and the flexibility of it. Victim, murderer, or cowriter, Nicole was willing to turn everything into a story.

"We can write the book together," Nicole said. "I'm a brilliant writer. The only thing I've lacked is the right subject. Now I've found it. I'm going to write about the murder, and I'm going to turn it into a bestseller. But I have to find out who did it. The last chapter. And you can help me."

She went over to the whiteboard, grabbed a pen, and wrote in big letters all over the only blank space: NICOLE WAS HERE.

Then she suddenly looked embarrassed. She was about to erase it when Berit shook her head. "Leave it here," she said.

"It's like I said. People tell you stuff. Even Commissaire Roche asks you for help."

"No."

"The only thing I need is a small lead. I know there's competition out there. Everyone here will write about the murder in one way or another. I must be the first if I'm to make an impression. If you help me solve the murder, I'll do everything else. We'll split fifty-fifty. Royalties, TV interviews…both our names on the cover. In alphabetical order obviously."

Of course. Archer before Gardner.

"And then what?" Berit wondered. "Have you thought about what would happen if we solved the case together? One of the people on the retreat turns out to be a killer. Everyone else has all their secrets revealed. Don't you care about that?"

"Why would I? I don't know anyone here. Sure, I like them, but we're not *friends*."

"You should write about something else. Something real. Instead of using someone else's death as PR."

"It's hardly going to hurt him now," Nicole reasoned. "He's just another dead author."

For a split second Berit was almost drawn toward the insane project. Not despite the insanity, but because of it. It had been much too long since she did something crazy and irresponsible and…

She realized Nicole reminded her of the young women she had shared a flat with when she first came to London. They were always off on some mad adventure, and they always dragged her along. Especially one of them had possessed an infallible ability to land herself in catastrophic situations varying from comical to dangerous, and she always expected Berit to rescue her. And what adventures they had been through… They'd given her material for at least three books.

Nicole Archer had exactly the same drive. Berit had always stayed within the given confines of life. She had largely accepted the way the world worked and tried to create her own space within it to the best of her abilities. People like Nicole, on the other hand, redrew the boundaries completely.

"I never know what you're thinking when you're looking at me like at that," Nicole said defensively.

"Why don't you write a different book?" Berit suggested. "A book that's more…*you*. The one you would have written if you'd never heard of John Wright."

"But you don't understand, this book *is* me. Everything I've experienced in my life has led me to this book. It will practically write itself. And it will sell, I guarantee it. The media will be there at the release party. The police too." She looked at Berit triumphantly. "You see, I'm not going to reveal who the killer is until the last chapter. Not even to them"

Berit had a really bad feeling. "What do you mean?" she said slowly.

"Exactly what I said. I will solve this murder, before anyone else, finish the book, get an obscenely big advance, and not let anyone read the last chapter in which the murderer gets revealed until just before it gets sent to print. I might even invite the murderer to the release party. Just imagine how fun it would be if the police made their arrest on my party! People would talk about it for years."

43

THE RESTAURANT WHERE ROCHE'S DAUGHTER worked closed at midnight. At one in the morning, Gabrielle came out the back door.

Philippe detached himself from the wall he had been leaning against.

She looked at him in surprise. It was only a couple of hours since they'd met but she didn't seem to recognize him. And why should she? They'd only said half a dozen words to each other when she came out to the table to talk to her mother.

She looked over her shoulder, toward the bar inside where a burly male bartender was tidying up after closing time.

"I was here earlier tonight with Commissaire Roche," he said quickly.

Gabrielle relaxed. "My mother's new lapdog." She smiled to take the edge off the joke.

"Her new guard dog," he corrected and did his best to look wild and dangerous. He was surprisingly pleased to hear her laugh.

"Let me guess," she said. "My mother sent you to tell me I work too much and should have left sooner? Or has she suddenly decided that I shouldn't walk home alone late at night?"

"Believe me, she has no idea I'm here. Fancy a glass?"

She hesitated. "Why not?" she said.

She knew a restaurant that would stay open another hour if she asked them. It was run by a grumpy man from Bretagne, who served them some snacks and a drink at the bar himself. He spoke a dialect Philippe could hardly understand.

It always made him feel ill at ease, all these parts of the country where people couldn't speak properly. He felt excluded, as if they shared a history that didn't include him, which, of course, they did.

Roche's daughter spoke it perfectly. She slipped easily into it when she spoke to the grumpy man. When the man looked at Gabrielle, there was almost a hint of a smile in his eyes.

"We worked together for six months in Noirmoutier, for Alexandre Couillon. He runs the only Michelin star restaurant on the island."

Not as in Lyon, where it was crawling with them. If you went out in the street with a chunk of bread in your hand and threw it randomly in any direction, there was a good chance you'd hit one.

There was something in Gabrielle's tone of voice, the way she spoke about that Couillon. "You admire him," he said.

"Sure, don't you? He's a man who takes his roots and his family seriously."

Philippe didn't admire roots. He admired heritage. People in the past who had accomplished something, achieved important results. Roots were nothing more than a name for people who had married their cousins for generations.

But he smiled anyway. "And yourself?" he asked. "What are your roots? Where do you belong?"

It should have been an easy question to answer, but she replied: "I don't know. I only really think of the future. I'm more interested in where I'm going. I'd like to travel. Work in Japan, Korea, or Vietnam, South America, Svalbard…"

"I guess you'd be cooking polar bear then," he suggested half-jokingly.

"Probably whale," she said. "Isn't that what the Norwegians catch?" She looked like she would have liked to prepare it. "There's so much food to discover. Life is too short for all the food I want to cook." Gabrielle smiled, and then she said: "In the kitchen. I belong in the kitchen. Isn't that where they say a woman's place is?"

Philippe had some of the smoked eel, even though he wasn't hungry.

In secret he distrusted everything that came from the sea. He preferred the land. Fields, wheat, vineyards, cows, pigs, truffles, mushrooms, olive groves, tomatoes…

"They're wrong," he said and raised his glass to her. "A woman's place is in a Michelin star kitchen."

She laughed. Then she regarded him seriously. "Are you flirting with me? Because that's not a good idea, you know. It would never work."

"I'm only here to find out more about your mother. I'm hoping you'll help me figure her out."

"Haven't you done so already?" she asked.

"Would I be here in the middle of the night if I had?"

"She's my role model," Gabrielle said earnestly. "She always has been. She's taught me that you can be tough but have a sense of humor. Be successful but be a part of the gang. Did you know she gave me a course in self-defense when I was fourteen?"

"*Good*," Philippe said emphatically "All young woman should take one of them."

"Then she taught me how to diffuse a situation so I wouldn't have to use what I'd learned. How to prevent and analyze risks."

"But what's important to her?" he asked.

Gabrielle shrugged. "Work. That's what's important to her."

Philippe looked more closely at her. "Do you resent it? Did she work all the time when you were a kid?" His father definitely had.

"Sure. Evenings. Weekends. She was called away for a murder on my seventh birthday. I think she feels bad about it, but I don't mind. I admire her for it, I always have. She's…she's the good guys. Out there, catching the bad."

"She calls me The Mayor." It slipped out before he could stop himself.

"But only to your face, right? Never behind your back?"

He thought about this. As far as he knew it was true. "How can I make her trust me?"

Gabrielle shrugged her shoulders. "Be trustworthy."

He grimaced. "It might be too late for that. I made a mistake." He clarified, "Not on purpose, but…"

"So your question is really how to regain her trust." She nodded to herself. "Admit your mistakes. And be loyal. My mother values loyalty above everything else."

"You mean, not criticize her then? Agree with everything she says?"

"If you think that, you don't understand what loyalty is. At least not my mother's version of it. More smoked eel?"

Philippe accepted. It was a small price to pay for advice on how to handle the boss.

Then he suddenly looked at her. "Why wouldn't it work out between us?"

She laughed. "Don't tell me you think it would."

"Why not?" he said, even though dating his boss's daughter probably topped the list of mistakes he would never make. He just didn't understand why it was at the top of *her* list.

"I will work nights all my life."

"Me too."

She looked at him, from top to toe, with a humorous look in her eye that made the gesture seem less insulting. "You? You'll be chief of police in no time. You'll need someone who can mingle at events."

He shrugged. "So you could be responsible for the catering at these events then."

"Every time you took me out for a date, I'd spend the whole time reviewing the food," she said.

"Surely that would be the restaurant's problem, not mine."

He was actually fascinated by the way she ate. Like every mouthful was worthy of her attention.

Even when she spoke to him, some part of her was always focused on what her mouth was experiencing at that moment. Tastes and textures seemed to register and get archived in her head for future reference.

He would just mechanically eat whatever was put in front of him. He was used to dinners as networking events. You ate, you smiled, you went through your next move in your head. You saved the really important conversations until the cognac.

She laughed and shook her head. "We would work so much we'd never even see each other."

"Sounds like the bedrock for a perfect marriage. At least you'd never tire of me."

"I would prioritize my work over my relationship." She held her hand up before he could say anything else. "And so would you, admit it!"

"But is that so awful?" he asked.

"Not really. But we would both be married to our work, and that's not a great foundation for a relationship. What you need is a pretty little girl who understands."

"You would understand." He smiled. "But not all the self-defense courses during my whole police training have made me brave enough to call you either pretty or little."

She laughed, a remarkably charming sound similar to a snort that started somewhere in her stomach and ended through her nose.

"Wise," she said. "Very wise."

They looked at each other for a moment.

"Disagree," she said.

"What? With what? You?"

"My mother. When you think she does something wrong. Do your job properly, be passionate, but put your foot down. She respects hard work and people with their own opinions."

YOUR GREATEST FEAR

DO YOU REMEMBER THE FILM *Trainspotting*?

The main character has just stolen loads of cash and is on his way to Amsterdam or some other city, and he looks straight into the camera and explains he's going to become just like you.

The job, the washing machine, the pension, low cholesterol, TV, mortgage, golf, washing the car, Christmas with the family, the list of things he's determined to get is long, and just thinking about it now gives me a panic attack.

Do you want to know what my greatest fear is?

Exactly that. Being content. To endure life, to soldier on. Do your best to contribute to the increase in emissions and global warming. Pat yourself on the back because you're driving an electric car but flying to Thailand once a year because "you need it." Read a chapter of some book club pick before you go to sleep and post pictures of a backlit glass of rosé on Instagram.

Biggest fear? *To become just like you.*

Biggest dream? To have created something.

Oh, how I've missed it! The intoxicating feeling of having created something. The possibilities dance before me in the evening sun. The fields and the future lie wide open in front of me. In the lilac twilight over the hills, anything can happen.

I take deep breaths. Get drunk on the freedom of it all. I realize I've been too passive. I let my life shrink until there was almost nothing left of it.

But in the end, I defended it. I stood up for my dreams, and I was prepared to kill for it. No one can ever take away from me the knowledge that I'm capable of so much more.

Before you judge me, ask yourself: Are you really living the life you dream of? Are you fulfilling your own potential, or have you let other people say, *you can't, you shouldn't, you're not allowed?* Are you playing by their rules, making yourself smaller just so they can feel better about themselves?

What would you do to have the life you'd always dreamt of?

And to how far would you go to defend it?

44

THE SUN WAS SHINING ON Lyon's resplendent facades, and every member of the Writing Retreat That Will Change Your Life seemed to have caught the holiday feeling.

After lunch they had gathered in Place Bellecour, the only square that had been destroyed during the French Revolution. It had clearly been rebuilt afterward, complete with the mandatory statue of a king on a horse that no European city could do without.

Emma encouraged them to use this opportunity to explore, observe, and take notes. The students spread across la Presqu'île, or the Peninsula, the part of Lyon situated between the rivers Rhône and Saône.

Alex and Julian were drawn to the charming rue Mercière, where bars, restaurants, and cafés lined both sides of the narrow street. They found a spot outdoors and ordered two coffees, and while Alex watched the people ambling past, Julian got his computer out and started writing.

Julian was writing.

Nothing else mattered. That was it: Julian was once again writing words in a Word document that he refused to let Alex read.

During their whole life together, five years of it, practically an eternity, Julian had been writing. That's who he was.

Alex's own identity was more fluid. It changed depending on who he was talking to. He was a social chameleon, but at least he was aware of it. Blurred at the edges. No solid sense of self behind the smiling facade.

But not Julian. He'd always had his dream, no, not a dream, that implied that it was unreal. He'd always had this certainty. One day he would write a book. One day he would be published. One day his real life would begin.

Their real life, Alex corrected himself. Julian was right: They weren't like everybody else. Others might work for a salary; they worked in order for Julian to write.

The only time he'd stopped writing was those first days after John Wright's death. He had been inaccessible and pessimistic and refused to speak to Alex. But something, Alex didn't know what, had restored his energy, and now he was once again crouched over his computer.

Alex called the waiter over and ordered two glasses of champagne. Why not? It was after one o'clock and Julian was *writing*.

Alex turned to face the sun and relaxed for the first time since they'd got back from the wine-tasting trip, and he'd seen Julian's ashen, shocked face. Whatever happened they'd get through it together.

Berit moved slowly along the same winding streets she'd wandered through years ago.

To her, Lyon had always been a vibrant, *living* city, much more so than Paris. She wondered if it was because students were such a big part of the town. *There was something about students that kept a city young at heart*, she thought. Unlike tourists, who only made it cynical.

She was sweating in the sultry heat, but she was used to that too. Lyon in the summer was like a cauldron surrounded by mountains. Thunderstorms were always brewing over the horizon. It would rain torrentially for a brief moment, and then you could breathe again.

Without thinking, she moved toward the bohemian quarters of La Croix-Rousse. It had always been her favorite part of the city, but today even this charming part of town couldn't chase away the ominous feeling she'd had ever since the conversation with Nicole.

Nicole was young, enthusiastic, convinced of her own immortality—exactly the type of person you could be sure would put herself or others in danger.

Somehow Berit would have to stop her interfering in the investigation of the murder. But how? Berit longed to grab her by the shoulders, give her a good shake, and tell her not to be a bloody idiot…

She smiled ironically at herself. That would only make a woman like Nicole even more determined.

Now there's a thought.

If saying no wouldn't work, perhaps she should try the opposite strategy… It could work, but only if Nicole was prepared to swap short-term gain for long-term one.

At first Berit thought her worries had provoked the uncomfortable feeling of being followed, but the more she listened, the more she was convinced she wasn't imagining it. It was hard to be sure among all the tourists. The constant hum made it tricky to identify one set of feet among so many others. But most crowds had their own rhythm and movements. Today was a warm, sweaty summer's day. People moved idly, without haste. So Berit increased her speed. Then she suddenly stopped, waited, started walking again, stopped. Every time she changed tempo, someone behind her did the same thing.

She took a few random turns into one of the many narrow, winding back streets that were everywhere in this part of Lyon. Now and then a square or cathedral suddenly appeared, but neither her nor the person behind her stopped to admire them.

She realized she'd ended up near Place des Terreaux, where once there had been a cloister full of nuns who had run amok, taken lovers, and generally refused to toe the line. In the end they had to choose between following the rules or leaving the church, and faced with the choice of security or freedom, most of them had chosen freedom.

She turned. Her feet seemed to remember the direction themselves. But was it still there? Then she saw the colored lights and smiled.

Broc' Bar. She still remembered all the magical evenings beneath the gigantic mulberry tree that watched over and shaded the outdoor seating area. The front of the building was a delightful shade of red, the chairs bright yellow.

Berit ordered two cups of coffee.

Nicole sat down in the chair next to her. "You knew I was following you," she said.

"I guessed." Berit had a sip of the excellent coffee.

"I thought you were investigating something or doing something interesting," Nicole said. Her voice sounded reproachful and appreciative at the same time. "But you wasted my time on purpose."

"Not wasted," Berit said. "We need to talk."

"About what?"

Berit looked at her gravely. "You can't go around accusing people of being the killer," she said.

"Why not?"

"Because you might accidentally be *right*."

Nicole looked completely baffled.

"I'll agree to work with you." Berit raised her hands. "With conditions."

"What conditions?" asked Nicole suspiciously.

"Let me take care of the practical investigation," Berit said. "If I manage to find out who the killer is, I'll tell you first. After Commissaire Roche," she added conscientiously. "She'll need to know before you."

Nicole objected: "But then everybody will find out as soon as she arrests the killer!"

"But you will get all the details. I'll tell you everything I did." She got to the irresistible part: "And you can take the credit. You can write the whole book about how you and no one else solved the murder."

Nicole looked at her suspiciously. "What's the catch?"

"No catch. Like I said, a condition."

"What condition?"

"As soon as everyone is back at the château, you'll tell them that you're going to stop investigating the murder. At dinner, perhaps. Make a big declaration that you'll leave everything to me or to the police to solve."

Berit didn't like the thought about Nicole running around telling everyone she knew who the murderer was. At least this way Nicole would get out of the murderer's crosshair until Berit had time to solve the murder.

"But then I won't get the credit!" Nicole complained.

"Yes, afterward," Berit promised. "Afterward you will. We'll tell everyone you solved it. It's just a…just a ruse."

Nicole thought about this. Then she nodded. "Okay," she said. "Let's do it."

Berit stood up. "Shall we go back to the others now?" she asked.

Nicole smiled. "You go ahead. I'll stay here for a bit."

Nicole sneaked stealthily across the red bridge toward Vieux Lyon.

Berit had already crossed the stunning bridge over the Saône to the town's old quarters, and this time she had no idea she was being followed; Nicole was sure of it.

In front of Cathedral Saint-Jean, Berit slowed down. Nicole hid behind a postcard stand. Berit might be telling the truth about being willing to give Nicole all the credit for solving the murders, but it might just have been a ploy to get her off the hunt. Nicole sure as heck wouldn't take her word for it. She'd be following in her footsteps, looking over her shoulder, finding out who the murderer was right along with her.

This time, she'd been careful to give it enough time before crossing the bridge after Berit. In the crowded, narrow streets, she stayed as far back as she dared. She was convinced Berit hadn't noticed her, and the thought of her just walking along, completely unaware of how close Nicole was, filled her with extreme satisfaction.

It was like they were attached by an asymmetrical link where only one of them knew they were connected. She wondered if this was what being a stalker felt like. An intoxicating feeling of power and an all-seeing knowledge. Almost…almost like when you were writing, the few times when it all flowed freely.

Beyond the cathedral the hordes of tourists dwindled. The buildings became lower and more run-down. Berit suddenly stopped in front of a red door. Nicole darted into one of the steep side streets. What was she doing?

Eventually, a young girl came out of the door, and Berit gave her a friendly nod, grabbed hold of the door before it shut, and sneaked in.

Nicole only had a few seconds before the heavy door slammed shut. She threw herself at it and pried it open before it locked.

Behind it was a dark and gloomy tunnel, leading toward a bright light. She walked past a row of mailboxes. Water was dripping from somewhere, and despite the heat outside, it was deliciously cool. She looked around, fascinated.

She was standing in the middle of a stunning courtyard. But where was Berit? She must have carried on... Up ahead was an opening suggesting an alleyway. Nicole listened. Footsteps ascended a staircase at an impressive speed.

Nicole lingered in the lovely cool stillness. She looked up at the clear blue sky high above, framed like a painting by the buildings around her.

Someone punched her in the back.

Nicole was indignant at first. Then she was hit again, and again, and before she had a chance to orient herself, someone had wrapped an arm around her. She saw something shiny underneath her, cold steel, and then she was punched in the stomach instead.

Not punched, she thought, as if she was editing her own thoughts. *Stabbed.*

She stumbled. For a moment she was held up by the arm around her chest. She caught herself feeling grateful for the support.

No, not grateful.

Then the arm disappeared. She fell down on her knees. Her whole body was in revolt. Every breath tore through her. Her back broke out in a cold sweat. She had to call for help, get her mobile out, do something.

The ground was cool to her cheek. She closed her eyes. She just needed a little rest. Just a short, sweet little rest.

Her last thought before she blacked out was: *I didn't even find out who the killer was.*

45

BERIT WALKED QUICKLY UP THE stairs.

She knew she was being followed. She had waited for the unmistakable sound of the door slamming shut behind her, but instead had heard the faint squeak of it opening wide again.

She nodded, pleased. Soon Nicole would see one of the best and privately owned *traboules* of Lyon. *Traboules* were narrow, secret walkways linking different streets in the old part of Lyon, originally built as a practical solution to the many steep hills and winding streets. Goods had to be transported quickly up from the river to the weaving factories.

Since then, they'd been used by religious sects, alchemists, secret societies, the French Resistance, and of course, these days, by tourists. There were hundreds of these walkways in Vieux Lyon and in the old book printing quarters around La Croix-Rousse. Some were renovated in collaboration with the city and open to tourists, others were still private and only open a few hours in the morning to receive post and deliveries.

This one, at 2 Montée du Gourguillon, was Berit's favorite. The round stairwell led up, up, up, until she reached a new courtyard, then continued even farther. In front of the charming blue doors were doormats saying *Welcome*, but the yellow walls had notes here and there asking people to *Respect the residents!*

She stopped to look through a small opening in the wall. The rooftops in the old silk weaving quarters spread out below her in a jumble of orange-colored bricks, chimneys, and beautiful skylight.

Soon, she was on her way again, slightly panting on the steep stairs. Once you'd reached the end, you were almost at the top of Fourvière Hill, with its antique Roman theatres and dramatically lit-up cathedral. She hoped Nicole would think it was worth the climb.

She froze.

Her subconscious realized something was wrong before her brain did. Something had changed. She turned around. Listened.

No footsteps.

She told herself that it was nothing to worry about. They were in a locked apartment block. No one from the writing retreat even knew where they were. Nicole must be safe.

But the sudden silence made her panic.

She turned around and hurried down the stairs. She followed her own trail, in her mind going over the times she'd stopped to admire the view. Had she heard the footsteps then?

Think, Berit. The door. She'd definitely heard the door. And on the first set of stairs, the gentle echo of Nicole's tentative steps.

Were they still there after the second courtyard?

She was running now. Down the winding staircase, round, round, across the courtyard and down the next set of stairs. This time she didn't stop to admire any rooftops. Instead, she leaned over one of the walkways and looked down on the courtyard below.

She saw the motionless shape lying there far down on the ground and prayed that it wouldn't be too late. *Why do people do that? Pray, even though you don't believe, even though it never helped, completely pointless...*

She went down the last stairs three steps at a time and knelt beside Nicole on the ground.

The young woman was lying face down with her cheek against the ground. She was alive, but barely.

Her breathing was shallow, and her eyes were wide open in pain and surprise. There was blood underneath her. Blood all around, a pool slowly spreading. Berit took her in her arms and carefully turned her over. She wasn't sure if it would make things worse, but she didn't want her to lie there with her face on the ground.

"*You...*" Nicole said.

Berit wasn't sure if it was an accusation or a prayer for help.

"Everything's going to be all right," she said. "I'll call for help. I'll...fix it, somehow. I promise."

She felt a hand on her arm. It was surprisingly determined. "Stay."

Berit nodded. She got her phone out and called 999. An ambulance. Quick. A woman stabbed.

Nicole closed her eyes. "I didn't even see who it was."

"It doesn't matter."

The grip on Berit's arm tightened. "The ending of my book. You have to write it."

"Don't think about that now. You'll get help. You'll..."

"Promise." Nicole's voice was so weak it was only a painful breath.

Berit put her hand on hers. "I will finish it," she said.

"My name..."

"All over the cover. Bigger than the title."

A faint laugh turned into a painful cough. "You'll still have to do all the TV talk shows... For me."

"Anything," Berit promised.

The smell of blood overwhelmed and confused her until she could hardly remember where they were or why they had come here.

"I used to think you knew everything," Nicole said. Her voice was barely audible. "That you saw...everything. But you didn't see this coming. Not even you can fix this."

She focused her eyes on a point beyond Berit's shoulder. Her eyes dimmed. It was like her soul just slipped away. Everything that Nicole had been—stubborn, intelligent, ambitious, driven—disappeared from her face. All that was left was a vague semblance to her person, and Berit, alone, next to a lifeless body.

She lay down, exhausted, as if all her powers had been used up in the failed attempt to keep Nicole alive.

Clear blue sky. Framed by the beautiful buildings. The last thing Nicole ever saw. Something stung her eyes, and she realized in surprise, she was crying.

Outside the door, she could hear the usual sounds of the city. Busy footsteps. Laughing people. Sirens. She thought she could hear a door opening on one of the floors above and thought to herself that the murderer hadn't respected the residents.

She slowly stood up.

A few yards away was a bloodied knife, carelessly tossed away. She recognized it from the kitchen at Château des Livres. She could see Antoine chopping carrots. Emma with the pile of root vegetables. It had been so cozy.

Pointless thoughts. Illogical thoughts.

Something else on the ground caught her attention. Nicole's notebook. She bent down, picked it up, and put it in her jacket pocket.

46

THE FORENSIC TEAM LOOKED LIKE ghosts moving around the crime scene as they documented, marked, and collected everything of interest. White plastic overalls. White face masks. White shoe covers.

There was something disturbing about their completely covered shapes. Roche couldn't escape the feeling that perhaps they were perfectly dressed to investigate murders, but also to commit them.

The body had already been taken away. Laurent had personally been at the scene for a preliminary examination. He had glanced quickly at Roche's face and promised to perform the autopsy immediately. For a change, neither of them had made any jokes. He'd inspected and photographed the knife before forensics sent if off for analysis. Almost certainly the murder weapon, he'd agreed.

They had cordoned-off an area as wide as possible around the scene of the crime, but they'd had to leave a small corridor for the residents to come and go. Roche looked up at the walkways. So far, no curious faces were looking over the railings, but that would come. She wondered if going door-to-door would lead to anything and decided to task Janvier with it. If his mother-in-law was still visiting, he would be pleased with the assignment.

It soon got too crowded in the little courtyard, so Roche went outside to let forensics work undisturbed. She had placed uniformed police outside to make sure only residents got through and put police tape around the actual door.

Roche looked around.

To the right, Montée du Gourguillon led up toward Fourvière; to the right, three side streets met and formed a small square where tourists, students, and the people from the writer's retreat had started to gather. An outdoor seating area overlooked the square, and everyone there was following the police's work with keen interest.

The police cars and the forensic van had parked up in the alleyways nearby. *Old Lyon was a nightmare to work in*, Roche thought. The one-way streets were narrow, and the area was heaving with people.

Instinctively she looked for bloodstains on everyone who was there. How could the killer stab their victim several times without being covered in blood? She would have to ask all the participants if they'd noticed anyone changing since they'd last seen each other. But even if the killer had brought a spare set of clothes, where would they have changed? You couldn't just pull a bloodstained jumper off in the middle of the square.

She looked around. The outdoor seating area belonged to l'Alchemiste. They probably had a bathroom, but that didn't really solve anything. You couldn't exactly go in there covered in blood and ask if you could use it.

Across the street was a kiosk selling postcards, water bottles, and cigarettes at tourist prices. The owner, a fancy lady in her sixties, was standing in the doorway observing everything.

And on the other side of the square was a puppet theatre. A poster advertised daily performances at two, four, and six. A man was smoking at a rickety table in front of it.

That's right, Roche thought. Guignol came from these quarters. The famous figure in the Punch and Judy show was created by an unemployed silk weaver.

At the edge of the police cordon, Berit Gardner was standing with some other people from the retreat. She wasn't hurt—physically, at least. The paramedics had been first on the scene, and they had examined her, and forensics had already taken samples from her clothes. She'd tried to wipe them clean,

Roche noticed when she got closer, but there was no point. She knew from experience that blood didn't wipe off that easily.

As always, there were a thousand things that demanded her attention.

She should say a few calming words to the English people from the château. Maintain their trust in the police and all that, now that another one of them had been murdered. She wondered if that's what they were thinking: that someone was killing them off one by one. Did they imagine they were next? But their faces didn't convey fear. They were horrified, excited, curious, sad, all the usual feelings people experienced in a crisis. One looked sick. Berit hid her hands behind her back.

"I can't stand blood," the young guy said gratefully. Pale face, black hair, obviously dyed. Julian, that was his name.

Inspector Janvier had begun examining the area around the door. He shouted from a bin just outside the police cordon. He held up a scarf in a beautiful light green color. Everyone from outside the restaurant stared at it.

The scarf was covered in large, dark stains.

Blood.

Sally looked instinctively at Berit.

"Is it yours?" Roche asked Berit.

"Yes," she replied. She neither explained or excused herself.

The man outside the puppet show lit another cigarette and leaned forward. He followed it all with a chillingly greedy interest. Roche suddenly remembered that Guignol had become so popular by going around bashing authorities on the back of their heads. His favorite opponents were priests, politicians—and the police. Maybe the man outside the puppet show had an urge to do the same.

"Take Gardner to the station," Roche told The Mayor.

She turned to Janvier. "Knock on all the neighbors' doors. See if anyone's in and has seen or heard something. And good work with the scarf. Make sure it's sent off for analysis."

"Yes, boss."

She ignored the man outside the theatre.

Berit sat motionless and expressionless opposite them. Said nothing. Asked nothing. Didn't even complain about having to wait.

"Tell us what happened," Roche said and realized she sounded as tired as she felt. "Start from when you first arrived in Lyon."

Berit told them about the day, about Nicole following her, about the coffee at Broc' Bar and the walk they had taken together at a distance, so to speak. All the time, Berit's notebook remained shut next to her.

"It sounds like you were playing some kind of game," Roche said irritably. "A killer's on the loose! This is not the right time for childish games."

Berit looked down at her hands. They were only steady when they rested on the table. As soon as she lifted them up, they started trembling.

"And then you found her," Roche continued wearily. "Did she say something to you?"

"She said: *You.*"

"What? As an accusation?" It was The Mayor asking.

"I don't know."

Roche wiped her face with her hand. She didn't like the expression on Berit's face. It was shocked, yes, but also stubborn. Roche thought that the murder of the young woman should have made Berit realize she needed to stay the hell out of the police investigation. At least it had been a brutal awakening for Roche. She had given Berit too much freedom, but all that needed to end right now. If Berit had any sense she would realize that too. And answer all their questions promptly.

Yet she still had to drag ever word out of her.

"Your scarf," she said impatiently, "when did you last have it?"

Berit thought for a moment. "I know I had it in the kitchen yesterday. I must have hung it up on a chair and left it there. I was helping Emma chop vegetables for dinner and took it off."

"You recognized the kitchen knife, you said?"

"It looked exactly like the one they use at Château des Livres," Berit said. Roche nodded. She'd already given The Mayor the task of calling the cook to see if a knife was missing. The killer could have found the scarf at the same time they took the murder weapon.

"Do you know of anyone who might have had a reason to kill Nicole?"

"Nicole was…reckless. She wanted to solve the murder to write a book about it. I should have stopped her. I tried to, but…"

"So you think she might have got too close to the truth? She found something out that caused her death?"

"Maybe," Berit said hesitantly.

"Did she have a specific theory she was working on? About who the killer was, I mean."

"I would have thought she had several. But I got a feeling she wanted me to believe she knew more than she actually did."

"But she didn't share her suspicions with you?"

"No." A strange smile formed on Berit's lips. "Yes. She told me about one suspect she had."

"Who?"

"Me."

When Laurent came out of the autopsy room, Roche was waiting for him. The forensic department was attached to the university hospital, so he was preceded by a bunch of students dressed in white overalls, turquoise face-coverings, and boots. Laurent came out last, saw her leaned against the wall, and sighed.

"It's always worse when they're young," he said, looking as tired as Roche felt. "This ramps up the pressure on you, doesn't it?"

"The second murder in a week. A young woman killed. No real progress to talk about. Yes, you could say that."

He walked ahead of her to a corridor where he hung up his protective clothing and took his boots off. On a shoe rack were row after row of boots, some marked with only the shoe sizes for visitors and students, others with names.

She followed him into his office.

"You know I called the last murder merciful?" he said and sank down into his office chair.

Roche nodded.

"This is completely different," Laurent said. "Not refined at all. Attack from behind. Wild stabs. Excessive force. As if the perpetrator was surprised by their own brutality. You often see it in first-time offenders."

"You're not saying we're dealing with two different killers?" Roche objected.

"No, not necessarily. But it's probably the first time he or she commits such a physical and violent murder up close. The first was made from a distance. He or she never had to witness the consequences of their deeds."

"He's stepping up," she said. "That is, if it *is* a man. Any signs pointing in either direction?"

"The perpetrator wasn't much taller than the victim, but that doesn't give us much. According to my measurements she was five feet eight inches. You don't need to be particularly short if you're a man to be roughly the same height."

"A certain strength is needed to stab someone in the back," Roche pointed out.

Amateurs always underestimated how much strength it took. Certainly, there were soft parts in the back, relatively unprotected parts, kidneys, the spinal cord. But there were also many ribs. Easy to get it wrong and have the knife slip against the hard bones.

Laurent nodded. "What do you think about…regret?" he asked.

"Seven stab wounds in the back, doesn't sound to me like someone who feels much guilt."

"He—and I'm using the word for simplicity, spare me your feminist principles—has got himself worked up in order to be able to commit the murder. He attacks with speed. I think the energy of the movement helped him with the first cut. It's considerably deeper than the rest. An arm around her neck or upper part of her chest—a bruise has started forming—and then a deep stab to the kidneys, none of it enough to actually kill her."

Killing someone with a knife was unreliable. If you wanted to be sure to kill a person, you used a gun. Or at least slit their throat.

"No wounds on the front of the body?" she asked.

"Two. Stomach, pointing up. Punctured the spleen and the liver. Heavy internal bleeding. More deadly than the stab wounds in the back."

"But you're certain the perpetrator was standing behind her the whole time?"

Laurent got up, went to stand behind Roche, and put his arm gently on her shoulders and collarbone. "Stab one, two, three, four, five," he counted. Each time he touched her lower back lightly. She closed her eyes and imagined how Nicole's body had been pierced by the kitchen knife.

"She didn't necessarily feel any pain, you know," Laurent said. His breath was sour from coffee and nicotine. "Adrenaline. Surprise. Many people who are attacked by a knife report that they don't feel anything initially. The first thing they notice is the blood."

"How much blood would have ended up on the perpetrator?"

"Enough to stain his clothes, but not a blood bath. He was partially shielded by her own body."

"He or she covered themselves with a scarf."

Laurent nodded. "That should be enough."

He put his hand under her arm which she had instinctively raised to try and remove his arm from across her shoulders and chest. *That's how Nicole would have stood*, she thought. *She would have tried to fight them, even if it had been quick.*

"Six, seven," he finished. Two light prods with his fist against her stomach. Soft, unprotected, lots of inner organs that could be ripped to shreds. "She died from internal bleeding," he said and let go of her.

"Not immediately?"

"No, she would have been conscious for at least a couple of minutes."

"But you're saying she might never have seen her assailant?"

"I don't think so. He didn't want her to see him when he killed her, that's how I interpret it. Stab wounds to the back are rarely lethal. The stomach is much worse. But then you must be able to face the person you want to kill, eye to eye."

"So, you think deep down the perpetrator didn't want to kill her?"

"That's what I believe. When it's about revenge, they want the person to know who did it. Knife stabs to the stomach. In the back? It's almost apologetic. Did you notice how I held you?"

Roche nodded. "I could breathe."

"Exactly. It's almost like he didn't even really want to hurt her. A professional would have throttled her so she couldn't call for help."

"So you're saying we're dealing with an overly enthusiastic amateur who's ashamed of what he's done?" she concluded.

"Something along those lines, yes," Laurent said.

47

"YOU KNOW THE BOSS DOESN'T like you, don't you?" Janvier said. He was ridiculously dressed in jeans that were too tight and a leather jacket he probably thought made him look young. When they walked up all the steps at 2 Montée de Gourguillon, Philippe noticed with satisfaction that the bald patch on the back of Janvier's head had grown.

Philippe was dressed correctly in a suit jacket, and *his* hair was still reassuringly thick.

"Otherwise, she would never have sent you on such a meaningless mission," Janvier continued. "Door-knocking has never resulted, and never will result, in any sensible information surfacing. All that happens is that we get to talk to some crazy people."

"She sent you as well."

Janvier shrugged. "Someone has to keep an eye on you." He carried on his monologue while they ascended the stairs. "In cities, half of the people are here illegally, and the other half are up to something illegal. Most people are smart enough not to open the door when we knock. But not the crazy ones. Oh no. They've always at home, and they never have anything better to do than waste our time."

Philippe had to admit that at least Janvier was fit. Despite complaining about all the immigrants and the state of the world nonstop while running up the stairs, he wasn't even out of breath when they reached the top. Philippe had started to sweat on the first set of stairs.

They worked their way through every door in the stairwell that overlooked the spot where Nicole Archer had died, but to Philippe's chagrin, Janvier proved to be right. No one had seen or heard anything, apart from an elderly woman who had seen Jesus in the Cathedral Saint-Jean and who heard God talking to her every day.

"What does he say?" Janvier asked irreverently. The whole flat smelled of incense. Philippe thought about his old Catholic school and shuddered.

The woman pursed her lips. "That's between Him and me."

"What did I say?" Janvier said to Philippe before the woman had even closed the door. "Mad as a hatter."

Back in the street, they stood for a while in Place de la Trinité and looked around. Paintings of two of the figurines from the Punch and Judy show livened up one of the facades, and above them the statues of the Madonna and Petrus watched over them.

"We should talk to people out here as well," Philippe suggested.

"Listen, lad," Janvier said. *Jesus, he was barely five years older than Philippe.* "Cities are like a river. No one ever steps in the same river twice. Look at them. Tourists. Students. None of them were here three hours ago."

Philippe pointed at the restaurant, the kiosk, and the puppet theatre. "The people working there might have been."

"She's not going to respect you more for wasting your time." Janvier sighed, but he followed him into the restaurant.

Philippe showed a busy waiter his police badge. "We were wondering if you've seen two women here earlier today," Philippe said. He described Berit Gardner and Nicole Archer. "Some time just before two. Say from one forty-five to two. They entered that door across from your outside seating area. We think a third person followed them in."

The waiter looked at him with disdain. "How would I remember two women in a crowd?"

"One," Philippe corrected. "They entered one after the other. The older one first. Then the younger."

"Ah, well, you should have said. Of course. I keep track of every middle-aged woman who walks past. After all, it's not like I have anything better to do with my time, is it?"

"All right, all right. I get it," Philippe muttered.

Janvier smiled patronizingly.

The owner of the kiosk didn't remember anything either, but she was more than happy to talk to them. She offered them coffee from her machine and even seemed to admire Janvier's leather jacket.

"I would love to help if I could, handsome," she said apologetically. "But people go in and out of that door all day long. Mainly students."

Philippe nodded. There was student accommodation over at Fourvière too.

"These people had no key," Philippe said. "Perhaps they hung around the door and waited for the right moment?"

"Some do," the woman nodded. "They want to see *les traboules*. They don't know they have to be there before noon. A friend of mine lives there, and it drives her insane, all the activity."

"Could she have seen something?" Philippe asked with hope in his voice.

"I doubt it," the woman said. "She's in Montpellier visiting her grandchildren."

A group of tourists walked past on a guided tour, and Philippe stepped aside to let them pass.

He looked around the square.

There was a simple trestle table set up outside the puppet theatre where a middle-aged man was sitting. He seemed to be on a break. Philippe wondered if he'd been there when Berit and Nicole walked past too.

"You want to ask me about that murder, don't you?" the man shouted from across the square.

Philippe walked over to him and showed him his police badge. He looked around for Janvier, but he was still busy with the kiosk owner. She had made him another espresso.

Philippe swore to himself and turned back toward the man.

"This is not the first murder," the man professed.

His voice was strong and articulate. Every line he uttered sounded like a line from a play. There was something slightly surreal about him, as if he'd worked in theatre so long and didn't quite feel at home in the real world. The windows behind him were covered in posters that made Philippe feel like he risked ending up in a play if he wasn't careful.

"No, we're investigating it in connection to…"

"I meant, it's not the first murder that has been committed at that address. No one can forget the first one. It was gruesome. He chopped her up. They never found all the parts."

The man's voice was hypnotic.

Philippe had an unnerving feeling of being pulled into something he couldn't control.

"Philippe!" He flinched and saw Janvier waiving at him from the kiosk.

"I have to go back," he said, without being able to fully hide his relief.

"The rabbits made him do it!" the man called after him.

"Monique's offering us some *pain au chocolat*," Janvier hollered.

Philippe looked over his shoulder, but the man had suddenly disappeared. At first he thought he'd imagined the whole conversation, then he saw the sign in front of the theatre. PERFORMANCES AT TWO, FOUR, AND SIX EVERY DAY. It was five to four.

"For God's sake," Janvier said. "Why are you encouraging these lunatics? Here, have a pastry."

Philippe shook his head. "I'm heading straight out to the château," he said. Superintendent Roche was already there.

"Good. You can report back with all your progress," Janvier suggested.

Philippe would have told him to go to hell if the owner of the kiosk hadn't been there. He nodded curtly, ignored Janvier, and left.

The last thing he thought before he crossed Passerelle Saint-Georges was: *What the hell did he mean, the rabbits made him do it?*

48

WHEN PHILIPPE REACHED CHÂTEAU DES Livres, Béatrice Roche had already addressed the whole group. She was on her own in the library going through the list of participants in preparation for the interviews this afternoon.

"How did they seem when you spoke to them?" Philippe asked.

"The ones who knew her best were upset. As expected. The rest were… interested. A bit too interested, if you ask me."

"Anyone mention going home?"

"No, no one. Can you believe it? A murderer has struck twice, and none of them are even considering going home. They've got five days left, and they don't want to miss out on anything."

"Five days," Philippe said. "Not much time."

"Thanks, I realize that," Roche said. "Did the door-to-door give us anything?"

"No."

She shrugged her shoulders. "It had to be done," she said and got up and started pacing across the floor of the small room. "What do we know?" she asked.

"We know that feminist chick"—he realized he started to sound like Janvier after only an afternoon with him and made a face—"Claudia

Ramirez," he corrected himself. "We know she was in John's room. And there's something she's not telling us."

"True. And don't forget Rebecka and Charles. Those two still have the strongest motive."

"Now that there's a second murder, we might be able to eliminate more people from the investigation," Philippe said, sounding hopeful. "Some of them should have alibis."

"There's no such thing as a perfect alibi," Roche said. "That only happens in films. In reality no one remembers where they were or who they were talking to."

"Sure, sure," he said quickly. He made a mental note not to annoy his boss by being too positive.

Nicole Archer seemed to have been killed at precisely the moment when the group had maximum freedom, Roche thought despondently. The guided tour was over, and Emma had sent them away to "observe and take notes." Most of them seemed to have interpreted this as finding the nearest bar with outdoor seating and having a drink. Roche didn't blame them. By that time they'd been dragged halfway across town in the sweltering heat.

Most of them had chosen one of the tourist spots in Old Lyon, very close to where Nicole had been murdered. A simple thing, in theory, to notice Berit and then Nicole slipping inside the door and seizing the opportunity to follow them.

The killer had brought Berit's scarf and the kitchen knife, so they must have been waiting for an opportune moment to arise. And when it did, the killer acted quickly and violently. The murder had been both planned and impulsive.

Roche asked everyone she interviewed if they'd seen someone suddenly get up, excuse themselves in the middle of a conversation, or just disappear, but they all looked at her as if it was unreasonable to expect them to remember something like that. People got up all the time. They went to the toilet. Ordered another glass of wine. Got postcards from the souvenir shop across the road.

Nicole Archer had died sometime between twenty to two and ten to two, a fairly specific time frame that didn't help them at all. Several of them believed they had been at a bar at that time, but they couldn't be sure. Others had been on their way to one, but when pushed, they couldn't even remember which street they'd been on.

As Roche questioned them, one after the other, the sun set over the fields and a whole evening passed without her getting any closer to identifying who had killed Nicole.

"Who's next on our list?" The Mayor asked.

Roche thought for a moment. "Let's try Rebecka Linscott and Charles Tate again."

"Him or her?"

"Him. He feels like the weakest link."

Nicole's murder seemed to have finally made a crack in Charles Tate's confident surface. His eyes were wide open, and his hair stood on all ends as if he'd run his fingers through it in frustration or desperation several times.

"You can't seriously think I killed Nicole for, well, what? To protect my agency? For God's sake…"

"Tell us again about Rebecka Linscott's relationship to John Wright," Roche said.

"Haven't we talked enough about that?" Charles said.

"She embezzled his money."

"Not knowingly, I swear. It was just negligence on her behalf. You can't expect a person like Rebecka Linscott to know about bookkeeping. She was naive. It was a mistake."

"John Wright wanted to report her to the police," Roche said.

"Olivia averted that." He sounded exhausted suddenly, as if it had drained his energy just to admit that Olivia had helped him. "But after that, he obviously refused to have anything to do with Rebecka. Or me."

"What were you doing between twenty to two and ten to two today?"

"I was with Rebecka, at a bar."

"In Old Lyon?"

"No, on the other side of the river. By a square. A roundabout, I think. There was as sculpture of some kind… No, wait, it was a fountain. And it was close to that other big square," Charles said without certainty.

Roche got a map of Lyon on her phone and managed to work out that they'd been at some outdoor bar near Place des Jacobines.

"What did you do? Talk? Drink? Have lunch?"

"If you must know, we were working. Rebecka had been given a manuscript to read. She thought it had potential. She wanted to know what I thought."

"And what did you think?"

"The first hundred pages needed cutting—she was totally right about that—but, yes, there was something there."

"And you were with each other all the time?"

"Yes."

"Neither of you left? To go to the toilet, perhaps?"

"No."

"Did Nicole find anything out? About you or Rebecka?"

"I've told you we didn't have anything to do with that. Neither of us. My God, why would we want to hurt her?"

Roche was wondering if maybe he protested a bit too much. Could he really be sure he could speak for both himself and Rebecka Linscott, or was he trying to convince himself as much as Roche? When she looked closer, she could the see the pearls of sweat on his forehead.

"I know someone who definitely disliked John," he said. He sounded very eager to, what was it the English said, *throw someone under the bus.* "She even threatened to kill him."

"And who was that?" Roche asked.

"Claudia Ramirez."

"Why didn't you tell us this before?"

He shrugged. "I thought that was just something you said. He wrote an absolutely scathing review of her book. She was upset. You know how writers react if you criticize their books." He seemed to be thinking fast. "And I saw her yesterday. She was talking to Nicole. And it didn't look like a friendly chat either."

Roche paced across the library floor.

"That's a motive," she said. "A clear motive. And we already know she was in his room."

This could be the breakthrough they'd been waiting for.

The Mayor looked at her skeptically. "A bad review? Is that really something you'd kill someone for?"

"No, not normal people. At the beginning of this investigation, I would have thought it sounded ridiculous. But after a week in the company of these maniacs, I'm not too sure. Who knows what they're capable of?"

It looked like The Mayor was about to say something else, but he didn't. "If you say so, boss," he said eventually, but he didn't sound convinced.

Claudia Ramirez was clearly nervous, and she channeled her fear into aggressive confidence. After an initial glance around the room, she walked resolutely over to the armchair, sat down with her legs apart and leaned forward, hands on her knees, and stuck her chin out.

She seemed to be prepared to meet all their accusations, Roche thought.

"Tell us about your death threat against John Wright," she said.

Claudia looked at her in surprise. "My what?"

"Your death threat. After he'd reviewed your book."

Claudia looked at them in turn with an amused smile. "Is this what it's about? Who told you? My dear agent Charles? Remind me that I really need new representation."

"Just answer the question," The Mayor said harshly.

"Sure. Okay. Yes. I said I wanted to kill him, but that's just something you say? I only meant that I was… That I really couldn't stand him. I wouldn't have used physical violence, even if he'd been standing in front of me then, and this was more than six months ago. I still think he's an arsehole, but if you went around killing every male writer who's a jerk, the industry parties would be very poorly attended."

"He slated your book?"

"He 'reviewed' one of my books. He took pleasure in destroying me."

"So you made a death threat against him," Roche said.

"I was upset, I admit it, but not enough to actually *kill* him. We writers might be a bit crazy, but we don't go around killing people for one bad review. We channel it through other things instead. Like binge drinking or gossiping at parties."

"Which one did you choose?" The Mayor asked.

"Alcohol. Any more questions?"

"Did you have an affair with him?" he blurted out.

"Jesus, what is this? Why does everyone think I've slept with him?" She sighed and got her phone out and showed them her screensaver. "Look at this. A picture of my *wife*. And our two children. Can I go now?"

"Where were you between twenty to two and ten to two?" Roche asked.

"Same place I was all day. At a table in the shady part of the kitchen garden where it's dark enough to see the screen on your laptop. I was working, if you must know."

She sounded both defiant and proud at the same time.

"You didn't go to Lyon?" Roche asked. "How come?"

"Like I said. I was working. All the trips are voluntary. The teachers are expected to hold their workshops or lectures, but apart from that, we're free to do as we please."

"Can anyone confirm that you were here the whole time?"

"Well, the cook. She worked only a few meters away from me all day. Just before two, she treated me to a tuna salad for lunch. It was delicious."

Ten minutes later Roche had to admit that at least one person on the retreat had a perfect alibi: Claudia had been writing all day. She'd been right where the cook could see her.

"She was just writing, writing, writing," the cook said and shook her head. "She was lost in her own little world. She heard or saw nothing. She even forgot to have lunch!"

The cook flung her arms wide open as if to say: Have you ever heard anything so crazy?

"But I would have none of it, so I made her a tuna salad. When I'm in the kitchen, no one skips meals, I can assure you."

Roche was standing in the idyllic evening sun outside Château des Livres cursing quietly.

"Another fucking dead end," she said, more to herself than to Philippe. "This case is slipping away from me, I can feel it. We've got two deaths, and we're no closer to identifying the killer. In five days they all leave, and if we haven't solved it by then, we're not going to."

"I might have something," Philippe said. The words came out of his mouth before he'd had a chance to think. He should have kept his mouth shut, but he didn't like his boss's explosive restless energy as she paced up and down before him. It was almost worse than the fatalistic resignation earlier.

"A possible witness," he said. He already regretted it, but there was no going back now. He steeled himself for the ridicule he expected and added: "That man from the puppet theatre."

She stared at him. "The puppet theatre," she repeated.

"I noticed him when Janvier and I were going door-to-door. The theatre has performances at two, four, and six. Janvier and I were there just before four, and he was outside. If he was outside just before the show at four, he might have been…"

"There between just before two as well," Roche said. "Worth a try, I guess. Bring him in. See if you can make any more sense out of him in an interrogation room."

"Me?"

"It's your witness. Do it when you have some spare time. And when he's not performing, I suppose. But not first thing in the morning. A man from the English consulate wants to see us then. He wants to know what progress we're making."

"What will you say?"

"The truth, I guess. That we're not making any."

HEARTBEAT

I COULD HEAR THEM.

The whole time. Thump-thump, thump-thump, thump-thump. Hard and fast against my body. And they never *stopped*.

Why didn't she die? I knew someone could appear at any time. Her body was pressed against mine in a morbid embrace, and the smell of blood and perfume and sweat sickened me.

There was no time.

I felt no satisfaction about this murder. The murder of John Wright, it had some kind of finesse, elegance to it. Not this one.

But it had to be done. I had no choice. And it had to be done quickly. She was like a bloodhound on a trail. She would have exposed me, and she wouldn't have any qualms about doing it. Her book was all that mattered to her. I did what I did to protect everything that matters to *me*.

In the end I couldn't wait any longer. I pushed her away from me and escaped. And then the bloody door wouldn't open. I pushed the button several times, heard the buzz from the lock, but every time I pulled the handle, it remained locked. I could hear my own heartbeat then. It beat as fast as Nicole's had done. It took me several seconds before I realized I had to hold the buzzer and pull the handle at the same time.

What if I got caught because I couldn't open a goddamn door? Like I said. No elegance.

It wasn't until I'd thrown the scarf away and disappeared into the crowd, that I realized I should have stayed and looked for the notebook.

I can see her in my mind now, just as she was when she was alive: smiling, cocky, always with that bloody pen and notebook in her hand. She haunts me in death just as she did in life.

But how could I have looked for it? She was still alive when I left. Her heartbeat was still echoing in my head.

What did she write in that fucking book?

49

A YOUNG POLICE OFFICER DROVE Berit back to Château des Livres. She'd hardly got out of the car before Emma came running toward her. Her face was frozen in an unnatural smile, presumably meant to calm people down, but it looked more like a terrifying grin.

"What did the police say?" she asked as soon as she was close enough to Berit.

"Did you have anything to do with this?"

Emma flinched. "What do you mean?" she asked.

Berit's voice was stern and merciless. "Nicole," she said. "If you were involved in any way, if you hurt her... Or if someone else did on your behalf..."

"Berit!"

"John Wright threatened you," Berit said. "What did he have on you?"

Emma hesitated.

Berit grabbed her arm. "Listen," she said. "I never allowed myself to suspect you when John Wright was murdered, but I promise that if you had anything to do with Nicole, I will find out, and I will take you down. Your only hope is to tell me everything."

"But, Berit! I could never hurt her!" Emma objected. "Not Nicole. She was here for the retreat, for God's sake. I promised I would help her fulfill her dreams. I promised all of them. How could I have killed her then?"

Her face was honest and vulnerable. But Berit saw something else in her eyes as well, a reflection of her own feelings. *Guilt.* Neither of them had managed to protect Nicole.

"What did John have against you?" she insisted.

"It was Rebecka. He found out that she was also a teacher on the retreat the same day she arrived, and he did not like it, not at all. And…" Emma swallowed, and then rushed through it: "And we'd written in the welcome pack that we would offer all the participants a deal with Linscott Publishing at the end of the retreat. Only if they wanted to!" she added quickly, as if she anticipated Berit's reaction.

"Emma…" Berit said and shook her head.

"It was Rebecka's idea. I know what you're thinking. I should never have agreed to it. But it was totally up to them! And several of them were over the moon at being offered a publishing deal."

"With a woman who's embezzled money from another writer? And before they'd been given any advice from an agent, or even a chance to talk to other publishers?"

"That's exactly what John said," Emma said grumpily. "And then he said he would reveal everything in that book he was writing. After all I'd done for him…the ungrateful, hypocritical bastard."

Her voice trembled with anger. "But I didn't kill him for it. Jesus, I can't believe you think I could kill someone. I thought we were *friends.*"

"There's no place for friendship in a murder investigation," Berit said. Yet another thing she had learnt from DCI Ahmed. "What are you going to do now?" she asked.

"If it was up to me, I would send them all home immediately," Emma said. "I swear. I would never knowingly put them in any danger. But the police have asked me to continue as usual. And the participants don't want to go home, not even after this. They've all worked so hard…" She looked at Berit pleadingly. "The last five days are the most important! This is when they can really start to write, work on their own projects, and—"

"Even if you had nothing to do with Nicole's murder," Berit interrupted, and she was by no means certain that she hadn't, "she talked to you, didn't she? Just before her death?"

Emma swallowed. She licked her lips. Her voice cracked. "Yes, somehow she'd found out that John Wright had threatened to report me to the police."

Berit nodded. Nicole had seen Berit and Sally talk to Annie and done the same thing herself. And Annie had probably told Nicole everything. She wouldn't have stood a chance with her.

"But everything else Nicole said was completely incoherent," Emma complained. "She claimed to have seen me, just before your lecture, down by the stairs, where they think the murder took place. She threatened to go to the police if I didn't confess and tell her everything."

Emma grabbed Berit's arm. "But I didn't do it. I was serving coffee with Antoine. Everybody saw it."

Berit felt mentally and physically exhausted, but she couldn't rest now. Instead, she went up to her room and changed. Then she swam until her legs and arms hurt and she could no longer remember the metallic smell of Nicole's blood.

Not until then did she pull herself out of the pool with trembling arms. She looked at her phone. Quarter to six.

After getting dressed, she went to the kitchen and got herself a scalding hot cup coffee and went outside to the garden.

She had failed to protect Nicole, which should have been her top priority, but at least she could find out who did it.

Nicole would have wanted answers, and Berit would find them for her.

She shivered, even though the evening was warm, and had a sip of coffee. Then she reached for Nicole's notebook.

A life of writing had made her an expert on notebooks. This one was new and cheap, made to look old and expensive. Dark waxed cloth resembling leather, cream-colored, thin pages, unlined. Bigger than an A5, more square than an A4. Berit nodded in approval. A practical choice. She could have used one like it herself.

Berit opened it. There was something childish about Nicole's handwriting and her softly rounded letters. Her style was impulsive and seemed to change according to her feelings. Sometimes the words were neatly written, like it was the first day of school. Berit could practically smell the sharpened pencils and erasers (metaphorically speaking; just like Berit, Nicole only wrote in ink).

BERIT GARDNER'S LECTURE it said at the top of one page for instance.

And below a surprisingly moving account of Berit's thoughts about the writing life. *I want it!!* Nicole had written. *And I'm going to have it.*

Then her handwriting got more untidy, in some places unintelligible, from eagerness, inspiration or haste.

Why do women have affairs with men they can't stand? it said on one page, on the diagonal, words overlapping each other and the handwriting floating across the page every which way.

Berit remembered Roche's questions about another mistress on the retreat.

She had some more coffee and parked the thought temporarily.

Sometimes there was an unexpected sharpness and contempt in Nicole's notes. She had a way of finding out people's weaknesses and pretensions and making fun out of them.

She called Mildred *Elizabeth Taylor,* and she was dismissed with the words "mostly harmless."

And she constantly glorified herself, something Berit recognized from speaking to her.

Berit shook her head but couldn't help being drawn in by the confidence that danced across the pages. Even when Nicole was wrong, she saw it as a sign of her own excellence: She knew she'd been wrong before because she was right now. Conflicting interpretations were crammed in on the same pages without any excuses.

Berit found her own nickname and smiled despite herself: *Sherlock.*

Someone else was simply *The Writer.* Whoever it was, Nicole seemed to have got along with them. *The Writer says… The Writer thinks… The Writer means…*

Berit wondered what type of person Nicole would give that nickname. It was clearly more than a literal title. After all, the retreat was full of people who considered themselves writers. No, from what Berit had read in Nicole's notebook, it was more likely that it was someone who *didn't* write. Or a person who used to write, but no longer did?

Even though it was late, Berit stood up and got another cup of coffee. She doubted she would sleep much tonight. This time she also brought a glass of brandy. She needed it.

Berit opened up the notebook again and looked at the last pages.

The final entry read:

What did she do with the wine glass?

Telegram: Flee, everything has been exposed!

Who could walk around with a bottle of wine in broad daylight without drawing attention to themselves?

At least Nicole had answered that question herself with a sarcastic: *Writers!*

50

THE MAN FROM THE CONSULATE *was in his fifties and radiated such resentment that it seemed to have become chronic,* Philippe thought. Whining eyes. Whining lines around his mouth. Whining lips. His voice was loud and shrill and seemed to be constantly heading toward a new complaint.

"The foreign office is constantly on my back. Two British citizens have been murdered within a week of each other without even a suspect in sight! And one of them a young woman."

"We're doing everything we can," Roche assured him. Her voice was respectful but impersonal. "And we'll naturally keep you informed of our progress every step of the way."

"What progress?" the man said grumpily. He seemed to make every effort for his clothes not to touch anything around him. He sat with a straight back, his hands on his lap, his shoulders as far away from the dirty gray walls as possible. He couldn't avoid his shoes touching the floor, but he looked as if he would have liked to.

"Mrs. Wright is still in town," he said, "and hasn't been given any information about when she can expect her husband's remains."

"I'm afraid it will take a little longer," Roche said.

"And the media," the man from the consulate continued as if he was working his way through a list of his own suffering. "What are you going to do about them? The tabloids will make this seem like it's our fault somehow, mark my words."

Philippe was wondering if he wanted Roche to repeal three hundred years of the British freedom of press.

"So far none of the writers on the retreat has spoken to the media," Roche said. "Any information that is released goes through us. It helps."

"They're going to talk to them sooner or later," the man said gloomily. "Writers can never resist free advertising. I should know. My aunt is one." He shivered. "Poet," he added in a disapproving tone, as if that made things even worse.

Roche managed to get rid of him eventually. He left with slouching shoulders, tall, thin, and defeated by life.

"I don't know what the hell he wants you to do," Philippe said.

Roche shrugged. "Everyone's got their problems."

"The lab report is back," Philippe said. "About the knife. No fingerprints. But the cook has confirmed it came from the kitchen at Château des Livres. She's missing one. She identified it from a photo."

Roche didn't even comment. Her face was tired and haggard.

The on-duty receptionist called her mobile. "Commissaire Roche? There's an English hiker down here who wants to see you. Says it's about a Berit Gardner."

DCI Ian Ahmed from the Devon and Cornwall police looked around the office with professional curiosity. Roche pulled out an extra chair and placed it by her desk. He put his backpack on the floor and sat down.

"I got your message," he said. "You said you wanted to talk to me about Berit Gardner?"

"I didn't think you were going to show up in person," she said. It felt strange having him there all of a sudden. Just when she needed him the least as well. She had a new investigation to focus on and didn't really have time for courtesy visits.

Then she remembered the stubborn expression on Berit's face and decided not to get rid of him right away like she had first planned.

"What can you tell me about her, Detective Ahmed?" she asked.

He held his hands up. "Please, call me Ian. I'm on holiday, after all."

His face was tanned from weeks of hiking, and his body was fit. Muscular arms and legs. Black T-shirt, black hiking pants.

"Okay," she said. "So what do I need to know about her?"

Ian thought for a minute. He seemed to choose his words carefully. "She…notices things. She's one of the best observers I've ever met. Naturally curious, I think. And an intuitive sense for detail. She values loyalty, maybe too much. She's driven by a longing for community, which doesn't altogether sit well with her clear perception of human beings."

"You seem to know her well?"

"I've read several of her books now."

"Is she a friend of yours?"

Ian hesitated. "I wouldn't exactly call her a friend. But…have you ever met someone you felt an instant connection with? You're not friends, but you're not strangers either?"

"Yes," The Mayor said suddenly from his desk.

Ian and Roche looked at him, and he shrugged in embarrassment.

"She contributed invaluable insights during my investigation," Ian said more formally. "But she also drove me insane. She can be a bloody nuisance."

A bloody nuisance. Roche repeated the words in her head and filed it away for later. The French were experts at vulgar language, but the English had a fantastic way with everyday insults.

Ian looked back and forth between the two officers. He seemed to take in their attentive faces and tense body language. The department was bustling with life. There was a special atmosphere in the air, like at the beginning of an investigation when everyone is slightly overexcited.

"There's been another murder," he surmised.

"A young woman," The Mayor said. "Stabbed."

Ian looked intrigued. "Any suspects?"

"A whole château full of them," The Mayor said.

Roche cleared her throat. "I really appreciate you taking the time to come and see us," she said.

Ian smiled knowingly. "But you'll appreciate it even more when I leave?"

"As you said. There's been another murder."

He nodded. "I understand," he said.

She stood up. "What will you do now?"

"I might as well go and see her, since I'm in the area. If that's okay?"

Roche nodded. "Do you need a ride?" she asked.

"No, save your resources. I'll walk." He smiled hastily. "I've managed so far, after all."

He got up and picked up his backpack but lingered in the doorway. He threw a longing glance at the efficient but familiar chaos around them. For a moment he reminded Roche of one of those English foxhounds, alert, eager for the hunt to begin.

But this chase was not his. She held the door open for him cordially; he got the gist and left. She swiped her card and sent him down to reception. Just before the doors of the elevators closed, he said: "Don't trust her."

She put her hand between the doors, they opened again.

"Are you saying you think she might have something to do with the murders?" she asked.

"No, of course not. I'm just saying you should keep her as far away from your investigation as you possibly can."

Roche pulled a face. "Too late," she admitted.

"Then watch over her like a hawk," he said. "I know it feels like she knows our work when you talk to her. She has a way of asking questions that makes us believe she really understands. But she's not one of us. She'll do what *feels* right, not what *is* right."

51

BERIT STARED AT THE WHITEBOARD.

She had scribbled down all her thoughts about the first murder on it, and now she'd come back to compare it with her thoughts on the second one.

The first murder had been impulsive and unplanned. Berit had concluded it wasn't about revenge for something that had happened in the past. If someone had traveled all the way to France to revenge a wrongdoing in the past, they would have planned it better. Revenge involved dwelling on some kind of obsession, which she felt would resulted in meticulous planning rather than improvisation.

No, this murder was not about the past. It was about the future.

The way she saw it, there were two main alternatives: The murderer either wanted something to happen, or to prevent something from happening. Both were equally plausible.

She added the words *The creative life*. The whiteboard was so full of scribbles, she had to squeeze it in. She circled it several times. After all, that's where it all started, and it was the reason they were all there.

A dream, a longing, an urge—of writing, success, money?

Had John Wright stood in the way of some deeply felt desire or need? Had Nicole?

Berit ran her hand over her head. There were too many old and new thoughts in there, labyrinths and dead ends, semi-dismissed ideas that came back to haunt her. She got a headache just from looking at the chaos in front of her.

In the only remaining empty space she listed all the things she didn't understand:

Why steal John Wright's computer and notebook? (And why hide the bag in Rebecka's room?)

Who was the "mistress" Nicole wrote about in her notebook?

What the hell did she mean with "Flee, everything has been exposed"?

She couldn't work out what the killer could possibly gain from stealing John Wright's briefcase. A random idea that someone had wanted to get their hands on John's next manuscript was dismissed. Even if John, against all odds, had finished it, it wouldn't be of use to anyone, not without John Wright's name on the cover. The same book by an unknown author wouldn't exactly receive an advance of a million pounds.

And what had Nicole meant by the woman who had an affair with someone she couldn't stand? For a while Berit toyed with the idea that Rebecka could have had an affair with him when they were still working together, but she dismissed that as well. Neither of them had been interested enough in sex or some old-fashioned idea of romantic love to risk what was most important to both of them: their work and John's books.

But why had Nicole thought another woman could have had an affair with him? What had she misread?

Berit tapped her pen against her lips. Paced up and down. Her steps echoed in the silence. Down here it was dark and cool even in the middle of the day. She needed the stillness and coolness to think.

Suddenly she was acutely aware that she wasn't alone and quickly turned around. A tall shape appeared in the doorway. What little daylight there was came from behind him, so at first she couldn't see his face.

Once she had, she thought it was her brain overheating. That her subconscious had summoned him because she needed him.

She squinted. DCI Ahmed. It really was him.

"I was in the area," he said.

He looked like he'd walked all the way from England.

"Have you come to tell me to stop interfering with the investigation?" she asked. It was meant as a joke, but she realized how defensive she sounded.

"A bit too late for that now, isn't it?"

He walked up to the whiteboard without even removing his backpack. A tent was rolled up and attached to it at the top.

He seemed to try and follow all her thoughts on the whiteboard. His gaze was alert and focused, and as he was reading her chaotic scribbles, he looked more and more interested. For a moment he seemed to want to grab her pen and add something but caught himself in time and hooked his thumbs to the shoulder straps to avoid the temptation.

"I've only come to see if you have a washing machine," he said without tearing his eyes away from the whiteboard for even a second.

52

CHÂTEAU DES LIVRES HAD THREE washing machines and while Ian washed his clothes, Berit was standing by the work top where all his belongings were spread out. She seemed fascinated by how little you actually needed in life. Tent. Sleeping mat. His lightweight sleeping bag. Freeze-dried spaghetti Bolognese. Flashlight, pocket knife, first aid kit.

Half a book, brutally torn apart halfway through.

Berit picked it up. She couldn't help herself. It was one of her own. "If you didn't like it, you could have just stopped reading, you know," she said.

"It's for the weight. I only keep what I haven't read. A tip from Cheryl Strayed." He smiled. "Your books are too long."

His thoughts constantly went back to the murders. He was physically strengthened by his long holiday, and even if he was loath to admit it, Berit's whiteboard had kickstarted something he seemed unable to turn off.

He reminded himself it was Roche's investigation. He'd been impressed by her calm, confident demeanor. She clearly led a competent and close-knit team in a skillful way, and he knew better than to interfere.

Still, he couldn't deny that he felt tempted to go out there and solve the mystery. Curiosity was a big part of his work and personality, and he seemed unable to switch off even when he wasn't working. On the contrary, the extended holiday had given him more energy.

Maybe I can be of some use.

He was convinced Berit would continue to interfere. He also knew she was stuck. *She had started the jigsaw puzzle before she had all the pieces.* The solution was always to step back and start answering the different questions, one by one, until the tangled threads unraveled and you could go back and see the full picture.

But she couldn't do it alone. She needed fresh eyes, and he could help.

Berit knew the people here, he knew investigations, together they could offer Roche some useful help. He already had an idea based on what he'd seen on the whiteboard.

He shook his head. Roche needed their help as much as she needed a broken leg.

He blamed it on the holiday; it did strange things to him. And he wasn't used to being on the sidelines of an investigation, just observing. He felt like an athlete on the bench, and even though intellectually he knew Roche would do just as good a job, it wasn't the same as being out there on the pitch himself.

While he was thinking, he looked at Berit. There was something fragile and vulnerable about her that he hadn't seen before. It bothered him more than he cared to admit. Until today, he'd been sure that no one in the world needed his protection less than Berit, but when he looked at her now, her eyes said *help me*, loud and clear.

He wondered if she was aware of it.

He had met many people like her, who were hurt, but didn't realize it themselves. He'd seen a person lose a hand to just stand there in shock without even realizing it. Same about the soul. Someone could be fatally injured and believe they could carry on as normal. If you didn't watch them, they could trick themselves and everyone else into thinking they didn't need any help. No thank you, no need to call anyone. Oh, no, I don't need to talk about it, I'm just fine.

But they weren't fine. They never were.

It was probably best if he stayed around for a couple of days. It wasn't like he had anything better to do. All he needed was somewhere to pitch his tent.

They offered him a room instead, a simple room with a narrow bed, a wardrobe, and a stool that doubled up as a bedside table. After three weeks in the mountains, it felt like luxury. He put his clean clothes on a shelf in the wardrobe and went to find Berit.

He found her on the terrace with her nose in a notebook.

He got them each a beer and put her glass down on the table in front of her. He remained standing looking out over the fields and the endless sky above them. She didn't even look up from her book. He presumed she was already used to the magnificent view.

He shook his head, sat down next to her, and took a deep sip of his beer and sighed contentedly.

"One thing you realize when you've been out hiking for a while is how incredibly delicious it is to just sit down with a cold beer."

Berit didn't even seem to hear him. When she started talking it was like she was in the middle of a train of thought she'd mulled over many times.

"I know what kind of person I am," she said gravely. "I'm judgmental, condescending, convinced of my own excellence…"

"Not just that," Ian said. He could list plenty of other, more positive traits as well.

"I'm so used to being on my high horse, I could be a circus performer. I criticize people for being obsessed with status, of maintaining a successful appearance. But what do I know about the real world? I moved to a cottage in Cornwall to get away from it. The truth is I judged Nicole because she wanted to be famous, and because I didn't take her seriously, I put her in danger. But how was I to know the killer would act so quickly? I thought everything would be fine as soon as she told them she wasn't interested in solving the murder anymore. Stupid. Stupid!"

She told him about the circumstances regarding the murder and finished bitterly: "So you see. If I hadn't led her away, if I hadn't lured her into that stairwell… It's my fault she's dead."

Ian grabbed her arm, hard enough to make her flinch. He didn't let go.

"This is unworthy of you, Berit," he said. "It's the killer's fault she's dead. No one else's. Blame must be placed where it belongs."

"Perhaps. But I should have done more. Talked to her. Made her understand. Convinced her how dangerous it was to interfere with a murder investigation."

"Do you think it would have made any difference? I hear writers can be pretty stubborn."

Berit didn't smile. "It would have mattered to me. So you see, I owe her this. The ending to her story."

"We don't owe the dead anything. We can't reach them anymore. Our only debt, if we have one, is to the living."

"Okay, then let's say I owe the ones who are still here an answer."

Ian stood up and walked over to the railing with his beer.

"I'm stuck," she said, from over at the table. "There are too many loose threads, too many possibilities. I've become blind to the material. Do you remember that time when you came to my cottage to…what did we call it?"

He nodded without turning around to look at her. "Go over the cast of characters. Yes, I remember."

"That's where I am now. I need a sparring partner. I have to say things out loud and take myself out of my own head."

"Tell me about John Wright and his notebook," he suddenly said. "That was on top of the list of things you didn't understand."

"They were missing after the murder. The briefcase they'd been in were found in one of the rooms, but the computer, the notebook, and some other notes are still missing."

"Have they looked for them?"

She told him about the room and body searches.

"If something doesn't fit, it's always possible it's not related to the murder. I know policemen don't believe in coincidences."

"Writers are even more skeptical."

"But sometimes they do occur. The trick, when you're stuck, is to go through everything systematically. Dismissing the false leads so you can remove them from the investigation."

"And how do we do that?" Berit asked.

Ian hesitated. "We need the lists of all the things that were found in their rooms. But Roche would never give anyone outside the investigation access to them."

Berit stood up and went over to him. For a long time, they just stood there next to each other in silence and watched the sun embed the fields in a warm soft light.

When she spoke again, her voice was distinctly neutral. "She might let a visiting colleague go through them though."

"Berit…"

She looked at Ian, really looked at him, and for the first time it seemed she allowed him to really see her.

"I don't think I can do this without you," she said.

53

YOU'RE A BLOODY IDIOT, IAN Ahmed, he said to himself.

Up there on the terrace, in the warm evening sun, with the view over the vineyard, the hills and infinity, for a short moment he'd thought it wasn't that much to ask. Not when you thought of how much she needed it.

In the cold light of the police station, the sheer thought of it seemed absurd.

What would he say?

Excuse me, Superintendent Roche, but I was wondering if you could let a civilian friend of mine read parts of your report?

When Roche came down to meet him in the reception, it became even clearer what a crazy idea it was. She looked tired after a long day at work. She moved resolutely but without wasting any more energy than necessary. Went from A to B in an almost military fashion, as if the body was a power tool whose energy should be preserved.

"What can I do for you, DCI Ahmed? It's pretty late."

This time he didn't ask her to use his first name. Perhaps he needed to remind himself where his loyalty lay.

"Nothing. Nothing at all," he said. He hesitated, but he had to think of a reason for his visit. "I just came to see if I could be of any assistance?"

"You've seen her?"

He nodded.

She looked at him with something akin to understanding. "And she managed to persuade you to do something? That's why you're here interrupting my work?"

He smiled apologetically and shrugged his shoulders.

She shook her head. "What did you promise her?"

"I said I would ask if she could see the lists of what you found when you searched the rooms."

"No." The answer came immediately. "Out of the question. I have a great respect for you and the English police, but Berit isn't... Madame Gardner is a member of the public. I can't pass any information on outside of the investigation."

"Of course. Naturally. I completely understand. I...I just said I'd ask."

Superintendent Roche ran her fingers through her hair. "I questioned her just after she found the body," she said. "So I understand you. I do. I just can't help you. Tell her to stay away from the investigation. Otherwise, I'll arrest her."

"She's not going to let this go."

"Tell me something I don't know."

"It was just a shot in the dark anyway," Ian said when he met Berit at the château. "It might not even have worked. But I thought that since they didn't search the people at the same time as they searched the rooms, there was always a chance they didn't link the two searches together."

"What do you mean?" she asked.

"A computer, a notebook, those are non-specific things to look for in this environment. Everyone's got one. If you find a computer in one of the rooms, you would check that it wasn't John Wright's, but would you also double-check that the person hadn't brought a computer to Vienne? Perhaps not. Same thing about his notebook. People can have several, after all... I wanted to compare the two lists, that's all." He shrugged. "It was just a thought."

Berit considered this.

"Yes," she said. "And a very good one too. Maybe…" She looked around. Most people were changing for dinner, except Claudia, who was in the garden writing as usual. "I wonder if we might just have to do it the hard way," she said.

"Excuse me?"

"Don't worry. All you have to do is keep an eye out."

A while later Ian was keeping watch in the door leading to the hallway, manically listening to any sound that suggested someone was coming. Berit breezily assured him no one would.

"They're in the middle of dinner," she said and checked her watch. "They haven't even finished the main course."

"*I* should be in the middle of dinner," he said. "Instead, I'm here as an accomplice to burglary."

"You'll thank me for it later," Berit said. "The cook has made andouillette. And you're not much of an accomplice. You're just standing there."

She held up Nicole's notebook. "What you said made me think of something else as well. Another thing I didn't understand. Nicole wrote that John Wright was having an affair with a woman who couldn't stand him. I was always convinced he wasn't. John didn't like women. One affair was unlikely, two affairs almost impossible."

"I'm sure his wife is grateful," Ian muttered.

"Show, don't tell," Berit continued. "It's advice usually given to writers. Instead of telling the readers that someone is angry, for example, you show him raising his voice or slamming his hand down."

"Sure. But if it's a lecture on writing we're after, we could have done it somewhere else. At dinner, for example."

"I told you I asked the cook to save you a portion. Not that I recommend having it, so don't come crying to me later."

Berit turned her back on him and continued her search of the room. She went through the wardrobe, the desk, looked under the bed, in a decidedly unprofessional manner.

Ian was itching to take over to make sure it was done properly. Berit hadn't even checked the jacket pockets or the shoes.

"In any case," she said while looking. "Nicole clearly didn't believe in show, don't tell. She wrote down her own interpretations, not what she'd actually witnessed. So, what would make a person like Nicole think that someone was having an affair with John Wright?"

"Looks between them?"

"Too subtle. I don't think she was that much of an observer. She was really only interested in herself."

"Standing close to each other talking?"

"Maybe. But there's another possibility: She could have seen her coming out of John's room."

"She could have seen anything," Ian pointed out. "Impossible for us to know."

"Sure, that's why I focused on the last part of the sentence. We're looking for someone who couldn't stand him."

"From what I've understood it doesn't narrow down the field much," Ian said.

"Again. It must have been someone who made it obvious enough for Nicole to notice," Berit said as she picked up a power cable and a laptop. She opened it up and turned it on. A picture of Claudia Ramirez prompted them to put the password in. "Look outside. We're not the only ones missing dinner."

He scanned the hallway before leaving the room to look out the window. In the garden Claudia Ramirez was on her own at a table. A plate of food was untouched next to her.

She was writing furiously.

On a computer.

"Just like you suggested," Berit said.

54

IAN AHMED WAS HOLDING A plate of andouillette sausage, gravy, and potatoes. Berit was holding Nicole's notebook.

"Can we sit down?" she asked.

Claudia looked like she wanted to say no, but eventually she shrugged her shoulders and said: "Do as you please."

Berit and Ian sat down, and Ian got to work on the sausages.

Berit glanced at him before she turned to Claudia and nodded toward the computer. "Clever, putting that sticker on the computer. Together with the pink case, it was enough to make anyone believe it couldn't have been John Wright's. But you still took one hell of a chance."

Claudia froze when Berit started talking, but then it was like she came to some sort of acceptance and relaxed. In the end she looked almost relieved.

"I didn't exactly have a choice," she said. "I didn't even think it through before I stole the briefcase. It was pure impulse. And then, well, I had to deal with it the best I could."

"What did you do with his notebooks and the other papers?" Berit asked.

"Oh, I destroyed them immediately. I couldn't run the risk of anyone finding them. The notes were easy, of course, but the notebook was a bloody problem. Eventually, I buried it under a rock in the darkest part of the kitchen garden. But the briefcase was too big to bury."

"So you planted it in Rebecka's room. Did you know she'd embezzled John's money?"

Claudia shrugged. "She'd rejected two of my books. And I had to hide it somewhere. I was sure the police would search our rooms sooner or later."

Ian suddenly cursed next to them. He'd swallowed the first bite and his face twisted in disgust.

"What the hell is this?" he asked. He cut another slice and smelt it suspiciously. "It smells..."

"Like shit," Berit said. "It's a sausage made from intestines and offal, what had you expected? The large intestine by the look of it. Bon appétit." She turned toward Claudia again. "Did you steal the briefcase in order to destroy the diary?"

Claudia hesitated. "I'm not sure what I was thinking," she admitted. "He was so condescending and talked about how he would out everyone with his diaries, and I was convinced he'd written something about me... I guess I just wanted to know what it was."

"Did you destroy the notebook before you buried it?" Ian asked suddenly.

"Yes, I cut it up." There wasn't a hint of remorse in her voice. "And dissolved it in water. Then I buried the remains. It's harder than you think to destroy a book, but I can guarantee that no one will ever read that crap again."

"And then you killed him," Berit said. Her voice was harsh and merciless. "I don't really care what pathetic excuse you came up with in your head. But Nicole Archer. What had she done to you? How could you?"

She could see Ian shaking his head in the corner of her eye, but she didn't care.

Claudia stared at her in panic. "No," she said. She grabbed Berit's arm. "You have to believe me. I'd never kill Nicole."

"And John Wright?" Ian asked.

"I wanted to kill him. I'm not going to deny it. But I didn't. It was only a fantasy. You know what it's like," she added and turned to Berit.

"Sure," Berit said and wriggled her arm out of Claudia's grip.

Ian looked at her strangely.

"We're writers," Berit said to him. "We're used to imagining things. What would it be like...what would happen if..."

"Like: What would it be like to kill John Wright?" Ian said. "What would happen if he died?"

"Sure," Berit agreed. "We imagine ten things before breakfast. That's why I never understand writers who say they could never have dreamt of their books becoming successful. You're not much of a writer if you can't even imagine that, are you?"

"Exactly!" Claudia said excitedly. "But they're just thoughts. You wouldn't do it in real life. And never Nicole! Never!" Claudia leaned forward and said pleadingly: "I admit Nicole suspected me…"

Berit made a face. "She seems to have suspected most of us," she said.

"She saw me leave John's room and thought I was having an affair with him." She shook her head.

"She wasn't a particularly good judge of character," Berit said.

"But no matter how much I fantasized about killing John, I never even thought about killing Nicole. She was so young and driven…"

"I know," Berit said. She believed Claudia.

"And…what happens now, with the computer? Will you tell Roche about this?"

Berit shrugged. "The theft is none of my business," she said. "And, after all, I've promised Superintendent Roche not to interfere."

"So suddenly it's fine wanting to kill middle-aged men?" Ian commented afterward. He had managed to finish his dinner, and they were on the patio outside the kitchen having a beer. For the first time since arriving at Château des Livres he felt almost relaxed, but that in itself worried him. Somehow, he'd allowed himself to be drawn into Berit's investigation. He smiled wearily at himself. It hadn't taken much persuasion, he had to admit. In fact, he'd willingly thrown himself at it, and no matter how much he wanted to deny it, he was pleased and proud about the progress they'd already made. They were a good team.

Berit had a sip of beer. "He was a very difficult person to deal with," she said.

He looked at her briefly. "Did *you* ever…?"

"No, I actually liked him in his own kind of way. People can be jerks but still be interesting. And surprise you with a sense of humor and some self-awareness when you least expect it. Doesn't mean he was a good person, obviously."

"But at least multifaceted?" Ian suggested.

Berit nodded. "Most people are, if you dig deep enough."

"Do you believe Claudia? That she didn't kill them?"

"I think she told the truth. Not just because she sounded very convincing when she spoke about Nicole, I remembered something else as well. In the notebook Nicole jumps backward and forward all the time. I think she meant for her notes to be thematic rather than chronological. And right next to where she'd written about the affair—that we know was about Claudia, only they never had an affair—she'd added: What did she do with the wineglass?"

"The wineglass that contained the poison that killed John Wright?" Ian guessed.

"Exactly. I think Nicole realized what I just thought of: If she saw Claudia leaving John's room with his briefcase, where had she hidden the wineglass? She couldn't have thrown it into the case with everything else. And wouldn't it have been easier to give him the wine in his room?"

"That's true," Ian admitted.

Berit got up. "I'm crossing that lead out. The theft of John's briefcase had nothing to do with the murder."

It didn't appear to be a positive realization. Her voice suddenly sounded sad and dispirited, and very tired. "All this time since Nicole died, I've asked myself what it was she knew. But it occurred to me today that she might not have found out *anything*."

"What do you mean?"

"It was enough for the killer to believe she had. Nicole bragged to everyone about how much she knew. She kept saying she had 'information that the police didn't even know about.' She claimed she was going to solve the crime before…"

"Before the police?" Ian suggested.

"No," Berit said. "Before *me*."

Ian looked at her suddenly. "What did you mean when you were talking about what was in Nicole's notebook? How do you know what's in it?"

Berit looked at him in surprise. "Because I've read it, of course."

"But…when? Don't the police have it? If it was in her room, they must have found it straightaway. Surely, it must have been the first place they looked?"

"It wasn't in her room."

"Berit, have you withheld important evidence from the police?"

"I've got a better chance of understanding Nicole's notes than they have. I've only had it for a day, and I've already deciphered several things in it. I even think I understand what she meant by '*Flee, everything has been exposed.*'"

"That's beside the point. You can't…"

"She was twenty-five, Ian. And she thought she was invincible, like so many twenty-five-year-olds do. She died in my arms because I failed to protect her. I'm not going to let her down now."

"I hope you're not going to use her in a book."

The words came out of his mouth before he could stop himself. She looked hurt, but she didn't say anything. Instead, she just walked off and left him alone with his guilt and conflicting loyalties.

You can be such a bloody idiot sometimes, Ian Ahmed, he said to himself for the second time today.

WHAT DOES BERIT KNOW?

WHAT HAS SHE FOUND IN *that notebook?*

That's the only thing I can think about right now. I see her bent over it, and I break out in a cold sweat about what she might find in there.

The murder of John Wright made me feel mighty as a lion. The murder of Nicole makes me tremble like a hare. What a cliché. Can you see what Nicole's death has done to me?

No wonder I can't write.

I've waited for an opportunity to steal that notebook, but Berit won't let it out of her sight for a second. She probably sleeps with it under her pillow.

Nicole was a threat that needed eliminating, but Berit is much more dangerous.

When Berit looks at me, I'm convinced she knows exactly what I've done. The temptation to confess overwhelms me. *Just tell her. Maybe she'd understand.*

It's the anxiety talking. And the loneliness. The longing to confide in someone. Sometimes she looks at me with kindness, then the temptation grows stronger.

Why can't she just let it go? Why does she have to stick her nose into everything?

If only Nicole had let it rest too. Then we could have continued this writing retreat as if nothing had happened… Everybody would have been happier then, wouldn't they?

And now Berit's talking to that English policeman. If she forces me to, I'll… I don't know what I'll do. I just know I've come this far, and I'm not going to give up.

Only four days left to go.

Why won't she stop interfering?

55

PHILIPPE'S NICKNAME FOR HIM WAS the Dollman, and even though it was late, he was still sitting outside the theatre in Place de la Trinité.

It was seven in the evening, and the square was busy. The outdoor seating area was bustling with tourists and students. Yet the man noticed him straight away. It was like he'd been expecting him.

"You want to know more about the first murder, don't you?" he said when he saw Philippe.

"I want to know if you saw something yesterday between twenty to two and ten to two."

"A man walks into a police station in Paris. Doesn't say a word. No matter what the police asks him. Not a word. Eventually they find a letter in one of his pockets. It's a letter to his wife who lives at…"

"Number 2 Montée du Gourguillon," Philippe said.

"You catch on quickly. In the letter he confesses to a horrific crime and asks for forgiveness. The police call your station here in Lyon and the police go over and knock on her door."

"Let me guess. They find the wife murdered in the flat?"

"Oh, no. They find her very much alive."

"So what's the crime?"

"It was the mistress he had murdered. Chopped her up into seventeen pieces and cast her into large concrete blocks. He had a workshop in the flat. That's where he did it. The police searched it and found pieces of her. But not all of them. The head was never recovered. But do you know what the weirdest thing was?" the Dollman asked.

"Where you out here between twenty to two and ten to two yesterday?" Philippe said. "Did you see anything? Two women, they would have walked straight past you."

"The entire workshop was full of rabbits. It was crawling with them. That's when he told the police. Why he killed her."

"What did he say?"

"Because the rabbits told him to."

Philippe shuddered. He was an idiot wasting his time, and even worse, he wasted valuable investigation time. He decided to not even mention this visit to Roche. She had enough on her plate as it was.

He was just about to leave when the man said: "Don't you want to know what I saw then?"

The Dollman was called Bernard Corbin.

He had agreed to come to the police station the following morning, and removed from his natural environment, he looked much more normal. He was dressed in a creased thin shirt that was already damp with sweat. His hair was unkempt. His nails stained with nicotine. He came across like a man who lived on his own and didn't look himself in the mirror often enough. Philippe promised himself never to turn into him.

"Tell us about the murder," he said.

Roche was in the interrogation room too, but she let him lead. *It's your witness*, she'd said.

"The current one," he hastened to add.

He had checked out the case Bernard had talked about. A man by the name of Léon Collini had indeed confessed to the murder of his mistress, Maria Corigliano, but the murder had happened in 1936, so it wasn't exactly current. He hadn't mentioned it to Roche, and he didn't want to go into it now.

"I sit there often," Bernard Corbin said. "In the square, that is. I work in the theatre box office, so I sell tickets to the shows and check them when people go inside."

"And you were there yesterday?" Philippe asked.

"Sure. And I see things. You notice things that stand out if you're in the same spot all the time."

"And something stood out?" Philippe guessed.

"There are mostly students and old people at that address. Either or. They come and go at different times."

Philippe imagined he probably kept a close eye on the young female students.

"And then you have the tourists. You recognize them immediately. Tourists walk slowly, they carry their phones in their hands, and look up at the buildings. Students walk fast, have their phones in their hands, and look down at them."

"Clever," Roche said admiringly. Philippe presumed she had come to the same conclusion about Bernard Corbin and wanted to see how he reacted to flattery.

The man straightened. "It was the rhythm, you see. A woman walks through the door. Middle-aged. She slipped in when a student came out. Nothing unusual about that. She looked around, so I thought she must be one of the tourists who sometimes sneak in to see it. The *traboule*, I mean."

"We know," Philippe said impatiently.

"But there was a younger woman close behind, who also sneaked in, and that's unusual. I mean what are the odds? It felt like they were linked."

Roche leaned forward eagerly. "And after that? Did you see anything else? Did anyone follow the second woman?"

"I wouldn't know. I went inside. The show was about to begin."

Roche swore quietly to herself.

"She had a notebook in her hand," the man said suddenly. "I thought she might be a journalist. She had that energy. Hungry. Curious. Was she?"

"Writer," Roche said. "The middle-aged woman with the notebook. She's a writer."

"What? No, she didn't have the notebook. It was the second one. The good-looking one."

Roche stood up and left the room.

Philippe concluded the interview quickly and hurried after her.

He found her by her desk, where she was going through the documentation of the investigation. Over her shoulder he saw how she went through the photographs from the scene of the crime, and then the list of things found in Nicole's room.

"That bitch," Roche said. *"That bitch."*

She slammed the file shut and grabbed her jacket from the back of the chair.

Philippe ran after her, threw himself into the passenger seat of her car, and had hardly closed the door before she'd swung out, switched on the blue lights, and drove off.

Less than half an hour later they skidded onto the gravel track outside Château des Livres. They hurried around the building to the garden where people were having their breakfast. Roche went straight up to Berit.

"Berit Gardner," she said. "I'm arresting you—"

"Boss," Philippe said hesitantly, but Roche ignored him. "For obstructing a police investigation, interfering in things you have nothing to do with, and being a fucking idiot. Philippe, handcuffs, please."

"Are you sure that…" he began, but she took them off him and pulled Berit up by the arm.

Berit didn't object. She didn't even say anything. Just placed her hands behind her back and let Roche handcuff her.

Philippe led her to the police car. He put his hand on her head as he placed her in the back seat. For a moment a sad, almost melancholic, expression came over her. Then she smiled ironically and shook her head.

"First time I'm arrested, and I can't even take notes," she said.

56

CHIEF SUPERINTENDENT PELISSIER WAS *NOT* a happy camper, as the American expression went. She had been forced to come in on her Sunday off, and she was glaring at Roche from behind her desk.

"I understand you were angry that she'd withheld evidence," she said. "But did you have to go and arrest her? Soon we'll have a lawyer here or that sour man from the consulate."

"She's a Swedish citizen," Roche reminded her. "Swedish passport."

"Either way, I don't want to be involved in this, do you hear me? I don't want any trouble. Especially not with The Mayor involved in the case."

"My name's Philippe," The Mayor politely pointed out.

"Of course it is," Pelissier said and glared angrily at Roche as if it was her fault that she'd accidentally called him The Mayor to his face.

"I'll release her tomorrow," Roche promised. "Twenty-four hours in the cell might calm her down, and at least it won't hurt."

"You release her the same second a lawyer gets involved, okay? We don't want them accusing us of harassing tourists. There's no worse police brutality than disrupting tourism; you know that as well as I do."

"Sure."

"Don't make me regret I'm giving you free rein here."

"You won't regret it," Roche said. "Trust me."

"Nothing good has ever come of the words *trust me*."

"I know what I'm doing. I promise."

The boss's look told her she didn't believe in it for a second but sent her away with an annoyed wave of her hand.

Roche was by her desk, mechanically eating an uninspiring salad straight from the plastic container. All morning she'd waited for Berit to demand to speak to a lawyer, but nothing happened. She found her phone in the mess on her desk and called up custody to find out what was going on. Everything's fine, the bored voice on the other end reported back. *Relax, we know how to deal with middle-aged tourists.*

Roche hung up. She spent a couple of hours on the notebook, then reached out for the phone again but changed her mind. Better to check in on her in person. She went down to the custody building and met the duty guard just after he'd done his rounds. Everything was quiet.

"What's she doing?" Roche asked. "Is she talking? Complaining?"

"She's lying on her back. Every now and then she gets up and stares at the wall. That's it."

"She hasn't demanded to see a lawyer? Contacted her consulate?"

"She's saying nothing. See for yourself."

Roche did. She went over to Berit's cell and slid open the little hatch in the door, where a tray could be placed or you could check up on the detained.

Berit lay on her back on the narrow bunk. Her eyes were open, and she was staring at the ceiling with such intensity that Roche automatically looked up herself. The ceiling was painted a pale green color some overpaid consultant must have decided was calming. Hardly worth the attention.

She closed the hatch.

"Report back to me if anything happens."

The call came, not from jail, but from the reception at the police station. "We've got a girl down here who demands to speak to you," they said. "We've told her you're busy, but she won't leave until she's spoken to you."

For a split second, Roche thought Nicole had been resurrected and was there to haunt her, but it was Sally Marsch, Berit's agent, and it turned out, defender.

When Roche met her in reception, she was upset: "Where is Berit? Is she okay? I demand to speak to her!"

"She's not accepting visitors at the moment," Roche said dryly.

"In that case, I'll talk to a lawyer. Or the media. I'm sure they'd be interested in knowing you've arrested a famous writer."

They probably would be, Roche admitted to herself. "Okay," Roche said. There was no point in creating unnecessary trouble. "I'll see what I can do."

"Don't make me call my mum about this!" Sally shouted after her.

Roche was back ten minutes later. "She's not seeing visitors," she said.

Sally made herself look tall and resolute.

"You give me no other choice than to…"

"You misunderstand," Roche said. "I spoke to Berit. I told her you were here and offered to let you see her. She says she's thinking and doesn't want to be disturbed."

Roche was at her desk all evening, hunched over the photocopied pages from Nicole's notebook. At the opposite desk, Philippe was hunched over his copies of the same pages.

He looked as tired and frustrated as she felt. His skin was pasty, and he had dark rings under his eyes. Next to the photocopies was a deserted half-eaten baguette.

He looked up as if he could feel her eyes on him.

"We're not getting anywhere," he said.

She was acutely aware of this. "What's with this telegram?" she said for the fourth time. "'*Flee, everything has been exposed?*' What's exposed? Is she talking about the murder? Something else?"

"Rebecka's embezzlement? But who was she going to send a telegram to?"

"Are you sure she's not sent a telegram in the last few days?"

"We've gone through her phone and her computer. Nothing in the search history on how to send a telegram. She hasn't visited any of the pages you can send one from. We're still waiting for the bank statements from the English police," Philippe said.

They would have to wait a while, Roche thought. Bureaucracy across borders always dragged on.

"But there is nothing that suggests she's paid for one. And why a telegram? Why not just an email? Or a text message?"

"A bloody good question," Roche said. She rested her head in her hands and massaged her aching forehead with her fingers.

He waved the photocopies in the air to attract her attention. She looked at him through her fingers.

"Do you think she's found something in here?" he asked.

There was no need to ask who "she" was.

Berit Gardner was still lying in her cell staring at the ceiling. Roche had checked three times. In the end the duty guard had told her off and asked her to leave them alone. She wondered if Berit would get any sleep at all.

Hardly anybody slept on their first night in custody. It normally took two, three days for exhaustion to overcome the uncomfortable bunk, the strange noises, the desperation, and the fear.

One night won't harm her, Roche reminded herself.

"You know I've said all along we should keep her away from the investigation," Philippe said.

"Might as well come out with a 'I told you so' if it makes you happier," Roche muttered.

"Nine times out of ten it's best not to involve civilians. No more like, in ninety-nine times out of a hundred it's a mistake. No, in—"

"Thank you, I get it. You were right, I was wrong. What do you want? A fucking medal?"

"No, the opposite." He leaned across the table. The light from the lampshade made his eyes glimmer with newfound energy. "The point is, these are not normal circumstances, right? We've got four days, then all our suspects will disperse, and our killer goes back to England. The only thing we've got is a notebook that neither of us understands. We need her."

"You saw her face just after the murder," Roche said. "She'll do something reckless. She'll put herself in danger."

"She'll cause problems no matter what you do," he said, which was absolutely true. "This way, at least we can keep an eye on her. And, big problems demand big solutions."

"What are you, a management consultant?" She nearly said politician but managed to stop herself just in time. He couldn't help who is father was. She stared at him. "You want to use Berit?"

"Boss, we're getting nowhere with this notebook."

"No. Never. Out of the question."

"I've been staring at it all night, and it tells me nothing. I've read it backward and forward, several times, and the only thing I keep thinking is that the girl didn't have a clue what she was doing."

"But somebody killed her," Roche pointed out.

"I know, so she must have found something out. But we're not going to find it. Our only hope is that Berit Gardner can extract more information from Nicole's notebook than we can. After all, they think the same, they're both…" He seemed to consider how to describe them both and chose the diplomatic: "Writers."

"You want to give Berit back the notebook? The investigating judge will never agree to it. It's evidence."

"Not exactly. I've got an idea for…let's call it crime-prevention surveillance. Follow-up, you could say, of Berit Gardner's release."

She looked at him. "I hope you know what you're doing," she said, but by this point she was so desperate she'd try anything.

"You won't regret it, I promise," he said. There was a hint of a smile in his eyes, and he added: "Trust me."

Roche scoffed, the closest to a laugh he would get with two unsolved murders hanging over her. "The boss was right," she said. "Those are two fucking ominous words."

57

THE RENTAL CAR WAS PARKED outside the police station when Berit Gardner stepped through the doors.

She stood in the bright sunshine and blinked at freedom, as if she'd only then realized she'd been deprived of it. Then she checked her jacket pockets to make sure that all her belongings had been returned.

Ian Ahmed waved at her to catch her attention. She crossed the car park, opened the passenger door, and sat down without commenting on his presence or her night in a cell.

Was she really that indifferent? he thought irritably. But then she closed her eyes, and he realized she was just exhausted.

Berit Gardner may be tough, but she wasn't invincible, and he was pretty sure her head ached, her body was stiff, and that she was more tired than she'd been in a long time. She was dressed in yesterday's clothes.

"Stop at a tech shop on the way back," she said without opening her eyes.

It took him fifteen minutes to find one, and when he did, she left him in the car, went inside, and came back ten minutes later with a small plastic bag in one hand and her jacket over her arm.

Ian Ahmed put his hand out and kept it there until she gave him the plastic bag. In return he gave her a takeaway coffee and a small paper bag with croissants from the bakery opposite. She took the coffee and put the bag on top of the folded jacket.

Ian opened the bag from the tech shop. It contained a small cheap voice recorder. It wasn't quite old enough to have an actual tape for recording, but almost.

"Berit, what are you doing?" he asked. "Is this part of some new plan?"

"No plan," she said and had some coffee.

He didn't believe her. "What are you going to use it for?"

She closed her eyes and didn't answer.

"If you're planning on using it for eavesdropping or recording something, forget it. It's only in old films you can carry a voice recorder in your pocket as the killer just happens to confess everything."

"It's not for me."

He waited.

"I had a lot of time to think in my cell, and one thing I thought about was voices. How unnecessary it was that Nicole's had been silenced. How unnecessary it is that others, who are still alive, silence themselves. I might not be able to do anything for Nicole, but I can help Mildred."

He had no idea who Mildred was, but he didn't like the look on Berit's face. There was something about how she avoided his eyes that made him feel uncomfortable.

When they were back at Château des Livres, she went straight up to the table where the oldest woman on the retreat sat, put the bag down in front of her, and said: "There you go. Now you can record your thoughts while you're knitting. You have a unique voice, Mildred Wilkinson, and it's about time you use it. No one else sees the world in exactly the same way as you do. If nothing else, you can impress us with all the swear words you have learned."

Ian and Sally waited outside Berit's room while she had a long shower and got changed. They had chatted a lot when she'd been away, and both agreed that they needed to keep an eye on her.

They knew it was going to be difficult. From the time they'd got back, Berit had radiated a disconcerting form of reckless resolve.

When she came out of her room and saw them waiting there, she raised one eyebrow in amusement. "Let me guess, you are my new prison guards?" she asked.

"Bodyguards," Sally corrected.

"Whatever you're planning on doing, we're joining you," Ian said firmly. It was the only way he could think of to protect her from herself.

Berit shrugged her shoulders. "Please, don't let me stop you," she said.

The first thing Berit did was to find Antoine in his office and ask to borrow his printer.

Sally and Ian followed. They stood behind her and looked over her shoulder as she sent photos to the computer from her phone and printed them out. Page after page of softly rounded letters.

Antoine looked worriedly at the pages but said nothing.

When they were finished, Berit led them down into the basement room with the whiteboard. She grabbed a cloth and erased everything on it. All her previous thoughts and theories and lists of questions and suspects disappeared in front of their eyes.

Berit turned toward them.

"Roche doesn't know it herself, but she actually did me a favor when she arrested me. She gave me the time to think. She detached me from the place where my old thinking had got stuck. I had to start from scratch."

She turned around again and wrote on the blank whiteboard:

Love.

Dreams.

Self-image.

"That's where I started," she said. "What's struck me with these two murders is how fast and furiously the killer attacked both times. I asked myself what could make someone react so instinctively, and the answer I kept coming back to was that the killer was protecting something. Something worth protecting. Love, dreams, perhaps the image of who they wanted to be—positive things leading to something horrible."

"You think someone killed John Wright out of love?" Ian asked.

"It is after all a stronger driving force than hatred. And I dismissed revenge early on. I asked myself: Why here, in that case? Why now? There's no time limit on revenge. It can be served hot or cold. No, the murder wasn't about something that happened in the past, but about preventing something about to happen in the future. That's what I was thinking, but it was only partly true."

Berit's phone pinged. She got it out, read the text, and nodded to herself. Sally sneaked up next to her and looked over her shoulder.

"It's from my mum," she said, surprised.

To Ian she said: "It has the answer to two questions. Berit must have sent them when she was in her room having a shower and getting changed. When we couldn't check up on her."

"What does it say?" he asked.

"To question one: yes. To question two: even more yes."

It pinged again and Sally read the next message too: "'It was merciless,'" she quoted.

"How do we know what's going to happen in the future?" Berit asked.

"We don't," Sally said.

"We make educated guesses from previous experiences," Ian said slowly.

"Exactly. We predict the future based on the lives we've lived. The motive was the future, but a clue could still be in the past."

At the top of the whiteboard she stuck the pages she'd printed, side by side, until they filled the whole board.

"Nicole's notebook. You photographed it," Ian said.

"Of course. It's important evidence. I couldn't risk letting anything happen to it without having copies."

"Just don't forget to take them down when we leave," Ian said dryly. "Otherwise, anyone, including our killer, could read them when we're not here."

"I'll take them down," she promised. She pointed at the last page of the notebook. "Look at this. Who could walk around with a bottle of wine in broad daylight? Writers."

"Not just writers," Sally said. "Agents too."

"Or organizers," Ian said.

"Exactly. But Nicole forgot one question. She forgot to include John Wright's personality in her calculations. The most important question isn't who could walk around with a bottle of wine without drawing attention to themselves. It is, who could offer a glass of red wine to John and *get him to drink it.*"

Ian looked from Berit to Sally. He'd never met John Wright and hadn't felt the tense atmosphere he'd created at the château before he died.

"He wouldn't accept it from an unknown participant of the retreat," Sally said slowly.

"No," Berit agreed. "He'd refuse to drink it."

"Not from Charles or Rebecka either," Sally said. "Unless he wanted to throw it in their faces, of course."

Sally hesitated. She looked at Ian pleadingly.

He sighed and said: "He would accept it from Emma." Sally had told him about Emma, and from what he'd heard, John Wright was used to being served food and drink by her.

"There's something you have to see," he said to Berit.

He led Berit and Sally up the small steps from the basement and over to the spot where John Wright had been poisoned. Beyond the dark corner, behind the grand staircase leading up to the second floor, was a small door leading to a winding corridor, the type of hidden walkway that would have been used by servants in the old days. A few turns and some storage rooms later—in no more than a minute—they were in the large, cozy kitchen.

Lunch preparations were already underway, and they left so they could talk in private.

"Someone could have stood here toward the end of the lunch break without being seen," he said. "During the last fifteen minutes, perhaps, when everyone had already got their coffee and they were putting things away. I spoke to the cook when you were in custody, and she said Emma left just before the lecture started, but she couldn't swear to exactly when. It would have been possible to sneak out, wait for John below the staircase, give him the wine, and continue on toward the lecture as if nothing had happened."

"It doesn't mean she necessarily did it," Sally said. "Just…"

"Just that she *could* have done it," Ian concluded.

Berit nodded thoughtfully.

"I've got a plan," she said. "But I'm going to need your help."

"What shall we do?" Sally asked.

"Tomorrow, you hold your workshop with Emma as planned," Berit said and continued to Ian: "They're talking about how you create and nurture a lasting career as a writer. All the teachers are supposedly involved, so they'll all be distracted while you break into Antoine's office."

He didn't even object, which was a sign of her bad influence on him. "And what will you be doing?" he asked.

"Me? I'm going to flush things down the loo, of course."

58

THE YOUNG OFFICER WHO'D BEEN given the thankless task of listening in on the conversation from what they called *la chambre de la tableau blanc* put his headphones down.

He was sitting in a white van without windows, parked at the back of the building. It was the kind of van that would have people in middle-class areas call the police immediately, but everyone at the château was so used to the forensic vans coming and going that no one had noticed one had been left behind. The young officer had a flask of coffee and a ham and mustard baguette with him, and a tree-lined avenue if he needed to relieve himself. He was prepared for a long wait and flinched when the van's door suddenly opened behind him.

"Heard anything yet?" The Mayor said.

"They think Emma Scott did it," the officer replied without even turning around.

"Interesting," Roche said.

The officer jumped up. "Sorry, boss," he said. Damn, he thought The Mayor had been on his own. He continued, "They were discussing who gave John Wright the red wine." He quoted them in English with a strong French accent: "'Who could have given him a glass of wine and *got him to drink it.*'"

"He wouldn't have accepted it from just anybody," Superintendent Roche said enthusiastically. "Not based on what I've learned about him anyway."

"That's what they said," the officer agreed. "But he would drink it if Emma Scott gave it to him. Then the man said, the English inspector, that he wanted to show her something."

"What?"

"I don't know," he admitted. "They left."

Roche patted him on the shoulder. "Well done. Continue listening. Call me if you hear anything that seems important."

He hesitated, torn between his eagerness to impress Roche and the fear of making a fool of himself.

Roche leaned against the van and nodded encouragingly. "Spit it out," she said as if she could read his thoughts.

"Yes, boss. There's one more thing. I think they're planning something."

"I wouldn't be surprised," Roche said. "I didn't like the way Berit looked when she lay there in her cell. I think she was already planning something then."

"As I said, they went to a different room, so I couldn't hear what they said. But I'm pretty sure they were talking about the plan on the way back. Toward the end they were standing outside the whiteboard room, just within reach of our microphones, and I think Berit Gardner is planning on getting rid of evidence!"

He just blurted it out, and now he looked at Roche with equal measures of anxiousness and anticipation.

"What exactly did she say?" Roche asked impatiently.

"She said she'd flush some stuff down the toilet!"

MOMENT OF DEATH

BERIT'S BACK.

I saw her being led away in handcuffs, and I wasn't sure if I should be worried or relieved. One thing reassures me: If Berit knew who the killer was, she would have told Superintendent Roche by now. Surely? No one spends a night in a cell unless you have to.

It's ten o'clock in the evening when Berit and the English inspector come out of the château. I've waited for them in the shadows. Everybody knows they've been holed up in the cellar working on the whiteboard all day, but no one knows what they've discovered.

The English inspector leaves almost immediately, but Berit lingers. She seems to enjoy the relative coolness of the evening. She doesn't know I'm here, only a few meters away, keeping her company in the dark.

The flood lights illuminate her. In the bright light, all her wrinkles are revealed. She's old, tired, and weary. The night in the cell has broken her, and I will walk out of this the winner.

When she turns to leave, she stumbles, that's how tired she is.

She doesn't notice that she's dropped one of the bunch of paper she's clutching in her arm. One single sheet, falling silently to the ground.

I wait until I know she's not coming back, then I go over to the piece of paper and pick it up. I read the words on it, and feel my world shake, threatening to come crashing down, only to stabilize itself again, like a house of cards that almost tumbled.

She doesn't know that I know. That makes all the difference. I'm almost there. I can't hesitate now.

A second of tiredness. That could be what decides everything. An otherwise brilliant mind fading after a long day, competent hands turning clumsy after a night in a police cell.

Berit Gardner continues up to her room as if nothing had happened. But in reality, she's already dead.

59

IT WAS THE SECOND TO last day of the writing retreat, dedicated to how to establish a long career as a writer by developing and strengthening your network. Emma held the workshop together with Sally, and then led at a talk with Claudia, Rebecka, and Charles out in the garden.

Alex drank Campari and soda with the other plus-ones at a table nearby, and even the cook stood leaning against the doorway watching it all with a smile on her face.

Berit was sitting at the big kitchen table going through everything that needed to be done. Through the open kitchen doors, they could see Sally standing next to Emma in front of the students. She looked like she belonged there. Calm, kind, attentive, ready to answer any questions or concerns, confident of her task and her place.

Berit thought of her own task and felt decidedly less confident. There were so many things that could go wrong, it was almost better to assume they would. But she would do her utmost. Whatever happened she'd be able to put a face to the person who'd killed Nicole. She would have answers. That was all that mattered.

She went through it in her head.

Sally was safe. Ian was safe. She would take all the risks herself, and that's how she wanted it. But she hadn't expected it to feel so sad, that the knowledge of the danger would paint the day in a bittersweet shade, like the autumn light, especially beautiful because it was fading.

At least she was used to being alone. It was fitting, in a way, that she was doing this on her own. For a moment, she looked out at the community outside. She could still be a part of it. It would be so simple to stand up and step out into the sunshine. So simple and tempting, but she resisted.

She'd already thought it all through that night in the cell. All that was left was an acceptance which was remarkably similar to freedom. Who said freedom was just another word for nothing left to lose? Kris Kristofferson, that was it. But it had taken Janis Joplin's raspy voice to really convey the meaning.

Antoine hurried past with rubber gloves and sink cleaning brushes, muttering about clogged toilets. She nodded at Ian Ahmed who left the periphery of the workshop and made his way up to Antoine's flat above the kitchen.

She took a sip of coffee. Reminded herself that she had to stop and smell the wisteria on the way back to the whiteboard. There were certain things in life you just had to do, and smelling the wisteria was one of them.

And if the worst would happen?

Well. Say what you may, but today was a beautiful day to die.

"It's happening," Philippe said to the young police officer in the white van.

The officer had just started his shift and was hunched over the screens. Philippe and Roche were waiting behind him. Every time they said something, he looked anxiously over his shoulder. They'd brought coffee, water bottles, and pastries.

"You both know what you're doing?" Roche said.

Philippe and the young officer nodded. They had no backup. Officially, this was a surveillance operation to follow up a previous offense. They were there to make sure there were no more hiccups in their investigation. Roche had assured her boss they could handle it.

Their whole plan was based on a few fleeting words about a toilet blockage. If she got away with this with her career intact, she would dine out on it for a long time.

She looked at her watch. Time moved forward at a snail's pace, as it always did before an operation.

No one knew when Berit would act, and until that happened, they were locked in the dark van while the sun was shining outside. It was a glorious day, but they saw nothing of it.

They prayed that the air-conditioning wouldn't fail.

Berit put up all of the pages from the notebook on the whiteboard again, but at the bottom of the board this time. At the top she wrote across the entire empty space:

NICOLE WAS HERE.

When she heard footsteps in the narrow corridor outside, she nodded to herself. She was ready.

"Hello, Alex," she said.

60

ALEX STOPPED RIGHT IN FRONT of her.

Once there, he looked around as if he'd just woken up from a dream. He wet his lips. His eyes took in her, the printed pages on the whiteboard, and all the junk in the cellar.

Berit waited. She hardly dared to breathe in case she disturbed him. Right then she felt as if the odds were on her side, that her crazy idea might just work...

Then it turned.

She witnessed the exact moment he gained control over himself. His posture became more confident. His shoulders relaxed. Suddenly there was even something amused in his eyes when he looked at her.

"I've always been annoyed with those endings in books where the villain just *has* to confess to his crimes," he said. "There's something so unrealistic about them, isn't it?"

Berit nodded slowly.

"Why do they always become so talkative?" he continued. "They've been clever and meticulous throughout the book, but in the last chapter they just have to reveal everything. And preferably somewhere the police can easily hide or where they've planted some microphones."

As he was talking he observed Berit as if he was expecting some kind of reaction from her. When there wasn't one, he nodded, impressed. At least she hadn't revealed any hiding place with an involuntary look. It seemed to please him that she hadn't given in to the temptation.

"I've not organized the room to be tapped," she said truthfully, and Alex smiled again.

"*You* haven't," he repeated and nodded. "An interesting choice of words."

She assumed he thought she'd got someone else to do it. She hadn't. No one knew where she was at that moment. She was alone with a murderer, just the way she wanted it.

Alex seemed to think hard. He tapped his fingers against his thigh, the only thing that revealed something of the turmoil that must be going on inside him. She looked at his hands. It was only now she became aware of his other hand. It was hidden underneath his long shirt, turned upward. She thought she could see something shiny underneath it, something sharp and dangerous.

"I think… I think I feel like going for a walk," he said slowly, as if he weighed each word before he pronounced it. "If you want…we could continue our discussion outside." He smiled. "Who knows, I might even have the answers to all your questions?"

Then he turned around and walked over to the steps.

Berit didn't hesitate for a second. She followed him immediately.

When they crossed the empty garden, she automatically turned around and looked up to the windows of Antoine's flat.

She thought about Ian who was up there. Would he react if he saw her follow Alex, heading for the fields? He knew better than to think that they were just out for a walk, but he was too far away to help in case it was needed.

Alex led her out into the fields. They walked through the perfectly straight path between the vines. The sun was hot on Berit's back. The vines were only chest-high and offered no shade. Far behind them at Château des Livres, the workshop was still underway. No one seemed to notice or care where they were going.

"Here is fine," Alex said eventually. He put the knife on the dry ground and walked up to her. "Put your arms out," he instructed. He was looking for some kind of hidden wiretap, and when he couldn't find one, or even a mobile, he nodded and walked back to the knife.

She made no attempt to take it off him. She hadn't had any answers yet.

"So," she said. "No one can hear us. You've got the knife. Now we can talk like equals."

He laughed at her view of equals, but it was obvious the thought appealed to him. "You know there are writers who plan everything down to the last detail, and then there are writers who throw themselves at it with no plan at all," he said.

Berit nodded.

"What type are you?" he asked.

"Oh, I never plan," she said. "Patricia Highsmith once said that she had to think of her own amusement when writing, and she liked a good surprise herself."

"I don't plan either," Alex said. "Not when I write, and not when I commit murder. I just hope there aren't too many gaps in my story… But I think it's going to work. You had a knife. You forced me into the fields. We started fighting. Somehow I gained control of the knife. Don't worry, they'll find your prints on it too. I'll have to see to it afterward. And obviously I'll have some cuts too. I was wondering why you killed Nicole? She was getting too close, I guess."

"She did accuse me of being the killer once," Berit said.

"She did? Amazing. You have to admire her."

"You did it out of love, didn't you?" Berit said.

He hesitated. He seemed to be torn between worrying that any delay would foil his plan, and the very human urge to confide in someone, brag, show someone what a genius you are. The sole reader of his amazing murder story.

He looked over her shoulder toward the château but clearly couldn't see anything that worried him.

"He was supposed to comment on Julian's manuscript. He bragged about it, you see. John Wright. Said he could determine Julian's future in only five pages."

"You had to act quickly," Berit said.

"I just did what I had to do," Alex said. "The only thing I regret is not stealing the notes first. Afterward it was too late. He was already dead when I realized they were gone. I'm pretty sure Claudia or Nicole took them. They were the only two I noticed come to the lecture after John. But it could have been Mrs. Wright, too, or whatever she calls herself. Buy my biggest fear was that Nicole had them. She hinted at it."

"It was Claudia," Berit said.

Alex nodded. "I realized that as soon as they found the briefcase in Rebecka's room. I had seen the way Claudia glared at her. After that I could be pretty sure the notes were destroyed. But I was really worried that day in Vienne. I was terrified that the police would find Julian's manuscript and that John had already read the pages and written some damning comments. That he would return from beyond the grave and ruin Julian's life."

"And yours."

"Our life together. But when they found the empty briefcase, I relaxed. I had gotten away with it. I felt euphoric. Like when you've finished writing a book against all odds. You think you're never going to finish it, and then suddenly you have."

"But then Nicole found something out?"

Alex brushed away some hair from his face. The other hand squeezed the knife tighter. "I didn't want to kill her. I liked her. But she refused to give up. She was constantly talking about solving the murder before you did. It was like an obsession. I knew it was only a matter of time before she found something that connected me to John Wright."

"She knew you'd written a book, didn't she?"

The first question she'd texted Olivia was: **Has Alex Spencer written a book under a pseudonym?**

"I slipped up. It meant nothing at first. She just thought it was funny that I had written a book but was no longer writing. She said I was like a sober alcoholic. But then she put two and two together. She found John Wright's review online. She thought I'd killed him in *revenge*."

Another one of Nicole's shots in the dark. She must have threatened half the retreat. *I know you did it. Flee, everything has been exposed.*

"She never understood people," Berit said. "That was one of her biggest flaws as a writer. You did it out of love, not revenge."

"So you do understand," he said.

There was gratefulness in his eyes. The human yearning to be seen at any cost.

"You were worried he would do to Julian what he'd done to you."

"We'd planned our whole life together. I would provide the inspiration and the funding, he the creativity. I would be both muse and sponsor. Together we would take over the world. Force our way into the literary salons and shake up their small little heterosexual lives. I wasn't going to let John Wright stop us."

Berit nodded. "But you had to act quickly, before he'd read and commented on the manuscript. Did you find the hemlock by accident?"

"I knew how Socrates was killed. I did study history and philosophy at university after all. When I found the hemlock, I improvised the rest. Even when I was writing, I did my best work under duress. I need deadlines. The Socrates angle amused me. Some part of me still admired John, I think. He was one of my biggest role models. It was what made the review so devastating. So, in a way, you could say I gave my mentor the chalice. I was going to do it before his own lecture. I would have liked to see him collapse up there, center stage, in front of all those people. But he and Mrs. Wright went down there together. I didn't have the opportunity to ask him to try the wine then."

"Instead, you waited below the staircase after lunch."

"Before your lecture," he nodded. "I was going to keep on trying until he turned up alone. And then, just like that, he did."

Something caught Alex's attention behind her. Berit turned her head.

Commissaire Roche and Philippe were running toward them, but they were too far away, much too far away, to be able to do anything.

Alex shouted: "Hurry up. She's got a knife!"

He held the knife close to his body, out of sight of the police at that distance, and took a few steps toward Berit. She couldn't take her eyes off it. This time she didn't have a library between her and the killer, no pile of books by her side to use as a weapon. It was just her, him, and the knife, and he looked alarmingly confident with it.

She reminded herself that he'd done this once before.

It just strengthened her resolve. He had to be stopped. If it required a sacrifice, a rather large sacrifice, so be it. She had gone into this with her eyes wide open. Unlike Nicole, she'd been aware of the risks.

And unlike Nicole, she had lived a long and rich life. Her books would survive her. A part of her, how she viewed the world and humanity, would exist long after her death. It was a consolation no one could take away from her.

She tensed up in preparation for the inevitable pain and hoped it would be quick. But she kept her eyes open. When the end came, she wanted to see everything.

Therefore, she saw the sudden explosion of movement a second before Alex did. She took a step back, just as he was brought to the ground by a strong and supple body, hardened after three weeks of tough hiking.

The knife fell to the ground with a thud, but Alex refused to give up. He fought as if his life and freedom and all his dreams depended on it. Ian Ahmed was just as stubborn. He was driven by a barely contained rage she suspected had a lot to do with worry and relief.

Berit quickly stooped down, picked up the knife, and took several steps to one side. Ian and Alex rolled around on the ground, but, as long as Alex didn't have the knife, he couldn't do much harm. The French police came running from the other direction. Roche reached them first. She pulled Alex away while Philippe took care of Ian.

It wasn't so bad having backup after all, Berit thought.

Then she realized they were all staring at the knife in her hand.

61

"YOU'RE AN IDIOT," IAN AHMED said.

"No, no," Roche objected. "She's a bloody idiot."

"You put yourself in an unforgivable danger—"

"You put my investigation in an unforgivable danger."

When Berit didn't say anything, Ian sighed. "You could have been killed," he said.

"And worse," Roche added. "You may have ruined our chances of securing a conviction for the murders of John Wright and Nicole Archer. He could go free because of you!"

"I wasn't there in time to hear him say anything," Ian said, almost apologetically. "I had to approach him from the other direction for him not to see me, and there were loads of vines between me and you. I can't even swear he was the one holding the knife."

"He claims you murdered Nicole and forced him out into the fields," Roche said. "The only thing anyone saw was that you walked behind him. You were hardly there against your will, not if you could have called for help at any time or just stopped following him."

"He was quick-witted," Berit admitted.

"We tapped the whiteboard room, but he didn't say anything in there a skilled lawyer couldn't explain. I do hope you realize that. If that was your plan, you were…"

Berit held her hands up. "Thank you, I know," she said. "A bloody fool."

She was sitting at the kitchen table, leaning on her elbows so she wouldn't collapse. The doors to the kitchen garden were open, and from the cooker, delicious smells of lunch being prepared wafted over. Everything was calm and still. She felt like laughing out loud at the absurdity of it.

Sally and Emma's workshop was still going on. Apparently, they had managed to keep everyone's attention, even when the police ran past the château and into the fields, and on the way back, Roche had been careful not to let any curious future writers see Alex.

It occurred to Berit that Julian still didn't know. He needed to be told, of course. Should she offer to do it?

She was overcome by immense fatigue. It was like the suffering of all of humanity, their stupidity, and infinite ability to hurt each other landed on her strong shoulders. They couldn't carry such an enormous weight.

She swayed and would have fallen off her chair if Ian Ahmed hadn't steadied her.

She nodded wearily toward the shelf above the knife stand. "There's a camera there," she said.

Commissaire Roche fell silent, in the middle of a tirade about how irresponsible Berit was.

"It will have filmed him when he got the knife," Berit continued. "It will be hard for him to claim that I threatened him with it, if he was the one who stole it." She smiled at Ian. "I bought it in that tech shop."

"The jacket," he said out loud to himself. "You had it hidden under the jacket."

"You would have tried to stop me, if you'd known." Berit turned to Roche again. "And I think you will get him to confess."

She patted her pockets, got a business card out, and pushed it across the table to Roche. "Give him this and remind him he's got the right to make one call. Tell him to say hi from me. You'll get your confession, don't worry."

Roche looked at the card. *Olivia Marsch—Senior Literary Agent*, it read.

"He's not going to be able to resist the temptation to write a book about this, and once he's started, he won't be able to stop."

"It was his debut novel that started it all," Berit said.

She was sitting with Ian, The Mayor, and Roche in the shadow under the wisteria in the château's garden. In front of them was a jug of ice-cold lemonade. Berit had already drunk two glasses. Then she'd asked for coffee, hot, strong, and lots of it. She was ready to tell it all.

As soon as Roche had secured the video recording, she began to look more philosophically on this whole crazy story. She had a suspect in custody, a video recording proving how he'd retrieved the intended murder weapon, and a Swedish writer who possibly knew all the answers to the questions Nicole's notebook had raised.

"John Wright," Berit began, "wasn't a man belonging on a pedestal. There are some people you can worship in relative safety, whereas others are downright dangerous to admire too uncritically. John Wright was that kind of person. He took a young, insecure, pretentious, perhaps slightly ridiculous, debut writer and crushed him. His essay was titled "Some Arguments Why No One Under the Age Of Fifty Should Be Allowed to Publish a Book," and one of the arguments was Alex Spencer's debut. Published under a pseudonym, it was praised before it came out and heavily criticized after. After John Wright had slated it, Alex never wrote another word. It wasn't until he saw John Wright here at the retreat that he decided to kill him."

Berit looked older and more tired today. No, not more tired. More serious. Roche was reminded of the photo from outside the court after the Great Diddling murders. Berit Gardner wasn't a person who took murder lightly. Roche got the feeling that she empathized with everyone's feelings and paid a high price for her empathy.

"I said earlier that this murder wasn't about the past but the future, and I was both right and wrong," Berit continued. "Alex saw John Wright talking to Julian, heard how he offered to read the first five pages, and saw history repeat itself: a young, starry-eyed hopeful writer, and an older, merciless cynic. By this time Alex lived for Julian's writing. Together they would have the creative life Alex had always dreamed of."

"Unless John Wright crushed that dream," Ian said quietly.

"Exactly. Alex had to improvise. From the moment he discovered the hemlock, he was trapped in a story he hardly understood. Gradually he lost control over the plot and the characters until he had to kill again to protect himself and his secret."

"Nicole Archer," Roche said. "I have so many questions about her notebook. First of all: Who was the mistress?"

"There wasn't one. Just like I always thought. John Wright wasn't a man who was particularly interested in sex. And Nicole Archer wasn't a particularly good judge of character. She saw Claudia Ramirez enter his room and assumed they were having an affair."

"And the telegram? '*Flee, everything has been exposed*'?"

Berit shook her head. "It's an old story about a man who sends a telegram to four of his closest friends: *Flee, everything has been exposed.* The next day three of them leave town. Nicole thought she could do the same in a murder investigation. Accuse everyone…"

"And see what reactions she could provoke," Ian concluded.

"She was, I said, still so very young," Berit said.

"But she never found out who the guilty person was," Roche said. "Laurent said she never saw her killer's face."

Berit nodded. "It upset her. But I'd like to think she knows now."

As she spoke, she gradually relaxed. The worst of the tension in her shoulders lifted. Roche noted that Berit was once again speaking with a calm confidence, now that she was telling a story whose ending she knew.

"Did it never occur to you that you could have been killed?" Roche asked.

Berit smiled feebly. "It did. But you would have found the video camera in the kitchen. You would have had definite proof." She looked at Ian. "The only thing I didn't understand is how you were out there in the field all of a sudden. You were supposed to be in Antoine's office. How could you catch up with us and overtake us without Alex noticing?"

"I was never in Antoine's office. If you really had believed that the solution to the murder lay in Antoine's office, I would have been the one blocking toilets while you did the breaking and entering. I knew you were up to something, so I kept close to you all the time. When you came outside,

I followed, parallel to you. Alex paid his attention forward and backward, never to the side."

"I had to make sure you and Antoine were somewhere else," Berit said. "I didn't want anyone to get in the way when Alex tried to silence me. I knew he would have to. I made sure I dropped the last page of Nicole's notebook. He knew 'the Writer' referred to him, and he couldn't run the risk of me finding out."

"But what about the wine tasting?" Roche remembered. "I thought he was together with the plus-ones when the first murder was committed?"

"The power of that little word *we*. They talked about how we discussed the wines, we packed our stuff, we went to the wine tasting. We always assumed it meant all three of them, but all it meant was that they were more than one. My guess is that they separated when they all went to get their things before the trip. A few minutes, that's all it took, but it wouldn't have been something they'd recollect. Ask the plus-ones now. They'll probably confirm that they weren't together the whole time."

"And Julian?" Roche said. "Will he tell us how Alex left to do something in Lyon? In the interviews they said they were sitting outside a bar writing."

"He wouldn't have to be gone very long. Julian might not even have noticed if he was in the middle of writing. That's why I had to do something. There wasn't enough evidence against him."

"Just don't do it again," Ian said. "I think I aged ten years in those few minutes. At one point I didn't think I'd get there in time."

"But you did," Berit said.

Her face lit up as if by a new inner strength, and when she looked around, it was as if she saw everything for the first time. The fruit trees. The rosemary bush. The beautiful wisteria over their heads.

She was memorizing it all to use in a future book, Roche suddenly realized. She sat up straight. "Am I going to find myself in a book one of these days?" she asked suspiciously.

Berit met her gaze. The laughter lines around her eyes came back. She nodded toward the students in the garden.

"In more than one, I'd imagine," she said.

EPILOGUE

THEY'D PUT THE TABLES IN the glade among the trees, and at every table was an agent, publisher, or writer opposite a student.

It looked as if they were speed dating, and in a way they were. It was the last day of the retreat, and everybody would get the chance to pitch their project to the publishers and agents and get feedback from the writers. Berit had declined to take part. Instead, she sat at her own table in the shade from the fig tree and observed everything.

Charles Tate was at the first table. He'd already heard five students pitch their "original" idea—a crime novel in which a writer is murdered in a French castle—and was fighting back his yawns. His only goal was to get through the day and be able to go home.

Mildred was taken aback by his disinterest. Everyone else had spoken enthusiastically, as if they thought they could keep him interested by talking so fast he couldn't understand what they were saying. They'd stared so intently at him, he'd been worried they would grab his hand.

Just like on a speed date.

Not Mildred. She clutched her hands on her lap, leaned back, and said nothing. He was wondering how long she'd sit there in silence if he didn't say anything and was tempted to give it a go. But he could feel Berit's eyes on his neck. *Why don't you just do your job? You used to be good at it.*

He sighed. "Tell me about your crime novel," he said.

"It's not a crime novel."

"No?" he said.

"At least I don't think so. Even though it is possible someone dies. Do you want to hear it?"

She got out her voice recorder. He put the little earphones in his ears while Mildred found the play button.

"*Chapter one,*" her sweet, grandmotherly voice said. "*People I fantasize about killing whilst tending to my begonias…*"

Julian was on his own at the edge of the group.

No one knew how much he'd suspected about his partner's activities. But everyone knew that Alex had done everything for his sake.

Rebecka sat down opposite him and took off her sunglasses. "I've read your manuscript," she said.

Julian looked at her. There wasn't a single feeling in his face. It was like they had all dried up.

"I have no idea what I'm supposed to do now," he said. "I have nothing left."

She shrugged. "I have worked in this industry for more than twenty years, and the only thing I've got in return is a pitifully low pension. All my savings went to buying my way out of John's accusations. I don't even have an office anymore. I work from home in a house in Putney I inherited from my parents. So, I guess that makes two of us."

"Alex was on the contract of our flat. He paid for it all. I don't even know where I'm going to live now."

"The whole manuscript needs editing," Rebecka said. "You must get rid of the first hundred pages, that's for sure. And large sections need rewriting. But I still have a publishing house, and I want to publish your book."

Far back in Julian's eyes was a small glimmer of reluctant interest. "What has to be rewritten?" he asked.

"First of all, we need to strengthen the narrator's perspective. I can tell you were searching for your voice when you wrote it. You found it in the end. You've got something unique to tell the world, and I will make sure they listen."

It was like life itself grabbed him and forced him to come back to it. "So it has something, my manuscript?"

"I just said so, didn't I?" Rebecka said. "Otherwise, I wouldn't want to publish it."

"I can't edit a book," Julian said suddenly. "I've got nowhere to go."

Rebecka waved away his objection. "Don't you understand?" she said impatiently. "We could create something together. Something that will *last*."

"But where will I live?"

"Well, I guess you'll have to move into my basement while you're writing. Who knows, the house can be part publishing house, part literary salon." She looked at him sternly. "Just as long as you don't expect me to cook for you."

Charles grabbed hold of Rebecka's arm when she walked past. "Did he say yes?"

"Of course," she said.

"And he has potential? Could he be a new John?"

"He could be a new Julian Aubrey," Rebecka said. "We're going to do it all from my house in Putney. We can probably squeeze a desk in for you as well. It could be the beginning of a new life for all of us. With the freedom to create something good…"

"Of course," he said. "The lad's going to need an agent."

He realized he was still clutching her arm. She seemed to realize at the same time. They'd known each other for more than ten years, and all of a sudden he felt like an insecure school boy.

"The manuscript needs editing, of course. But you know what, Charles? I think we've found it. I think if we only cross…"

He pulled her close.

"We'll have to edit later," he said and kissed her.

Sally was just changing into her evening outfit ahead of the big closing party when someone knocked on the door. She quickly buttoned up her blouse and opened the door.

Claudia was outside, with a nervous expression on her face. Sally couldn't understand how anyone could be nervous talking to her, but she opened the door wider and asked her to come inside.

Claudia sat down on the little stool which was the only place to sit and said quickly, as if she was throwing herself over a hurdle, "You represent John Wright, don't you?"

"My mother does, but I work for the same agency. As a junior agent," she added conscientiously.

"So you know he was working on a new project before he died?"

Claudia continued without waiting for an answer. "And you probably know that...somebody stole John Wright's computer and his notes in connection with his death?"

Sally nodded.

Claudia signed. "Me," she said. "It was me who stole them."

Sally nodded slowly. "Okay," she said.

Claudia seemed confused at the lack of a reaction. "The diary is destroyed, and I can't do anything about that even if I wanted to. But I have his notes on his new project. He hadn't started the actual manuscript yet, but everything else is there: the story, characters, setting, the historical research. I can send it all to you."

"Okay," Sally said again.

"I read it," Claudia continued. "Believe me, I hate to say this, but it's *good*. Brilliant descriptions of the milieu already. Suggestive. Detailed. The character descriptions are spot on. I could never have written anything like it. Maybe John was right that I don't have any talent and shouldn't be writing."

"Not write the way he does, obviously," Sally said. "Berit always says that no one can tell a story the same way as someone else. We all have a unique way of looking at the world."

"Berit says that, does she?"

"Yes."

"And what do you say?" Claudia wondered.

"I say his descriptions of men might have been brilliant, but I wonder what his descriptions of the women were like."

"Well, as a matter of fact, there weren't any. It's a historical novel. As soon as male writers place their stories in the past—or the future!—they can pretend women don't exist."

"I imagine you could change that. What do you say? A female food taster for Henry VIII, perhaps?"

Claudia leaned forward enthusiastically. "I've been thinking the same thing," she said. "A Black, female, lesbian food taster. Someone who really understands what it means to be marginalized and who cares about the poor and the downtrodden when no one else does. It could *work*."

"It could be fantastic," Sally said. "I know my mother is looking for someone to finish what John Wright started. I could give her your name. If you would consider sharing the credit with him."

"He would turn in his grave," Claudia said.

Sally said nothing.

Claudia reached for her computer.

She opened John Wright's old folder *Better than Mantel*. Then she clicked on change title and wrote: *Better than Wright...*

Sally pushed her business card across the table. Marsch Agency, Sally Marsch—Junior Literary Agent. "Call me when you've got something," she said.

Sally got out her phone as soon as Claudia left. She really should go over to the party, but instead she made a short phone call. When she'd hung up, she made another one.

"Hi, Mum," she said when Olivia picked up. "I know who can finish John Wright's book."

"Berit?" Olivia guessed. "You'll never be able to persuade her."

"Claudia Ramirez."

The phone went silent. "Who?"

"She's already started. She's added new notes to his folders. She calls them *Better than Wright*, and I think it could be. A modern historical novel. Like nothing you've seen before. A genuine societal engagement. A young female food taster at Henry VIII's court. Lisbeth Salander meets Tudor-England."

"But what will Mrs. Wright say?"

"She said: 'Do what you want.' I just spoke to her."

Silence. "I presume you want to be promoted to senior agent, in that case?"

"Well, someone will have to represent Claudia Ramirez. And junior agent wouldn't be fitting for a project of this size."

Olivia laughed. "We'll talk about it when you get back. And, Sally? Well done."

Everyone had dressed up for the closing party. It was like they were all determined to create something better to remember about the two weeks at the château than the murders.

Roche and Philippe were also invited, and Roche had brought her daughter. Roche was standing next to Berit, watching Gabrielle come out of the kitchen, rosy-cheeked and with flour on her black dress. She hadn't been able to resist giving the cook a hand.

"She'll be just like me." Roche sighed.

Berit smiled. "It's not the worst that could happen," she said.

"Just work, work, work all the time. No time for anything else."

Gabrielle accepted a glass of champagne from Philippe. "Perhaps not only work," Berit suggested.

Roche tensed. "They got to be kidding," she said darkly. "Over my dead body."

"What was it you said?" Berit asked. "That she should fall in love with someone completely inappropriate?"

"I didn't mean a *police officer*." It looked like she was about to march straight over to them, but Berit stopped her.

"He's not a bad man," she suggested.

"I guess there are worse." Roche sighed. "I guess she has to make her own mistakes in life."

"You've raised a good kid. She'll be all right."

"At least there's one consolation."

"What?"

"If he hurt breaks her heart, I can make his life miserable."

Gabrielle sipped the champagne and said with a smile: "You see what would happen. You wouldn't be able to take me anywhere without me ending up in the kitchen."

"At least I'd always know where you were," he said. He frowned. "Why is your mother staring so angrily at me?"

Gabrielle shrugged. "Who knows? You're not afraid of her, are you?"

"What do you mean, not afraid? Of course I'm afraid. That woman terrifies me." He tugged at his shirt collar. "Do you think I should go over and talk to her?"

Gabrielle held out her glass. "I think you should top up my champagne," she said.

Berit was standing out on the terrace, watching Antoine approach Emma. He had one bottle in his hand and another under his arm, and he seemed determined that she should celebrate properly.

She wondered if she would ever be able to think of Emma without seeing Nicole's face. Perhaps their friendship was yet one more sacrifice this retreat had demanded. It couldn't be helped. People changed. At least she was pretty sure Emma would do all right in life.

Berit leaned against the railing of the terrace and looked out over the vineyard that nearly took her life.

"Heartbreakingly beautiful, isn't it?" Ian said quietly, suddenly by her side. "You can't tear your eyes away, despite everything that's happened."

"Too beautiful," Berit said. "Anyone can appreciate a French vineyard in the evening sun. That's why I've always been drawn to the rugged and slightly broken. Someone has to appreciate those as well."

Yet she couldn't tear herself away. She stared at the view as if she was trying to memorize the exact light of a French sunset. *A pointless exercise*, she thought. It could never be captured in a book anyway.

"I feel the same way about people," he said. "The perfect ones always bore me."

Berit laughed. "That, too. But at the moment I'm thinking about places. You should see the Stockholm archipelago on a stormy day in November. Everything is gray, dark, and cold. When you're in a dinghy, in the middle of the sea and you can feel the sleet whipping your face, all on your own because no one else is stupid enough to be out there, well, then you definitely know you're alive."

"I'm stupid enough to be there," he said with absolute certainty. "In fact, I think I'd appreciate it."

Berit looked at him and tried to imagine him there.

"Perhaps," she admitted.

WINDFALL FOR BOOKS ABOUT REAL-LIFE MURDERS

Press release from Marsch Agency

Marsch Agency is proud to announce that HBO Max has bought the rights to the autobiographical book *Memoirs of a Murderer* by Alexander Spencer, the Englishman who was convicted of killing bestselling author John Wright and a young female journalist. The book spent ten weeks on the *New York Times* bestseller list and was hailed by critics as "a harrowing insight into a murderer's psyche" (*The Guardian*) and "gripping, raw, terrifying" (*New York Review of Books*).

Netflix and Shondaland have already bought the rights to Nicole Archer's posthumously published book, the international bestseller *The Hunt for a Killer*. It's based on the true story of a young woman's fight for truth and justice, and the price she paid for it. The book was largely written by the Swedish-English writer Berit Gardner who witnessed both murders close up.

This summer also sees the publication of one of this year's most talked about novels: the sensational collaboration between the late John Wright and Claudia Ramirez. It's a unique historical novel unlike anything you've read before. Set in Henry VIII's court, we see it through the eyes of his Black, lesbian food taster and follow her struggle to survive amidst court intrigue, hierarchies, and rapidly replaced queens.

For foreign rights inquiries, please contact Sally Marsch, senior literary agent.

READING GROUP GUIDE

1. Upon arriving at the retreat, Berit is struck by how inspired she feels by the place. "There was magic in the air, a creative energy that seemed to come from the earth itself." Have you ever experienced such a place? If so, where was it, and how did it affect your mood or your creativity?

2. While observing John Wright's condescending and scornful treatment of the would-be writers at the retreat, author Claudia Ramirez remarks to herself that success rarely comes to those who deserve it. By all accounts, however, John Wright is a brilliant, once-in-a-generation writer. Is someone like John less deserving of success because he's a loathsome human being? Why or why not?

3. Berit thinks to herself at one point that the opposite of freedom isn't obligations; it's comfort. What does she mean? Do you agree? Why or why not?

4. After John Wright's death, Julian says to Berit: "We cling to the illusion that a life is worth something, that it matters what

happens to individual specimens of the human race, but the reality is that we're all disposable. The only thing that matters is what we leave behind. What we have *written*." Do you agree with his assessment of the value of an individual life? Why or why not?

5.   "Freedom could be extremely revealing. When you were unable to hide behind your everyday life and your set identity, you might accidentally reveal the murkier parts of your personality that were normally kept strictly under control." Have you ever been in a situation where you felt unconstrained by your own identity to do or say whatever you wished? Or in a place where no one knew you and you felt free to "go wild"? Did you learn anything about yourself? Were there any consequences to your behavior, positive or negative?

6.   Have you ever met one of your idols? Were you inspired by the meeting or disappointed? Why?

7.   Writing retreats give aspiring and established authors time and space to work without the distractions of day-to-day life. Would you find such an experience valuable? Why or why not?

8.   No one at the writing retreat chooses to leave after the first murder—or the second. If you were in a similar situation, do you think you would be able to disregard the potential danger and remain, or would you catch the next train home to safety? Give reasons for your answer.

9.   Alex states that he killed John Wright to protect Julian and the future they had planned together. Have you or would you ever consider committing a crime in order to spare someone you love from disgrace or danger? Or to preserve your lifestyle?

10. Sally's mother, Olivia, is a powerhouse, take-no-prisoners agent who seems to offend a lot of people in the course of doing her job well. Do you think it's necessary to be ruthless in order to be on top in such a competitive field? Why or why not? Have you ever felt that your own success has been affected either by your own ruthlessness or the lack of a "killer instinct"? Give details.

A CONVERSATION
WITH THE AUTHOR

Your books are translated into English from the original Swedish. Do you ever worry that subtle nuances, moods, or certain words and phrases will be lost in translation? Being fluent in English, have you ever considered writing or attempted to write a book in English?

I don't worry, not at all. Quite the opposite, really. For me, a translated manuscript is a great opportunity to revisit a work that is already finished in Sweden. Most of the changes I do concern plot or character development, and when I do suggest specific changes in words, I am keenly aware that it's the translator's skill and hard work that makes the subtle nuances possible.

You've said in an interview that Berit is based on "the idea of a person I would like to be." What about your other main characters? Is Sally based on an actual agent? Emma, a bookseller you've met? What or who inspired the character of DI Ahmed and his relationship with Berit?

Most of the characters are not based on a specific individual but are more an amalgamation of different people and experiences. With Sally, for example, it's the experience of being new at your job and eager to prove yourself. With Emma, all the many, many hardworking booksellers I've met, who devote so much time and energy to books and reading, and the nagging feeling I sometimes have that in the end, they don't receive enough credit for it. DI Ahmed is a bit different: There, it is about showing how many competent, hardworking police officers there are out there. One of my pet peeves when it comes to books about amateur sleuths is when the author tries to make her sleuth seem smart by making the police incredibly stupid. Instead, I wanted to show how Berit and Ian Ahmed were both competent and just had different approaches to solving murders and how those approaches can complement each other.

When you begin a new project, do you have any underlying themes in mind to explore via the story? Or do the themes present themselves during the writing process?

A bit of both, I think. I have a situation that interests me, and that situation often implies certain themes. But I don't think about them when I write, at least not the first draft. The first draft is almost exclusively about putting a number of strange people together and seeing what they get up to. The themes mostly present themselves in the editing process.

If you had to pick, what is the single most important element to a story to make it "unputdownable" for readers? What do you focus on as you write to ensure that readers will engage and relate to the tale?

I think what makes a book "unputdownable" is pacing and micro cliff-hangers that sort of force the reader along in the story. But I'm not sure I want to write books that are "unputdownable." For me, it's more about creating characters and worlds that you long to return to if you do have to put the book down—characters that feel like old friends, settings that transport you, and of course, a murder mystery to keep things interesting.

What has been your personal experience with writing retreats, either as a teacher or a student? Do you feel they are a useful tool for aspiring writers, or are they, as John Wright believes, not worth the price of admission?

I've never been to one. Like most things in life, I don't think they are inherently good or bad, it's more a question about how you use them. On the one hand, writing is a lonely profession, and I think partly has to be. You have to be willing to put in the long hours of hard work, and at worst, retreats can distract from it. And I think many of our ideas shouldn't be shared too early. Something happens when we talk about ideas very early in the process. They lose a little bit of the magic. And new ideas are often too fragile for both negative and positive feedback. It's like how very young plants sometimes need protection even against good things: too much sunshine or too much water or too-rich soil. But at the same time, precisely because writing is such a lonely profession, having teachers and colleagues can make all the difference. And even if art perhaps can't be taught, craft certainly can be. And while you have to discover your unique, individual voice by yourself, fellow writers and colleagues are essential in helping you hone it.

What are you reading now?

Death and Fromage by Ian Moore, which is every bit as great as it sounds.

ABOUT THE AUTHOR

Katarina Bivald grew up working part-time in a bookstore, dreaming of becoming an author. In 2013, the dream came true when she published her *New York Times* bestselling debut, *The Readers of Broken Wheel Recommend*. She lives outside of Stockholm with her dog, Sam; still prefers books over people; and has just found out that life is so much more fun when you're plotting to kill someone.